TRULY ARE
the FREE

TRULY ARE
the FREE

Book Two of the
Sweet Wine of Youth Trilogy

Jeffrey K. Walker

Ballybur

Also by Jeffrey K. Walker

None of Us the Same

Printed in the United States of America
First Printing, 2017

ISBN 978-1-947108-02-8

Published by Ballybur Publishing

Cover and book design © John H. Matthews
www.BookConnectors.com

Text divider design by freepik.com

Edited by Kathy A. Walker

Author photograph by Paul Harrison

Poem by Roscoe C. Jamison and
cover photographs in public domain

For Kathy

These truly are the Brave,
These men who cast aside
Old memories, to walk the blood-stained pave
Of Sacrifice, joining the solemn tide
That moves away, to suffer and to die
For Freedom—when their own is yet denied!
O Pride! O Prejudice! When they pass by,
Hail them, the Brave, for you now crucified!

These truly are the Free,
These souls that grandly rise
Above base dreams of vengeance for their wrongs,
Who march to war with visions in their eyes
Of Peace through Brotherhood, lifting glad songs,
Aforetime, while they front the firing line.
Stand and behold! They take the field to-day,
Shedding their blood like Him now held divine,
That those who mock might find a better way!

"The Negro Soldiers"
by Roscoe C. Jamison (1917)

CHAPTER ONE

Adèle

The French insisted on throwing open their windows even in the dead of winter. He found this both odd and cold, lying naked on the bed as Adèle unlatched two windows and pushed back the wooden shutters. She stretched over the sills to fasten them back on rusty iron hooks and he squinted past her into the brilliant morning sky. Such unadulterated blue came only on rare winter days. Sometimes it was all you could see looking up from the trenches, if you were lucky and it wasn't raining. This morning, the freshness and clarity made up a little for the iciness of the air. He pulled the crumpled quilt tight around him.

"Don't snug yourself," Adèle said, kneeling on the mattress while yanking at the bedclothes. He pulled back in a feigned tug-of-war, but soon surrendered. Adèle crawled across to him, the loose front of her old silk peignoir falling open. She placed a chaste kiss on his mouth, thinking to signal an end to the morning's lovemaking, but he ran the back of his fingers over an exposed breast. This earned him an insincere slap to his arm, just below the puckered skin left by a German bullet. He caught her wrist and kissed the underside, feeling her pulse against his lips.

"I have to return to the Machine Gun School this afternoon," he said, tongue following a turquoise vein to her elbow. "Who knows when I'll be able to beg another pass." He continued up her arm and slid his hand under the dressing gown, pushing it off one shoulder. She sighed with showy exasperation, knowing he'd scarcely missed a weekend with her since they met. The school was less than ten kilometers away and officers were not subject to restrictions. She kissed him again, less chaste this time.

"Oooh, my Neh-deee! Yoo are zo beeg, zo *formidable*! *Mon Dieu*!" She fell back on the pillows as he rolled to his side and untied her robe.

"Much as I love that Frenchy girl talk," he said, kissing her neck, "it's a little disappointing that you usually sound like an English schoolgirl." Adèle wrapped her leg around his hip and nuzzled into his chest. Ned slid the watered green silk from her other shoulder.

"My granny would have something to do with that," she said. "After Maman died, we spoke French only when Papa was home. Otherwise, it was proper English." Adèle gazed out at the perfect sky and smiled with the memory of her indomitable English grandmother.

Ned inched down the bed and placed a moist kiss just above her navel. He mumbled into the smooth skin of her stomach, "How did the old girl come to marry your grandfather anyway?" Adèle ran fingers through his hair, not near long enough to twirl. Better for dealing with the lice, although he'd kept himself clear of the trenches these last months.

"She was governess to some petty English aristocrat with a sickly wife. Went with the family to Vichy while the mother took a cure." She squirmed and lifted her hips as Ned brushed his nose through the patch of hair between her legs. "Grand-père was there on holiday with some friends, I suspect for the casino. He saw her airing the children along the boulevard and was smitten at first sight, so he claimed. He spent the next month on a quest to woo her and…" She gave a sharp inhalation followed by a low moan as he moved back up to her breasts. "…it seemed to have worked."

Ned discovered this high school *maitresse d'école* after she'd rescued him struggling to order dinner in unintelligible French. His previous brushes with French women consisted of a few prostitutes and the surly daughter of the owner of a grubby *estaminet* where they'd drank bad wine when out of the trenches on the Somme. They were quite different from American girls, unfussy and confident in their sexuality. Adèle wasn't much like them, more discriminating to be sure. Once Ned proved he was interested in more than another *française* for his wartime brags, she'd become quite fond of him. There weren't many Americans in Amiens, just a few volunteers with the British and Canadians. He'd joined up with the Newfoundlanders, a regiment from that remote British dominion with long connections to Ned's New England home.

He intrigued her, this man from Boston. Americans seemed to her, unlike the English or French, a people without any fixed place in life, endlessly reinventing themselves without a thought it might not be the most natural thing in the world. In Ned's case, he wanted her to teach him French, thinking an officer—even a newly minted one—ought not sound like a Tommy from east London, massacring the language with jovial impunity. Then she'd taken him into her bed without regret, which had proven delightful to them both.

Her legs were loose about him as he melted inside her. He kissed her neck, letting his tongue run along her skin, tasting the saltiness from her sheen of perspiration. He pulled himself up and was drawn into her eyes, dark as chestnuts, saying in a thick whisper, "You're the loveliest woman I've ever known, Adèle Chéreaux." He spoke with such wistfulness it made her wonder what his life had been before. "I'm afraid I'll never meet one more lovely. You think that makes my future somehow disappointing?"

She let out an incredulous burst of laughter. "It would seem rather bad form for a gentleman to muse over future prospects with unknown beauties, having just deposited his seed within a woman he claims is the loveliest he's ever seen."

A blush of pink rose in his cheeks. "Seems they may have overlooked the 'gentleman' in my hasty promotion." He tumbled off her and onto his back, easing her head down on his shoulder. She placed a palm on his chest as she settled, accepting his tacit apology in smiling silence.

Glancing over him at the chiffonier against the wall, she pointed with her chin at a small framed portrait sitting there. "You're sure that picture of Gilles doesn't annoy you?" The hand-tinted photograph had been atop the old mahogany dresser since Ned first came to her apartment. He'd examined it closely once, just able to make out the regimental numbers on the young officer's collar. He wore the old uniform with which the French began the war. The red kepi and trousers—so crucial to *élan*, it was thought—made easy shooting for the Germans, as Gilles discovered at Charleroi before the war was even a month old.

"No, not at all. He looks like a decent fellow. Was he?"

Adèle smiled, not sure she could even answer. "I suppose he was. Decent is a good word," she said. "We hardly knew each other as man and wife. We married in such a rush after the mobilization."

Ned felt a kinship with the poor French officer, dead more than two years, just as he did with the *poilus* at the front when he was still a private soldier. Their country needed defending and the French infantrymen fought with a stoic resolve, resigned to their fate. Pity this fellow died so early. Or maybe it was his good luck.

"I like to keep the picture up," Adèle said. "I wake with a start sometimes, afraid I've forgotten what he looks like. I've long forgotten his voice."

Ned rubbed her arm. "He deserves that much, not to be forgotten. Keep the picture up."

Adèle craned her neck and kissed his cheek. "That's very kind of you, Ned." She then raised her head and smiled until he turned his face to hers. "We've made love many more times than Gilles and I ever managed."

She peeled herself from under his arm and rolled to her feet in a fluid motion. Ned watched her cross the bedroom, bending for the robe he'd tossed against the yellowing plaster wall. She slipped it on, the cold silk pleasant against her skin. "This is my last day of freedom before the *lycée* commences, where I'll again be tortured by ninety girls speaking the worst English imaginable." She bent and kissed him, chaste again, on the mouth. "I expect my overpaid Allied officer to treat me to a fine luncheon at a fashionable café." She wrapped the robe tight. "The least a girl can ask in exchange for her virtue."

Ned rose from the bed and wrapped his arms around her, warming her with his body. "You're a scandal, Adèle." Releasing her, he went to the wooden washstand across from the bed, peering into the small mirror as he ran a hand over his chin. "I'll need a shave. An officer must not present himself unshaven in public." She nudged in front of him and poured from the pitcher stored below the basin.

"I need a good wash after my morning calisthenics," she said, elbowing him and fingering the water in the basin. "Brace yourself. It's bloody cold." He kissed her on top of her head while wetting a shaving brush. She soaked a small sponge, then reached for a bar of soap.

She slapped his arm with the wet sponge and said, "And now that we're up, it will be French only, *s'il vous plaît*. You need the practice."

"*Oui, commandant! Je suis à votre service!*" he said, lathering his chin while she bent to wash between her legs, shaking back her thick sable hair.

"*Ah oui, chéri.* You've done very well this morning *à mon service*," she said with an improper glance back at him.

CHAPTER TWO

Chester

For as long as either could remember, their father had hidden behind the reliably Republican *New York Tribune* during breakfast. In their younger days, they made faces at him through the newspaper when their mother was in the kitchen with Maddie, their cook. Maman's was the only voice for which he'd glance above the newsprint. After she died, they left him to his reading, waiting for him to emerge in his own good time. It was small consolation for him, after all.

Chester flipped through last week's *Chicago Defender*, a publication Chester had mailed to their Harlem address and his father thought so radical he barely tolerated it in the mailbox. Lena scribbled notes from her pedagogy textbook for the morning's lecture. Both looked up when they heard the familiar rustling that signaled their father had finished consuming his *Tribune*.

"Pop, I ran into Genevieve Harrison walking home yesterday. She's very pregnant," said Chester. "How come you never mentioned it? We were kids together."

Clarence Dawkins peered over his glasses and said, "Didn't know m'self. She must be seeing another physician." He smoothed the refolded paper and rose. Patting the front of his vest, he produced a heavy gold watch and gave it a perfunctory glance. "Off to work," he said with a wan smile.

Lena gave her brother a worried look and made to say something, which he quashed with a discrete shake of his head. She pretended to look over her notes until their father left the dining room. They could hear him rummaging in the hall closet for his hat and umbrella, then the sound of the front door. Lena leaned toward Chester across the table and said, "The Harrisons have been Papa's patients forever, the whole family." She didn't want the cook to hear, so she switched to French. Chester saw his sister's panicked face. He was worried, too.

"He's been distracted since we lost Maman, that's all. You know that he adored her."

"She has been dead four years now." Her worried look was undiminished.

Chester met his sister's eyes with forced calm, but she'd known him too long for this to be convincing. He sighed, then said in French, "I do not know what can be done for him. His patients are losing confidence, abandoning him. Only the oldest remain."

Lena closed her notebook and gathered her things from the table. "Well, you must complete your studies with M. Davis and take admission to the Bar. We could be without a home before I finish my studies." She stacked her books and notes then said, "At least you had your time at Howard, like Papa."

"Let me speak with him, Lennie. He must know what's happening to his practice. He is just too proud to say anything."

Returning to English, Lena said, "You think you can talk to him without turning it into one of those fights you two love so much? You're not to mention New Negroes or Dr. Du Bois, you hear me? You know how that sets him off."

"Not respectable." Chester said, an octave lower in imitation of their father. "Have to keep our heads down and shoulders to the wheel. Back to the plantation."

"For pity's sake, Chester, we haven't had a slave in the family for more than a century. And that's exactly the kind of talk doesn't sit well with Papa." Lena pointed a finger at him and narrowed her eyes in mock threat, although she'd never been able to tell him anything.

"You need to speak with him before he gets into the brandy," she said in whispered French.

"That's becoming earlier and earlier," Chester replied.

"And what if you're sent to France? You've been with the regiment since last year, since the beginning," Lena said. "Isn't it likely you'll have to go? Then I'll be left alone to look after Papa."

The recent declaration of war on the 6th of April was not unexpected. German submarines had brought a little of the violence raging in Europe across to America. Even a reluctant President Wilson had been pushed too far when the Germans proposed a Mexican invasion of the United States, no matter how far-fetched it was in reality. All the National Guard units across the nation, white and black, expected to receive word of their mobilization for overseas duty any day.

Chester hadn't been enthusiastic about joining the new National Guard regiment when it started recruiting six months ago in Harlem. The 15th was formed after repeated attempts in the state legislature to approve raising a unit from the Negro population. The old lawyer he clerked for, Mr. Davis, had thought it a fine opportunity for Chester to show himself a young leader in the community. When Chester, ink on his diploma scarcely dry, was offered a second lieutenant's commission, his father likewise thought it a laudable addition to the family escutcheon. With the two most influential men in his life pressing him, Chester bowed to their wishes and had been drilling with the 15th on nights and weekends ever since. They had no armory, few rifles and not enough uniforms, but the regiment recruited a remarkable band that played dances all over Upper Manhattan and Brooklyn. And Chester's tailored uniform with its high collar and tall brown boots impressed the ladies of Harlem, too.

"I need a few hours in the library this morning before lecture," Lena said. She bustled around the table and kissed her seated brother on the top of his head, then wrapped an arm around his neck and squeezed him against her waist.

He patted her arm. "We'll get by, Lennie. You know we will." She kissed his head again and turned to leave.

"Lennie?"

She looked back to her brother, "Yes?"

"I still miss her."

Lena bit her lower lip through a trembly smile and said, "I know. Me, too."

Their mother was the daughter of the noted Dr. Antoine Villere, who taught their father pharmacology at Howard Medical School. Grand-père Villere, the scion of a colored Creole dynasty of pharmacists in New Orleans, had studied medicine in Paris. He was an exemplary medical scholar, but he'd also delved into chemistry while in France. Having seen for himself the inexactness of the concoctions sold at his family's pharmacies, he sought to apply the rigors of laboratory chemistry to the compounding of drugs. Upon his return, he joined the family business while building his new medical practice. Ten years later, he was offered the chair of pharmacology in the medical school of the new and prestigious Howard University in Washington, D.C.

Their father, from an old freeman family in New York City, arrived at Howard as a seventeen-year-old, eager to begin his medical studies. He met his pharmacology professor's daughter at a Sunday reception. There was never to be another woman, in his eyes, after that day. He begged to stay on after graduation as Grand-père Villere's assistant, much to his own father's consternation. He wasn't particularly interested in pharmacology or chemistry, but he had ulterior motives. It required two years of courting, but Maman finally agreed to marry him.

As a child, Chester thought there could be no other woman more beautiful than his mother. She often retired to her room soon after supper to answer letters or read. Chester and Lena would sit with her at night as she shed her daytime dress behind an intricate Chinese screen. She'd perch in her dressing gown on a small cushioned stool before her vanity mirror and unpin her hair. As it fell to her shoulders, Chester sometimes twirled his finger in the long, glossy curls. She was very fair and at a glance, her hair pinned up, white people often took her for one of their own. It was in the evenings when Maman spoke French with them. As they grew to school age, she'd read with them in French and supervise writing letters to cousins in New Orleans.

Lena inherited her mother's lustrous skin—just a shade darker, the palest caramel—as well as Maman's jet-black ringlets. When Chester was five or six, he'd sometimes hold his forearm against Lena's or Maman's and rub to see if his darker brown would wipe off.

He favored his stouter father in both stature and looks. His mother's features were finer than Lena's, almost sculpted from marble it seemed to him, but Lena also had some of the Dawkins's height and wide shoulders. Still, the similarity was profound, and Chester's breath caught sometimes when his sister entered a room.

When he was eleven or twelve, Maman gently banished him from their evening rituals. He understood as he grew that this intimacy wasn't deemed appropriate for a young man whose desires were awakening. Instead, his mother expanded the use of French into the dining room and front parlor. Although this annoyed her husband a little, she didn't want her son to lose his mother tongue from want of use. Maman and Lena began sharing quiet words in French and Chester felt pangs of exclusion when they giggled over some nonsense.

However, having been banished from his mother's boudoir, Chester was able to see her with more detachment. The fineness of her beauty was somewhat overwrought. She was what people called delicate when they meant she had tenuous health. He'd heard passing comments about the difficult time Maman had delivering Lena and how she'd never recovered her strength. Sometimes, his mother appeared to him as ethereal as the carved angels he'd seen standing watch over the tombs of distant relatives in a New Orleans graveyard.

In the end, forty years was all she was allowed. Her last illness was a matter of a few days and Chester learned of it through the brief telegram announcing her death. On the train up from Washington, mile upon mile of awakening green countryside sliding by, he couldn't understand how his beautiful mother could pass in such a lovely season. He was never quite sure why she slipped away. His father could never speak of it. When he arrived home for the funeral, she was simply gone. The absence was yawning, echoing. Lena was just fifteen, devastated yet expected to run a household that would never be the same.

Chester shook himself out of his bittersweet daydreaming, realizing with a start that he should have left for the office ten minutes ago. He stuck his head through to the kitchen to let Maddie know he was off, then retraced his father and Lena's footsteps out onto the morning streets of Harlem.

CHAPTER THREE

Ned

From below erratic grey eyebrows, the gruff commander examined Lieutenant Tobin with suspicion. The order from British Expeditionary Force Headquarters lay heavy in its officiousness on the desk between them. The colonel, indignantly recalled to active duty from a boozy retirement, had tossed the paper there to demonstrate how unimpressed he was that one of his junior officers might possibly warrant such a thing.

"Seems HQ wants you at the American Embassy in Paris toot-sweet, Tobin. More's the mystery to me as to why." He sniffed at the paper as if it emitted some unpleasant odor. Although he treated his junior officers with public contempt, he looked after them with vicious protectiveness when it mattered. "Mightn't it have something to do with your damned dilatory countrymen deigning to join our little shivaree?"

Ned took the order from the desktop and returned to a position of attention, where the commander always left his junior officers, regardless of the length or breadth of the ensuing conversation. Something about teaching respect for rank.

"That seems likely, sir. However, I've scheduled a swing through some of the battalions to inspect machine gun companies. I was meant to depart this morning."

The commander did not like complications of any size or description and assumed a most aggrieved look. "That order says to report within seven days to your bloody embassy. I see no need to disrupt the workings of my unit." He sniffed again at the order in Ned's hand. "They damned well took their time getting into this donnybrook. They can wait a day or two for you. Proceed with your inspections."

The colonel sized Ned up anew, the slightest softening around his mouth and eyes. "Damn it, Tobin, you've been a serviceable enough officer and I don't like losing men I've spent so much effort training up. Nothing more important than machine gunnery, not in this bloody trench war we've bungled into," the old officer said, harrumphing to regain composure after this uncharacteristic eruption of decency to a subaltern. "Damnable waste, really."

From the contemplative look on the commander's face, Ned knew there was more to come. He stood silent, eyeing the pink leave-and-railway ticket sitting at the colonel's elbow.

So he already had the orderly room arrange my travel, Ned thought. *I'll miss the old bastard, even with the regular rations of shit.*

"Whatever the outcome of your *tête-à-tête* with that bloody American attaché, you've done a man's work here with the British Expeditionary Force, Tobin. Not many of your countrymen can say that." He rubbed a finger under his mustache and searched the desktop for some nonexistent paperwork, covering this flicker of emotion. "Stout fellow, Tobin, damned stout fellow. We'll not forgot your kind when this bloody cotillion is over." The colonel shoved the leave card across and nodded for Ned to pick it up, then fell into a silent funk of indignation. Ned took this as his cue to exit.

"Will that be all, sir?" The old colonel's head snapped up, perturbed at being roused from his tetchy reverie.

"Yes, yes, that will be all," he grumbled, then returned to his thoughts. Relishing the chance to tweak the old gent, Ned cocked a parade-ground salute. He held it until the colonel returned it with a desultory wave at his forehead.

Outside the headquarters, Ned wandered around the forecourt packed with vehicles, finally recognizing a large hatless corporal lounging against the arcing fender of a green Peerless lorry. He was smoking in an admirably relaxed manner.

"It is customary for a soldier to wear a cover when out of doors, Corporal King," he said in as pommy an accent as he could manage. Geordie King's head snapped up and he jumped to attention. Seeing it was Ned Tobin, he broke into a toothy grin and tossed his cigarette into the pea gravel.

"Why as I live and breathe, 'tis a walking silk purse stitched from a sow's ear!" he called out, forgoing a salute. No one would've expected much else, these being Dominion troops.

Ned shook his head and smiled back at the big, bluff Newfoundlander. "You're the only soldier in France who finds this damn war a great relaxation, Geordie."

"Like a summer's holiday, b'y."

Ned offered his hand and Geordie grasped it with a crush. They stood for a moment, recalling in the brief silence the last time they were together on the Somme. Geordie slapped Ned's shoulder and hooked a thumb at the open driver's compartment of the lorry. "Up we go then, Lieutenant Tobin," he said, stepping up on the running board. Ned circled around and climbed to the passenger's side of the long bench seat.

"Three units to visit, if we've the daylight. I don't want to spend a night in a dugout, so we may cut this short," Ned said. "I thought we'd start with Will Parsons's Glamorgans. They're just north of here, near some burg called Belmarais."

Geordie shifted the idling lorry with a great grinding and set off. "Strange when our William left us after the Somme that he ended up with a Welsh battalion," Geordie shouted over the roar of the four-cylinder laboring along the rutted road. "But his ma's English, so the Royal Army had equal dibs. Divided loyalties, eh?"

Ned looked out over the plowed and seeded fields, their winter brown broken by new green shoots, low hills undulating toward the horizon. Spitting rain fell from the overcast, just enough to keep the roads in their perpetual state of muddiness.

"That's right," Ned said, his mind turning to the changes coming his way. "Divided loyalties."

The young lieutenant seated behind the gilded Louis Quatorze table in the Hôtel de Crillon's lobby scanned Ned's orders. "You'd best see Major Waller. He seems to be behind most of these drop-ins. Main stairs to the fourth floor, then left, last room at the end of the hall. Number 410. Knock before you go in—no anteroom or secretary."

Ned nodded his thanks and made his way to the switchback marble staircase, running his hand along the curving brass balustrade as he climbed to the fourth floor. He knocked twice on the door, the sounds of a telephone conversation and a clacking typewriter leaking out through the dark wood. The door flew open almost as he lifted his knuckles and a broad-shouldered officer with short-cropped salt-and-pepper hair filled the opening. He seemed to Ned rectangular in every way—square head, jaw, shoulders.

"What can I do for you, Lieutenant?" the major said, bursting with bustle and efficiency.

Ned offered his orders and said, "Lieutenant—'lef-tenant'—Edmund Tobin, sir. Ordered to report to the American attaché's office."

The big American officer looked over the order, then studied the British officer with the Boston accent standing in front of him. "Took your time getting here." He examined Ned's lapel insignia and sleeve rank. "You're the Boston man with the Newfoundlanders," he said, adding so Ned knew he was home, "Isn't that correct, Loo-tenant Tobin?" The square major broke into a large, rectangular grin.

"I've been with the British forces for over two years, Major. You'll have to allow me some slippage."

The American stuck out his large quadrilateral hand and said, "Major Wally Waller, and no tittering. My dear mother thought it a fine name." He motioned for Ned to enter, then nodded to a chair by a very utilitarian desk standing before a very large window that overlooked a very grande Place de la Concorde. Cigarettes were lit.

Could've watched the guillotining not so many years ago, Ned thought.

"I expect you've a good idea why we asked the Brits to send you along, Ed?" the major said with deliberate informality.

"Has to do with the declaration of war, I suppose?" Ned returned the relaxed attitude. *Yep, just us Yanks here.* "My friends call me Ned, sir."

"We're in it now, Ned, and our forces are as unprepared as they could be. We're starting from scratch with almost no officers with experience of this kind of warfare. Hell, only combat I saw in the fifteen years since I graduated West Point was chasing *banditos* back across the Mexican border. I'm trying to locate all the American volunteers here and bring 'em home to the colors." Leaning forward and giving Ned his best recruiting-poster stare. "Your country needs you, Lieutenant, and trusts you'll not disappoint her."

So there's the pitch. Ned intended to play a little ball before agreeing.

"I've been with the Newfoundlanders since December of '14, Major. I was wounded on the Somme with them. They made me an officer and I'm doing important work at the Machine Gun School." Ned paused to make a show of agonizing. With a dejected and confused look, he added, "I don't see how I can leave the lads now, Major."

Anticipating nothing but enthusiastic acceptance, Major Wally Waller stared across the desk, fidgeting with his cigarette. Ned stared back, placid as an iced-over pond. It was the major's move. Knowing this was an officer with experience the U.S. forces desperately needed, the major leaned back in his chair, counting his chips in this bluffer's game, and blew out his cheeks. "Now I understand loyalty to a unit you've fought with—hell, bled with. I truly do." He eyed the cocksure lieutenant with a little suspicion above his ingratiating smile. "But the United States is your home, and you owe her your loyalty, too."

Ned looked back at the major and, silent and calm, went on smoking his cigarette.

"Seeing how you've gained so much experience with the Newfoundlanders and at the Machine Gun School, I'm authorized to offer specific rank with a U.S. commission."

Here comes the payoff.

It looked like this was physically paining Wally Waller. "So let's say you come back home as... *Major* Tobin?"

Ned sat with a genial smile and said nothing. Major Waller's growing impatience was very evident on his square face.

"I'd be honored to accept, Major."

The angular man relaxed into his chair with a self-satisfied smile. "Perilous times we're facing. All the peacetime rules out the window. Hell, they're promoting me to *colonel*." Major Waller pursed his lips and raised his eyebrows, telegraphing that he'd not given away half as much as young Lieutenant Tobin thought. Ned returned a slight nod and leaned back in his chair, flashing Major Waller an admiring smile.

The two understood each other now. They sat with the congenial smiles of two well-fed diners awaiting their *digestifs*, while taxis dashed around the Egyptian pylon protruding from the wide traffic circle below.

It took a genuine effort for Ned to stay engaged with his work at the Machine Gun School. The attaché's office instructed him to return to his British unit while awaiting orders. His commander reacted with a put-upon pout when Ned informed him of his decision, congratulated him on his impending promotion to field-grade rank, warned him not to forget he was still a subaltern under his command, then poured whiskies to toast the imminent arrival of American forces in France.

With an open-ended wait stretching before him, Ned took every advantage to spend as many nights with Adèle as he could manage. He decided not to tell her of his impending departure until he had orders in hand. All too familiar with the vagaries of military administration, he had low expectations of heading back across the Atlantic anytime soon. No need to upset her until he knew when that would be.

Adèle was thrilled to see more of him, although the concierge continued her cold, fish-eyed inspection whenever he turned up for an overnight visit. No matter, since wartime rules applied, particularly to romances. Reveling in this time together, they hid themselves away from the daily horrors to the east.

Harboring the secret of his imminent departure was a strain, but Ned was too happy to agonize much. Nevertheless, the wheels of Army bureaucracy ground relentlessly onward and his orders arrived in mid-June. After six weeks without a word, the U.S. Army now wanted him at Le Havre for transport in forty-eight hours. Tomorrow would be their last night together until the American Expeditionary Forces arrived in earnest, bearing Major Tobin back with them.

She sensed as soon as she opened the door something was strange. Ned kissed her and handed over a tin of coffee with a sheepish smile. She turned the tin over in her hands, noting it was American. "A gift from home?" she said, wary that he was bringing food. He'd never done so before.

"Picked up a few tins on that trip to Paris last month," he said, in a glancing attempt to introduce the unpleasant topic. "Thought you might like some."

She left the door open and turned toward the long thin table she used as a kind of kitchen, tucked into the back corner of her sitting room. It held a small gas ring, a kettle, and a few cups and dishes. Trying to shake off the awkwardness saturating the room, Ned walked up behind her as she fussed at the table and wrapped his arms around her. She relaxed into the smooth worsted of his uniform, the familiar smell of him, the feel of his chin resting against her hair. Then it all went away.

Looking down at her hands, not turning, she said, "Out with it, Ned."

Slumping from the ineffectiveness of his jittery affections, he turned toward a half-open window. An early hint of the looming summer mugginess rendered the people on the street a little indistinct, their sounds muffled by the thick humid air. He turned back, reluctant and slow, and saw her eyes filled with tears. His chest constricted.

"Adèle, the U.S. has been in the war over two months," he began. She remained very still. "That's why I was called to Paris, to see the American Attaché at the embassy." Almost imperceptible at first, she began moving her head in little oscillations. "They offered me a commission, as a major. They need all of us back, all of us who volunteered here." The shaking grew wider and faster while she looked over his shoulder, out the window.

He was becoming frantic at her reaction. "We... they... the Americans..."— casting about, he struggled on—"there's no one back home with any idea how terrible the fighting is here. They'll be lambs to the slaughter unless some of us go back to help train them."

She began to sob, hands to her face and shoulders curling down around her chest, collapsing into herself. She choked out, between heaving catches of breath, "You've... you've done your... bit and now you're... you're safe here. It's not... fair."

Hearing her voice, meek as it was, steeled him. He rushed to her and pulled her close against his chest. The rise and fall of her shoulders as she breathed, ragged and uneven, steadied him. "I'll be back. They won't keep me in the States once we've got some divisions trained. There are so few officers with any experience. I'll be needed back here, you'll see." He rocked her in the middle of the echoing room, a place where they'd known such pleasure and contentment.

She pushed away, wiping the back of her hand under her nose, then glared up at him. "Do you think I want that? For you to come back to be shot and bombed in a different uniform?" He saw the shocking look of disappointment at how little he understood her. "I want you to cling to America with both your hands. Do anything you can to remain there. Stay alive, Ned!" She grabbed his upper arms and held them tight. "For God's sake, be shed of this bloody war once and for all!"

When he answered, his voice came thick and shaky. His vision clouded, her face a soft aura as he gazed down at her. "Adèle, if I stay home, we'll not see each other again."

She clung to his arms, her weight hanging from him now. "I buried a husband I hardly knew, Ned. I'd rather lose you to home than bury the first man I've truly loved."

They held tight to each other on her bed, not making love this last night. Neither slept, although she pretended, matching his breathing for long stretches to deaden her dread of the creeping morning. First, she could just make out the shapes of her familiar furniture, hulking black forms in the greyness, like shadows on a cave wall. Then she began to perceive colors, blues and greens, then the yellows and reds. Finally, she could count each of her black hairs spread loose across the white pillow.

Then he was gone.

CHAPTER FOUR

Ned

WAR DEPARTMENT
PERSONNEL PLANS OFFICE
WASHINGTON

August 30, 1917

MEMORANDUM FOR Major Edmund Tobin

Re: Enclosed orders, Officer Assignments Branch (29 Aug 17), assigning you UFN as Liaison & Training Officer, 93d Infantry Division.

I feel obliged to enclose this letter with your orders, by way of introduction to your unit of assignment. Secretary of War Baker, with the concurrence of the President, is keen to see all Americans participating in the war effort, including the Negro population. In furtherance thereof, two combat divisions have been authorized, the 92d and 93d Infantry Divisions, to be comprised entirely of colored soldiers and non-commissioned officers.

A majority of junior officers in these divisions will be Negroes, drawn either from the officer ranks of colored National Guard units or from graduates of the Negro Officer Training School recently established at Fort Des Moines. The commanders, field-grade officers, and (with few exceptions) captains will be white. The 93d Infantry Division will be comprised of colored National Guard regiments from Ill., N.Y., and Washington City, as well as separate colored companies from Conn., Mass., Ohio, and Md.

The Divisions will not be mustered until reaching France, with their constituent regiments training at separate locations to minimize impact upon local white communities. I understand you are a Boston man and will therefore bring a more open attitude toward this difficult assignment. You are being sent to the 15th New York, which is to commence training at Camp Wadsworth near Spartanburg, S.C.

You were recommended for this assignment by the Military Attaché's Office in Paris. Col. Waller highly commended your excellent French and experience in training with the Allies.

Although unstated in your orders for reasons you will appreciate, you are to keep this office informed of any peculiar difficulties arising during the 15th New York's tenure in South Carolina or at any other training depot in the United States. Once the unit embarks for France, they will no longer be of pressing interest.

> I wish you the best of luck and Godspeed,
> Philip R. Newsome
> Lieut. Col.

Encl: assignment order

Summoned to Washington while the 15th New York awaited relief from their temporary duties, Ned lingered more than two weeks in the capital without much to do but attend a few useless meetings. He'd slept late, ate long meals full of things rationed or unavailable in Europe, and drank his way around the District of Columbia. Being of that still rare breed of American with experience in the trenches of France, he seldom paid, drinking off his compendium of war stories. He was finally released for a few weeks' leave and jumped a Friday overnight train. Arriving at South Station, he walked across the

Summer Street bridge, hoping to rouse himself after too little sleep and too much drink in the club cars of the four trains it took to reach Boston. The September morning chill made it clear another New England summer had run its course.

Ned arrived at the house on 5th Street, a short walk from his father's three stores strung along East Broadway, right at breakfast time. He could hear the uproar from the front steps, his throbbing head already the worse for it. Fortifying with a few deep breaths and a good stretch, he hefted his bag and stepped inside.

Arrayed around the big dining room table sat the family he'd not seen for almost three years. No one heard the door or his footsteps through the arguing and clinking. He looked through, drinking in the familiarity, not quite ready to intrude. His father sat at the head of the table, back to Ned, easy to pick out from his thick head of hair.

He's going fast to white, Ned thought.

His sister Irene—Renie inside these walls— sat at the other end, from where she'd run the household from the age of fifteen, ever since they'd lost Ma more than six years ago. His big brother, Bobby, sat next to a striking woman with sweeping blond hair of suspect provenance. His youngest brother and sister sat on the other side of the table. In profile, Ned scarcely recognized the smaller ones.

Renie was reaching across to slap away the hand of a younger Tobin when she happened to glance through to the parlor and caught a glimpse of her brother. "Holy Mother of God!" she gasped, leaping to her feet. She clutched at her throat and clapped the other hand over her mouth as her eyes filled.

"What the divil are ye on about, Renie Tobin?" her father shouted down the table, turning to follow her with annoyed eyes as she flew from the room. Emmett Tobin caught a snatch of his son's face over Irene's shoulder.

"Ned! Praise be to God, ye've come home t'us at last!" he said, rising with such force that several coffee cups sloshed over into their saucers.

Irene was already in the parlor, her arms around her brother's neck, sobbing into his shoulder. Emmett stood back, antsy to greet his son, but knowing his daughter wouldn't be denied. He pulled out a crumpled handkerchief and blew his nose with deliberate gusto to remind her he was waiting. Bobby joined him, draping an arm over his father's shoulders.

Ned looked from his sister to his father. The two locked eyes and Emmett nodded both recognition and welcome. Ned smiled in relief. Easing his sister away, Ned stepped to his father and offered a hand. Emmett grasped it with both of his. "Oh Ned, my own dear boy," he said, barely able to choke out his endearments. "We thought to never see you again this side o' heaven, so long were you away from us."

Seeing so close the whiteness of his father's hair and the deep lines of his face, it struck Ned that he was becoming an old man. But the malachite eyes still shone with mischief and that was both a comfort and a warning.

Ned reached for his brother Bobby's hand and received a crushing reply. Bobby had been the bigger and stronger since grade school, but the handshake challenge was something they'd done even longer. Ned was the first to wince and pull away. "Still the runt of the litter, Ned boy," Bobby said, slapping his brother hard on the shoulder, "even with that fancy uniform."

The blond woman from the table sidled to Bobby and slid under his arm, batting large eyes. Bobby scarcely noticed her.

"Edmund Tobin, at your service, ma'am," Ned said, offering his upturned palm to the woman. She placed her hand lightly in his, sighed, then unleashed a shining smile.

"Marion Gillespie. Pleased to make your acquaintance, Colonel Tobin."

Ned flushed crimson from the electric charge that jolted through his hand. He hesitated, holding her fingers longer than proper, then said, "I'm afraid it's Major Tobin and I certainly hope you'll call me Ned, Miss Gillespie."

Bobby slapped Ned's shoulder again, oblivious to the flirtatious exchange between Marion and his brother. "Get yourself to the table and put some breakfast in you. Looks like you could use a good fry-up. They not feedin' you in either of those armies of yours?"

Renie bustled about the dining room and kitchen, producing a chair and place setting. "Bobby's right. Sit yourself down, Ned Tobin, and tuck into a proper breakfast with your family." She disappeared into the kitchen, muttering about eggs.

Emmett straightened his chair and reclaimed his place at the head of the table. He glanced along the faces, settling everyone with a sweep of his hand, his composure fully recovered. "We weren't expectin' you 'til tomorrow, Ned. You gave us quite a start."

Ned plucked a half-slice of toast from a small rack and slathered it with store-bought blueberry jam. They'd eaten the last of the preserves put up by his mother, gone almost four years by then, before he left for Newfoundland. Renie had decided it would go bad soon, so they might just as well eat it.

"I'd enough of Washington and managed to take the overnight train."

The youngest of the Tobin boys, Charlie, couldn't contain himself a second longer. Gawking across at his big brother, eyes wide as saucers, he blurted, "How many Germans did you kill, Ned?"

Although it shouldn't have surprised him coming from a twelve-year-old, Ned stopped chewing and looked over to his father. Emmett was examining him with intensity in light of young Charlie's question. He'd been wondering the same thing, it seemed.

"It's an odd sort of fight, Charlie. We hardly saw any Germans. We sat in our trenches, dug deep in the earth, and they sat in theirs. Then we lobbed shells and fired machine guns at each other. It's a strange war." He took a long draught of the coffee Renie poured for him. He could still feel his father's eyes on him. "And all the more deadly for it," he said. "Too many good men gone."

Charlie seemed satisfied with this answer, so he returned to his food with renewed vigor. Emmett continued studying his soldier son while Bobby and Marion slid back into their chairs.

"You wrote of your woundin', son. Was it somewhat bad? You look hale and hearty enough now."

"Not so bad as many, Pa. I was hit early the first day on the Somme. I got pipped behind our own lines, long-range machine gun fire, so didn't have to lie out all day and half the night waiting for a stretcher party." Irene returned with hot eggs and took her seat again. She went quite pale at the thought of poor men left bleeding in the dirt for so long.

"Oh, Ned. It must have been terrible," she said.

"It was worse than anything I'd ever imagined, Renie. The worst kind of nightmare and more." Charlie was rapt again, while little Bessie, youngest of them all, sat with a trembling lip and watery eyes at the very thought of what the worst nightmare imaginable could possibly be. "They sent us against uncut barbed wire. It was almost untouched after eight days' shelling. The Germans had kept their machine guns underground until our bombardment stopped, then hauled them back up and mowed us down like green hay."

This knocked the flirtatiousness from Marion and she sat with terrified eyes, mouth agape. Bobby belatedly noticed and slipped an arm around her. She collapsed into him with a great show of emotion.

"We had almost eight hundred men jump off the 1st of July." Ned's voice was as sharp and cold as a knife blade. "One of the lucky lads from the regiment told me months later that sixty-eight answered roll the next morning." Renie crossed herself. Bessie let out a tiny sob. Marion wept copious tears into Bobby's shirtsleeve. And Emmett understood a little of what had become of his second son.

Bobby slapped the table, palms each side of his plate, breaking the horrified silence and leaving Marion to dangle over his chair back. "Well, it's a grand thing that we're in it now to put an end to all such foolishness. The Yanks are comin' and the Kaiser will be goin' soon enough."

Emmett leaned a little toward Ned and said, "You think that's right? You think our boys'll make the difference?"

"Maybe by weight of numbers," Ned said, picking up another slice of toast. "The Germans and the French and the Brits, they've bled themselves dry and it's all at a standstill. Has been for over a year."

Bobby blew out his cheeks and said, "One American's worth five of them Froggies."

Ned stuck a knife in the jam pot and said, calm as he could manage, "The French die brave as any. It's their country bein' burned and bombed, after all." He hated the quick reemergence of his local accent.

Bobby rose and lifted Marion by an armpit. "Well, we'll see who's right soon enough, won't we?" Marion shouldered away from him, smoothed her dress and patted her hair, the adjustments necessitated by her turbulent emotional display. "It was an honor to meet you, *Colonel* Tobin," she said, extending a limpid white hand. Ned took it with his fingertips and gave it a gentle squeeze.

"We're off for the shoppin', my sweet girl bein' in need of a fine new hat for my fight next Saturday," Bobby said, giving a large wink to his little brother Charlie, who stared back with a puzzled look. With that, Bobby and Marion were out the door.

Renie stood and gathered their plates. "Bessie, be a good girl and help me clear away." Bess slid sideways from her chair and took her own plate to the kitchen. "Lord knows Her Highness there wouldn't lift a finger," Renie said, jerking her head at Marion's empty chair. "Bobby spoils that one and he'll pay the price for it soon enough. And a Presbyterian to boot, not that she's darkened the door of any church for a month of Sundays." She pushed the swinging door harder than needed with her hip and set about washing up with a deliberate clatter.

"Charlie, why don't you run along and find your mates outside," Emmett said. Charlie moved closer to look over his brother's fine uniform, gave Ned a tight hug, and jogged to the front door.

Ned produced a green packet of Lucky Strikes from an inside pocket and offered one to his father, then smiled at this reflex. "Your mother would be pushin' you out the door with those," Emmett said, smiling back at his son. "I never developed a taste for the tobacco, what with the asthma as a young one."

Ned lit the cigarette and said, "They were a comfort to us in the trenches. Settled the nerves when there was shellin'." He looked around the familiar room, so much of his mother still in everything.

Ned's father was well known throughout the Irish neighborhoods. He'd built a fine grocery from the fruit-and-vegetable cart he'd bought with a little money raised from pawning his grandmother's locket when just off the boat from Ireland. After moving his trade into a proper greengrocer's store, he'd always extended credit when some poor soul fell on hard times, never forgetting how he himself started out. Building on the resulting loyalty, he opened a tobacco store and then a sweet shop, staffing them with sons of neighbors and the odd distant cousin over from Tipperary. But first and foremost, he was the father of the middleweight champion of all the New England boxing clubs, just turned professional, known to all and sundry as Bobby "Tearin' Tip" Tobin.

"Ned, I know you were anxious to get into the fightin' and that's why you left us for the north. You fought for the English against my very wishes, as you well know." The older man said this without accusation or any intent to dredge up old hurt, merely restating the facts as they both knew them. "You did your bit and took a bullet as proof of 't. There's no need to prove anythin' more to yourself or any man."

Ned knew this conversation was bound to occur but hadn't thought it would be within an hour of his arrival. "Our country's in this now, Pa. I can't turn my back, knowin' all that I do. I had months in the trenches and was at the Machine Gun School for seven more after I was made an officer. There's a need for men like me, powerful need."

Emmett frowned and looked out the window opposite. Charlie and his pals were kicking a rusty can down the street in a wild gaggle. "Our country or no, 'tis more blood shed for an English king. And this isn't our only country."

Ned sighed and took one last long drag from his cigarette before stabbing it into a saucer. "Ireland's not my country, Pa. It was once yours, but it's not any more."

Emmett straightened in his chair, color rising. "There's not a drop of blood in your veins isn't that of a good Irishman, Edmund James Tobin, including that you spilled on the fields of France, mind you." Emmett was not about to let this matter drop, no matter how tired his son might be. Ned sat passive as a stone and let his father ramble.

"'Twas a Tipperary man I was born. And your dear mother's parents straight from the County Clare, they were." Emmett tapped a long finger into the tabletop as he spoke. "If you've a nose for the fightin', there'll be plenty to be had in Ireland, soon enough. Sure, hasn't it already started? And in a righteous cause."

Ned unhooked his high collar and loosed the first few buttons on his tunic, slumping with exhaustion. "That's not my fight, Pa."

"More so than when you took the King's shillin' three years ago, my boy." The bitterness from his Republican leanings was burning clear and bright. "You bled for him, now 'tis time to bleed for Ireland, if need be."

Irene burst out of the kitchen and began swooping up the remaining plates on the table. Seeing the ashy saucer before Ned, she tut-tutted at her brother and whisked it away. "Now stop your yammerin', you two," she said in a manner that brooked no dissent. "Ned'll be needin' a bath and a good rest, Pa. He has to be sharp and look smart for his homecomin' tomorrow." She rubbed her brother's shoulder, then looked minutely at his tunic. "That uniform will need a good brush up. Leave it out for me. And those boots, too. Charlie'll be over the moon polishin' a real soldier's boots."

Ned looked up with a deep sigh and pained expression at his sister. "Renie, tell me you haven't planned some big party. You know full well I hate that sort of fuss."

Renie gave him a terse back of her hand. "Then think of it as a duty for the honor of your family, Ned. The whole South End wants a look at you and they'll not be denied. Tomorrow afternoon at Saint Brigid's parish hall."

"For the love of Mike…" Ned grumbled back at her.

"Now hush yourself!" she said, swatting his complaints away like a late-season fly. "Didn't our councilman want a parade all the way to the Fenian Hall? Count yourself fortunate it's just to be at the parish." She stood, arms crossed, at her end of the table. Both men knew there was no hope in resistance, so like her mother had Renie become.

Ned went out to the long front stoop and sat on the steps. It had turned to a fine cool morning. After milling about the house to no discernible purpose, Emmett came out and sat behind his son, a few steps higher. With lingering discomfort at how their conversation had turned, Emmett remained quiet. Finally, Ned spoke.

"They already have an assignment for me, the brass hats at the War Department."

Emmett sighed at the granite stairs. "Then it's back to the fightin' with ye."

"I'm to join up with a National Guard regiment in ten days, down in South Carolina. The plan is to mash three or four Guard regiments together into a new division."

"They just announced the same with our Massachusetts boys," Emmett said. "They've gathered them out on the Cape for trainin' and such, before shippin' them off to France. So what state are these battalions from?"

"From all over."

"Strange for the Guard, wouldn't you say? Them bein' state militia."

"Yep, strange indeed, Pa."

"Seems a lot of nonsense, especially those from big states," Emmett said, suspecting there was more to this than his son was letting on.

Ned studied his feet, brushed off his sleeve, and fished for another cigarette.

"Speak your mind, lad. I know well enough when you're himmin' and hawin'."

Exhaling a long blue stream, Ned straightened and said, "None of the state Guard divisions will have them. They're Negro regiments." He fished a few shreds of tobacco from his lip. "It's to be a colored infantry division."

His father stood and came down the steps. The calm and control had sloughed away revealing a bright red face. "Jayzus, Ned! Are ye daft? How could you agree to such a thing, ever in the world?" Emmett sputtered, spreading his hands for an answer.

"It's got the Secretary of War's attention, Pa. He's determined to have all the people supporting this war," Ned said. "There're millions of Negroes in this country."

Emmett rubbed a hand along his mouth and around to the back of his neck. "There damned well are, more's the pity."

"They can fight and die as well as white men."

Emmett shook his head and scoffed. "So you're to train these darkies how to die like white men then? More's the fool y'are."

"I saw Negroes from the African colonies fight with the French, and right well, too."

"And you'll not lift so much as a finger to help the cause in Ireland, but you'll parade yourself around with a gang o' niggers, playin' at soldier?" Emmett spat at the pavement and said, "What a fine time you'll have with those jolly white fellas down there in the Carolina states, too."

"We could put a million Negroes in uniform." Ned tried to steer the conversation to less dangerous waters. "You've no idea how many men we'll need to end this bloody mess."

Emmett turned his back to his son and jammed his hands deep into his pockets, shoulders bunched and tense. "Well, have the decency not to tell anyone while you're here. Sure not that brother o' yours. Mouth like a bargeman and less like to keep a secret, too. Boy could never hold his liquor nor his tongue."

Emmett brushed past and pulled the front door hard. He turned and added, "Some of us have to carry on livin' and doin' business here."

CHAPTER FIVE

Chester

By nightfall, the soldiers were nodding in and out of restive sleep, rocked senseless by the clack-clack rhythm. After the first half-day in packed train carriages, all anyone smelled was sour sweaty wool and the permeating acridness of thousands upon thousands of cigarettes. Their commander made enough of a nuisance that they'd received movement orders along with the units of the all-white Empire Division, now finally traveling as a regiment. Somehow, somewhere within the War Department, someone thought it a fine idea to send two thousand colored New Yorkers to South Carolina for training. Word had gone ahead and everyone from political leaders to the poorest whites was in an uproar. Unruly northern Negroes, after all, were sure to be unfamiliar with the folkways governing the relations of the dominant and subordinate races in Dixie.

By the time they reached Spartanburg, in the environs of which sat Camp Wadsworth, the men were listless and hungry. The cool October air of New York City had not dropped this far south and the omnipresent odor of pine-forest decay was cloying to men more accustomed to the grittier smells of a well-drained and paved cityscape. Their first several days were spent repairing the rundown or unfinished facilities they were assigned. As was the way with soldiers, once this flurry of immediate work was completed, the men wanted off the post. There was no justifiable way to keep them confined to the installation, but each man knew, like it or not, he'd be under constant scrutiny as a representative of the Negro race.

Into this tense situation Ned Tobin arrived from Boston. After locating the regiment's mess hall, he begged coffee and a sandwich from the cook sergeant, an animated railroad porter from Poughkeepsie who appeared from his girth to be a zealous devotee of his own cooking. The sergeant escorted Ned to the back. "Officers' country," he said, spreading his beefy arms before two less battered tables with place settings and a carved regimental seal as a centerpiece.

By 4:30, men began straggling in for evening chow, exhausted and sweaty, forming a dusty green serpentine of scraping feet and razzing voices. Ned knew by long tradition the officers would eat after their troops, so he waited for the platoon lieutenants to follow behind the flow of privates. Soon enough, two men in Sam Browne belts pushed through the double doors and followed a mess orderly toward the officers' tables. They conversed easily, turning their heads to emphasize occasional points. Neither was much younger than Ned, though he looked some years older. They walked with confidence, trim and fit in their khaki green uniforms. One was clean shaven, but the other had a well-tended black mustache and brilliantined hair that radiated rakish fastidiousness. As they closed on the back tables, both pulled up short at the unfamiliar white major sipping coffee behind a plate of half-crusts.

Ned set down his cup and stood. The two lieutenants made no move, not sure what was expected of them. "Major Ned Tobin." He extended his hand a bit further with a nod of encouragement. The clean-shaven officer moved first.

"Lieutenant Dawkins, sir."

Ned nodded again and pumped Chester's hand. "Pleased to meet you, Lieutenant."

The other lieutenant followed, offering his hand. "Lieutenant Sharpe, sir. Benjamin Sharpe," he said, flashing a smile the ladies of France would find very fetching.

Real flapper's delight this one, Ned thought.

"Glad to make your acquaintance, Lieutenant Sharpe. Please join me, if you haven't any other place to be, gentlemen. The mess sergeant has been plying me with enough sandwiches and coffee for six majors, but I hope you'll enjoy your supper."

Chester pulled a chair back from the table and moved around to seat himself. He glanced over his shoulder toward the kitchen and said, "You've met Sergeant Ames then? The men would mutiny if the Army transferred him to any other unit."

Benny Sharpe added, "The Sergeant has taken Napoleon's admonition regarding armies traveling on their stomachs as a point of personal honor, sir. The 15th could circumnavigate the globe on Sergeant Ames's efforts."

Steady, lad. Don't need to impress the new major all at once.

The mess orderly returned with two plates and the lieutenants went at their meals with vigor. After listening to several minutes of clinking cutlery and rapid chewing, Ned spoke again. "I suppose I should solve the mystery. I've been attached to the 93rd Division as training and liaison officer."

Both lieutenants gave a quick look up, deciding to commit Ned's face to memory since he'd be sticking around for awhile. Then they returned to their food without a word. There being no signs of interest, Ned continued, "Since the 93rd Division exists nowhere but on paper, the War Department detailed me to your regiment. Seems you were closer to Washington than the 8th Illinois. Didn't seem to be any better reason than that, far as I could tell."

Ned picked up his coffee and studied the contents. Both lieutenants stared at this odd major. Then Benny gave out a nervous laugh. Chester smiled in turn.

There, we're all friends now.

"So that explains how a Boston Irish boy finds himself in deepest Dixie," Ned said. "How about you New Yorkers?"

Chester gave Ned a curious look, all raised eyebrows and cynical smile, and said, "Begging the Major's pardon, but isn't your question actually how did we *colored* New Yorkers find our way to South Carolina?"

Straight to it, this one. We'll get along fine.

"Alright, fair play to you, Lieutenant... Dawson is it?"

"Dawkins, sir."

"Lieutenant Dawkins," Ned repeated. "It did occur to me there might have been a more… judicious choice for the 15th New York, given your peculiar… circumstances."

"Colonel Hayward's thoughts exactly, Major… Tobias was it?" Chester said, a hint of insubordination. Ned smiled and nodded in appreciation of the cheekiness.

"Tobin. Major Ned Tobin."

"Of course, Major Tobin. Very sorry, sir," said Chester, not sorry in the least.

Lieutenant Sharpe said, "Are you regular Army, sir? You don't seem old enough for your rank."

"Nope, not a day in the U.S. Army before July, when I returned from France."

"You were in France, Major?" Chester asked, finding this new white officer much more interesting. Ned nodded a little too modestly. "If you don't mind my asking, sir, what were you doing in France?"

Now I've got you, Lieutenant. You and me are going to be fine.

Ned pushed back his chair and crossed his legs, his boots the cleanest in the mess hall. He removed a cigarette and, the lieutenants still eating, returned the pack to his pocket. He lit the cigarette with great care from his worn trench lighter, so the other men would notice. "I signed on with the Newfoundlanders in December of '14. Spent two-and-a-half years with them in the BEF. Missed their turn in Gallipoli, but was with them on the Somme." His two new colleagues stopped eating, sitting in rapt attention, as any green lieutenants would. "We lost so many junior officers in the fighting on the Somme that they commissioned me straight from the hospital," Ned said, adding with a self-deprecating smile, "demonstrating the depths of our British cousins' desperation."

"You made major awfully fast with them, sir," Benny interjected, always keen on rank and precedence.

"Just to first lieutenant"—the purposefully affected 'left-tenant' again—"and lucky to make that. 'Twas dear Uncle Samuel leapfrogged me to major." Adding to his humble bona fides, "Made the old neighborhood back in Boston right proud, too."

Just one of the lads, see? And a Yankee, not one of these crackers.

The two lieutenants struggled against appearing wide-eyed. This strange new major had the real knowledge and they wanted to hear everything. They swallowed the hundred questions that were on their lips, but it was easy enough for Ned to read their thoughts. He'd been this green not so long ago, overflowing with excitement and trepidation. He pulled out his cigarettes and tossed them with casual camaraderie across the table. After they'd each extracted one, thinking it akin to an order to join the major in smoking, Ned slid his trench lighter over with melodramatic reverence.

Benny picked it up like a religious relic, examining each knick and scrape, turning the brass cylinder around and around in his fingers. He fumbled with the wick cap, then with the thumb wheel. Ned didn't want to embarrass him by retrieving the lighter, so he let him struggle. The lieutenant finally managed to raise a flame, lighting his own cigarette, then holding it out so Chester could bend in, too. Benny slid the lighter back to Ned.

"That lighter's seen some duty, hasn't she?"

"Too much, maybe," Ned said, looking over his lighter with a rueful pout. "Glad to see you smoke. Helps steady you during bombardments or before jumping off. Can't let the men see you nervous, after all."

"Of course not, sir. Have to set an example for the men at all times," recited Chester. Hearing his own rote response, he twitched an uneasy smile and searched desperately for somewhere to look other than at Ned.

He's learning, that's what matters. He'll make out. The other one's a little puffed up. That tidy mustache is a giveaway.

Ned decided the war stories had lasted long enough. "So tell me, gentlemen, how has your settling in with the locals been proceeding?" Both lieutenants were disappointed the talk of France had ended, but there would be future opportunities.

"Tense, as everyone expected," Chester said. "Colonel Hayward, the commander, ordered the men to ignore insulting words and actions. He enjoined all the officers to enforce his order."

"How's that gone?"

Chester exhaled a long stream of smoke and tapped his cigarette into an ashtray. "None of the locals take kindly to colored soldiers in general, let alone on their sidewalks or in their stores. Even our officers."

"We've had some tense situations," Benny said. "The commander's detailed officers and sergeants to patrol the streets whenever our men are off post. Short of restricting everyone to camp, there's not much more we can do."

"They'll be restrictions enough once they get to the front. No need to hurry things." Ned stubbed his cigarette and uncrossed his legs, elbows on the table. "How's the training regimen?"

"As rigorous as can be expected, given the strains of the mobilization. Shortages of everything," Chester said.

"We've gotten all the men into new-style uniforms. We started with half in Union blues," Benny said. "And we finally received our full issue of Springfields yesterday."

"What exactly have these men been training with?"

"For drill, wooden facsimiles and broomsticks. We collected some surplus rifles in New York City," Chester said.

"And we got a few new Springfields when we were in camp up in Peekskill," Benny added. "We had to rotate the weapons to men on guard duty, but we held a dozen or so back to get some riflery in each day. Most city boys don't have much experience shooting, after all."

Ned pushed down his rising disappointment and anger before speaking again. "So we have a full issue of rifles now"—two nods across the table—"and can get every man on the range at least a few times each week?" More nods across the table.

"If we have the ammunition," said Benny.

"And if we can get range time from the other regiments," Chester said. "We get lowest priority for resources, Major." He looked Ned square in his green eyes, his own serious and unwavering, until he was sure this new white officer understood.

"I'll take that challenge, Lieutenant Dawkins. The War Department sent me to assist you with training. The firing range seems a fine place to start."

"That would be widely appreciated, Major."

"One of the few advantages the Newfoundlanders brought to the field was their dedication to riflery. We were the finest shots in the BEF, certainly among the New Army battalions." He eyed each lieutenant in turn, riveting their attention, then continued, "I believe this regiment can match that skill. It'll serve them damn well in France. Are we in agreement, gentlemen?"

The two lieutenants sat ramrod straight and barked in unison, "Yes, sir!"

As Ned rose to leave them to their close dissection of every word he'd just spoken, he noticed Chester's face radiating excitement and… hard to tell what else.

Maybe relief.

Why are memories of smells so strong?

On order from the range sergeant, twenty rifles fired in ragged syncopation. The biting smell of smokeless powder began to rise on the breeze.

So much time looking, always looking. Sights ought to be strongest, Ned thought.

The sergeant barked again and the popping ceased. The men bent to retrieve their brass, the spent rounds clinking as they dropped into an empty ammunition case. Twenty new men stepped forward to the firing line.

Whiff of rose water sends a grown man right back to grandma's lap.

Having succeeded in getting the men on the range daily, Ned had time to ponder such things. Maybe he'd become too thoughtful since his return to the States. Some smells he'd love to forget— rotting flesh, smoking gun cotton, sweaty wool on terrified men's bodies. But for some reason, he'd always enjoyed the sound of a rifle. The Lee-Enfield was what he carried on the Somme, like every other poor Tommy who drew the short straw that day. Now here he was, jolly friends with the American Springfield. What intrigued him was how he could distinguish the sounds of each. He'd never thought about it in France, so much a part of the background these noises had been. Rifle shots were just staccato grace notes between the ominous rumbling bass of the big guns. The chunky Springfield made a curious *snick* when fired. The sturdy Lee-Enfield said *crack*, while the long French Lebel *chunked* with each round. The differences puzzled him, since the intended result was always the same. Maim a leg, kill a man, grieve a family. The German's Mauser had its own sound, too.

He was on the range with Lieutenant Dawkins's platoon, redeeming a promise to follow their progress. It also gave him a chance to converse in French. Chester had learned at his mother's knee but Madame Dawkins had overlooked "barbed wire" and "howitzer" and "machine gun." Ned knew none of the names of wild flowers or embroidery stitches, but thought his vocabulary the more serviceable given their current circumstances.

Ned and Chester ambled behind the firing line, giving only passing attention to the soldiers. This pleasant languidness was interrupted by the dusty arrival of a transport truck with a nervous orderly room clerk leaping from the passenger side. The skittish corporal tripped toward them, arms flailing in an unmilitary manner. "Major! Major Tobin!" the clerk shouted, his pitchy voice carrying a surprising distance. He was panting like a blown horse when he reached the officers, threatening to tumble at their feet. He came to disordered attention with a wobbly salute.

"Commander's compliments, Major Tobin. He wants you in town right away. Meet him at the city jailhouse, he says." He urged Ned toward the truck with waving arms, retracing his dusty footprints.

"Can your platoon sergeant handle the rest of the riflery, Lieutenant?" Ned asked.

Knowing this meant an invitation, Chester said, "Of course, sir." Turning toward the firing line, Chester bellowed, "Sergeant Freeman!" The no-nonsense platoon sergeant quick-stepped to his commander and, with a few words and an exchange of salutes, trotted back to the men.

"Let's see what the commander needs, shall we?" Ned said, heading to the truck belching grimy exhaust into the thick morning air. Chester followed, falling into step.

Camp Wadsworth sat three miles west of Spartanburg. Unlike much of South Carolina, the town had done well after Reconstruction, ballooning from a thousand souls to nearly 18,000. The city was chock-a-block with textile mills running full bore with War Department orders for everything from overcoats to underwear, all destined to clothe the mushrooming American Expeditionary Forces.

The jittery clerk jumped into the bed of the truck, leaving Chester and Ned to crowd in with the driver on the bench seat in front. When they reached town, none of them knew where the city jail was located, so Ned hailed a few pedestrians along Main Street. Being seen with two Negroes next to him and another tumbling around the back, the only reply he received was a desultory point and nod from one ancient man loitering in front of the Farmer's Bank, too blind to recognize the mixing of races. Turning off Main, they found the police station and jail a block south. As soon as they made the corner, Chester spotted a crowd lining the sidewalk and spilling onto the street. A military truck stood in the middle of the road.

"We have a little trouble, Major," Chester said, nodding toward the crowd, all of them in uniform and all of them colored.

Ned pointed for the driver to pull next to the first truck, then turned to Chester with none of his usual easiness. He grabbed the roof frame and prepared to jump down while the truck was still rolling to a stop. "Lieutenant, take the truck and that nervous clerk back to the post." Chester began to protest, but Ned cut him off. "Get back to your men, Lieutenant. Word's going to spread about whatever the hell is going on here. And your troops are the ones holding rifles."

"Sir, my men would never for an instant…"

More insistent, Ned said, "They're good men, Chester. But good men lose their heads when there's trouble." He slapped the brick pavement with both feet and gave Chester an urgent wave. "Go. Your place is with your men."

As he reached the edge of the roiling group of green uniforms, Ned could make out the commander on the steps of the jailhouse, speaking with agitation to a short wiry man wearing a saggy gun belt. The soldiers opened a begrudging path, forgoing military courtesies and following Ned's progress with hot glares.

"Colonel Hayward, sir," Ned called out as he reached the steps.

Breaking off with the sheriff, the commander turned, anxiety evident in his tensed posture. "Tobin, good. We need to calm the men. Gather up whatever junior officers are in this crowd and get some discipline restored." With that, the colonel returned to the sheriff.

Ned saw two lieutenants at the front of the crowd, attempting with limited success to keep the men away from the sidewalk, sensitive turf in this town. When one turned in profile, Ned recognized half the immaculate mustache of Lieutenant Sharpe.

"Sharpe!" Ned barked, "To me!"

Benny looked over his shoulder and rushed over.

"What the devil's going on here?"

"Word got around the sheriff has three of our men in there," Benny said. "Arrested for loitering or some other nonsense."

"Who are they?"

"No knowing, sir. Colonel Hayward is trying to find out."

The sheriff stood arms akimbo, shaking his head with a sneering smile. The colonel loomed over him, but this had no visible impact on the intransigent sheriff. Ned could see this was the situation everyone from the Secretary downward had either feared or desired.

Not on my watch, Ned thought.

Stepping up a few stairs to get his head above the men, he reckoned the crowd at fifty or sixty. Coming to attention, he let out a back-street bellow redolent of his younger and tougher days in South Boston.

"Fall in! Five ranks!"

The men made no move to obey, but the surprise of its delivery silenced them. Ned knew that wouldn't last long. "You will demonstrate to these… Southern gentlemen… exactly what the 15th New York is made of!" Some of the men straightened themselves a little, looking around for direction.

"Form up! Five ranks!" Ned repeated. "At Lieutenant Sharpe's command!" He was betting the cocksure Benjamin Sharpe would play his part.

Benny had snapped to attention at Ned's first bellow. He executed a drill-manual about-face and called out in an adjutant's voice, "Fall in! On me! Five ranks!" The men complied, forming lines and stiffening to attention.

Benny spun on his heels and mounted the steps to face Ned Tobin. He popped a crisp salute and said, "Company assembled in good order, Major." Ned returned the salute and gave Benny a tiny wink of encouragement. He turned and stomped up the steps to the mulish sheriff and vexed commander.

"Just because ya'll command a bunch o' darkies paradin' themselves 'round my town playin' soldiers, that don't give you a right to demand nothin' from me." Colonel Hayward was struggling to maintain composure with the petty little lawman and said nothing. "You want some advice from me? White man to white man? It'd be best for all us here 'bouts if you kept them boys at the camp diggin' ditches and choppin' wood. That's what they good for. Keeps 'em busy and tuckered out so they don't make trouble. For you or me or any of our women."

The colonel was steaming from his stock collar upward, crimson creeping up his neck and under his cap. "These men are soldiers of the United States, Sheriff McCall," the commander said with clipped precision. "They will behave as such under my command. But we have a right to know if three of their comrades are wrongly incarcerated in your jail."

The sheriff shook his head again, reveling in his power over the misguided Yankee colonel. Ned slapped his heels, startling the commander who turned to face the major a few steps below.

"Command assembled and in good order, sir," Ned reported, sneaking a glance at the sheriff, who had just noticed the well-formed ranks. There were sixty pairs of eyes glaring back at him in menacing anger. The sheriff's arrogance drained away like rain down a storm gutter.

Sheriff McCall said in an aggrieved grumble, "I got none o' yer negrahs in my jail, Colonel." He looked over the ranks in one last show of disgust, then stalked into the building.

The commander murmured, "Put the men at parade rest, Major."

Ned relayed the order to Benny Sharpe. The formation executed the command with a synchronized *frumph* as they slapped their feet to the bricks, elbows out and hands crossed in their backs.

"This was very close to disaster, Ned," the commander continued in a hoarse whisper. "We cannot keep the lid on this pot much longer."

"I agree, sir."

Hayward ran a palm over his clean-shaven upper lip and thought for a moment. "You and I are going to Washington tonight."

"I'm not sure what I can…"

"Don't start with me, Major. I know damn well you were sent here as much to keep an eye on things as train the men. Might as well make use of you to better effect."

"Whatever I can do, sir."

"I'll have to lodge another protest regarding the treatment of the men. I'll work the chain of command." He smiled, his eyes turning to mischief, and added, "And you will work your particular contacts at the War Department."

I may have misjudged this one. Lot of gumption.

"It would be my pleasure, sir," Ned said, his back to the men. "Sir, you might say a few words to the troops."

Hayward nodded. "Of course, to be sure, Major."

Lieutenant Sharpe made an about-face and took a deep breath, calling out, "Tench-hut!" The reply was a synchronous snap of sixty pairs of heels. The men stared ahead, their anger banked, not extinguished. Benny spun and saluted. "15th New York awaiting your orders, sir."

Standing at the commander's shoulder, Ned looked over the ranks. *Not a slacker or complainer among them. Just angry as hell at all the guff they've had to swallow.*

The colonel cleared his throat and said, "Men of the 15th! You have today, in the face of grievous provocation, shown yourselves men of substance. Men of honor and character, upon whom this nation can rely in her time of need."

Lieutenant Sharpe looked as if he were growing inside his boots. The faces of the front ranks were cooling from their rage, eyes telegraphing pride.

"I can think of no men I would rather lead to the fight. I can make no greater boast than to say, 'I command the 15th New York!'"

The Old Man can rise to the moment. He'll be a steady one in France.

"All I might add is God help those bastard Germans when the 15th comes over!" The colonel's voice hitched a little with emotion. *Time to finish*, Ned thought.

"Lieutenant Sharpe, dismiss the men," he said quietly.

Benny spun a final time and shouted, "Three cheers for the commander! Hip-hip!" The hooraying rolled up and over the two men on the steps. Ned motioned the colonel to his waiting truck, not wanting the men to see tears shining in their commander's eyes.

Too much to be done. Plenty of time for that at the victory parade.

1842
29/10 rbl

HEADQUARTERS
UNITED STATES ARMY
WAR DEPARTMENT, WASHINGTON, DC

October 29, 1917

From: The Director, Personnel Division/Manpower Plans
To: The Commander, 15th New York Infantry Regiment

Encl.:   (A) S.O. #17259, Change of Operational Control, 15th
N.Y. Inf. Reg.
        (B) S.O. #17442, Movement and Embarkation, 15th N.Y.
Inf. Reg.

Effective date of Special Order 17259 (Oct. 28, 1917)(Encl. A),
15TH NEW YORK (NATIONAL GUARD) INFANTRY REGIMENT is
assigned UFN to operational control of Headquarters, American
Expeditionary Forces, Chaumont, France.

2. 15TH N.Y. INF. REG. is designated a constituent unit
of 185th Brigade (Infantry), 93rd Division (Colored) upon
constitution of the division in Theater of Operation. A.E.F
Commander is delegated authority to reassign unit as deemed
necessary and operationally prudent.

3. 15TH N.Y. INF. REG. to depart Camp Wadsworth, S.C.,
ASAP and report for embarkation, Port of Bayonne, N.J., NLT
November 4, 1917, to await next available transport, per Special
Order #17442 (Oct. 28, 1917)(Encl. B). Direct liaison with U.S.
Navy authorized. Upon arrival in Theater of Operations, forward
movement and lodgment will be at the discretion of H.Q. A.E.F.
(REAR) OFFICER COMMANDING (Brest, France).

4. SPECIAL INSTRUCTIONS: Per Secretary of War Baker,
92nd Division (Colored) and 93rd Division (Colored), with all

constituent units, shall be deemed combat units of the American Expeditionary Forces and treated as such. This directive has the endorsement of the President.

WILLIAM T. HARRELL, Col.
FOR THE DIRECTOR

Form 1204

WESTERN UNION TELEGRAM
NEWCOMB CARLTON, PRESIDENT
GEORGE W.E. ATKINS, VICE-PRESIDENT   BELVIDERE BROOKS, VICE-PRESIDENT

New York, N.Y. 11:20 AM Oct. 31, 1917

RECEIVED AT   SPARTANBURG, S.C.

Lt. Chester Dawkins 15 N.Y. INF. Reg.
        Camp Wadsworth

Papa passed in sleep last night STOP Funeral Nov 3 STOP Come home need you STOP

Lena

CHAPTER SIX

Ned

It was all so familiar. Her pale green robe lay crumpled in its accustomed pile on the floor next to Ned's side of the bed. Gilles still gazed down in benign nostalgia from his frame on the chiffonier. Winter was creeping up, rendering the sky outside the open-shuttered window more often grey than blue, but that was not to be counted anything new.

"Oooh, Neh-deeee! 'Ow I meeeesed yoo zees *six mois*! Yoo must promees yoo weell nayfer leefe me ageen, yoo nah-tee, nah-tee booy!" Adèle squealed in her silly French girl voice. He still loved it. And he still adored her.

She shoved herself up on an elbow, one breast pressed against his side, the other resting against his chest. She reached a hand for the edge of the bed sheet bunched across Ned's waist. Lifting it with her thumb and finger, she rolled her eyes downward. "Appears the old boy's gone limp," she said. "Bit disappointing. He's only been at it the whole of the morning." She laid the sheet back with pantomime solemnity and patted his crotch. He opened his mouth to protest, but she slapped her hand over it. He peered over her palm with the eyes of a kidnap victim, then reached for her exposed breast.

She rolled away and onto her feet, standing beside the bed, naked except for the shawl of glossy black hair covering her shoulders. It had begun in the thick braid he loved to unloose, the slow progress electrifying them both.

Putting up a palm, she said, "No, no. Too late. I'm so bloody famished I could even eat English food."

He sat up, his back against the cold iron of the bed frame and ran his eyes up and down her nakedness. She stood at the foot of the bed, not the least uncomfortable under his gaze.

"Now that my fancy man is back, I'd hoped to get a few proper meals again." She shuffled on bare feet across the cold floor to his side of the bed and gathered her peignoir, slipping it over her arms and gathering it around her. Ned let out a sigh of surrender and hauled himself up as the old bed complained in a chorus of squeaks and rattles from its relieved springs. His tunic hung from the back of the familiar wooden chair in the opposite corner.

"Not much different than your old British uniform, is it?" Adèle said while sponging herself at the washstand. "Suppose the Americans really are the cousins. And you big Yanks would make a right music hall troupe if you dressed like our dear little *poilus.*"

"Always thought those helmets made them look like turtles," Ned said.

She pointed with her head at the photo on the dresser. "When Gilles marched off, they were very dashing in their red breeches and kepis, not like the British in that muddy green kit of theirs. Anyway, they say you're panhandling—isn't that the word?—our French artillery as well," she said, a little unsure of the term she'd heard him use. "So much for the industrial might of America."

Ned, having already gotten into his underwear and shirt, pulled his breeches up and began buttoning them. "Just give us a chance to gin up the factories. Then wait and see." He ran a hand over his chin while she watched in the small mirror over the dry sink. She'd seen this gesture every morning they'd spent together. It reassured her, made her feel safe. Maybe just the normality, something she might see every day even into old age. After the war.

"I better shave before we head out, if you ever finish." She was rebraiding her hair and he watched as her slender white fingers appeared and disappeared within the black cords.

Lord, she's lovely. I'd almost forgotten.

She tossed the braid over her shoulder and it swayed a few times across her bare back before settling. He tested the braid's heaviness in his palm, rubbing it between his fingers. He slid his free hand around her waist and pulled her to him. Adèle reached back and placed a hand around his neck as he leaned in to kiss hers. She gave him a last squeeze and slid away to the armoire, leaving him the mirror and basin for his shave.

There was a shortage of everything involving cloth, the first priority being breeches and coats for the army. On Adèle's modest salary, she could afford little new clothing even if it was available. Still, she attired herself smartly from her pre-war wardrobe. She tended to her clothing with fastidious care, not knowing how long the deprivations would continue. Ned didn't have to fret over his dress. His American kit was only a few months old. Little of it was government issue, as was the custom with officers. He'd procured his uniforms from a specialty tailor in New York City during a week's stay on Governor's Island. Even without a soldier servant, he tipped the staff wherever he billeted to keep himself presentable. So when Ned and Adèle strolled the streets of Amiens, they appeared a young couple as well-turned-out as any in the wartime city.

They strolled down the street, her arm light in the angle of his elbow. The royal purple sleeve of her box jacket was an attractive contrast to the dark khaki of his tunic. Like any young French woman in 1917, almost three years into the war, Adèle had shortened her skirts to mid-calf. This was now the fashionable length, established by the shorter "war crinolines" that were all the rage. Requiring much less material, they had the double virtue of being fashionable and patriotic. As a result, even old skirts from happier times needed their hemlines raised. She'd had to settle for black accessories—gloves, boots, the ribbon on her small grey hat. Even in these austere times she thought they cut fine figures on the boulevard this Saturday. The finest *accoutrement* a young woman could be seen sporting was, after all, an officer of acceptable appearance. Especially one as exotic, at least for now, as an American. It was dry on the streets but with a slate overcast. Depressing as it might be to one's mood, the filtered autumn light made Adèle's outfit gleam—almost scandalously so—like a faceted amethyst. She was euphoric at feeling fashionable and attractive and smitten with a fine man again, cloudiness be damned.

They stopped to exchange a few pleasantries with one of Adèle's students and her parents. The teenager's eyes were wide and awe-struck at the soldier—an American major!—upon whose arm her English teacher was appended. Ned's French had not atrophied, Adèle was pleased to hear, and the father complimented him. After bidding the appropriate *tu* and *vous* farewells, they continued on their respective promenades.

Adèle squeezed his arm and said, "Thank you, Ned."

"What have I done to earn your thanks? Other than earlier?"

She looked up with a wicked smile. "That young lady will spread word to every one of her classmates by Monday morning that their dear Madame Chéreaux, *maîtresse d'école* by day, is a *femme fatale* by night. Weekends, too, I suppose. And I have ensnared a most mysterious American officer in my romantic web."

"All that from one three-minute chat on the sidewalk?"

"Oh yes, Major Tobin, all that and more. By Friday, I shall have been kidnapped and ravaged by an infamous American buccaneer, a plunderer of the Spanish Main."

"I've never been a teenage girl," Ned said, "so I cannot fathom what you're on about."

"And I was, I can assure you, never a teenage boy," Adèle parried. "I cannot even recall why we teenage girls were in the least attracted to you spotty little satyrs."

Ned wrapped his fingers around the gloved hand and felt her warmth through the calfskin. The day was not very cold, so he'd left his overcoat behind.

"Spotty little satyrs grow to big satyrs, you know," he spoke low, almost in a whisper. She gave his arm a light slap. They'd caused enough scandal on the street for this afternoon, so she thought a little circumspection in order. Not that many persons, other than the Allied soldiers, would understand in the slightest what they were saying.

They reached the café, one they'd frequented while Ned was assigned to the Machine Gun School. Adèle stood aside to allow him to open one of the double doors, heavy with its long brass handle and thick beveled glass. He smiled with nostalgia for a place that knew him well in earlier days. They entered and waited on the tiles, a particolored depiction of an angry little rooster, the café's eponymous *Le Coq Nain,* and old Marcel scurried over. As the ancient headwaiter approached, an enormous gap-toothed smile spread across his fleshy pink face when he recognized Ned. The jolly man hailed him in French, still so pleased that this American had bothered to learn the language.

"Ahh, Lieutenant Ned, you have returned to us!" The waiter clapped a beefy hand on each of Ned's shoulders and kissed his cheeks.

"It's a great joy to see you again, Marcel, my old friend," Ned replied, long past embarrassment at being kissed by a Frenchman. "But now it is necessary to call me *Major* Ned."

He tapped the gold oak leaf on one shoulder. Marcel beamed with paternal pride. "So the British have learned finally to distinguish a *bonhomme* of great bravery and daring, eh?

"Ahh, but you would be wrong, my friend," Ned said, smiling with honest affection. He tapped the U.S. insignia on the collar of his tunic. "I fear the British never found such a high opinion of me."

Marcel studied Ned's collar, his face screwed up in puzzlement until he recalled that the Americans' insignia would, *bien sûr,* be in English. "Ahh, I am a stupid old man, Major Ned. It is U-ni-ted States, not *États-Unis!*"

Ned took his hand and pumped it, as he always did after any Frenchman kissed his cheeks. *Just leveling the field,* he always thought. "But no, Marcel! You are neither stupid nor old. You are the wisest among all the young men of Amiens."

"If I were the President of the Republic, I would make you *Marshall* Ned!" exclaimed Marcel, repaying Ned's outrageous flattery.

"But then you would no longer be the wisest man in Amiens, *mon vieux.*"

Marcel held Ned's hand in both his, fighting bittersweet tears. Two of his grandsons had been lost at Verdun, along with so many other grandsons. "Now, to your table," the old waiter said. "There is a perfect one here, near the window and out of the draft. We must display you so all can see Major Ned and his charming Madame Chéreaux."

"So you have not forgotten me after all, Monsieur?" Adèle said, placing a hand on his forearm. "I had feared you were blinded by the Major's radiance."

Marcel scolded with a wagging stubby finger, "Only when a Frenchman is in his grave would he forget such beauty, *mademoiselle*." He lifted her hand from his arm and made a bow over it. After they settled and the curious murmuring of the nearby diners ceased, Ned ordered lunch and champagne. After Marcel cracked the bottle, he retired with more effusions over Ned's unrivaled bravery and Adèle's incomparable beauty. Adèle took a long, slow drink and closed her eyes, the dryness and effervescence bubbling up memories. She thought for just a moment of her very first champagne, not so many years ago, while a student at the convent school in Albert. Of course, she'd drunk more and better champagne during her university days at the *École normale supérieure* in the old royal porcelain works at Sèvres. Paris was within such easy reach then, in so many ways.

She turned her attention back to Ned after he lit a cigarette, the tang of the smoke filtering through her daydreaming. She took a deep breath, then opened her eyes.

"You were gone for a moment." There was no offense in his voice, affirmed by his indulgent smile. They both respected these moments. His came more often, carrying him to less pleasant times than her old school days.

"Yes, the champagne…" He didn't need her to finish. She wouldn't have bothered anyway. There would be time enough for explanations someday. After the war.

CHAPTER SEVEN

Lena

So few people had come and she couldn't let that go. All Maman's family were in New Orleans, but that couldn't be the excuse for Papa's people. Just a few old cousins even bothered. What cut Lena deepest was the pitiful handful of his patients, past and present, who'd come to the funeral.

Chester couldn't attend. There was a war on, the Army told him. All personal matters came a distant second to defeating the Germans. As an officer, he had no license to bemoan the arbitrariness of the Army. Terrible loss for you, Lieutenant. Need to set an example for the men. Buck up and soldier on. Lena had felt his absence at the muddy graveside like a severed limb. She'd imagined the feel of his arm around her shoulders as the priest eulogized to the tiny group of mourners gathered around the opened earth that would soon surround their father, welcome him next to Maman, and turn him just as surely to dust.

"I am afraid I have little but disappointment for you, Lena." The office smelled of musty books and sadness. Arid law and troubled neediness, mournful wills and hopeful contracts, court papers indecipherable to all but the anointed at the Bar. Behind his wide desk, Henry Davis looked as desiccated as his surroundings in a somber, decades-old suit.

How did any of us think Chester could survive here, she thought.

Lena swallowed hard, then again, as Papa's long-time attorney tiptoed around the sad facts of her father's estate in his clumsy attempt at delicacy. His sonorous voice vibrated in the pit of her stomach, aggravating her rising nausea.

"We have the house at least," she said, more question than statement. The lawyer found a pressing need to rearrange objects on his desktop rather than meet Lena's disbelieving stare. He moved some pens from one side of his blotter to the other. A stack of file folders near the edge of the desk demanded immediate straightening.

"It's the house Chester and I were raised in, Mr. Davis. It's *Maman's* house."

There was no ethical way to soften the blow, so Henry Davis stopped his fidgets and rearranged himself. The loud creaking from his swivel chair shattered the tense quiet. He placed his fingertips on the faded baize blotter, as if to push himself toward his troubling duty. "The house has two mortgages against it, both in default. It will be only a matter of days before both banks exercise their liens against the property. Your father's practice was moribund for some years. After your mother passed, you must have seen how... lost he was, how... distracted... he had become. We heard rumors of his... other problem... as well."

As each halting word emerged from the old lawyer's pinched mouth, Lena saw the clear truth of every one. She and Chester had refused to accept Papa's deterioration, so crippled by grief, rationalizing everything with inexcusable blindness these past five years.

"All his patients drifted away, for the sake of their families and themselves." He reached to move a paperweight, but felt the pang of his weakness and looked back with an effort. "I'm ashamed to admit my wife and I quit him, too. He was hardly able to care for himself by the end, my dear, let alone anyone else. Surely you and Chester could see that?"

She'd cried very little during the funeral mass or at the graveside. Without Chester, she told herself, she had to see to the thousand things a death in the family demands. There was no time to indulge her grief. She was her mother's daughter and would not disgrace her memory by acting the spoiled girl. Now, in the drab light of a gloomy law office, she could no longer help herself. There was no need for restraint and she gave way to tears, her sobs stealing her breath. Mr. Davis waited in agonized silence, unsuited to these sorts of scenes since his earliest days in practice. His deceased partner Daniels had been much better at consoling afflicted clients. After a time, her sobs slowed and she blew her nose as she regained a little control. The old lawyer had rearranged every item on his desk in the interim and was now concentrating on his sleeves and waistcoat.

Get hold of yourself, Lena Dawkins. With a final wipe, she shoved the handkerchief back in her mother's black-beaded string purse and said, "How long can you keep the bankers at bay, Mr. Davis?"

He spread his bony fingers, palms out, and shrugged a little. "They have the legal right to foreclose immediately."

"I understand that, Mr. Davis. I asked how long you can keep them away from my home. I need some time."

Davis was not fond of pressing bankers on such matters, on any matters really, but her steady challenging stare demanded a satisfactory answer. "I might be able to… with the general fondness for your father… and your brother away in service… they might be a little lenient in this matter. I can't imagine they would allow you more than six weeks, perhaps two months at the most." He shook his head in dread of the effort even this short reprieve would require, bankers not being much inclined to charity.

"Then get me those two months, Mr. Davis." Lena rose, knowing she had many things to do and little idea what those things might be.

30th of November, 1917

Dear Chester,

I don't know if this letter will find you. I'm sending it to Camp Wadsworth without the slightest idea if you're still there. Let's hope the Army's post office can find you, wherever you might be.

Thanksgiving was yesterday and Maddie and I made all the things we had on the table when we were children. I shooed her home to her husband after we washed up. She should have been home all day but wouldn't hear of leaving me alone. It's a pity they never had children of their own.

The ragamuffins came like always, so I was running back and forth between the kitchen and the front door for most of the morning to see them off with their treats. Some of them were dressed like Uptown swells—tiny Vanderbilts and Astors in cast-off opera hats falling over their eyes and threadbare gowns dragging behind them. In our day, we only dressed as hobos and urchins, didn't we? There was still a large contingent of those, but times are changing even on ragamuffin day. There were even a few motley little soldiers. The children decided to forsake their candy this year and instead collected coins for the YMCA to help the soldiers in France. Maybe you'll see some of their rest rooms and canteens? I'm sure they'll set up places for the colored soldiers, too.

Do you remember that wonderful divinity candy the Dixons across the street used to give out on ragamuffin day? That recipe their grandmother brought with her when she came north from Georgia? Maddie and I got to talking, so I went over and asked old Mrs. Dixon if she could write down the recipe. She dictated it to her granddaughter Genevieve, who was my year in high school. The poor old dear said it was because her eyesight is failing, but I suspect she doesn't write well or maybe not at all. I felt awful that I might have embarrassed her. Maddie and I thought if we wrapped the pieces in a few layers of waxed paper, the divinity might keep and we could send some to you in France. We'll see if we can find time to make up a batch before Christmas.

Life at home isn't nearly as exciting as yours. The house is so quiet at night after Maddie goes home. Sometimes I imagine I can hear Papa's chair squeaking in his study. I miss him so very much. My days are full of the usual lectures and studying, so there's really nothing of importance to report. Mr. Davis helped me settle Papa's affairs and sends his regards. You're not to worry a single moment about Maddie and me. We're looking after each other just fine. We'll keep praying that this war is over soon. Please bring yourself home safe to us, Chester. I can't bear the thought of losing you, too.

With my dearest affections, I am as always,
Your loving sister Lena

"*Mon Dieu*, these greens are *délicieux*, Maddie!"

Lena cringed whenever the lodger indulged in her execrable put-on French. *Sitting at Maman's table, of all places,* she groused to herself. It was a small price to pay, as Maddie had reminded her several times since Madame Arnaud had moved into her mother's old room. She paid her rent every week in advance, which was recompense enough in the old cook's reckoning.

Babette Arnaud—not the name given by her parents—occupied most of any room in which she happened to find herself. She was not a large woman, neither fat nor tall, although what there was of her seemed all bosom and *derrière*. It was rather her excess of personality that consumed space well beyond the requirements of her physical stature. She had mentioned in a vague way a deceased husband from Quebec to provide her French *bona fides*, although the few times Lena attempted a fluent conversation, Babette was quite deficient in both vocabulary and comprehension. Still, she was never late with her rent.

Maddie, the family's longtime cook, had been more aware of the deterioration of the household's finances than either of the Dawkins children. Over the past few years, there had been too many hushed discussions between her and the doctor over late wages and past-due butcher's accounts. Still, when Lena spilled out the full extent of her desperate circumstances, Maddie was shocked. However, coming from a long line of women who'd survived all manner of adversity, by the next morning the old cook proposed a solution.

The house had five bedrooms, as well as a small maid's room in the attic. At Maddie's urging, Lena moved to the little room under the eaves, allowing for a fifth room to let. It took less than a week to fill them with lodgers. The war had brought a rush of colored workers into the city, all making good money on military contracts and looking for places to live. She was hardly the only one converting rooms into lodgings for hire. By paying half the rent she collected each week to the banks, she covered the interest on the mortgages. Still, she was making no headway against the principal of the loans and was working herself ragged for the sake of the bankers.

Chester will be home when the fighting ends and things will be alright, she told herself.

Supper finished, the lodgers retired to the sitting room with their coffee and, for the men and Babette, their cigarettes or cigars. Maddie and Lena were clearing away the last of the dishes when someone pulled the front doorbell. It was not a vigorous tug, but rather a meek and tentative one that scarcely rang the bell. Lena opened the door to a very uneasy Mr. Davis who stood studying the sidelights.

"Mr. Davis, what an unexpected surprise. Please come in."

The old lawyer stepped into the house just far enough to allow the door to close behind him. His black overcoat was soaked with rain and he turned his hat between his hands as he dripped on the front hall floor. He'd arrived without an umbrella, which given the old lawyer's fustiness rather surprised Lena.

"We're just having coffee. Would you care to join us?"

"No, no. I would not impose unannounced. I… I felt the need to stop personally on my way home… before you heard from anyone tomorrow."

The January dampness that she hadn't noticed before now penetrated to her marrow. She knew her father's old friend well enough to realize he was bearing bad news with this visit. "Who might I be hearing from tomorrow, Mr. Davis?"

He reached for her elbow, thinking it might be the proper thing to do, then thought better and withdrew his hand. "Guaranty Trust, I'm afraid. They have decided to call the loan and demand payment in full."

She might have cried or wailed. Mr. Davis was expecting it, but what she felt was smoldering anger. Although her father had put her in this predicament by twice mortgaging their home, she'd developed a bitter loathing for bankers. They were here at hand, not cold in an unassailable grave like Papa.

"I've paid the interest on both mortgages without fail since just two weeks after our discussion, Mr. Davis. How can they do this?"

"The mortgages are in default due to the many payments your father missed, I'm afraid. The banks are within their right to demand payment in full. Guaranty Trust is, I believe, seeking capital to invest in war industries and has decided to call all mortgages that are in arrears." Finally mustering the resolve to look up at her, Davis thought how much of her mother he saw before him. Perhaps he had loved Delphine Dawkins just a little, but he could do nothing for her daughter.

"How long?" Lena asked, defiant more than afraid.

"I would venture to say no more than ten days. I am truly sorry. Perhaps you can go to your mother's family?"

She felt her spine stiffen, although she knew the lawyer was trying to offer her a lifeline. "This house belongs to my brother and me, as it did to my father and mother before us. I shall remain until ejected."

He stood looking at Lena, knowing there was nothing left for him to say. He'd delivered the unfortunate facts of her situation and she'd rejected them. Time would tell what would happen to her. He let out a slow breath through his nostrils and gave her a tiny nod. Slipping his hat back on his head, his thin ashy fingers stark against the black felt, Mr. Davis turned to the door without another word and stepped back out into the misting twilight.

When Lena turned, she found Babette Arnaud posed against the frame of the sitting room doorway, the slender tortoise-shell cigarette holder between her fingers emitting a long thread of smoke that snaked above her coiffed head. Her knowing look told Lena how long she'd been standing there. Babette took a slow drag, then pointed the holder at Lena. Without a trace of *faux* sophistication, she said, "You and me has somethin' to talk over, sister." She turned without waiting for any reply and headed for the kitchen, confident Lena would follow.

"Maddie, could you give Lena *et moi* a moment, *s'il vous plait*?" Maddie got the gist and headed for the dining room to busy herself without straying far from the kitchen. Lena motioned to a chair at the plain wooden table in the middle of the large kitchen. Babette remained standing and made a grander motion to a chair for Lena, who sat without taking her eyes off the lodger.

"You got yourself into a world o' hurt here," Babette said. "And I see through the tough act you just gave that lawyer man."

Guess I don't rate the fancy manners now.

"Other than apologizing for your boorish eavesdropping, *Madame Arnaud*"— deliberate and perfect pronunciation—"what else do you have to say to me?"

Babette stood assessing Lena Dawkins anew. She continued to smoke with languid motions, choosing her next words with great care. In a sign of resolution, she perched herself on the chair opposite. "If it'll make you any less snooty, I'm Beulah Tubbs. My people is all back in South Carolina. That's where I come up, but I was the smart one found a way out." Lena shifted in her chair and crossed her arms with impatience. Babette cut her off before she could say anything. The disdainful look on Lena's face spoke enough. "Now you hush 'til I'm done speakin' my piece. I'm your best boarder, so you can least ways hear me out." Lena nodded and, with an annoyed sigh, cocked an eyebrow as an invitation to continue.

"Let's you and me get the cards on the table. You stop me when I get somethin' wrong." Babette extracted the cigarette end from its holder and, not finding an ashtray at hand, dropped it with a short hiss into a cold cup of coffee on the tabletop.

"Your daddy left you high and dry by borrowin' against this house. By the sound of that lawyer, more'n once. And brother man is off killin' them Germans. And you ain't never had to fend for yourself in your entire life, have you, sugar?"

Lena's anger at the bankers was fast being supplanted by rage at this phony woman's presumption. However, her resolve began to crack knowing her desperate situation was so transparent.

"Since you're not denyin' what I said, let me get right down to the nub," said Babette, moving in closer toward Lena. The bluntness of this woman whom she had until five minutes ago only seen as an annoying *poseuse* was throwing Lena off balance, as was Babette's incongruous businesslike look as she leaned across the kitchen table in her emerald silk dress.

Whatever's coming can't be worse than what old Davis just told me.

"I'm currently working as an occasional *chanteuse* and, well, a kind of *hôtesse* at a private club up on 147th," she said, Babette returning in full pretension. "I have made the acquaintance of some gentlemen who have expressed an interest in setting up a similar establishment under my oversight. Since my current employer takes a shocking portion of what I earn, he being a rather sharp *homme d'affaire* with a long nose for money, it would be in my best interest to keep more of what I make."

Lena found it fascinating watching this canny woman flip between characters—and that's exactly what Babette and Beulah were, she had no doubt. No telling which was by now the more authentic, not that it mattered much.

I know just what kind of a "hostess" you are, Beulah Tubbs.

"What has this to do with me?"

"It might have a lot to do with you, *Mademoiselle* Dawkins. And more to the point, with your house." Babette snapped open the small clutch purse dangling from her wrist and extracted another cigarette from a tasteful enameled case. She twisted it into the tortoiseshell holder with dainty care, then produced a friction match and dragged it along the underside of the table with a loud scratch. She lit her cigarette, tossed the wooden match over her shoulder into the sink behind her, then lounged with one arm hanging loose over the back of her chair. She waited with unconcerned patience while Lena pieced it all together, as Babette was sure this clever girl would do soon enough.

It didn't take long. Lena leapt to her feet and paced about the kitchen in exasperation. She turned on Babette and, fists jammed to her hips, said, "Are you suggesting we turn my mother's house into a bordello?"

"It ain't your mama's house now, sister girl. She's dead and gone, just like your daddy. It's your house now, 'cept it'll be the bank's tomorrow. Unless you got a few thousand dollars buried out back there." Babette gazed through the kitchen window. She'd let Lena think over her unforgiving position a little longer. In the meantime, she pondered just where you might hide that much money in the back garden.

Chester, why aren't you here?

Facing eviction—it might as well be tomorrow—there was no other option at hand. She could leave the house with nothing or she could save her home until the war's end. Lena dropped back into her chair and traced the patterns in the oilcloth table covering. Although her only choices were obvious enough, she hesitated a long minute or two before saying, by way of surrender, "Was there ever a *Monsieur* Arnaud?"

A surprised laugh burst from around the cigarette holder and Babette turned back from her contemplation of the backyard with a satisfied smile. This looked to be the way Lena would accept her offer.

"Oh, there was—still is—a Sidney Arnaud." Might as well be friendly and familiar now. "He was from Quebec City but wasn't exactly a husband to me. More of a mentor in the trade, shall we say? I left him near dead in a Buffalo hospital two years ago. He was, among his many other weaknesses, a dreadful cheat at cards, you see."

Lena sat back in her chair, sizing up the woman opposite with new eyes. Babette let her take as long as she needed, not at all uncomfortable under the younger woman's scrutinizing stare. After a prolonged silence, Lena put her feet flat on the floor, patted her legs with both hands, and said, "So how do we operate this partnership, Madame Arnaud?"

"Three ways. Me, you and my money man."

"What would be my obligations, besides handing over my home?"

"Keeping up the house, providing the food. That old Maddie can sure cook like home. I'd expect a lot of our clients might enjoy that, both the colored ones with a little war money in their pockets and the rich white ones looking for something *authentique*. We'd handle the cash and the books together, since I'm not feeling much trust between us."

It was Lena's turn for a sharp laugh. "I'm feeling a lot more than distrust right now."

"It'll pass. My job will be entertainment and overseeing the girls, umm, the *staff* shall we call them? Our money man will see to supplying the booze. I know all the best musicians in Harlem, at least the ones that damn fool Jim Europe didn't drag away to the war with him. We'll make this a place where a discerning gentleman can find his heart's desire, as my present boss likes to say."

Babette scratched her temple with the end of the holder. "You'll need to get the other lodgers out of here. We'll be needing those rooms."

"And the money man? When can I expect to meet him?"

Babette shook her head with an indulgent smile. "Better you not know him. Best for all of us."

CHAPTER EIGHT

Ned

The trip to Washington had ended with their "problem regiment" ordered overseas without delay, so Colonel Hayward had dispatched Ned to find immediate passage to France in preparation for their arrival. The commander added the codicil, "without annoying anyone of importance, if it can be helped." Because of the ambiguous nature of his early posting to France, he didn't exactly belong anywhere and this suited Major Edmund Tobin. Arriving the second week of November after an uneventful crossing, he'd made his way straight to Paris and begged assistance from the attaché's office, renewing his acquaintance with now-Colonel Wally Waller. The put-upon Assistant Attaché had not gotten command of an infantry brigade as he'd hoped. Instead, he inherited the crushing protocol responsibilities that the American Expeditionary Forces commander, General Pershing, abandoned when he left Paris and established his headquarters at Chaumont, a hundred miles to the east along the Marne. Colonel Waller was now indispensable to the AEF right where he was, keeping nosy visiting delegations ensconced in Paris where General Pershing preferred them to stay.

Ned convinced the despondent Waller that he should be attached to the attaché's office as a kind of freelance interpreter, available to shepherd visiting delegations whenever "regimental business" allowed. Colonel Waller jumped at the extra manpower and approved a room at the Hôtel de Crillon. Major Tobin could, of course, always conjure some conflicting "regimental business." As soon as he settled into his oversized Empire-furnished room on the top floor of the grand hotel, he fired off a telegram to Adèle.

This is not to say he neglected the regiment. There was not much to do while the 15th awaited embarkation. After rushing the entire unit to Bayonne in less than a week, they became victims of the inevitable bureaucratic neglect of an overtaxed War Department. Ned knew Colonel Hayward was burning up the wires between New Jersey and Washington, but thus far not even the well-connected commander had secured any reliable promise of transportation for his men.

A week after his chummy agreement with Wally Waller, Ned made a short trip to Tours, the Loire Valley city to which Pershing had banished his burgeoning supply staff. Upon his return to Paris, Ned stopped at the front desk of his hotel and the clerk slid his room key across the marble counter on top of a familiar cream-colored envelope. Ned ran a finger under the flap and pulled out the telegram, going first, as always, to the signature, "Col Wm Hayward." The regiment had departed two days earlier while Ned was in Tours. They'd be in Brest by the 29th, Thanksgiving for the Americans, if all went to plan. Brest sat at the tip of the long finger of Brittany that pointed accusingly across the Atlantic toward the tardy Americans. The French had gifted the old city to their new allies for the duration, anything to get the Sammies into the fight and relieve their battered *poilus*.

Ned took just enough time in his room to wash, shave and change his underclothes before heading off to catch the next train from the Gare Montparnasse. He hailed a taxi and tossed his valise, mostly containing unwashed clothing from Tours, on the back seat and climbed in after. Two long days later, an unwashed, unbrushed, unpressed and underfed Major Tobin sloped out the door of his first-class compartment onto the train platform in Brest. He made his way to a reception desk for American troops manned by a sergeant with a bull neck and a huge grizzled mustache sitting next to a suspiciously clean-shaven lieutenant. When Ned approached the table, the young officer leapt to his feet. Ned shot an indulgent smile at the lieutenant, which set the boy to inspecting his tunic with jittery urgency. After asking his business, the firmly seated sergeant offered up the officer as an escort.

"Shall we be off then, Lieutenant?" Ned said, relieving the poor lad from self-conscious scrutiny of his uniform. "Any need for a taxi?"

"No need, sir. A little airin' will do the l'tnant no harm," the sergeant said, toneless and condescending.

The skittish boy-officer bounded for the door like a springbok pursued by hungry lions. Ned quick-walked behind him, adjusting his hat as he neared the door. As Ned caught up, the junior officer made to outpace again, but Ned grabbed a sleeve.

Good God, he even has freckles.

"Lieutenant, what's your name?"

"Mowbray, sir, Bert Mowbray."

"How long have you been in Brest?"

After a short cough, Bert said, "I landed six days ago, sir. They assigned me to Sergeant Morgan at the train station... until they get the base headquarters opened. We're to operate the port."

He doesn't know what's hit him. Poor kid's in a daze.

"Where did you come from, Lieutenant?"

"My family's in River Forest. Chicago," Bert said. "I was at University of Illinois studying engineering, in the cadet corps. They gave us our commissions early, after war was declared."

Half-trained baby officers leading half-trained men against machine guns. Different army, same damn stupidity.

"And how old would that make you, Lieutenant Mowbray?"

Bert started for his tunic again, but caught himself. "I turned twenty in July, sir."

I've watched younger men die. No reason to spook this one.

The neighborhood changed when they turned off the rue de Château. The three-and four-story houses and shops that lined the street running up to the old castle gave way to sooty workshops and warehouses. They walked along the docks to a brick building with an American flag hanging limp over the doorway, its fold creases still visible in the new fabric.

"The whole base establishment's topsy-turvy, sir. If anyone's in charge, likely we'll find them here." They stepped into the noise and smell of dozens of men jammed together two to a desk. Some were working off upended packing crates. Cigarette smoke hung above their heads in an acrid blue-grey miasma. The heady scent of damp wool and fresh ink added to the stifling atmosphere. An orderly corporal sat at a tiny schoolroom desk next to the door. He rose to ask the major's business.

Lieutenant Mowbray spoke right up, surprising Ned. "This is Major Tobin, from the Military Attaché's Office in Paris, Corporal. He's seeing to some details regarding the arrival of a unit from New York."

Quite a serviceable junior officer, with a major at his back.

"The movements officer is away, sir. Believe he's at the new headquarters building in rue Voltaire."

Ned looked to Bert for some sign that he recognized the street name. The lieutenant shrugged and shook his head. "We'll need a little assistance finding that, Corporal. Maybe swing by the military docks on the way?"

Grabbing his overseas cap, the corporal held open the door and said, "This way, sir." They headed down the waterside street and turned onto the pier of the Port de Commerce, lined with stone warehouses. There were several cargo vessels tied off to the long pier. Ned pulled up with a start, watching the unloading of the first ship. Bagged cargo—wheat or oats, some kind of grain—was being moved by hand. And every pair of those hands belonged to a Negro soldier.

"Didn't know there were colored troops in France," Ned said, indifferent as he could manage.

"Thousands, sir," the corporal said. "Draftees from the South and dumb as bricks, most all of 'em." The corporal turned to Ned and continued with a little familiarity. "Glad to have 'em, otherwise we'd be doing this work rather than the coon battalions. All we need do is feed 'em and keep 'em away from the French women."

"What kind of work are these battalions doing?"

The corporal stopped to consider. "All kinds, I guess, sir. Mostly stevedore work like this. Layin' rails to the supply depots out in the countryside. Buildin' camps, diggin' latrines." The corporal removed his cap and scratched the back of his head, then said, "Any work not fit for white men, I s'pose, sir."

The telegrams kept coming, Colonel Hayward's anger radiating from each successively terser message. The regiment's ship was turned back only a few hours out and, after a second departure, was damaged. Ned judged it a good thing when he stopped receiving telegrams. He assumed that meant the commander was finally at sea.

Bert Mowbray, loyal as a puppy, passed along what information he could by letters and the occasional phone call. His new job was overseeing a scrum of competent clerks who needed little oversight. This gave him ample time to poke around. With his mouth shut and ears open, he picked up a surprising amount of information— there were some advantages to being an invisible second lieutenant. With snippets from Bert, Ned pieced together that the regiment was packed aboard a rust-bucket freighter called the *Pocahontas* and would reach Brest on or soon after Christmas.

He still managed to spend weekends in Amiens, attending to his own priorities. His work weeks, however, had serious purpose. With Bert keeping an eye out in Brest for the arrival of the regiment, Ned began a quiet campaign, facilitated by travel authorizations emanating from the office of the ever-malleable Colonel Wally Waller. to discover the AEF's intentions toward his men.

After an uneventful and blessedly short train ride, Ned found himself in Chaumont, a town now overrun with Americans. Mass mobilization was a messy ordeal and the chaos extended right across the Atlantic to AEF Headquarters. From the moment he stepped from the train, Ned realized Chaumont would be a harder nut to crack, requiring more than coopting an impressionable lieutenant. Since all officers had to eat, the officers' mess seemed a good place to start. The French had requisitioned half the buildings in Chaumont for the Americans and the mess occupied the council room in the old town hall.

No matter the time of day, any officers' mess had coffee and some kind of food available, so Ned found a mug and a donut, then ate as slowly as he could without drawing notice. Officers began arriving around noon in twos and threes. Ned watched the tables fill, then made an inconspicuous arc around the edge of the room. He came back in through the entry hall, looking like a befuddled new arrival. A major stood and motioned him over. Ned walked to a long half-filled table, where the major pumped his hand.

"Melvin Singleton. Looks like you're new around here."

"Ned Tobin. That obvious?"

"We were all in your boots not so long ago, Ned," Major Singleton said. "You staying or just passing through?"

"Assigned to the attaché's office in Paris, so just visiting."

"Well, that's not too hard to take, is it? Gay Paree?"

Ned flashed an aw-shucks smile, not altogether natural for a kid from Southie, and said, "Guess not, but I'm hopin' to get to the fight soon, Melvin."

"Well, until then why don't you come and join us. No sense eating alone."

Ned took a vacant chair next to Major Singelton and nodded to the others around the table.

"Boys, this is Ned Tobin, from the attaché's office in Paris. You can introduce yourselves during lunch." Two mess orderlies appeared with bowls of soup, dispensing the first course with silent efficiency. They were young, draftees probably, their ebony skin in high contrast to the immaculate white linen of their mess jackets. No one took any notice of them except Ned. A year or even a few months ago, he wouldn't have noticed either.

One of the majors at the end of the table bawled out in a boarding-house voice, "What do you get up to at the attaché's office, Ned, other than seeing to the lonely *mademoiselles* of Paris?"

"Nothing as interesting as here." Ned paused for some soup, then as if an afterthought said, "Lately, I've been doing some liaising for a new division coming over, the 93rd. First battalions are on the way." Back to his soup, Ned cast a few side glances. No recognition from anyone except a buttoned-up lieutenant colonel across from him. He gave a sharp look, a little perplexed, then went back to his soup with silent purpose.

Now what's eating him I wonder?

The banter of small talk and war news continued, ebbing and flowing as the meat course and dessert came and went. Coffee arrived and a few of Ned's table mates began melting away, back to their fourteen-hour days. The lieutenant colonel lingered.

"You said you're helping out the 93rd?"

"Yes, sir," Ned said. "I was attached to assist with training in the States and now to liaise with the French over here."

"You know the 93rd only exists on paper?" the lieutenant colonel said. "And in the Secretary's fancy, some would say."

"I spent time with the 15th New York, giving them a few skills they might use over here, before I was sent ahead."

The other officer looked Ned over. "How did you determine which skills they would need over here, Major Tobin?"

Here's my ace of trumps.

"Until this last June, it was Lieutenant Tobin"—the affected 'leftenant' again—"from the Newfoundland Regiment."

"So now the War Department's sent you to look after the Secretary's colored division in France, is that it?"

"You might say that, Colonel. The 15th New York is at sea now, due in at Brest by Christmas." Ned considered the other man's icy hazel eyes and how they must bore holes through his junior staff. That'd serve him well commanding a battalion, which would be soon enough. "Sir, if you don't mind, what are your duties here?"

With a tight-lipped smile, the officer said, "Thought you'd never ask, Major. Sidney Prescott, Manpower and Training."

With all the appearance of an untroubled shrug, an ecstatic Ned said, "Explains why you know about my boys then."

A throaty chuckle came from Prescott, accompanied by another tight-lipped smile. "Major Tobin, let's you and me cut the bullshit, shall we? I know of the 93rd Division—the 93rd Division (*Colored*)— because the Old Man himself is seized with the matter. Let me assure you, General Pershing is not overjoyed at the addition of your Negroes—they're now the 369th U.S. Infantry, by the way—to his combat establishment. I happen to be his whipping boy on this issue, others more responsible not being near at hand."

What followed, Ned knew, would be either a disaster or a way forward. "Colonel Prescott, Secretary Baker's determined to get these colored troops into combat."

"Politics has no place at the front, Major."

"I'll grant his reasons are political. Doesn't matter to me. My job's to get them to the front in some sort of prepared state. And I won't have them used like every other Negro soldier I've seen so far in France. Neither will the Secretary."

Prescott ran a finger under his collar, as every officer wearing the uncomfortable wool tunics did a hundred times a day. He gave a long exhalation while staring at nothing in particular. "The Secretary of War can be a great nuisance to the Commander-in-Chief. I don't relish placing another burr under his saddle with your boys."

Ned decided to put a little more fear into this saturnine officer and let the chips fall where they may. "The commander of the 15th... the 369th... is the son of a former senator. He left his position as senior legal counsel to Governor Whitman of New York to take up this command. It was Colonel William Hayward who formed the regiment, with the governor's blessing. Like it or not, the politics are coming."

The lieutenant colonel leaned against the back of his chair. He said nothing and Ned hesitated even to breathe. Then Prescott let out a low glissando whistle. "They'd come at Pershing from all sides." He shrank inside his uniform, deflated by just how much worse this could get. Lieutenant Colonel Melvin Prescott looked a very stricken man.

Now we can make a deal, you and me.

"We both want something here, Colonel. We need to find a way we can both get it."

"Pershing won't have Negroes in combat, Ned." *Ahh, all friendly now.* "The South's always been overrepresented in the officer corps, especially in the peacetime establishment. Half his generals are Southerners."

Ned nodded along. This confirmed all he'd learned in South Carolina. Little hope of changing minds set since birth.

"Hell, probably half his Northern officers won't have them either."

Ned was well aware of the truth in that statement. "Well, sir, we have ourselves a problem. I need my men in combat and your commanders won't have them."

Prescott was looking desperate. "Jesus, most of my days are spent listening to the Old Man rant about colored infantry. And when he's off on inspection, it's the French whining about giving them our regiments for their broken-down divisions."

They sat in sullen silence, each sulking over his half of their mutual dilemma.

No time to train in the States and on their way here to dig latrines. Doing precious little liaising with the French.

Prescott produced a packet of cigarettes, took one, and tossed it over to Ned.

The French... the French...

"Colonel, you said the French are badgering Pershing for some of our regiments to fill out their divisions?"

Prescott nodded. "Every chance they get. General Pershing's railed against it to everyone from the President on down. He says Americans will only fight under American command."

"But Pershing doesn't consider my colored troops a combat regiment." Ned waited for the older officer to catch on.

"No, Major Tobin, I believe it's safe to say General Pershing would not consider *any* colored troops part of his combat establishment."

"Has Secretary Baker specified *who* our colored regiments go into combat with?"

Prescott loosed a satisfied guffaw, all at once enjoying the conversation very much. "I believe the only stipulation is that they go into combat *against* the Germans."

They sat finishing their cigarettes very pleased with themselves.

"Can you convince Pershing?" Ned said.

"I look forward to bringing the General some good news on this matter."

"Then all I need do is sell it to Colonel William Hayward."

Chester Dawkins's platoon sergeant was as trustworthy as the young lieutenant could ever want. He also refused to learn a word of French, clinging to an unshakeable belief that Frenchmen could be made to understand English by loudly speaking it, and if not then comprehensible, by speaking it louder still. The fact that Sergeant Lucien Barthold was the exception to his rule didn't discourage

Sergeant Freeman. In the case of Sergeant Lucy, as he insisted on calling the Frenchman, Willy Freeman added ecstatic gestures to sharpen his meaning. Lucien Barthold assumed Freeman's incomprehension of French could likewise be enhanced with added volume and equivalently extravagant gestures, rendering their days rather cacophonous from bugle to bugle. Beyond all reasonable explanation, this worked out fine for them. Once when the shouting reached peak intensity, Chester intervened to translate. The sergeants, to his astonishment, were much offended at his presumption, so he'd left them to their own devices. They argued without end throughout the day, although it was difficult to distinguish argument from basic communication. Nevertheless, both were incapable of holding a grudge and the sergeants shared a bottle of wine every night, becoming quite *sympathique*.

With the platoon keeping up a steady volley and the sergeants in a rare moment of agreement, the two officers strolled behind the firing trench without paying much notice to the riflery training.

"Back where we started, eh Major?"

Ned scuffed at the gravel and glanced along the revetted trench at the men below. A few fidgeted with their new French helmets, removing and readjusting them between volleys. "Seems that way, Lieutenant. Thankful we don't have to beg ammunition and range time over here."

"*Les français* are very generous, sir."

"Anxious to have us forward and getting ourselves shot *toute de suite*."

Sergeant Freeman barked an order and the men rattled out of the trench and lay prone on the ground, feet dangling back over the parapet. They settled in, ranging the flat wooden targets two hundred meters away.

They'd already stopped noticing the muffled *whoomp* of artillery to the east, although it never ceased. If it did, they'd notice.

The Berthier rifles were more slender than their old Springfields, but the French had little affection for riflery. From what the Americans could determine, their allies valued two things above all—hand grenades and bayonets. The French loved their long rapier bayonets and Sergeant Barthold, like most *poilus*, called his Rosalie.

Ned stopped behind one of the soldiers and asked Chester for his field glasses. The private kept up a precise fire, regular as a metronome, with mechanical efficiency. Ned went down to a knee and studied the target opposite for eight or nine shots. When the soldier paused to change an ammunition clip, Ned tossed a little gravel at his legs and the private jerked his head around to see who was pranking him.

"Haven't lost a thing changing rifles, have you McGowan?" Ned called across the trench.

The young private flashed a huge grin over his shoulder, shouting back through the racket, "No, sir. Frenchy rifles shoot good, too. Might pop a squirrel's eye at a quarter mile with this'n." Ned returned a smiling nod and Private McGowan went back to his shooting. Ned watched a half-dozen more rounds through the field glasses, all showing in a tight cluster on the target downrange.

"The French won't know what to make of shooting like that," he said to Chester. "Just need to bring the rest of the boys up to scratch. Safer killing at a few hundred yards than getting close enough to toss grenades or use those French pigstickers."

"Not many of the men will ever be as good as McGowan," said Chester. "He told me his granddaddy taught him two things—how to shoot and how to blow the jug. Gets a lot of grief for being too country, but none of the city fellows can shoot like that."

Ned shook his head and said with a smile, "Wasn't much call in South Boston for shooting your supper either."

"Hell of a coronet player as well. Says he can play anything that needs blowing," Chester said. "Think his granddad would be damn proud of him on both counts."

Jugs McGowan insisted on joining up with a company training for trench duty. Like many of the regimental band's musicians, including their commander, Lieutenant Europe, Jugs was adamant that he came to France to kill Germans, not play ragtime. While the regiment was on fatigue duties at St. Nazaire, however, the commander had sent the band to play in any town that would have them. They gained an immediate reputation as missionaries of jazz, that new American music. They even played a rag version of *La Marseillaise* and the French went wild for it after a few bars, once they recognized the tune.

As Ned and Chester turned at the end of the firing trench to retrace their steps, they spotted a thin, almost gaunt, French officer striding with great purpose toward them.

"Well then, what requires you to walk so fast, Fabien?" Ned called out in French. The captain's light blue tunic and trousers were tailored for a man several kilograms heavier, attesting to the length of the war and the inadequacy of a French military diet. But Fabien Aubert wasn't concerned with cutting a dashing figure for the ladies. He was a Catholic priest, called up like every other man of draft age by the anti-clerical Republic. His uniform was immaculate, however, with his kepi set in the regulation manner and his riding boots spotless. He'd studied in Montreal before the war and the English he acquired there was a skill the army found much more useful than administration of the sacraments. Spending the first three years commanding an infantry platoon, then a company, he'd been detailed as liaison to the 369th Regiment. He'd brought his company sergeant, Lucien Barthold, along with him. Since they'd survived this long together, the sergeant thought it a grand idea to accompany his captain, lest he disturb their enviable run of good fortune.

"Gentlemen," Captain Aubert said, saluting Ned.

"It's good to see you here, Captain," Chester said. "The men are making good progress with the new rifles."

"Yes, yes. To be sure," said the captain with uncharacteristic distraction. He fidgeted with a rolled piece of paper in his left hand.

Must be something bad to ruffle his Jesuit feathers, Ned thought.

Captain Aubert, switching to English, glanced at Chester as he unrolled the paper. "You're not going to like this, Major. You even less, Lieutenant. Just received from the French Liaison Mission at the American headquarters." With painful hesitation, he handed the paper over. The heading read '*CONFIDENTIEL AU SUJET DES TROUPES NOIRES AMÉRICAINES.*' Ned jumped to the bottom in search of a signature.

"Who is this 'Linard' then?"

Fabien puffed his cheeks and shook his head. "Colonel Linard, head of the Liaison Mission. He recruited me for this job. An embarrassing Anglophile—speaks perfect English—and he's very ambitious. His only orders to me were to get you Americans into combat, even if we get you all killed."

As the Frenchman spoke, Ned scanned the document. "Fabien, where's this been sent? To whom?"

"Every French commander with American troops assigned to them, every commander with any American troops in his sector, and the military governors of districts with any Americans."

Turning to Chester, Ned handed over the paper with heavy reluctance. Chester's eyes moved faster with each line as he read, pressing his lips together so hard they drained of blood. His hand dropped to his side when he'd finished as if the paper had the weight of stone. Turning away, he took a few labored steps and dropped it on the ground.

Hurrying to pick it up, Fabien gaped at Chester's back, then over his shoulder at Ned with an imploring look. His years as a priest had given him the reflex to console afflicted spirits, but as a military officer he looked to his superior for permission. Ned shook his head and held out his hand. Fabien handed the document over, the paper rattling in his grasp as if Chester's anger still lingered there. Ned read the paper again slowly.

Captain Aubert shifted his weight from foot to foot and said, "Major, this will mean nothing to the French. We're very accomplished at ignoring mindless edicts from far-away bureaucrats."

Opening his mouth to reply, Ned stopped, heat rising up his neck and burning his ears. He looked past Fabien, eyes on the horizon as it struck him like a slap.

I'd have written the same thing a year ago.

While Ned and Fabien conversed in half-whispers, like churchgoers before the Mass commenced, Chester paced—stomped almost—in tight circles only a few yards away but distanced from them by his roiling anger and bitter humiliation. He jerked his head from time to time, as if shocked anew by the awful contents of the paper, chest heaving from surge after surge of raging adrenalin.

After four or five minutes, Chester spoke in a quiet and tight-jawed voice. "Your Colonel Linard had nothing to do with that order, Captain. He was just the messenger for the American staff."

Then he focused on the syncopated firing, trying to empty his thoughts and let his anger dissipate. He had men to lead.

To: French Military Mission, stationed with the American Army.

Re: Secret information concerning Colored American Troops.

It is important for French officers who have been called upon to exercise command over colored American troops, or to live in close contact with them, to have an exact idea of the position occupied by Negroes in the United States. The information set forth in the following communication ought to be given to these officers and it is to their interest to have these matters known and widely disseminated. It will devolve likewise on the French Military Authorities to give information on this subject to the French population.

The American attitude upon the Negro question may seem a matter for discussion to many French minds. But we French are not in our province if we undertake to discuss what some call "prejudice." Recognize that American opinion is unanimous on the "color question" and does not admit of any discussion.

The increasing number of Negroes in the United States (about 15,000,000) would create for the white race a menace of degeneracy were it not that an impassable gulf has been made between them. As this danger does not exist for the French race, the French public has become accustomed to treating the Negro with familiarity and indulgence. This is of grievous concern to the Americans. They are afraid contact with the French will inspire in colored Americans intolerable aspirations. It is of the utmost importance to avoid estranging American opinion.

Although a citizen of the United States, the Negro is regarded by the white American as an inferior being with whom relations of business or service only are possible. The Negro is constantly censured for his want of intelligence and discretion, his lack of civic and professional conscience, and his tendency toward undue familiarity.

The vices of the Negro are a constant menace to the Americans. For instance, the colored American troops in France have, by themselves, given rise to as many complaints for attempted rape as all the rest of the army. And yet the colored soldiers sent us have been the choicest with respect to physique and morals, for the number disqualified at the time of mobilization was enormous.

Conclusion

1. We must prevent the rise of intimacy between French officers and colored officers. We may be courteous, but we cannot deal with them on the same plane as with the white American officers without deeply wounding the latter. We must not eat with the Negroes, must not shake hands or seek to talk or meet with them outside of the requirements of military service.

2. We must not commend too highly the colored American troops, particularly in the presence of white Americans. It is all right to recognize their good qualities and their services, but only in moderate terms strictly in keeping with the truth.

3. Make a point of keeping our native population from "spoiling" the Negroes. White Americans become greatly incensed at any public expression of intimacy between white women and Negro men. They have recently uttered violent protests against a picture in the "Vie Parisienne" entitled "The Child of the Desert" which shows a white woman in a "cabinet particulier" with a Negro.

LINARD

CHAPTER NINE

Adèle

She allowed nothing but English in her classroom after the first day when she gave instructions and expectations in French. She thought this very progressive. The girls found it horrific.

"Won't the war be finits…"

"Finished…" Adèle said, a rise on the last syllable.

"Won't the war be finished soon?"

"Very good, Marie," she said, the girl dropping back to her seat with visible relief. "What is your opinion, Josephine?"

Poor Josephine arose with a notable lack of enthusiasm. Her eyes darted from side to side, unnerved by her neighbors' tittering. She cleared her throat several times, reaching for the easiest English words that might fit the occasion.

"I think…the war will finish… in Febreeary." The girl looked with pitiable hopefulness at her teacher, eyes begging for the smallest encouragement.

"I don't believe the war ended last month," Adèle said. There was general snickering across the class and Josephine stood burning, wishing the wood planks of the floor would part and swallow her. Adèle silenced the titters with a stiff upraised palm.

Such a hard age for girls, she thought.

"Perhaps you might choose a different month, Josephine?" Adèle could never leave a student hanging in embarrassment. It was not so long ago she stood in Josephine's shoes. Never in English class, to be sure, but in Latin. And certainly in Religion, it still a mystery why her atheist father had sent her to a convent school.

"I think the war will finish in July." The girl tucked her chin into the front of her sweater as if the wool might shield her from further taunts.

"Excellent, Josephine," said Adèle. "And would that not be a wonderful thing?" Josephine sat down as the crimson began to subside from her round face. By graduation, most of the girls would be a little comfortable with the language. She knew a few of the bolder ones had already discovered the utility of their English while flirting with Allied soldiers around the main square on Saturdays.

I've done rather more than flirt with the Allied soldiers.

She'd not seen Ned since his regiment arrived on Christmas Day and she missed him. He sent short letters when he could, never more than a single page and much of that unfilled. He was working at a pace of which she'd not thought him capable. Unless he sensed something might benefit him personally, her American lover tended toward indolence. It was wonderful to be around him on a Sunday afternoon, but could be a little infuriating on more pressing occasions.

The handbell signaling the end of morning classes sounded down the hallways, bouncing off plastered walls and tiled floors, telegraphing throughout the building. Adèle's English class emptied with the usual commotion of gathering books and shuffling shoes. Taking her own coat and handbag, she made her way out of the *lycée* and headed for her apartment above the fishmonger's shop in rue Saint-Patrice. The modest flat had been her home for three years, ever since she'd replaced the English teacher called up the same time as her long-dead husband.

Papa was in Albert, where he'd returned as soon as the Germans withdrew and the opposing armies had dug in east of the town for their long stay. Situated up against a small hillside, his home was shielded from bombardment, more or less. Sitting just outside the western municipal limit, Papa blithely ignored the orders evicting the residents when they'd militarized the town. Found out by the British, he ingratiated himself with his fluent English and gratis use of the old barn and outbuildings for billeting some of the troops rotating back from their days-long stints in the trenches.

After several attempts at convincing him to relocate to Amiens or her sister's new home in Toulouse, Adèle left Papa to his memories of happier times. Filling the days with his vast collection of insects and plants, the fruits of four decades' tramping through the woods and marshes of the Somme, he was content enough. A few times a month he invited some British officers to dinner for a little intellectual companionship. He also tutored some children from nearby farm villages, although he knew it a poor substitute for regular schooling. Adèle visited from time to time on weekends, whenever Ned was stuck in Paris or God-knows-where and she could find transportation to take her the thirty kilometers. This weekend she'd have to make the effort again.

Were she being honest with herself, she knew in February, maybe earlier. Still, her cycle had been erratic in her teenage years and on occasion since then, so she hadn't been altogether self-delusional. A visit in February to a dotty old physician, too feeble to be conscripted, had confirmed the pregnancy. She would tell Ned face-to-face, but his current absorption with his regiment had precluded any opportunity. Not that he'd be surprised. They'd behaved like a pair of rutting rabbits the last year and a half.

She was pleased, truth be told, and thought she could conceal things at school with some judicious wardrobe changes. If not, she'd tell the headmistress she'd run off to Paris one weekend and married her American officer. That would do, as long as Madame Broussard didn't ask to see a certificate. Her students would think it terribly romantic and very much in keeping with the personality they'd assigned her mysterious American paramour. Still, she needed someone to say everything was fine, that the war had changed opinions by necessity. In the absence of the responsible lover, her religion-loathing father was just the man. It was Monday, so she'd push through the rest of the school week and travel to Albert on Saturday.

On Thursday everything changed.

The French and British were excited by the arrival of the Americans but the German General Staff was even more so. Knowing the vast manpower and countless factories of the United States would inevitably decide the war for the Allies, the Germans had planned a huge offensive utilizing their divisions freed by the withdrawal of Russia from the war under a new Bolshevik government. With a hundred thousand Americans and more arriving each month, time was not on the Germans' side.

On the 21st of March in 1918, the bloodletting recommenced along the Somme, the million casualties of two years before not enough to settle ownership of that bloody river. Six days later, Albert was overrun again by the Germans as they rushed toward Amiens and its important railway junction. Three days before that, Adèle fled the advancing Germans by wangling a ride to Paris with an Australian Medical Corps colonel who was scrounging supplies for his depleted field hospital. There was no way to locate Papa in the chaotic retreat from the German advance. She had to look after her unborn child, first and foremost, but she agonized over his whereabouts.

Adèle and her sister, Clarisse, had parted with unkind words when she'd left school to marry and move to the south, so Paris seemed the most suitable destination. She'd friends there from her days at the *École normale supérieure de jeunes filles* in Sèvres, halfway between the city and Versailles. Someone was sure to give her refuge in these circumstances, perhaps her dear friend Berthe.

There was, it turned out, a very good reason Adèle had trouble locating Berthe Fournier. She no longer existed.

They had shared a large room on the second floor with four other students at the *École normale supérieure*. The ceilings in the repurposed porcelain works were so high that each winter the girls shivered under the majestic plaster. Berthe was awful at English, a required discipline for her diploma, so the affable and bilingual Adèle had been her deliverance. In their last year, Berthe kissed Adèle on the mouth one winter night as they huddled in the same bed for warmth. It was not unpleasant, but Adèle was so surprised that her overreaction convinced Berthe to never chance a second kiss. After graduation, Berthe returned to her parents' home in Orléans and Adèle stayed an extra year to prepare for the *agrégation*. This was a national academic distinction to which Berthe had no aspiration whatsoever. But as the diligent eldest daughter of a radical father who valued education above all else, Adèle assumed from her earliest college days that she would endure the exhausting five-day written and grueling oral examinations.

Gilles Chéreaux was also preparing for the *agrégation*. During that hectic year, they'd been introduced by a mutual acquaintance one Saturday at a forgettable bistro in Montmartre. Soon they were spending together whatever free time they could salvage from the demands of their studies. Gilles had been raised within easy earshot of the bells of Notre Dame, in a comfortable apartment behind the city government's offices at the Hôtel de Ville. Gilles had an easy relaxed relationship with Paris and was thrilled to share his city with her.

In the middle of July, the official notices of their passing the *agrégation* arrived and they celebrated for the next three days, spending Gilles's father's money on theater tickets, brasserie meals and carriage rides through the Tuilleries. They were now *agrégés*, with all the prestige that title carried in Republican France. Each secured a position teaching at a fine *lycée* and looked forward to the coming school year with a mix of excitement and confidence. They never fell in love, not exactly. They loved each other's company, loved Paris, maybe loved that they loved the same things. It's unlikely either would have claimed to have found their one true love that summer.

Then a shabby little man shot an Austrian prince in a faraway place and the world came crashing down around them. Adèle couldn't quite remember who first had the idea they should marry. Probably Gilles, overcome with fear of being forgotten while off fighting the Germans. It may have been her idea, since he seemed so in need of reassurance. In the end, they presented themselves at the Hôtel de Ville for a proper civil ceremony, then strolled the few hundred meters to his family's apartment for champagne and a wedding luncheon. Gilles was nervous and dashing in his blue coat with gold braid and red breeches. He even wore a sabre for the ceremony. It was the first time she'd seen him in uniform.

Two days later, he was gone to his regiment. Three weeks after that, he was dead on a field in Belgium and she a widow. That led her back to Albert and a position vacated by a mobilized English teacher at her father's *lycée*. The Germans had their own plans for Albert, however, which moved her on to the girl's school in Amiens, where she was happy enough until the Germans intruded again.

Adèle knew Berthe had returned to Paris after the war began. They were no different than other friends who clung tight to each other throughout their school years, only to watch the intensity of their relationship fade with distance and the lengthening interval between letters. Adèle had a Paris address for Berthe, but when she found the building in rue Lecourbe, the second-floor flat above the *fromagerie* was occupied by a middle-aged woman with two teenage daughters and an absent husband off fighting or already dead like Gilles. The cheesemonger had a vague memory of an odd young woman from Orléans, but said her name was not Berthe as far as he could recall.

Her room in the dingy *pension* behind Saint-Sulpice was paid through the week, but Adèle had no money for longer. Berthe was the one person in Paris upon whom she was confident she could impose herself and her swelling belly without judgment or much complaint. Adèle looked up schoolmates for whom she had addresses to ask about Berthe. After two exhausting days, one woman who'd been somewhat close to Berthe at school provided a sliver of information. She'd spoken a few weeks ago with another classmate—the name didn't register with Adèle—who mentioned running into Berthe in Montparnasse, working in a gallery that sold "wretched avant-garde nonsense." The friend thought it was named after some Greek goddess or other. *Galerie Méduse* or something.

The next morning, Adèle trudged ten blocks south to the Montparnasse rail station. She asked around the shops until a gregarious and toothless old man in a kiosk across the boulevard helped her sort through her sparse clues. After a meandering discussion and the sale of several dozen morning papers to passersby, he sent her a few blocks up the boulevard to a small shop in rue Vavin, across from the new Metro station. The small sign over the red-framed door read *Galerie Myrmidon*.

The musty shop was chock-a-block with every imaginable kind of artwork, if you could call them that. Few contained anything recognizable as people or landscapes. The furious mix of shape and color had the intended disorienting effect on Adèle. Behind a tiny counter, perched on a high stool, a curious person sat flipping through a copy of *La Vie Parisienne*, sighing at each turn of a page.

"*Bonjour*," she said, awaiting some sign of recognition. There was none forthcoming.

"Pardon me?" she said.

The person—she thought a man, but wearing a woman's blouse—closed his risqué magazine with one last windy sigh, then deigned to gaze upon the intruder.

"May I help you?" he said with notable lack of enthusiasm.

"I hope you can. My name is Madame Chéreaux."

"Monsieur Fiantrien," the man replied, taking her offered hand by the very tips of the fingers and giving the tiniest pull. He smoothed the front of his blouse with the same hand, giving her the impression he might be wiping it.

What a curious name, she thought.

"I'm looking for a dear friend. We were at university together. I was told she might be working here."

M. Fiantrien smoothed the sides of his brilliantined hair with both hands, then stood from his stool. His head ended a few inches below her eyebrows. He assessed her through half-closed eyes and sucked in his cheeks. She noticed he was wearing a little lip rouge.

And a very curious owner of that curious name.

"What might the name of your dear friend be, *ma chère* Madame *Chér-eaux*?" He tittered at his little pun.

"Berthe Fournier. She's from Orléans but she's been back in Paris a few years now."

M. Fiantrien startled a little—Adèle didn't notice—then returned to his stool and magazine for distraction, working his mouth and jaw in a peculiar way as he riffled the pages.

Is he holding in a laugh? How very odd.

"I believe I'm acquainted with that lady," he said, looking back at her, his lips pursed tight and eyes moist with amusement.

"Do you know where I might find her?" Adèle was never good at cat-and-mouse and was growing exasperated.

"I do indeed," he said, coming around the counter again and motioning with two fingers over his shoulder. She watched him as he made his way to the front of the gallery with a strange rolling gait, as if his hips were stiff from sitting too long. His trousers were tailored tight as a matador's and over his shoes he wore spats the loveliest shade of lilac. He swung out the door with Adèle at his heels, then stopped before the upstairs residents' entryway adjacent to the gallery. He nodded at the doorway.

"Right up to the top. The room is on the right." He made no move, so she stepped past him and opened the door onto a dingy stairway. "It's six floors. Hope you're up to it in your condition."

I'm not showing much yet. How could he know?

She glanced up the narrow stairs. Turning to thank him, she caught just a flash of heels as he reentered the gallery. Adèle stopped to catch her breath at the fourth floor landing, feeling her pregnancy more than she'd admit. The landlord had fitted toilets on two landings, squeezing them into cabinets that required her to slide sideways between the thin wood-panel walls and the old iron balustrade. Smells from the makeshift water closets filled the stairway from top to bottom. She could see a small window two flights up illuminating the ceiling and continued her trudge toward the dim light. Gripping the rotting frame of the half-open window that hinged out from the mansard, she breathed the chill breeze to clear the sewage from her nostrils.

The strange M. Fiantrien had said on the right, so she crossed the landing and stood before a door that hadn't been painted since the last time the Germans had invaded France. In the weak light from the tiny window, she could read the card pinned to the door.

Léonie Déchaîne.

There was only one other door on the top landing. She turned and leaned close to the faded card on the door opposite to make out the name.

Mme. Leblanc…

Two days of searching and a hike up these awful stairs for nothing, Adèle thought with a self-pitying exhalation. She looked at both doors again, then went back to the window and breathed in the moist air to calm herself. After a few moments, she walked back to the first door and raised her hand to knock.

Perhaps Mademoiselle Déchaîne—another odd name!—has some information about Berthe. Not leaving without finding out.

Three knocks and Adèle paused to wait for a response. She heard nothing and pounded her fist three more times to vent her disappointed anger rather than expect a different result. A testy voice came from the apartment, random words filtering through the mildewing plaster and heavy wooden door.

"*Oui…attendez…merde…j'arrive…un moment…foutre!*"

In the midst of this staccato stream, the door flung wide. A woman—identifiable as such from the breasts exposed in the loose front of a white tuxedo shirt—stood in the doorway. The tail of the shirt made a poor job of covering her legs and backside. Flushing hot in the presence of the half-naked tenant, Adèle looked away and stammered, "I'm so very sorry, mademoiselle. I should not have intruded…"

Her hurried apology was cut off by the arms thrown around her neck and a loud squeal of delight. "Adèle! You've returned at last to Paris! Let me look at you." The woman pushed her to arms' length, beaming with pure joy. She had short-cropped hair hennaed to a shocking shade of red and jet-black penciled eyebrows.

Beneath it all was Berthe Fournier.

A shock of recognition, followed by equally unaffected joy, ran through Adèle. It was her turn to squeal and throw her arms around her old friend's neck. Wonderful tears poured down her face and she began to sob with relief in the familiar embrace.

"No, no, no! You must not cry!" Berthe fussed a little, smoothing Adèle's sleeves with affectionate rubbing, then leading her inside with an arm about her shoulders. "Sit and let me get you a cognac. It's very cheap, but it's what you need. We call those stairs *l'escarpement*."

Berthe looked down and noticed her shirt billowing open and stopped long enough to do up a few buttons before producing a glass and bottle. While Adèle wiped her eyes and blew her nose, Berthe poured a healthy dollop of brandy and handed it over. When Adèle reached to take the glass, she noticed for the first time a dark man sitting in a chair against the wall, brushing dust from a stout brass lens. His apparatus stood beside him on a tripod, draped in an expanse of black cloth, pointed at a threadbare chaise in the corner. The little bed was partially covered with a Persian rug and a pile of tatty pillows in various sizes and patterns.

"Don't mind Diego. He barely speaks French. Or English." Berthe curled her legs under herself as she settled next to Adèle on the faded divan. "We were in the middle of an exposure when you knocked." The Spaniard photographer grunted twice in varying intonations, then returned to his fastidious brushing. Adèle nodded and gave a little "ahhh" in reply.

"They all love coming here to work," Berthe said, sweeping her hand around the room. "The only good thing about climbing those terrible steps is my north skylight." She pointed to the steep ceiling and its big panel of grimy glass.

"The painters adore the northern light, although I've never quite understood why. I haven't seen anything they've made that might require actual light." She gave a little shiver, then slid a fringed shawl off the back of the sofa and wrapped it around her shoulders.

"They stay warm in their clothes while I freeze."

The pieces were coming together for Adèle. This was a new Berthe, one quite different from the provincial girl she'd known at the *École*, the girl with the stern and very devout parents.

Naked photographs and paintings? What would Papa and Maman Fournier think?

Berthe took Adèle's free hand, holding her long fingers loose in her own and swinging them back and forth. They sat smiling at each other, the old familiarity rushing back.

"You'll want to know about the name, I suppose."

"I was a little puzzled. And your colleague in the gallery downstairs did nothing to help."

Berthe kissed the back of Adèle's hand and held it for a moment to her cold cheek. "Signie can be such an obtuse little shit. He wanted more beatings as a child." Diego rose and fiddled with his camera. His back was turned, but they could hear the spotless lens threading back in place. He began shuffling a stack of wooden frames that held his photographic plates.

"So, your new name? Really, Léonie Déchaîne?" They both burst into fitful giggles. Diego grunted but did not turn.

"It's a wonderful name and I won't hear a word against it. Lord knows, I felt like a chained lion back in my parents' house. This war came just in time for me to make my escape. That and getting caught with the delicious dusty daughter of the *boulanger*."

"Caught?" Adèle's throat constricted as she sipped the astringent brandy.

"Yes, by her father. We were naked as babies, going at each other on a pile of empty flour sacks in his cellar." Léonie gave a sideways glance to see if Adèle was shocked. "My parents were not inclined to forgive and forget. Nor was the baker. I arrived back in Paris a most willing refugee and a little later I stumbled upon the gallery. With the avid encouragement of Signie downstairs, I reinvented my name, along with myself, here in degenerate Montparnasse."

Taking back her friend's hand, Adèle kissed it in return and held it to her own cheek. "You never were much interested in the boys, were you?" Berthe exhaled with relief at Adèle's open affection and acceptance. She was a provincial girl as well, but Adèle had been raised by a pair of radical atheists, not Catholic monarchists.

"I was cruel to you, that time in the winter, wasn't I?" Adèle said, "That night you kissed me?"

This probed a still-tender nerve. Léonie cupped her hand under Adèle's chin and studied the familiar face. Adèle's dark eyes, deepest color of *chocolat*, and her thick raven hair must have come from her father's mother, the daughter of an old family of Spanish *conversos*, she'd always thought. The wide round eyes and full arched brows held faint echoes of generations of exotic Jewesses.

"You had more right to be shocked than I did to be hurt. I know that now." Léonie reached around her friend's neck and laid the thick plait of black hair over Adèle's shoulder, then ran it through her palm. She'd braided it so many times in Sèvres. "I had no notion what I was doing. It wasn't fair to think you had any better idea." There was tenderness in Léonie's voice, not anger, this being the first woman she'd loved.

Their tableau was shattered when, without a knock, the door flew open. In stepped Signie Fiantrien, crossing the room toward them with his peculiar undulating walk.

"Ahhh, the happy reunion is over, I see," he said, sniffing back a bursting giggle. He bent and kissed Léonie's offered cheeks. As he pulled away, she slapped him hard across his face. Even Diego turned at the loud crack.

"You're a disgusting little *maquereau*. And you were perfectly rude to my oldest and dearest friend." Rubbing the rising red handprint on his cheek, Signie managed a wide smile to Adèle, took up her hand and kissed it with perfect aplomb.

He's rather handsome, under all that affectation, Adèle thought.

He flounced down into the tattered upholstered chair across from the two women. "That's not fair, *Berthe*," he said, arch as a teasing schoolboy. "I pimp out no one but myself. That doesn't really count, does it, *ma chère* Adèle?"

He's a disarming charmer, isn't he? She saw the indulgent look on Léonie's face. There was deep affection between these two extraordinary souls. Turning to Signie, Adèle gave him a lovely smile that melted his pretentious heart a little. "No, I should think that would not count, *mon cher* Signie." Her eyes did not waver from his. He made no move to avert his either. That sealed their newfound friendship.

Léonie jerked Adèle's thick braid. "Stop that! You are not permitted to make Signie fall in love with you!" Turning to him, Léonie added, "Adèle is a mourning war widow."

"Then your chastity will remain safe with me." Signie looked around the room and said as an afterthought, "I am an honored *blessé de guerre,* you know. A piece of Boche shrapnel took away half of my hip on the way in and all of my cock on the way out. I left my balls on the Marne." Léonie lit two cigarettes, walking across the room to place one in his lips. "Make a wonderful song lyric, wouldn't it? *I left my hip up in Ypres and my balls upon the Marne…*" He took a long drag from the cigarette and smiled across at the women, brittle with forced indifference. He sat forward on the worn edge of the chair, ready to change the subject.

"Where did you lose your *pauvre* husband then?"

Adèle handed Léonie the cigarette they'd been sharing, just like at school, and blew out a long stream of smoke. "He was killed at Charleroi, right at the beginning of things."

Signie straightened and made a show of raising his eyebrows and widening his eyes. "Why Madame Chéreaux, you have become much more interesting to me."

"What are you on about? I was just saying what an obtuse little shit you can be," Léonie said.

"What I find so very interesting, you testy bitch, is that the late lamented M. Chéreaux cannot possibly be responsible for our dear Adèle's present condition."

Léonie plucked the cigarette from her mouth and turned an appraising eye on the woman next to her. She pinched Adèle's chin between her thumb and finger, turning her head from side to side a few times. "I thought you looked a little plump for a war refugee."

Adèle pulled the collar of her blouse close around her throat and looked about the room with jerky glances. She settled on Diego's back as the safest place to focus.

"How far along?" said Léonie. There was no judgment in her voice, just a request for the facts.

Adèle turned her face from the Spanish photographer and looked at Léonie and Signie in turn. She found no disapproval, only honest concern and a little pity for what was coming soon enough for her. "I was told the baby will come around the middle of August, although I'm not sure that senile doctor could count reliably."

Léonie patted the back of Adèle's hand. "Then the Germans decided to chase you out of Amiens. Is your father still in Albert?"

"I've no idea. He'd never considered leaving again. And now the Germans are back." The tears were coming, both from relief at their welcome and horrible fear for her missing father. She fished in her bag for a handkerchief again.

"It's good you managed to find me"—Léonie looked over at Signie and saw the concern on his face—"to find *us*. You'll stay here and we'll form a tribe when the baby comes. Signie spends most of his indolent life here anyway. And there's dear old Madame Leblanc across the landing. We look after her, too. We're quite the little commune."

"You're as dear to me as a sister, Berthe."

"You've always been just a little dearer than a sister to me." Signie barked out an ironic laugh. Léonie silenced him with a much-practiced glare. "And if you want to show just how dear I am to you, never call me Berthe again." Signie was choking with suppressed laughter again.

"I'll find work first thing tomorrow. There's no lack of jobs for women these days, I'm told. Someplace where I can dress to cover things as long as possible."

Léonie tilted her head to one side. With a regretful smile, she said, "I wish you didn't have to work in your condition, but the gallery pays almost nothing. As you see, I'm making ends meet in other artistic ways." Diego grunted from his corner again. "With all these lovely American boys arriving, business is booming."

Léonie looked Adèle up and down again, this time with a more commercial eye. "It's a pity you're pregnant."

CHAPTER TEN

Ned

They were *les enfants perdus*, the lost children of the American Expeditionary Forces. Unwanted and unloved, General Pershing put his black foundlings in a basket and left them on the French Army's doorstep. The French were so ecstatic they rushed their foster children forward as quickly as could be managed. The last leg of their journey was on foot, the inevitable lot of the infantry, the men marching to a sing-song challenge and response. Ned couldn't make out the lone sergeant's call, but the men's reply was clear enough.

"Goddamn, let's go!" *Stamp, stamp,* "Goddamn, let's go!" *Stamp, stamp.*

From time to time, the cadenced tramping of three hundred-odd boots was muffled to a *squish, squish* as the company traversed waterlogged depressions in the sketchy country lane. Whenever the road turned to mud and the tramping silenced, Ned heard desultory shelling. The morning hate—some in, some out—keeping everyone on edge. They passed through tiny shattered villages that comprised the rubbly remnants of normal life in their assigned sector. *Avant la guerre,* the French always said, everything was different... before the war.

When will it ever be après *this bloody war?*

Ned hadn't spent long in the trenches, although it seemed quite sufficient to him at the time. After the Somme, where almost all the Newfoundland Regiment's officers were wiped out in less than an hour, he was commissioned in consideration of his brief tenure at Boston College. As a shiny new lieutenant, he was sent as the Newfoundlander's contribution to the BEF's Machine Gun School near Amiens, his sole qualification that he'd been wounded by one. That assignment allowed him the enviable opportunity to limit his time in the trenches to daylight only, never overnight if it could be avoided. He'd done a commendable job of avoiding it.

Why in hell am I marching back to the front?

After a few hours of rising fear that they were well and truly lost, Chester Dawkins spotted a church steeple standing somewhere near where Maffrecourt was alleged to be on their maps. "There's some luck," Ned said. "Germans usually shell the steeples to dust so we won't use them for observation."

After reaching the crossroad center of the village, Ned took charge, allowing the company commander some time to send messages to the rear announcing their arrival. "Alright, Lieutenants Sharpe, Dawkins. You're with me. Let's see if we can find two bricks still on top of each other."

The three men sloshed through the puddly mud, staying close to the ruts carved by vehicle tires to keep themselves on the road. Even *avant la guerre*, this village was little more than a crossroads, the church at the center and a few dozen houses and outbuildings strung like beads along the two intersecting roads. The streets were lined with pile upon pile of stone and brick rubble, any useful timber long since foraged by the French troops. However, it seemed to Chester the rubble was too neat and purposeful, so he picked his way between a pair of large piles.

As soon as he left the road, he saw some hand-lettered wooden placards in French, each beside a low timbered opening hung with a gas curtain. One read *les Folies Bergère*, its neighbor, *le Moulin Rouge*. There were five or six others. Chester ducked through one, his flashlight painting the walls of a dugout housing a dozen bunks piled with straw and a long table surrounded by supply-crate seats. The ceiling and walls were planked in wood, the floor paved with salvaged roof tiles. The French had even left a few nude postcards pinned to the walls as a housewarming.

Ned clambered through the rubble just as Chester was reemerging into the daylight, then broke into a wide grin at the makeshift alley of dugouts. "*Vive la France*, Lieutenant."

"Sergeant Freeman, fetch some lanterns!" Ned called out. "And get some cook fires going!"

It was difficult to think of Captain Aubert as a priest. The other Allied armies wouldn't have countenanced drafting clergymen as infantry officers, but the French took a different approach. Whereas the British had long ago merged their Church and State, a substantial slice of the French population had a deep tradition of active loathing for the Most Holy Roman Catholic and Apostolic Church. The Revolution had, after all, not only been against the King. The Radicals who dominated the Third Republic were determined to marginalize those mainstays of monarchist support, the bishops and clergy. So it was into a uniform with any priest young and healthy enough to serve. Since most were well-educated, that meant making officers of them. Just like Fabien Aubert.

"It may be perhaps too early for trench raiding, Major," said Captain Aubert.

"We have to blood them sometime, Fabien, especially the junior officers." Ned offered a cigarette from reflex civility, knowing full well the Frenchman would refuse. He hadn't shed his Jesuit abstemiousness, nor had he learned to curse like a proper soldier. Not that he ever chastised anyone, even for swearing like blue blazes. It puzzled the men in his infantry company, but they came to love him for his quiet decency and courage.

"They've been barraged a few times already."

Ned leaned against the sandbagged trench wall and took a long relaxing draw, exhaling through his nose. "That's not the same. Only teaches them to tolerate their helplessness."

"*Certainement, la mort est la mort.*"

"I'd prefer to keep as many of them alive as possible, if it's all the same," Ned replied. "That's a damn sad thing for a priest to say anyway." He kicked Aubert in the booted shin with his toe, smiling below amused eyebrows at the smear of mud left on the polished brown leather.

"*Alors*, we shall have a little show tonight then," Fabien said, wiping the spot of dirt from his boot with a blue handkerchief. Were Fabien not so dedicated to his men, Ned thought, his punctiliousness would be more than a little annoying. But like the *poilus* who'd served under him before, Ned was willing to forgive Fabien almost anything, even his scrupulously correct vocabulary in two languages.

"Pick fourteen men—two officers with two good sergeants and ten steady soldiers," Fabien said. "I'll bring Sergeant Barthold, so one of your sergeants better be Freeman or we'll never hear the last of it. I assume the Major wishes to attend the *soirée* as well?"

Ned tossed his cigarette toward a puddle and heard the short sizzle as it hit the slimy water. "Wouldn't miss it for the world, Captain Aubert."

Jesus, why in hell am I volunteering for this?

"Division headquarters has been complaining about a lack of prisoners for interrogation. With the Germans attacking up in Picardy, everyone is a little jumpy," Fabien said. "We'll snatch a few tonight and make our mark, eh?"

The only grumbling Ned heard was from men who hadn't been picked for the raid. Chester and Benny were ecstatic, so much so that Ned cautioned them to concentrate on keeping their men alive. Sergeant Freeman replied to the order with a single nod, paused to think things over for a moment, then spun on his heels shouting orders to the ten soldiers.

Waiting for darkness, the sun seemed to stop moving across the sky, no matter how hard they willed it toward the horizon. Chester and Benny had gathered the men in a single dugout, keeping them away from the distraction of bantering with those who would stay behind. The dugout was filled within half an hour by cigarette smoke and the thick smell of nervous sweat. They were set to jump off just before midnight. Captain Aubert arranged a short barrage for the fifteen minutes before to keep the

German machine gunners in their bunkers and give the raiding party a chance to get out into No-Man's Land unmolested. Their trench was so close to the German front line—only a fifty- or sixty-yard sprint—if they were held up even for a moment after the barrage lifted it would be very dangerous.

Two hours before sunset, Captain Aubert and Sergeant Barthold arrived at the dugout with two quartermaster's soldiers, each struggling under cumbersome bundles of horizon blue uniforms. The two privates dropped their burdens on the packed-clay floor and left without a word. Ned looked at the pile, then back to Fabien. "What the hell is this, Captain?"

"Headquarters says you must be in French uniforms when out on a raid. I've brought along two dozen trousers and jackets, various sizes." The men already had French gear—curved Adrian helmets, odd-shaped canteens, stout leather packs, their Berthier rifles and bayonets—but still wore American khaki.

"Officers and sergeants, too. No rank insignia on raids, in case things become complicated," Captain Aubert said to Chester and Benny.

The soldiers looked at each other, not sure what to do, so Ned extracted a uniform coat and pair of trousers that looked near his size. They weren't very clean, but he smelled the reassuring residue of delousing powder. He folded his khakis and laid them on one of the bunks, by which time all the men were sorting through the piles. The dugout resembled a parish rummage sale for the thirty minutes it took to try on uniforms, swap out ill-fitting trousers, and button coats. Sergeant Barthold walked among them, pipe glowing in the dimness, turning back jacket hems and distributing fat rolls of light blue puttees.

The conversation picked up again as the men finished their transformation into *poilus*, the usual gibes and off-color jokes gaining new variations at the expense of their temporary French clothing. Fabien leaned against the doorframe throughout the chaos, weak candlelight from a collapsible lantern providing enough illumination to see his bemusement.

"Quite pleased with yourself, Captain?" Ned said.

Fabien stood erect with a ranking officer addressing him, even if only Ned Tobin. "Just thinking of the Germans."

"You find the Germans amusing?"

"Not generally, Major. I was only wondering what they'll think if we're captured."

After the Americans swapped their uniforms, the two quartermaster's men returned, lugging a pair of wooden crates. They again plopped them in the middle of the dugout without a word and left. Sergeant Barthold pantomimed at a few men to pry open the boxes, then signaled with cautioning hands that they do so with care. Two of the men produced big Army-issue bolo knives and popped off the wooden lids. Sergeant Barthold motioned for one of the knives and examined it in the lantern light with a little whistle of admiration.

Sergeant Freeman patted the scabbard on Barthold's belt. "Rosalie?"

The Frenchman extracted the long bayonet with his free hand and said, "*Oui. Ma chère Rosalie*," kissing the blade with a wink.

Freeman pulled his own bolo and said, "Sergeant Lucy, I'd like you to meet my sweet Beatrice." He kissed the broad blade and winked back.

Barthold hesitated a moment, then smiled so all his tobacco-stained teeth were visible in the gloom. He kissed the knife the soldier had handed him and, rubbing the flat of the blade against his stubbly cheek, said with lascivious exaggeration, "*Ooh-la-la! La belle Béatrice!*" Both sergeants broke into hearty laughter, joined by the few men who understood the exchange. Ned smiled over at Fabien, who gave an amused shrug.

Sergeant Barthold stepped to the middle of the dugout, standing above the open crates. One contained green egg-shaped French grenades, the other a mix of ammunition clips for their Berthier rifles and longer curved magazines for their Chauchat light machine gun. Sergeant Barthold addressed the men in rapid French, so Chester stood beside him to translate. Willie Freeman stepped in to lend the silent support of an American sergeant to the discussion. Barthold explained through translated French and myriad hand gestures that they were to leave their packs, ammunition pouches and musette bags behind. They could get caught on the—Chester translated "clothesline" then looked in confusion to Captain Aubert.

"On the barbed wire," he interjected.

Sergeant Freeman jumped in. "Lucy, how the hell we supposed to carry all these damn grenades, let alone them magazines for the chow-cat gun?" The question coming from Willy Freeman, Sergeant Barthold somehow needed no translation and pulled a private toward him by the arm. Bending down to pick up some grenades, he hitched up the soldier's French coat and dropped the grenades into a deep inside pocket. He added another six grenades in the same pocket, followed by four Chauchat magazines in the opposite pocket.

"*Comme ça,*" the sergeant said, very pleased to be a Frenchman.

Having never before noticed the voluminous capacity of the *poilu's* coat, the men set about determining what ridiculous amounts of anything and everything they could stow in the pockets.

Fabien took over. "One canteen only, straps tight. Same with gas masks. Nothing that will jingle." The men nodded, sobered by the French officer's somber demeanor. "We'll take the one Chauchat, in case we are seen by a German patrol. Also for overwatch while we are in the German trench. Otherwise, it will be grenades and bayonets, understood?"

Sergeant Barthold broke into another toothy smile at the mention of the bayonet, a usefully bilingual word. Slapping Sergeant Freeman on the shoulder, the Frenchman said, "*Ce soir, les Boches ont un rendez-vous avec Rosalie… et Béatrice!*"

Willy Freeman slapped Lucien Barthold's back in turn and said, "That's right, them Germans will be steppin' out with both our best girls tonight!"

An hour before jump off, the men were given their wine rations, the beloved *pinard* that the *poilus* thought as much their birthright as *libérté* or *egalité*. They were as calm as anyone might expect of men awaiting their first raid. They could only wait for the barrage to commence now. Chester and Benny were taking turns checking their watches a little too often, Ned noticed.

Nervy enough, but they'll settle.

The edgy revery was interrupted by shrieks from a battery of the ubiquitous French 75mm field guns. The Germans hesitated before returning fire, targeting the offending artillery, not the forward trenches. Ned exhaled without a sound, hiding from the men his own relief.

Shelling's the worst. Never see what's killing you. Blow you apart, nothing to bury. He patted his thighs to distract from the coldness this morbid turn of thought brought over him.

Fabien nodded to Ned across the dugout, deferring to his rank although everyone accepted that the French officer was in command of the raid. Ned stood and spoke in an even voice, "Sergeant Freeman, get the men up to the trench." Sergeants Freeman and Barthold, their music-hall duet now muted to quiet seriousness, herded the men up the steps. Ned and Fabien were the last to exit, dousing the lanterns. The men arrayed along the trench in even intervals, stiff and erect with nervous anticipation.

With a nod from Fabien, Ned ordered the men to fix bayonets. Out came a dozen Rosalies, a few flashing in the sparse light as their owners locked them in place. Without checking his wristwatch, Fabien climbed up and squatted on the fire step. The men could make out his silhouette against the muddy tan sandbags in the moonless starlight. He sensed the last shell even before the eerie silence descended. In the faintest whisper, Father Fabien Aubert of the Society of Jesus said, "God keep us." With this fleeting benediction, he was over the parapet and gone in the darkness. Lucien Barthold, a socialist barrel-maker from the vineyards of Bordeaux, and Willy Freeman, a Negro longshoreman from the New York docks, repeated the captain's intent almost in unison.

"*Allons-y!*"

"Let's go!"

The dash across the narrow strip of No-Man's Land took less time than most had imagined during the barrage. Just a few yards short of the German parapet, they heard voices—unintelligible but German—and fell to the ground.

The lieutenants were to advance up the trench with four men on each flank to squeeze a few Germans between them, at which point the sergeants would wrangle the prisoners back to their own line. But they never encountered any Germans in the trench. Voices carry remarkable distances and at strange angles in the darkness, so there was no telling where the Germans they'd heard might be. After a few premature grenades exploded to each side, there was silence. Fabien knew this was a dangerous moment—separated groups of green soldiers meeting in the enemy's trench at night was an invitation to mistaken casualties.

The French captain jumped into the trench and, turning his head side to side, repeated in English, "Gather on me! Gather on me here!" Each lieutenant, a little more cool-headed than his men, led his group toward Fabien's voice. Ned left Sergeant Freeman with the Chauchat gunner up on the parapet to watch over their flanks in case the Germans gathered enough men to counterattack. Dropping down in the trench next to Fabien, Sergeant Barthold close behind, Ned could hear the tromp of men closing from each side. Fabien kept repeating his order in an impossibly calm voice. Soon, he could no longer be heard, drowned out by the heavy breathing and shuffling of the clustered group of raiders.

At least we didn't shoot each other, Ned thought.

Fabien gathered Barthold and Ned, speaking in French. "They heard the grenades, certainly, and not come up from their dugouts. This means either they are very nervous or they are gathering enough men to overwhelm us." Ned and the sergeant nodded agreement. "For the moment, we have two advantages. They are still underground and they do not know how many we are. So we must find a dugout entrance fast and make much noise while doing so." Ned grinned at the audacity of Fabien's improvisation. Headquarters wouldn't grumble if they declared the raid a failure and scampered back to their own trench. But Division wanted prisoners and prisoners they shall have, so saith the good Father Aubert.

Ned called for the lieutenants. "Chester, Benny! Get out your electric torches... your flashlights and move slowly up the trenches, back the way you came. Keep the lights on the duckboards to save your night vision. We're looking for dugout thresholds, understand? Make a lot of noise as you go—we want Fritz to think there are fifty of us, got it?" Two silhouetted heads nodded. "When you find an entrance, give a blow on your whistle, yeah? Now get going. The Boche will get wise to us soon enough."

Ned jumped up on the German fire step and said to Sergeant Freeman, "You heard?"

"Yes, sir," the sergeant said in his normal voice, abandoning his whisper. "Ballsy plan."

"Watch your fire, we're fanning the boys back out. Let's not mistake any of 'em for Germans, eh?"

"Don't you worry 'bout me and the chow-cat, Major." The gunner nodded in confirmation.

Chester stomped and laughed and yelled back to this men, holding his light in one hand and slapping his way along the trench boards with the other. The four men behind him whooped it up, calling to comrades across No-Man's Land, the pantomime relieving a little of their fear. They pulled up and fell silent when Chester's light illuminated a step. He mimed with his free hand to keep up the noise, then pulled his brass whistle out by its lanyard and gave a single, sharp blow. The others in the raiding party rushed to join, adding to the outsized shouting and clatter.

Captain Aubert pushed through the men to the dugout entry. He produced a grenade from his coat, signaled with a thumb and forefinger, then pointed to the grenade. Two of Chester's men produced their own. Putting a finger through the round safing pin, Fabien nodded to the others. He pulled the pin and tossed his grenade down the stairway. He heard it ping once as it hit a cement step, followed by wild shouting from below. He stepped aside and the two others pitched their grenades down the stairs in quick succession.

Bursts of warm air pushed against their faces as the shock of each explosion exhaled up the stairway and out into the trench. Sergeant Barthold pushed the grenadiers out of the way and charged down into the dugout, shouting in French. Chester fell in behind him, his flashlight hardly penetrating the dust and smoke. Six men followed on his heels, some coughing, the bitter explosive stench constricting their throats. It was over forty steps to the bottom, twenty-five feet deep.

The walls and ceiling of the concrete bunker—so much finer than their own planks and packed dirt—were unscathed by the grenades. The room, however, was a jumble of splintered furniture and personal gear, with two or three men lying still on the floor in unnatural poses. A few more writhed and moaned in pain.

Fabien and Ned swung their lights around the perimeter of the room. It was a large and ventilated space, the smoke and dust already clearing. As the two pools of yellow light moved around the line of the walls, a knotted group of soldiers huddled in a shadowy corner, a few clutching rifles but most just stunned faces staring into the flashlights' yellow beams.

Sergeant Barthold shouted one of the handful of phrases he knew in any language other than French, "*Ergeben sich! Ergeben sich!*"

The terrified Germans stood on unsteady legs, raising their arms and croaking through their fear, "*Komrade! Komrade!*" A few still held their rifles and Sergeant Barthold shouted, "*Nein! Nein! Nicht mit Gewehren! Nicht Gewehren!*" The armed Germans tossed their weapons to the floor without hesitation, one of them eyeing the sergeant's bayonet inches from his nose. The Americans stepped either side of the Frenchman, adding their bayonets to the threat.

Chester and Benny retrieved two kerosene lamps from the wreckage of the room, one intact, one with a cracked globe, and lit them. As the room filled with more substantial light, the Germans stared with wide incredulous eyes at the dark faces peering back at them from behind the array of metallic points. One German whispered to no one in particular, "*Schwarze?*"

"Lieutenant, these here German boys seem mighty surprised at seein' us all down in here," said Jugs McGowan, grinning at Chester.

"I'd say they are, Private. Mighty surprised."

The oldest of the cowering soldiers, a little grey at the temples and with a bit of black piping on his collar, mumbled to the others, "*Ja, Schwarze... Amerikaner.*"

CHAPTER ELEVEN

Lena

12th of March, 1918
Near the Marne

Dear Lena,

The Army mail finally caught up with us after our liaison officer, Major Tobin, made a special trip to Tours to tell the Service of Supply where to find us. We've been assigned to the French Fourth Army, since General Pershing didn't think us worthy to fight alongside his white soldiers. The two sacks of mail the major brought back held a wonderful surprise—three of your letters.

It's a great comfort to know you're safe at home with Maddie and that Mr. Davis has settled all Papa's affairs for you. You've always been the brave one and that's helped me get over my anger at not being at the funeral. It's a load off my mind here in France, too. You need to be concerned with your classes at Hunter, not worrying about bills.

The American Expeditionary Forces Headquarters set about humiliating most of the other Negroes here in France by making them do stoop labor when they all came here to fight. We've taken to reassuring our own soldiers that once we've done a man's work fighting the Germans, we'll come home to better treatment.

As soon as I read your letter from Thanksgiving, my mouth started watering at the thought of Grandma Dixon's divinity candy. Didn't she *always put pecans in it, too? Oh, how that would taste here! I sure hope there's some on the way right now.*

I'm keeping my spirits up. I'm too busy most days to think about much more than the tasks at hand, but I do miss Pop when my mind turns to home. It's just you and me now. Keep my old room ready, Lennie. I'll be home soon enough.

With my fondest affections and a hug,
I remain, your brother Chester... or rather,
Lieutenant Dawkins (for the duration)

"You gotta take what you can git, Miss Lena, and I'm what you can git," said Bunk Hill, "and I'm cheap as ol' yardbird chicken, pound for pound." The piano man slapped his belly and unleashed a big rolling guffaw, the kind of laugh you'd expect from a man of Bunk's girth and easy temperament. "Shoot, most the good players is off in France with that brother of yours. Like as not git themselves shot for the trouble, too."

Lena turned away at the mention of the danger Chester might face, tipping Bunk that he'd upset her. "Awww now, Miss Lena, I don't mean nothin'. You know I let my mouth run ahead of my brain most times." She turned back to Bunk, seated at the end of the kitchen table with his red suspenders pushed out around his paunch, the perpetual perspiration on his forehead shining, and squeezed the big hand resting on the oilcloth. She gave him a crooked smile.

Such soft hands, like Papa's, she thought.

The tablecloth hadn't weathered the changes very well. Lena had been with Maman when she bought it a few years before she died. Some of the big pink cabbage flowers had burns, punctuated by a few permanent rings from slopped coffee left out overnight by the girls trying to perk up for the last few hours of drudgery with drunk clients. Maddie tsked and mumbled each morning when she arrived to the half-empty cups and overflowing ashtrays, too late to save the tablecloth from another scar or two.

If it gets too tatty, maybe Maddie will let me buy a new one. We'll lose a little more of Maman.

It was close to ten when Maddie arrived. That was an unthinkable hour for her, but it was necessitated by the new late hours of the premises and the high demand, as Babette had foreseen, for her cooking. Still, Maddie laid down the law that her kitchen closed at 11:00 PM, come hell or high water. Her husband was none too pleased by this schedule change, but she told him to hush his mouth, showed him how to light the oven, and left him plates in their little icebox to reheat for his dinner. He adjusted quick enough when Lena insisted that floozy Babette double Maddie's wages and pay off everything Dr. Dawkins owed her when he passed on. Her man spent most of his evenings down at the cigar store now, smoking and playing penny-ante with his no-account friends. That suited her fine—least she knew where he was. And they weren't so no-account, truth be told.

The faithful cook began her scurrying as soon as she walked in the door, pausing only to hang her hat and handbag on a hook behind the rear door. Lena had already removed the previous night's debris to the sink. This reduced Maddie's tsking to the time it took to tie on her apron. She offered Bunk Hill a tight-lipped judgmental stare down her nose, then refilled his coffee cup from the pot Lena had going.

"You tell that man of yours to watch hisself, Maddie, or I'm gonna steal you away," his wide face providing ample space for his large smile. Maddie slapped the back of her hand against his beefy arm and turned to face another long day of frying and boiling and mashing. She produced a huge armful of greens from the pantry, delivered early that morning from the vegetable market, so Lena went to the sink to help wash and trim them. The cook returned to the pantry and retrieved what was left of yesterday's big ham, running it with only malevolence under Bunk's nose on her way past the table. She gave him another down-her-nose glare in passing.

Sure makes a show of not liking that man, Lena thought, taking the ham and setting it next to her on the counter. "Bunk, I've never asked how you got that name. Is it one of those musician's nicknames, like King or Buddy?" Lena knew this would get his stories started and help pass the time.

"Oh now, I've had plenty of those kinda handles over the years, Miss Lena, but I've outlived or outrun all of 'em," he said with another rumble of chuckling. "Hand to my heart, my daddy, God rest his soul, give me the name Bunker the day I was born."

Both women burst into laughter, Maddie despite herself. "You mean to say your name is… Bunker Hill?" Lena asked.

"Daddy was proud as could be of this country and tried to be somethin' of a readin' man, least whenever he could borrow a book. He only owned two—the Good Book and one called *My First Reader of American History*—and he near wore both out. He already had the last name my old granddaddy picked up in that Civil War. When granddaddy asked some blue-coat soldiers which way was freedom, that Yankee pointed north and said, "Over that there hill… and keep right on walkin'. So he thought Bunker went right well with Hill, too."

Turning around and pointing her knife in the big man's direction, Maddie said, "You keep lyin' like the Devil, he's gonna take you right down to Hell with him one o' these days." She did a poor job hiding her amusement, however, and spun back to the sink, not giving him the satisfaction of a smile.

Pleased he'd gotten a rare word out of Maddie, he added, "Well, could've been worse. Been born twenty years later, Daddy mighta named me… *San Juan*." They all laughed together, Bunk at the pleasure he took from amusing the women. He knew what a hardship this situation was to Lena. And Maddie was getting worn out by long days feeding the well-heeled clients in the front of the house, the same ones that tipped him with bigger bills the drunker they got. Two fine and good women and they deserved a little fun now and again.

As their laughter tapered off, the women wiped their eyes, one with a handkerchief and the other with the hem of her apron. At that moment, Babette slouched her way into the kitchen, tortoiseshell cigarette holder hanging from the corner of her lipsticked mouth. She was in a delicate japonais-patterned silk robe, but would not have contemplated arriving even in the kitchen without full makeup and impeccable hair. "Seems I missed the vaudeville," she said, heading straight for the coffee pot. "Good thing you can play that piano, Bunk, 'cause I sure's hell wouldn't pay good money for your jokes."

The women upstairs wouldn't be awake for a few hours yet, but Babette had to see to business. She also didn't spend half the night on her back anymore. Just a few men and only when she felt the money was right. Besides, Thursday was when she and Lena went over the accounts for the week, not that it took long. To Babette's surprise, Lena had two uncommon traits—accurate bookkeeping and shocking honesty. Of course, Babette was unable to fathom how such a misguided young woman would ever get on in life, especially now that their enterprise had turned into such a gusher of cash.

All of Babette's girls were cordial but not particularly friendly with Lena. The women came to their trade along different paths— born into it, economic necessity, fleeing abusive fathers or husbands. Most all of them had raging drug addictions that Babette monitored with great care, turfing out any girl who started to show wear and tear. For some it was cocaine to keep going, then a little reefer to settle at the end of the long nights. For others, it was morphine. For all of them, it was alcohol, drinking with the customers to loosen their wallets.

The customers saw little of Lena who only made brief trips into the front rooms. This was still her mother's home and Lena was proprietary of the house and its furnishings. Babette brought one of the big bouncers from her last club to keep everyone friendly and to turn away riffraff who couldn't afford their top-shelf booze, drugs, card games and companionship. Still, Lena needed to reassure herself a few times each night. Because Babette insisted on a high standard for anyone working the front rooms, Lena dressed every evening in quite fashionable clothes. This added to the notice many of the regulars took during her wraithlike appearances, enhancing the mystery surrounding the lovely young Creole woman who always spoke French to Babette in such a quiet voice. There were regular inquiries as to Lena's availability.

The partners adjourned to Dr. Dawkins's old study to go over accounts. Neither thought it a good idea to let too many people know, including Maddie and Bunk, just how lucrative the venture was. If word got around, they were sure to be burglarized or robbed outright. They also were careful to stay below the notice of the organized gangs—white or black, Italians or Irish. All of them were operating in Harlem, the white ones with compliant Negro front men, and all were looking to discourage competition.

The two women sat side-by-side at the green baize card table that occupied much of the room, the doctor's big desk having been pushed and heaved to the vacant walk-down apartment below. All the books and old prints remained on the shelves and walls, Babette convinced the scholarly atmosphere facilitated longer games and bigger pots— of which the house rake was a flat 15%.

Lena placed a locked cash box between them, then opened a long ledger. Both were kept in a safe she'd installed in the pantry soon after realizing how much cash would be flowing through her house every night. She'd also ordered a cash box with two keys from the old locksmith on 136th, just up the block from the Zion Church where Papa's relations worshipped, although he'd converted when he married Maman. Lena couldn't recall the last time she'd been to Mass, but two of the girls upstairs went to Baptist services every Sunday.

Extracting a single sheet of paper tucked behind the cover of the ledger, Lena said, "Before we get to the accounts, I made a few notes of things that came up this past week."

Babette, lounging back in her chair, swept her free hand across the table as she played the cigarette holder across her lips and said, "*Continues, ma chérie...*" This being one of the front rooms, Babette had switched without a thought from the South Carolina drawl she used in the kitchen.

"We'll need to either replace the bed in Chester's... in the Green Room or have a furniture repairman replace the slats and mend that splintered leg. That's Marlene's favorite room and she's a little... a little too... *vigoureuse et énergique* with her clients."

Coughing out a smoke-laced laugh, Babette said, "That she is. And worth every penny we charge for her." Lena gave a twitchy smile, then dusted the baize tabletop. Babette stilled Lena's hand with her own, amused at her partner's discomfiture. "How can you still be so edgy about what goes on within our little *affaires commerciales*? You don't blush over the alcohol, the gambling and the dope."

Lena turned back to her notes and smoothed back stray hairs that had escaped their satin ribbon, choosing to ignore Babette's observations, not for the first time.

"Sure is a shame. That fancy man was asking after you again last night. The gentleman is smitten—tall and pretty high-yellow girl like you…" Babette let her thought trail off, already knowing Lena's answer from a dozen similar discussions over these last several months.

"Bunk is asking for a raise again. Says he's here longer hours than you said he'd have to work and hardly has any life of his own." Lena checked Bunk off her list and looked up to Babette.

"He takes in enough tips after midnight to triple what we pay him. And you know he's getting a cut from the other musicians he brings in on the weekends to make up a trio for dancing."

She was right about Bunk, Lena knew. Fond as she was of Bunk, he was on the make like most everybody else in Harlem including herself. "I'll smooth his feathers, but I'll make sure Maddie feeds him first."

"If we started chargin' him for what he gobbles back in that kitchen, he'd be payin' us, child," Babette said, slipping back into Beulah. She caught herself, situated her rump on the edge of her chair with admirable posture, and said, "Go on, *s'il vous plaît.*"

Lena flipped pages until she came to the most recent entries. "We took in 8% more than last week, although our earnings from the card room were down. Still, a good showing. Total receipts were $1,428." Babette smiled under hooded eyes, nodding her pleasure.

"Our costs were also up, however," Lena continued, "and I'm especially concerned with what our supplier is charging for any liquor with a French word in its name. I'm suspicious he's on to the *à la française* brand we've developed."

Oh, Maman would be so horrified…

"It's part of what separates us from the competition, *ma chérie,*" Babette said, "and all you need do is speak a little French in front of the customers." She leaned back again in her chair, "I'll talk to that thief of a bootlegger myself."

"Total expenses paid out, including the set-asides for the ladies, were $653…" Lena retrieved a small key from a chain pinned inside her skirt pocket, "…meaning three shares of $258 each."

"Our silent partner will be very pleased," said Babette, fishing out a key from somewhere deep within her cleavage. They each turned their lock and Lena opened the cash box. Having already counted and separated the shares, she handed two brown envelopes over to Babette.

"As will two bankers," Lena said.

CHAPTER TWELVE

Chester

The sergeants sat on a rough-cut bench, leaning shoulder-to-shoulder as outgoing shells shrieked over their heads. Weak shadows cast by the steady flashes from the French artillery blinked along the trench walls. Sergeant Barthold passed a canteen to Sergeant Freeman who pushed aside the dangling cork stopper and took a long pull. Lucien had watered their wine for this occasion. The Frenchman drew on his pipe, while the American smoked one of the special-occasion cigars his wife sent from her cousin's shop in Brooklyn. Their faces were illuminated at intervals by the orange embers stoked by each puff. The men were only a little more anxious than the sergeants. They'd seen their share of barrages and counterbarrages, attacks and counterattacks. Still, this was never an easy time. Major Tobin leaned against the opening to the command dugout chain smoking through the barrage, a habit he picked up before the Somme. He lit another cigarette from the glowing butt, then held out a flat hand close to his body to check for steadiness.

"The barrage ought to lift soon," Ned said, resisting an urge to check his watch.

Fabien Aubert had long ago made peace with death and stowed away his impulse to minister to the afflicted until after the war. "Forty

minutes perhaps," he said, leaning against the sandbag wall next to
Ned and stretching out his arms.

Since General Pershing wouldn't let them fight alongside his
white American troops, they'd take the field again with the French
Fourth Army, with whom they'd faced the German's Bastille Day
attack along the Marne. The enemy had thrown everything into
this offensive, advancing all along the Western Front in five huge
attacks. The 369th had done their part halting and reversing the last
of these and several weeks later the opposing forces once again had
ended where they'd begun. There was one big change, however. The
Germans were near exhaustion and on the defensive. It was time
to start rolling them back behind the Rhine. Not that these grand
strategic notions had much direct relevance to their daily lives, only
to their future deaths. For this day, their concern was the Germans
hunkered down a few hundred yards to the east.

Ned and Fabien hoped the half-dozen new tanks assigned to their
advance might save some men from the slaughter. They'd seen the
little tracked vehicles waiting behind their trenches, the two-man
crews lounging against the caterpillar treads along the high front
end. The little Renaults were vulnerable to artillery and breakdowns,
but at least they repelled bullets.

The barrage lifted on schedule and the silence was, for a few
moments, terrifying. Then the low rumble of several cranky engines
rolled down the trench as the tanks inched their way forward. Ned
jumped to the fire step and saw the boxy turrets, three to the right
and two to the left. They'd lost one already and another on the left
was an unarmed communication tank carrying an artillery spotter
with his radioman. Still, it was cover they could walk behind.

With the tanks over their trench and into No-Man's Land, Fabien
nodded to the platoon commanders, Lieutenants Dawkins and
Sharpe, who replied with piercing whistles as they brought their men
over the top. They gathered in groups behind the tanks and began
their slow walk across the blasted ground.

As soon as the tanks made fifty yards, the German field guns
opened fire. Within a minute or two, the heavier guns farther back
joined the barrage. Ned watched from an outcropping in the trench
line, a machine gun team either side of him prepared for any German

counterattack. In the stark glaring white of the star shells, he could see both his platoons advancing with their tanks. Successive waves of explosions obscured the men and vehicles with smoke and flying dirt.

Then he lost sight of them in the darkness.

Chester spat the residue of the last explosion and dragged a sleeve across his face. His head was foggy, ears ringing, from the German shell. He ran his hand over the tortoise-head curve of his French helmet and felt a round dent along the right side.

Must have been a rock, not shrapnel.

Sergeant Barthold patted his back and asked with bushy eyebrows and an expectant look if the Lieutenant was alright. Chester nodded with a weak smile. The sergeant slapped his back again and shouted inches from his ear, *"Alors, allons-y!"*

Sergeants Freeman and Barthold had decided to accompany Chester Dawkins's platoon forward when one of their assigned tanks broke down, thinking the men could use some steadying. Willy Freeman was just visible through the haze, traipsing with a dozen men behind the radio tank. Lucien Barthold grabbed Chester under an arm and hurried him forward, catching Freeman's group before they vanished into the chaotic blackness. In the patchy light, Chester could see the silhouettes of another dozen men trailing the second tank.

Still have most of them. Maybe a few stragglers.

Through the murk, he saw faint flashes from the German machine guns.

Jesus, we're close now.

Sliding out from behind the tank, Chester scanned the German line. He caught snippets of detail in the mix of smoke and harsh flare light—barbed wire stanchions, a stretch of ragged parapet. He was interrupted by a bright flash, then a shell exploding into the dirt just a few yards ahead of the tank to his right. There was a second crackling bang, followed by a green streak of tracer and a loud slamming explosion as the anti-tank shell ripped through the thin armor. He watched as the turret floated up and back through the air, blown clear by the explosion of its own ammunition. The hulk was burning bright, soldiers scattering from the intense heat. A few moments later, one of them ran half-bent to Chester, soon followed by the rest.

"How many men with you, Corporal?" Chester asked.

Jugs McGowan moved close and panted, "Couple disappeared when the Germans lit that tank there, sir. Two wounded, but they can make they own way back to our trench. So countin' me, looks like seven." Jugs pushed and tugged, arranging his men behind the inadequate cover of the remaining tank.

They'll be moving that gun, now they've got the first tank.

Chester trotted to the front of his men and spread his arms wide waving them away. "Twenty paces back! Stay low!" His order was answered with disbelieving stares, the men not interested in leaving the deceptive safety of the remaining tank. The two sergeants took over, shouting and pushing. Chester caught another flash from the corner of his eye.

"Hit the dirt!"

He fell to the ground and wrapped his helmet with both arms just as the deafening crash of another anti-tank round exploded against the Renault in front of him. Metal fragments shrieked past, followed by a shower of dirt and stones. Even through his wool breeches, he could feel heat from the burning tank against the back of his legs. With the engine silenced, he heard machine gun rounds hitting all around them.

Pfft. Pfft. Pfft.

He crabbed toward the others, the handle of his revolver digging into the dirt. He found the sergeants first, both unharmed. Sergeant Barthold grabbed Chester's leather belt, turning the lieutenant to face him. The sergeant's face was animated with urgency but not a hint of fear. *"Il y a un moulin à café à gauche."* He spit some dirt, then added, *"Disons á une distance de soixante-quinze ou cent mètres."*

"D'accord," Chester said, giving the sergeant a few nods as he considered their situation. Sergeant Freeman slid in next to Sergeant Barthold.

"Sergeant Freeman, pick two men and send them around the far side of that machine gun. Sergeant Barthold thinks it's maybe seventy-five or a hundred yards up to our left. Make sure they've plenty of grenades." He repeated his order in French. Sergeant Lucien Barthold protested with a rapid torrent of words, most of them profane. Chester let the sergeant wind down, then squinted for a few moments toward the German trench. He could see the green streaks of tracer as the machine gunner walked his fire back and forth around the two smoldering tank hulks.

Grabbing Sergeant Freeman by the sleeve, Chester peered into the old longshoreman's face with an intensity that chilled the sergeant to his boots. With encouraging nods from the Frenchman, Chester said, "Sergeant Freeman, your friend Lucy says you and he won't send two men to do a job this dangerous. He says you'll do it yourselves."

Willy Freeman hesitated long enough for Chester to see a flash of regret. It passed as fast as it came, and the sergeants rose to a low crouch and were gone before Chester could say another word. Sliding a small notebook from his front pocket, Chester scribbled a message to Major Tobin by the light of a dying parachute flare, folded it, and detailed a soldier to carry it back.

Ned handed the crumpled paper to Captain Aubert, along with his small trench flashlight. Fabien grunted as he read Lieutenant Dawkins's almost indecipherable scrawl.

"Wait here, Private. We'll need you to run messages."

The young soldier looked at Ned and said, "If it's all the same to you, sir, I'd just as soon be gettin' back to my friends. Them that's left, at least. They got more call on my help than you do, Major." Without waiting for a reply, he hitched up his rifle and headed back down the trench.

Lieutenant Sharpe's platoon was having an easier time on the right, Ned could see. All three of his tanks slogged forward at their aching pace and had silenced the German machine guns in front of them. Ned had also seen the two colossal explosions on the left.

"We should relieve Dawkins," he said.

Fabien didn't reply right away, squinting through a machine gun port. He glanced back at the message from Chester, then said, "We let the sergeants have a chance. With that machine gun, we would be putting another three dozen men into needless danger."

By the faint glow of his radium watch, Chester knew the sergeants had been out over half an hour and the machine gun was still strafing them. He was surprised the German artillery hadn't ranged them yet. Caught in the open with their tanks destroyed, the scant cover they'd found would be useless when the big shells began dropping.

A German grenade popped with a flash and bang. Corporal McGowan shouted, "At 'em! They comin' for us!" Dark shapes appeared, the flashes from their rifle shots revealing faces in jerky moving-picture frames. A few held grenades, rearing back to throw. Chester and his men opened fire with rifles, pistols, and a single Chauchat gun that had made it forward. A grenade exploded in front of them, most of its charge burrowing into the loose earth. A few of the oncoming shadows crumpled and disappeared into the darkness. The rest scurried back to the safety of their trench. Seconds later, the enemy machine gun opened fire again.

Pfft. Pfft. Pfft.

The regiment's reserve troops were ready to go, strung in jittery clusters either side of Ned and Fabien. What Sergeant Barthold called the *"moulin à café"*—coffee grinder—was still burping bursts of fire every twenty or thirty seconds, pinning Chester's men. Fabien Aubert scanned the reserve platoon a last time and gave a nod. Ned blew his brass whistle and was first over, a half-step ahead of Fabien. The two officers moved in sprints between the sparse cover, three dozen men zigzagging behind them.

The German artillery opened fire with a terrific unified roar. Every man flung himself into the churned-over earth, rolling or burrowing in search of cover. Ned heard the staccato rhythm of the enemy machine gun to their left. He raised his head as a star shell burst, illuminating with its ghastly green-white glow a line of German soldiers advancing toward the crippled tanks.

Ned jerked around at the thunk of a flare, the light from its launch revealing in a quick flash Fabien's placid face. In the ensuing darkness, he heard the sound of crawling.

Fabien settled in beside Ned and said, "At least Chester will die knowing we tried."

Why's that barrage falling behind? Chester thought. *The Boche sure as hell know where we are.*

Swiveling to locate his remaining men, he saw a flare wiggle upward, swell to a pink ball as it hung for a moment, then flutter back to the ground.

Those must be our men drawing that artillery fire. Major has the reserves out.

The German machine gun spat into the dirt around him again, but Chester saw there was also fire coming from their right. In between the machine gun bursts, he could hear the more erratic cadence of rifles. Chancing a look above his inadequate cover, he froze at the sight of a renewed wave of Germans traipsing toward them in the peculiar into-the-wind lean soldiers adopt advancing into enemy fire. Somewhere in the gloom, he heard fresh agonies, another of his dwindling command wounded.

Corporal McGowan was within earshot and Chester called out, "McGowan, we've got no good cover." Both men buried their faces as bullets sprayed into the dirt. "They'll chew us up from both sides here." Jugs nodded, aware of their situation but understanding the young officer's need to say it aloud. "If I read that flare right, Major Tobin's got the reserves out, but they're hunkered down in the barrage."

"Don't look like they got much chance of joinin' the dance up here anytime soon," the corporal said. "Most men down to maybe twenty rounds after that last rush by them Boche. The chow-cat team got eight pans of ammo and they'll shoot that off right quick once they see 'em comin' again."

Chester readjusted his helmet and secured his pistol. "Tell the Chauchat gunner and his loader to make a dash for the tank hulk on the left. See if they can find a place to steady their gun. I don't want their fire spraying all over." Corporal McGowan crawled into the darkness, carrying out orders that would determine whether any of them would see another morning.

Come on Major, come on...

In a few minutes, Chester heard movement behind him as the brawny Chauchat gunner and his skinny loader made their way forward. Hopping up to a low squat, Chester led them to the blackened wreck of the radio tank. Since it would be suicide to use a flashlight, they'd have to clear a space for the gun by feel. The cloying smell from the fire, still smoldering in a few discrete places, reminded him in a rush that there were dead Frenchmen inside.

Sweet Jesus. Steady, steady.

He grabbed the loader, the crescent-moon ammunition pans strapped across his thin body, and pulled him along. He halted the gunner—they needed to keep the weapon away from the dirt and debris. This was no time to risk one of the gun's habitual jams. Chester groped his way into an opening in the front of the tank where a hatch had been. There was no body, the driver having been blown free along with the hatch, both now lying out in the sinister darkness ten or a hundred feet away.

"Bring up the gun," Chester said, hefting himself out of the gaping hole. He pushed the big gunner toward the opening. "Driver's position is clear—find a platform there. It'll give a wide field of fire." Chester held the long-barreled Chauchat while the gunner heaved himself up and settled into the crumpled space with shoulders touching the twisted frame.

The loader crouched along the right tread, keeping the tank between himself and the German machine gun. Chester scaled the side using whatever footholds he could feel in the darkness, then called down to the loader, "Give me your hand. I'll haul you up." With the prospect of being surrounded by metal, the loader leapt through an opening blown in the turret, then slid down behind the gunner. Soon Chester heard retching from below.

"Jee-zus! Get your skinny ass up here and stop that pukin'!" the gunner shouted. "Ain't nothin' but a burnt-up Frenchy-man anyways."

Breathing heavily, the loader clambered around inside. "Now put a few pans of that ammo in my lap—no room for you reloadin' from the side. Just keep puttin' a pan in my lap each time you hear me changin' one, awright?"

Chester straddled the remnants of the observer's perch swallowing back bile at the smell of burnt flesh mixing with gasoline vapors from the ruptured fuel tank.

"Lieutenant, you in there?" Corporal McGowan said in a loud whisper, slapping the skin of the tank.

"I'm coming down. See if we can find the rest of the men."

"Don't know if any more comin'. They either been hit or skedaddled back to our line. Hopin' it were the first." Jugs pulled his chin strap clear, lifted his helmet and ran a dirty sleeve over his drenched face.

Three men here, maybe the same at the other hulk, Chester thought. *Come on, Major. Come on now. Get him going, Captain Aubert.*

Chester realized with perfect clarity this is where they'd make their stand and likely be the place they'd die.

Lord, help us.

He willed his breathing to slow, pushing the rising panic back down. He drew his pistol to occupy his hands and thoughts. Six bullets left, just the ones in the cylinder.

Pfft, pfft, pfft. Plink. Pfft, pfft, plink, plink, plink.

The enemy machine gunner found them.

Why are they wasting ammunition on a tank?

He heard firing erupt from near the other tank hulk. Two or three German flares arced up, giving fuller illumination to fifty or more Germans heading toward the remnants of his platoon. While the flare light lasted, the Americans kept firing, their long days on the ranges in South Carolina and France paying off at what they expected to be the very end of their lives. The Germans scrambled for cover but would advance again as soon as the flares burned down. The persistent enemy machine gun was keeping Chester and his men out of the fight. Their turn would come next.

Shouting to the Chauchat gunner to save his ammunition, Chester and Jugs fired into the advancing Germans, hoping to distract them. They'd save the Chauchat for later. It was useless at this distance anyway. After emptying his pistol, Chester crept to the back of the burned-out tank from where Jugs had been firing. They knelt together beneath the twisted tailpiece.

"McGowan, looks like the sergeants didn't get that machine gun. You've seen what it's done. It'll do the same to the reserves when they break through the barrage."

"I 'spect you're right, sir. I got one clip left for my rifle, five rounds. No grenades. Got Rosalie and my bolo, too."

"I'm out of ammunition," Chester said, "but that machine gun crew doesn't know it." He saw the corporal smile weakly.

"You best do a powerful lot of wavin' that pea-shooter then, sir."

He squeezed McGowan's upper arm and bent to look him square in the face. "We're the only ones left to do this, Jugs."

"'Best be gettin' on with it then, sir. Maybe there ain't no Boche left in this end of the trench, gatherin' up like they done to get at the others."

Rising to a crouch, Chester said, "Only one way to know for certain."

He and Jugs headed for the German line, hugging close to the ground whenever a flare lit above them. They squeezed through a blown gap in the wire, slithering on their backs while they held up the tangled strands with their forearms. The barbs bit through the wool sleeves and dug into their skin, but they freed themselves and rolled down into the German trench.

On their stomachs, they tensed and waited for any sound. After ten or twenty long seconds, Chester tapped Jugs on the back. They rose and picked their way toward the machine gun emplacement, stopping every ten yards to listen again. With the switchback traverses that both sides built into their trench lines, sound was a poor indicator of distance.

Keeping a hand on the trench wall, Chester felt the turn of a traverse and flattened himself against the sandbags, sidestepping until the angle reversed. He knelt and peered around the corner. He could hear snatches of words in German and made out shadowy movements of four men just a few yards away. A trench lantern hung from a spike jutting from the sandbag wall, its light doors opened a crack. He jerked back when one of the shadowy shapes tossed an empty ammunition box down the trench. Pulling back, he whispered into Jugs's ear, "Three plus gunner. Lantern to right. No grenades.

Have to rush them. Lot of noise, startle them." He could hear Jugs breath whistling out his nose. "With me."

Feeling a pull on his sleeve, Chester hesitated as Jugs slid a thin bayonet into his hand. He nestled the grip in his fingers, hearing the soft slide of McGowan's bolo easing from its sheath. Jugs tapped his fingers twice against Chester's shoulder.

They leapt around the corner of the traverse, adrenaline turning their voices inhuman, growling. Jugs's shoulder brushed open the lantern, half blinding their night-accustomed eyes as the single candle wrecked the darkness. A shot sounded, the smell of the spent round hanging in the close air. Jugs leapt at the farthest German, burying the knife up under his ribs. The black frame of a Luger dropped from the dying man's hand and clattered across the concrete of the machine gun platform.

Chester lunged at a second German, shoving the slender bayonet into his side, deflecting off a rib. As he crashed into the mortally wounded soldier, his weight buried the long blade to the hilt. Chester jerked at the bayonet, but it stuck fast, the suction of the deep wound closing tight around the blade. He pushed the body aside and produced his empty pistol, brandishing it at the gunner who was fumbling to his feet, a hand on the holster of his own sidearm. The German held his hands halfway up in surrender.

Jugs wrestled against the trench wall with a third enemy, his knife flashing in the lantern light as the German blocked each slash with a bloodying forearm. Grabbing the wounded arm and twisting it back with a sharp jerk, Jugs spun the man around as the soldier let out a high-pitched scream, betraying the terrified youngster inside the baggy grey uniform. Jugs pulled back the soldier's head and plunged his knife into his throat, almost severing the spine. The dead boy slipped to the ground, head lolled at an unnatural angle as his tunic darkened with purple blood.

Eyes moving back and forth from the gunner to his corporal, Chester saw a wet bloom seeping through the knee of Jugs's breeches, already soaking the top of his puttee. He fumbled for a field bandage and pressed the fat pad hard against the wounded leg. Looking up to his face, Chester saw Jugs's eyes wide and fixed, straining to see over his lieutenant's shoulder.

Jugs shoved Chester aside and leapt at the German gunner who, kneeling by his machine gun, drew a bead on Chester's back with the discarded Luger. Distracted by the sudden movement, he wavered before pulling the trigger. Jugs, the dripping bolo still in his hand, threw himself across the intervening six feet and swung down hard as he could, burying half the knife in the gunner's skull.

The German's face froze in a puzzled expression, his thoughts severed by the thick blade. He stayed erect for a moment, then crumpled over his gun. Chester caught Jugs under the arms as the wounded man staggered from the sudden exertion, sitting him back against the trench wall.

Jugs's eyes were closed tight, grimacing against the growing pain, head back against the sandbags. As he was fumbling with a second bandage, Chester felt a hand on his shoulder. It didn't seem real at first, then he turned with a confused jerk of recognition.

In the guttering light of the lantern, Chester looked up into the sad brown eyes of Fabien Aubert, bending toward him with an otherworldly look of kindness and concern. As the captain knelt, the light spilled over Major Tobin, his agitated eyes searching the scene of bloody and intimate combat.

Fabien ordered ten men down the trench toward the fighting. Taking to the Germans' fire step, they came up behind the attacking enemy and commenced a fusillade with rifles and a Chauchat gun, breaking the enemy assault on the troops still pinned at the burned-out tanks. The remaining twenty-five men rushed to improvise some firing positions, facing back toward the German's second trench line and the inevitable counterattack. A Moroccan sister regiment would pass through and continue the assault once word reached them that the first trench had been taken by *les Américains*.

In a daze from the hand-to-hand fight, Chester Dawkins was in no shape to command. Captain Aubert fed the shock-stricken lieutenant gulps of cognac from a flask he carried into battle for wounded men, never drinking himself. Ned Tobin knelt beside him and spoke slow and even.

"Lieutenant Dawkins?"

Chester heard the words but his mind couldn't parse the meaning.

"Chester? You need to come back to me, lad. We need to find the sergeants," Ned said, holding the lieutenant's chin, keeping his face up. "Chester, are you with me? Jesus, lad, come on now. We need to hear what you know."

"The sergeants?" The importance of what was being asked of him penetrated the fog in his head, along with the brandy. He pushed the major's hand away with a tentative swipe. "They went after the machine gun." His eyes darted around the horrible scene again. "*This* machine gun."

"Yeah, they did, Chester. That they did," Ned said. He saw Chester fading again and raised his voice. "When did you last see them? Where?"

Blinking in quick flutters, Chester said, "Behind the radio tank. We were pinned and we had to take the… this machine gun." His eyes twitched around the space again. "They wouldn't send any of the men, said they'd go instead. Sergeant Lucy insisted."

Fabien listened to Chester's halting narrative, the expressionless face belying deep worry for his longtime comrade. They'd been to hell and back together, he and Sergeant Barthold, too many times to count. "In which direction did they depart, Lieutenant?" he asked in quiet French.

"*À gauche,*" Chester replied, "at an angle of forty-five degrees to the Boche trench. To flank the machine gun." Captain Aubert gave Chester the same quiet gentle look of encouragement he gave the men, nodding with an almost imperceptible smile, "*Très bien, Chester.*"

They could spare only a couple of men, but Ned and Fabien went, too. They'd consolidated the captured line with Benny Sharpe's platoon. The Moroccans had acknowledged their message and were advancing, so Ned left Lieutenant Sharpe in command of the seventy-odd men and went to find their missing sergeants.

The two officers used flashlights and the soldiers held scrounged German lanterns. It was slow going over the heaved-up ground pocked with shell craters. They heard tramping and jangling as the

Moroccan *tirailleurs* set off into the new No-Man's Land between the German's first and second trench lines.

"Major! Captain! Over here!" one of the soldiers called, waving his lantern. As the officers reached the little spill of light, the anxious private motioned down a shell crater. The three men slid down the deep indentation, just able to make out two crumpled shapes near the bottom.

The fading flashlight beams joined on the two sergeants, propped unmoving against the slope. "Willy! Lucy!" shouted Ned. The khaki-clad arm of Willy Freeman raised a little and dropped. Close in, they could see his other arm around Lucien Barthold, the Frenchman's head cradled in the crook of his elbow.

Captain Aubert rushed to his sergeant's side. Freeman had tried to feed his friend some wine, wrapping Lucien's hand around the canteen since Willy couldn't hold up his wounded arm. His sleeve was soaked and blood pooled in his lap where his hand lay useless now. The canteen was tipped across Lucien's coat, wine mingling with blood and gore from the gaping wound in his abdomen that had taken him slowly and painfully.

The two privates brought down their lanterns and opened them, revealing a ghastly grey Sergeant Freeman. The privates fumbled with their field bandages, awkward with shock and grief, wanting to do something, anything, for their beloved sergeants.

"*Ah, mon vieux,*" Fabien said, kneeling close to his sergeant. "*Il semble que c'est la fin, n'est-ce pas?*"

"He's OK, Cap'n Aubert," Willy Freeman said, his big voice weak as a sparrow's. "He just nodded off, tired as he is. He'll be OK." Fabien turned to Willy with a pained smile of reassurance.

A hard spasm racked the sergeant. There was no doubt an equally grave wound in Willy's back, but Ned saw no point in moving him. When the pain passed, Willy motioned for Ned to come close. Swallowing back the sick grief flowing through him, Ned leaned down, his ear close to the sergeant's mouth.

"If… if I don't make it home… would you look in on my Bea, Major?" Ned nodded as his eyes clouded. "She got a little trouble… with the sugar, you know? And her feet bother her somethin' fierce most days…" His fading voice stopped. One of the young privates dropped his bloody bandage and sniffed, rubbing a filthy hand across his eyes.

In the yellow light, Ned saw the soldier-priest begin a sign of the cross over his dearest companion, two fingers extended, so familiar from before the war—*avant la guerre*. Then with a gentle sigh and a nod of understanding, he curled his fingers into his palm. He would not dishonor his friend at the last, this proud socialist who hated everything to do with the Catholic Church. With one exception.

14th of November, 1918
New York City

Mon très cher frère,

I keep telling myself it's real, the war is over and you'll be home soon! I wish you'd been here to see the celebrations all over the City. It was scarcely dawn here when the Armistice began, but that didn't stop anyone once the church bells rang out at six.

I dressed fast as I could and went down our street to Mount Morris Park where people were already gathering. I joined with some other girls from the neighborhood and a dozen white soldiers in an Army truck came by, shouting and honking, with a big sign that read, "To Hell With The Kaiser!" When they saw us girls, they pulled us up on the fenders and the hood of their truck and rode us all the way Downtown. By the time they stopped, it was around ten o'clock. They didn't have much choice, since the crowds had taken over the streets and it was impossible to drive any farther.

When we climbed down off the truck, we joined a huge crowd and had no choice but to move whichever direction the thousands around us wanted to go. We ended up all the way down on Broad Street, flags poking out of every window and all the bankers and brokers showering ticker tape out the windows on us. Some of the girls kissed anyone in uniform, including a few policemen!

Write me as soon as you can, Chester, so I know you ended the war safe. When might you know what day the Army will send you home? It surely won't be too long, since they can't need so many in Europe now that the fighting has ended. And you were some of the first over there. Please write and tell me you'll be home soon.

Everything is fine here. My studies are going well although it's hard to concentrate on lectures when I know what you've been risking overseas. Maddie and I will be waiting for you at home when you return, of that you can be sure. You're not to worry even a little over us—we're looking after each other just fine. It's just that we've missed you so much.

Je t'embrasse… à bientôt!
Now as always, your loving sister Lena

CHAPTER THIRTEEN

Adèle

The baby squirmed inside her coat as she bent to pluck a dirty ring protruding from the soil, not yet returned to farmland with the end of the fighting. At least it had been dry since the new year began, so she could have a good walk across the once-familiar countryside. It was an alien place now, the hillocks leveled and meadows chewed to unrecognizable wastes, barren and pockmarked. She rubbed away some of the muck with the side of her thumb, exposing the brown-yellow brass and a little of the threads winding around the inside.

Part of a fuse. Small caliber, not French. Maybe British?

She'd clean it up later, see if there was any writing. It was lovely, in a way, still holding a little of its metallic luster. The baby wriggled again, swaddled in his blanket and held snug against her ribs by the buttoned coat. There was plenty of room for him. Until she needed the shabby winter coat, she hadn't realized how much weight she'd lost from the long shifts at the shell factory. She went back so soon after the birth in August, still exhausted. They needed the money with the prices for everything—bread, eggs, even horse meat—skyrocketing. Then little more than two months later, Èdouard just three months old, the war ended and her job with it.

She slid the brass ring into her pocket, then withdrew her ungloved hand and held it up to the weak winter sun. There was still a little odd color, even two months on.

Not so yellow anymore, just a little tinge.

When her old schoolmate, the self-christened Léonie, took her in without hesitation, Adèle had to find any sort of work with decent wages. Teaching would be beyond the pale, since she'd have shown in the proper clothes required. The waistbands of the three skirts she'd managed to pack in her flight from Amiens were already tight and she would've run out of material for letting them out with her inevitable expansion. There was endless demand for young and healthy women in the factories producing for the war effort, especially in munitions work. The ceaseless bombardments that had become essential to the generals since Verdun and the Somme in '16 consumed unimaginable quantities of shells—millions upon millions—and the French needed to contribute their share to the carnage.

To call her interview at the munitions factory in the Boulevard Saint-Jacques perfunctory would be generous. The grim-faced and broad-shouldered woman who appraised her like cattle grunted and nodded to the payroll clerk and that was that. Adèle half expected her to check her teeth and feet, but those did not appear to be disqualifying factors. The pay was twice what she could have expected from teaching. At that moment in the glorious history of France, there was much greater need for 75mm shells than properly conjugated intransitive English verbs. When shown the factory floor where she'd be working, Adèle was flooded with relief when she saw the hundreds of women filling and assembling shells at long tables— in the loveliest long and baggy grey smocks.

The baby shifted a few times inside her coat, stretching out his legs before settling with a tiny sigh. She was still in complete wonder at how anything so small could have so many means of expressing himself without words. Joining in with a deeper sigh, she looked across the barren mid-winter ground that stretched away in the distance from her family home outside Albert. A row of orchard fruit trees, pears and a few quinces maybe, had once grown along the town side of the abandoned field. There was nothing left of them, cut down by the British or the Germans for what little timber or heat they might yield. It would take five or six years for the pears to return if replanted this spring.

Yes, pears, she was sure, the trees she and her sister raided in the late summertime when they were young. No children stole pears these last summers, the pockmarks left by the barrages of last spring not yet eroded by time and plowshares. She headed toward where the tree line once stood, weaving her way between the eroding shell craters. During the few warm days left after the guns had stopped in November, the meadow grasses had begun reclaiming their old ground. Just a few dried clumps tossed in irregular patterns, but they'd soon obliterate the violence and death that profaned this peaceful countryside.

Stooping again, an arm across her chest to steady the infant, she tugged at a small angled piece of canvas. She pinched the edge and wiggled it back and forth to loosen the dirt, freeing a dirty wallet with a buckled band. Crouched on the balls of her feet, the baby balanced in her elbow, she unbuckled the strap with her free hand. She unrolled the canvas, revealing two symmetric pouches, and shook one end. A collection of a dozen or more brass buttons and some small skeins of green thread, one with a pair of needles stuck through, rolled out. Protected by the canvas, the buttons were clean but tarnished to dull and no two seemed the same. Holding one close to her face, it appeared to have a royal crest. She flipped through the others with her fingertip—some smooth, others with simpler designs or numbers. One with the ostrich feathers of the Prince of Wales.

She gave the other edge a jerk and some loose British coins rolled out, a few grey shillings and several big copper pennies. She could see an edge of stiff paper peeking out and slid it free. It was a photograph of a young woman—pretty enough, dark hair piled atop her head— holding a baby in her lap, perhaps eighteen months old. Both of them looked straight at the camera, the baby with a startled expression and open mouth, the mother with the sweetest smile and wide eyes full of longing. Turning the photograph over, the ink bleeding a little from the damp, she read, "Until you come back to us, Archie, your loving wife and daughter." Folding up the canvas, she placed it in her pocket with the brass fuse ring, then wiped away the wetness on her cheek.

Enough tears. Enough death and enough sadness. Perhaps Archie made it back to them. Perhaps he was a lucky one.

Her mousy younger sister, Clarisse, had died in September of the influenza brought over by the Americans. She'd lived far to the south in Toulouse where her young husband had taken a job as a government engineer a year before heading off to war. He survived and returned to their little apartment, unchanged since his departure four years earlier but for the yawning absence of his young wife. When Adèle sent a letter to her sister a month after the Armistice asking after their father, she received a terse note from her brother-in-law, containing a few short sentences informing her that her sister had died three months earlier, her father's whereabouts were unknown to him, and he wanted no further communication with her as it would be too painful for him.

So Clarisse had taken Maman when she was born and now the influenza had taken Clarisse. Without Papa, only her son was left to her. She'd not heard from Ned since his new regiment moved to the front in March and she'd fled the German advance on Amiens. The best she could do she'd already done, having sent a letter to the address in Boston he'd given her. After settling at Léonie's in Paris, she realized she didn't even know the number of his new regiment. Since he always managed to get to her in Amiens, there hadn't been any need to write him at his unit. The only address she'd ever used was at the Hôtel de Crillon in Paris. When she sought information at the attaché's office, she'd found only new officers with no knowledge of any such American major. The previous officer-in-charge had been posted to a brigade command somewhere along the Meuse in August and took his entire staff with him.

Her work at the munitions factory had been tedious and physically demanding. But it was also a place of support, where women from families who would never have crossed paths were thrown together. This was their war, their trenches, their struggle. Although Adèle was careful to hide her swelling belly under her voluminous work smock, she hadn't realized how impossible it would be to hide the other telltale signs from these women, many with two or three or more pregnancies of their own.

The walk from the top-floor flat off Boulevard Montparnasse delighted her, even under a battered umbrella dodging the showers of a Parisian spring. In her early days as a *munitionette*, the baby still tiny and unnoticeable within her, she cut through the Montparnasse cemetery with bouncing steps. She proceeded beneath the lanky ash trees and limes that overshadowed the quiet *allées* where she and Gilles had picnicked on bread and cheese during that last beautiful summer before the war. *Avant la guerre.* The cemetery had been filling with new graves, of course, for the dead sons of Parisian families wealthy enough to afford monuments for them. She'd tried a few times to find her beloved Baudelaire and had poked around the smaller annex for Guy de Maupassant, a scandal in life with his bleak stories of war and death. He was enjoying a great resurgence of late.

When she left the cemetery en route to the factory, she'd skirt around the deceptive little surface entrance in Place Denfert-Rochereau to the huge catacombs below, millions and millions of skeletons resting peacefully beneath the bleat of traffic and the rush of quotidian lives. When she bounded up Boulevard Saint-Jacques, the glass-peaked roofs of the factory buildings appeared above rows of two-story shops lining the road—a *boulangerie* below, the fat baker's family above. Or a *fromagerie* below, a young widow and her children above, scraping by on an insufficient pension.

With inevitable tedium, her steps grew heavier and the walk less lighthearted as the baby grew and shifted. With her back sore and ankles swollen in the summer heat, the other women conspired to shift her to lighter tasks, finally settling her into the job of filling 75mm shells with mustardy granules of *mélinite* explosive powder. Although she stood most of the day, others delivered empty shells to her work station and hauled away the filled casings to those installing the long cylindrical fuses. Like the other fillers, her skin turned a bright canary yellow, starting with her hands and spreading over her entire body within a few weeks. At least her black hair hid the tint, unlike her fairer *compagnes* who sported all manner of jaundice-tinged locks. They accepted their new patina with raucous and profane humor at work and on the streets wore their odd pigmentation as a badge of their important contribution to defeating the hated Boche.

However, when her baby was born bright as a lemon, the shocked expression of the midwife shook her a little. The infant seemed well enough otherwise, and after just a few weeks his skin began to pinken with ruddy good health. He was small, a month early, but vigorous and loud in his demands for food and attention.

There hadn't been so much fighting in this farm field, the trench lines not having stalled here with the gnawing stalemate that consumed endless shells and bodies. It was contested in 1914, shelled during the Somme battles in 1916, then overrun again during the Germans' final big attack last spring before the British pushed them back a final time. It was, as a result, sufficiently scarred and battered. Her father's home, pushed right up against a low hill, had avoided any direct hits from the German barrages, although the windows were almost all gone from nearby concussions. Not much was left of the furniture, either burned to warm soldiers or scavenged by people returning after the war.

Papa's collection cases were destroyed, the contents and glass tossed into corners or left where they'd fallen. She spotted a few identifiable remnants here and there when she'd inspected the house that morning. One delicate blue butterfly wing was stuck low on a damp wall, a torn card with three or four pinned beetles sat on the floor beneath the glassless frame of one of the long library windows. The plant specimens had vanished altogether, too fragile to withstand such bullying. She was sure the small mammals—the ones Papa paid M. Duchamp from up the road in Hénencourt to stuff with hemp wool and mount in much-discussed poses—had been taken as souvenirs by transient soldiers. It was the sad demise of the collections that distressed Adèle most, not the damage to her girlhood room upstairs or the gutted kitchen where she and Clarisse had sat near the warm stove doing their lessons. Papa's collections, the gathering of which had been such a regular part of her youth, underscored in such a vivid manner that her father was gone, too. And like his beloved specimens, there was very little trace of him left to her.

The baby was fidgeting and fussing, his little squawks of hunger tugging in their telepathic way at her swollen breasts. The tingle of her milk letting down told her it was time, so she turned back toward the house to find a place out of the weather to nurse. She reversed her winding route from the line of tree stumps, walking with a little faster purpose than when she'd meandered into the field. As she came from around the back of the house, thinking to use one of the window seats in the front sitting room where there were still a few panes of glass, she was surprised to see a black car—was it an Amiens motor taxi?—idling fifty meters away at the end of the narrow gravel lane. She waved to the driver but his back was turned as he pushed open the door. A man in green khaki was bending into the back seat, indistinguishable at that distance. In a few moments, the taxi putt-putted down the main road, heading back toward Amiens with a lingering trail of blue exhaust.

18th of July, 1918
16 rue Vavin, Paris

My Dearest Ned,

I'm writing to the address you left me for your family in Boston, knowing no other way to reach you. I fled Amiens when the Germans looked certain to overrun us in the Spring, settling with an old university friend in Paris. I must risk this letter being read by someone in your family before reaching you, I'm afraid.

The simple truth of the matter is that I am carrying your baby. I don't suppose you'll be surprised, behaving as we did. What's done is done and my only concern now is the safety of our child.

I don't know how this will reach you in France—I am relying on a woman I've never met, your sister Irene, of whom you spoke so often and with such affection. If she is half as formidable as you claimed, I can't imagine her letting a letter from France sit unopened for long.

My dear, I love you all the more now that your child grows within me. Come to me as soon as you find this. I need you so desperately now.

With all my deepest love,
Your Adèle

[Envelope stamped, next to the French postage: *Rec'd United States Postal Service, Port of New York, Aug 22, 1918,* and over the center: *Addressee unknown,* with the handwritten annotation: *Illegible/water-damaged in transit at sea.*]

CHAPTER FOURTEEN

Chester

The medal ceremony was impressive and Chester was glad the French had insisted he and Jugs be allowed to remain until properly decorated by a grateful Republic. In front of Les Invalides where Napoleon and the other heroes of France rested, they'd stood in line with a dozen officers and *poilus* on a fine April morning five months after the guns fell silent. As the clutch of generals and politicians inched down the light blue line toward the two men in khaki, Marshal Pétain moved back with a nod and General Gouraud stepped forward to present the medals to Chester and Jugs. Having left his right arm in the Dardanelles, their old *4ᵉ armée* commander fumbled with the long neck ribbon of the *Croix de guerre* until Pétain stepped in to assist. As the Old Lion leaned forward to kiss Chester's cheeks, copious tears ran down his face and wet his long mustache. Chester could only mumble a tight-throated, "*C'était un honneur de servir, Général...*"

They were the toast of the town for weeks afterward, not just heroes, but *d'exotiques Américains*. His fluent French tarnished a little his strange allure for the ladies of Paris, but what Chester lacked in aw-shucks accent, Jugs more than made up with his horn. With no more call for marksmanship—Jugs's only other notable skill— everyone was ready to hear some American jazz. Once he got over his innate fear of being seen in public with white women, Paris became a friendly place indeed for now-Sergeant McGowan. Without the need for wartime rank distinctions, Chester found it a very good thing to follow Jugs in his rounds of the older music clubs of Montmartre and the new ones springing up along Boulevard Montparnasse.

As with all good things in the Army, their Parisian idyll came to an end when someone at American headquarters finally noticed they'd no further good reason to remain since the rest of their regiment had returned to New York in January, and orders arrived posting them to Brest for shipment home. When they made their way to the port, the movement control officer attached them to a group of a thousand or so colored troops, a mishmash of companies and platoons, most draftees from Southern states and held over in France to provide stoop labor for packing out the American Expeditionary Forces. Unlike the thousands of white troops boarding ships for home, all the men in Chester's temporary command were ordered to disarm—rifles, bayonets, knives, anything that might be considered a weapon. They were fortunate to keep their mess utensils.

They left Brest a few days after the 4th of July in 1919. The French were wild to celebrate the American Independence Day, anxious to demonstrate their gratitude for the Sammies' help in forcing the Germans from *la patrie*. But the port commander ordered all Negro soldiers restricted to their tents while the white troops drank their fill of free wine and cognac. The men sloughed off what they were sure would be the last in a long line of slights, excited at the prospect of seeing home again soon.

Their plodding dilapidated transport—couldn't have colored men sleeping in liner staterooms soon to be returned for civilian use—was due in at Norfolk, the huge port in the Virginia Tidewater, in the early morning hours of the 20th of July. Chester planned to jump the first train heading north.

There had been one wrinkle in his departure for home. At assembly time for boarding in Brest, Jugs McGowan was nowhere to be found. Chester looked all around the quayside for him but, given his on-board duties as officer-in-charge of a thousand soldiers, he couldn't spend much time searching. It wasn't until a day out at sea when, chilled by the wind over the deck, Chester donned his overcoat and found the one-page note neatly folded into one of the pockets.

> *I hope you won't be mad at me, Ltnt Chester. Since nothing change all the time we was at the fightin, what with the white men lordin it over us still, you understand I wanna stay right here in France. They's no diffrence for the Frenchmans (or them French ladies) tween us an any other man done what was spected of them at the war. We both seen how that old General Goroad cried when he gave us our medals, so proud of the two of us. You seen too in Pay-ree how they crazy for the way I blow my horn. I can make a good livin out of my music here. Don't be angry at me, sir. Maybe you and me'll see each other agin one side of that big ocean or other. I sure hope so.*
>
> *Your friend, Srgnt McGowan*

No, he wasn't angry with Jugs McGowan. He wouldn't even bother reporting him missing when they got to Norfolk. He'd done his part, more than most, and now he was a hero of France. Let him stay there in peace, blowing his coronet and bedding pretty French women. Maybe he would see him again. Probably not.

When they lumbered into Norfolk under a hazy summer sun that barely penetrated the thick, clinging humidity, every man on board was relieved. The Negro citizenry of Norfolk, a sizable slice of the population in this bastion of the Old South, had organized a homecoming parade and street celebration the next day for their returning heroes. One more night under moldy canvas in the port's transient camp wasn't too high a price, so Chester was as excited as the enlisted men. This was more like the reception they'd each imagined in one form or another. For Chester, it might make up a little for the parade in New York City he'd missed with his own regiment.

After breakfast the next morning, Chester and a few itinerant sergeants managed to wrangle the disparate troops into a hash of a battalion and got them marching in a straight line, ready to parade the streets of Norfolk. Two other ships had docked the day before, each disgorging another thousand or more colored doughboys. They had enough to make a good show of the parade, joined by a regimental band from one of the other transports. As they stepped off at noon, they didn't notice the heat and humidity.

Chester's battalion, led by a captain who'd graduated from the short-lived colored officer's training school in Des Moines, was the second group in the parade formation. Fifteen or twenty minutes into their march, the leading battalion slowed, then stopped. For a minute or two, no one knew what was happening. The soldiers in front started to break ranks as shouting and screams filtered back to Chester and his men. Soon the people lining the sidewalks began running in all directions, the men toward the melee, the women and children away from danger. More and more of Chester's men fell out to join those streaming forward.

When Chester reached the epicenter of the confusion, what he saw stopped him in his tracks. Since the colored troops had their weapons stripped back in France, they were fighting with bare fists to fend off a hundred or more white sailors and Marines armed with rifles and bayonets, truncheons and billy clubs. Soon, dozens of local police streamed in from side streets and immediately set upon the Negro soldiers, dragging several away to waiting paddy wagons, all the while beating them without mercy. The captain who commanded the made-up battalion approached a Marine sergeant and demanded to know who was in command. The white sergeant answered with a big fist straight to the officer's nose. He motioned to two nearby sailors who bloodied the sprawled captain with boots and sticks.

Chester staggered back into the doorway of a diner, his disbelief at the unfolding scene depriving him of words. As he stood in the alcove entrance, the door opened halfway and a pair of strong hands grabbed his shoulders and pulled him inside.

"That street no place to be," said a stout man in a white cook's uniform and paper cap. He was alone in the empty restaurant, looking Chester up and down with both curiosity and concern. "You hurt any, son?"

"No, no. I'm fine," Chester stuttered out.

"Only a matter o' time 'fore somethin' like this gonna boil over," the old cook said. "Them sailors been itchin' for a fight ever since the first of our men come back from over to France. Can't stand seein' no Negroes walkin' 'round in a fine uniform."

Chester looked out through the big glass windows at the churning crowd. The sailors and Marines were getting the best of the fight, police hauling away anyone with dark skin in a khaki uniform who dared stand his ground.

"What started this? It was supposed to be a homecoming celebration."

The old man eased Chester toward a stool at the empty counter and went around the backside to pour him some coffee. "Couple o' them police tried arrestin' a colored soldier who wasn't in the parade, maybe had a few drinks in him. Them marchin' seen it and a few peeled off to rescue the soldier." He returned the coffee urn to a burner on the back counter. "Then all them sailors and Gyrenes showed up."

"How could they have known there'd be trouble?"

The old cook gave a little smile and a knowing shake of his head. "They was there 'cause they knowed either they'd be trouble or they'd make sure there was trouble." Chester stared down into the blackness in his coffee cup. He was startled to feel hot tears pushing against the back of his eyes. He'd seen men die, beat the Germans, made the world safe for democracy. And nothing had changed here. Nothing. He gave a sharp sniff, raising the coffee to his lips to camouflage his bitterness.

"You an officer? I see them shiny bars on your shoulders."

Chester nodded and sipped the coffee.

"Ain't nothin' beat that! A Negro officer! And you got yourself a medal or two?" The cook pointed to the red-striped green ribbon of Chester's *Croix de guerre* and the rainbow ribbon of his victory medal.

"One is French." Chester whispered.

"Can you 'magine that? French medal on a Negro officer?" The old man patted Chester's hand, then looked hard at him. "We all real proud of you, son. You'n all them men out there. What you all done."

Chester sniffed again, put his coffee mug down, and looked up at the old man across the counter beaming at him.

"Son, I was born in a slave cabin on a James River plantation up 'round Charles City way. Just old 'nough to remember, 'fore them Yankee soldiers come and said we was free." He produced a white towel from beneath the counter and commenced wiping the already spotless surface. "Seein' you wear them officer bars, well that tells me we come a long, long way. Even if them cracker sailors still tryin' to beat you down."

Chester nodded and glanced out the plate-glass windows again. The crowd was almost disbursed. "Doesn't feel like we've come all that far, mister."

"Ahhh, you better call me Billy, like everyone else do," he said, patting Chester's hand again. "I says we come a long, long way. Not one of mine, not one child or grandchild, ever seen a day other than free. That sure is somethin', ain't it?" He leaned against the back counter and assessed Chester anew. "You not from 'round here. You not even from the South, is you?"

"No sir, Mister Billy. From New York City."

Billy blew out a whistle and jerked his chin once to the side. "Well this ain't no place for you, son. Best get you back on up to New York, fast as we can."

Peacetime trains were much more comfortable than the *Hommes 40 ou Chevaux 8* boxcars in France, even sitting in a colored carriage. All the passenger cars—white or black, no difference—were sweltering in the summer heat as they crossed the broad Virginia rivers: York, Rappahannock, Potomac. As they pulled out of Baltimore, the segregated cars were ignored and Chester knew he was out of the South. He resolved on the spot never to return to those parts again.

The heat relented once they reached Philadelphia. He didn't think it possible after all he'd been through these last two years, but the old excitement at being close to home began to bubble up, just like when he returned to Papa and Lena—Maman, too, until she passed—on his school breaks from Howard. Soon enough, the train slowed, anticipating Pennsylvania Station in New York.

The huge building was brand new when he went off to college and he'd loved coming and going from there. Walking under the big arched ironwork of the train platforms into the cavernous vaulted station made you feel like you mattered, like you were somebody who counted in this city. It never had colored waiting rooms or drinking fountains. Everyone moved and mixed in a shifting crowd, never the same one minute to the next.

He carried the sturdy leather suitcase his father lent him when he left in 1917, now filled with military clothing, and his old dispatch bag from France. Chester figured the 2 Line was his fastest way home. The station and the line had changed since he left two summers ago, so he asked for help from a bootblack working the newsstand at 33rd and 8th, feeling like a rube.

New Yorkers are supposed to look after themselves.

He saw the indulgent smile of the shoeshine man, more patient than he would have been had Chester not been in uniform.

Need to get my bearings again.

The subway ride up to the Lenox Terminal crawled on forever. The cars had a little more wear on the seats than he remembered, clattering along through the northbound tunnel toward home.

A home without Pop.

He was relieved that Lena had taken good care of things, more than she should've had to do, but the war was hard on everyone. Her letters had been chatty and full of news of old schoolmates and neighbors. She might have been a little lonely, but that would change now that he was back to stay. Maybe they could visit Maman's family down in New Orleans before he went back to work at the law office. Lena would be starting her last year at Hunter in September, so she'd be free for the rest of the summer. That would make for a welcome break, remembering Maman with those who loved her. It would give him a chance to share with Lena all that had happened in France.

Not many people took notice of his uniform at Penn Station or on the subway. The rest of the regiment had been home five months already, had their parade up 5th Avenue all the way past Central Park, where they'd turned up Lenox for their final strut home into Harlem.

They'd been the first combat troops home, so even the white folks turned out to see them—the papers said a million of them, if that can even be imagined—so a Negro in a uniform wasn't likely to attract much attention now. It didn't matter to Chester. He'd had his fill of finger-pointing and cheek-kissing in Paris. He just wanted to be home with Lena, back among his old neighbors, Pop's old patients, even musty old Mr. Davis sitting in his crypt of an office. His valise weighed him down as he trotted up the steps at 125th Street. With each step up toward the bright street, he could feel the humidity pushing back against his face.

Forgotten how this place swelters in summer.

As he stepped up onto the pavement, the clackety noises of the subway were supplanted by the hubbub of the busy commercial road, jammed with noticeably more motor trucks and automobiles. The war had been good to Harlem, with jobs for anyone who could lift a crate or swing a hammer.

Back among the colored neighborhoods, he garnered a little more notice than he had in Midtown. A few men lifted their hats to him while the ladies on their arms flashed smiles more interested than their husbands would have liked. He smiled back with as neutral a look as possible, not giving away the ladies' little secrets.

By the time he made the last turn onto 123rd and home, the shirt under his tunic was soaked through and the stiff stock collar had wicked perspiration down from his neck. He could see the trees, heavy in full summer foliage, in Mount Morris Park at the end of their street, just yards from his front stoop. It surprised him how much detail he noticed along the block, things he never really noticed all his years growing up. His childhood memories were filled with ranging through the park with his friends, playing all manner of boys' games and adventures. That and sitting with Maman in her room.

How could she be gone? And now Pop, too?

Their house was larger than most on the block—three broad windows wide and four stories tall, plus the short-ceilinged attic rooms where the live-in maid from Maman's time had slept. There was also a walk-down office that had remained unoccupied, full of discarded furniture and forgotten crates, ever since the squat accountant tenant died six months after Maman. Papa never advertised for a new one.

He could see the grey granite steps leading up to the front entry, running right up between the twin columns that supported the little roof over the door. Without thinking, Chester picked up his pace. As he approached his house, he noticed a tall man standing behind one of the pillars. The column did little to conceal him. Dressed in a good suit and a blue necktie, he gave a sidelong glance to the soldier striding up the sidewalk, then returned to his own thoughts with eyes focused a thousand miles away.

Chester slowed to a shuffle, not taking his eyes off the big man. His thoughts ran at breakneck pace, careening off what he thought he remembered and the incongruity of this looming stranger very much at home on the front stoop. Pushing aside a little flash of apprehension that he'd forgotten his own address, Chester hitched up his valise and dispatch bag and treaded up the stairs.

"Dey's closed 'til after dark t'night, sodjer boy," the stranger said in a thick West Indian accent. There was not a hint of humor in his voice or on his face.

Glancing up at the house number, Chester said, "I don't know who you are, friend, but this is my parents' home and it's damn well always open to me." He took two more steps as the larger man moved across the front door and crossed his arms over his barrel chest.

"Come back after nine or ten o'clock, you welcome den if mebbe you have da money," the Jamaican said as he stepped forward.

A standoff had developed on the steps of his mother's house and Chester was not able to puzzle through what could be happening. The two men stood unmoving and unblinking, both firm in the righteousness of his claim.

"Ain't nothing going on this early, soldier." A more American and avuncular voice sounded from behind Chester, startling him out of his confusion. He turned to look down on another big man, older than the one blocking the door but just as broad. His width was attributable to softer flesh however. "Somethin' I can help you with?"

Leaning his valise against a step, Chester said, "Mister, if you have any explanation as to why this… gentleman is blocking the front door to my house, I'd like to hear it." Chester's tone was testy and exasperated, heading to angry. Bunk Hill looked him over and pieced things together. A big, unaffected grin crossed the piano player's jowly face.

"Why you brother-man, ain't you?" Bunk slapped his belly with his left hand while fishing out a handkerchief with the other. He ran it across his forehead then in circles over his round face. "Why Miss Lena thought you wasn't comin' home 'til August. She says you was havin' too good a time sashayin' your way 'round Par-ee to come sooner."

Stepping up the wide stairs and hefting Chester's valise, Bunk said to the doorman, "Aww, it's alright, Nigel. This here's Miss Lena's brother, Lieutenant Dawkins." Nigel slid back to his ineffective hiding place behind the column.

"He ain't much for talkin' but he's harmless 'nough to those who know him, Lieutenant." Bunk stuck out his free hand and said, "I'm Bunk, the piano man, and pleased as a hound with two peckers to meet you, Mr. Chester. Heard a lot of stories 'bout you 'round that old kitchen table, from your sister and from that Maddie. Now git you'self in here."

Chester followed Bunk Hill inside his own childhood home in a befuddled daze. Moving from the bright sunshine into the shadows of the entry hall, he blinked hard a few times before he could make out the interior. The sitting room was a study in contradictions. Maman's walnut-cased spinet, the one on which he and Lena had taken piano lessons, was still there, but reversed and turned out from the wall with a maroon brocade shawl covering the soundboard. There were a few chairs scattered to one side of the piano that looked to be from the dining room across the hall. Most of the furniture was still Maman's, but rearranged in clusters that could seat three or four. The curtains were new and of a much gaudier pattern than his mother would have allowed.

What was Lena thinking with those draperies?

Above all else, however, Chester noticed the permeating smell of smoke—cigarettes, cigars, something else—and the cloying telltales of a half-dozen varieties of perfume. Maman never allowed smoking anywhere but in Papa's study, and even then, only when there were visitors and with the library doors firmly closed. As soon as the last guest departed, his mother opened windows and aired Papa's sanctum. And neither Lena nor Maman would ever have worn such an excess of scent.

During Chester's confused survey, Bunk shed his coat and tossed it across one of the empty bentwood chairs, his hat atop the piano. "If your sister's round 'bout, she's like to be in the kitchen with Maddie." Not waiting for a reply, Bunk rolled down the hallway toward the back of the house.

Sure makes himself at home. And country as a corncob.

Chester followed the big man and encountered the first normal thing he'd seen since returning home—Maddie's back, bent over the sink and scrubbing out the big pot she always used for cooking greens. Bunk walked over and with surprising gentleness placed a big hand under her elbow. She started a little and Bunk said, "Maddie, they's someone here to see you and I 'spect you might remember him."

The old cook slapped away Bunk's hand and backhanded his red-suspendered chest. "Don't you be sneakin' up, Bunk Hill. Like to scare the life right out of me!" She commenced drying her hands on her wide apron, looking up to see who the visitor might be. Her first sight of Chester didn't register, him looking older—much older than two years away could account for. Then she saw Delphine Dawkins's eyes set above the strong jaw that emerged from a stiff collar sitting on broad khaki shoulders. She gasped as if she'd been stuck with a knife, throwing both hands to her face. Chester stepped toward her, tears already streaming, and spread his arms.

"Hello, Maddie."

The good woman, so dear to him for as far back as he could recall, collapsed into his open arms. He held her so tight he felt uniform buttons pressing into his chest. Maddie was sobbing, choking out disjointed words between sharp inhalations. "Oh sweet... Mr. Chester... home now...everything be alright... poor Miss Lena... sweet, sweet Jesus!" For the time being, Chester was happy to hold her and cry into her grey hair. She smelled like home and soup she made for him when he'd had chicken pox and measles. He clung to her until her breathing eased and she was able to speak again.

"Maddie, where's Lena?"

Her apron hem was up to her cheeks, drying her soaked face and runny nose. Bunk was dabbing at his own eyes with his big square hankie, too. Chester blew his nose and wiped his own face. As the room relaxed in a collective sigh, he picked up unspoken signals passing between Maddie and Bunk. The war had taught him about reading silences among frightened men.

Taking both Maddie's shoulders in a gentle grip, he asked again, "Where's Lena?"

Maddie gave a jerk of a nod that told herself to stop being foolish, smoothed her apron back down, and said, "She's down payin' off the last of them mortgages, and I hope the devil comes take them bankers away to hell with him, too."

"What mortgages? Papa owned this house outright," he said. Bunk and Maddie's glances telegraphed their discomfort. "And no offense, Mr.—Bunk is it?—but who the hell are you anyway?"

"Oh, I'm just the man play's piano in the front most nights. Suppose you could say I'm a friend of Miss Lena's and Miss Babette's, too."

There was no bottom to Chester's confusion. "Why do we have a piano player in our house? And who is Miss Babette?"

Reaching for Chester's hand with both of hers, Maddie chewed her bottom lip with such a look of pity that he found some of the fear he'd left behind in France. "Ohhh, there's been some hard times since you been gone, Mr. Chester. Hard, hard times."

There was a sound of chafing satin moving down the hallway. Chester ignored it, until it was followed by a surge of perfume and a testy voice. "I said I don't want no more of those no-account, broke-ass soldiers looking for cheap drinks and free jelly rollin'." Chester jerked around, coming face-to-face with Babette, her signature cigarette holder ensconced in a loose-wristed hand, appraising him with a languid leer.

"Oh, an officer! Well, that is something else again, *n'est-ce pas*? I'm afraid you'll need to return later tonight, *mon cher*." She swept past Chester and made for the coffeepot on the stovetop. He watched as she reached without hesitation to take a cup from the right cupboard.

Maddie squeezed his hand again and said, "Hard, hard times." She held his hand just below her chin and tsked a few times. In his own home, in his mother's kitchen, he was dumbfounded. When the front door opened, Maddie and Bunk's heads swiveled toward the sound. They stared at the kitchen door, nerves firing with every clicking step of Lena's heels in the hall. Chester felt the air pushed by the door as it swung open, spinning to see what new atrocity had come to defile his parents' home.

Lena was sliding a blue bank passbook out of her purse as she pushed the door open with her hip. When she looked up, the sight of a man in a green uniform, some strange version of her beloved brother, stopped her dead. The pocket book slid from her hand and slapped the floor. With the sudden and unexpected release of two years' care and struggle, she began to tremble. She was wobbling on her legs when Chester rushed to throw his arms around her. Like Maddie before her, she sobbed in uncontrolled joy and relief, burying her face into the smooth green worsted of her brother's shoulder.

Chester was cried out from his scene with Maddie, but he held Lena all the tighter from his lack of tears. The deep, intense emotion of finally coming home surged in his chest like opening a long-clenched fist, spreading the aching fingers wide. "Oh, Lena," was all he could manage.

There was a long scrape of a chair as Babette sat herself down to watch the scene unfold, finding it grand entertainment. *So triste, so authentique. Such happy-family horse shit*, she thought. *Ain't brother man in for a cold-water wake-up?*

Very gently, soft as he could, Chester released his embrace and held Lena around the waist. She was not much shorter than he was, so they were eye to eye when he said in a quiet and concerned voice, "Lena, what's happened here? You wrote over and over that everything was fine."

Babette screwed a new cigarette into her holder. Bunk backed himself all the way to the counter and wished he could fit himself into a cupboard. Maddie put a hand over her heart to soothe away the stabbing that came from how much Lena looked like her mother just now.

Chester handed his soaked handkerchief to his sister and she composed herself a little. With a few wipes and blows, her confident posture returned, shoulders back and chin leveled to the world. She took a final deep breath then said, "He hid it from us, Chester. We were living on borrowed money from just a few months after Maman passed. Papa mortgaged the house to pay for your time at Howard, my fees at Hunter, almost all our day-to-day expenses. His practice was a shambles and hemorrhaged patients every month. None were left by the end. He even owed Maddie back wages."

Looking over to the devastated expression on the old cook's face, Chester knew everything Lena said was true. He struggled with the dawning realization that he'd abandoned his sister to cope with the debris of Pop's desolating grief. It was worse than he would've imagined, had he the slightest idea. She'd hid it all under layer upon layer of cheery letters filled with chatty news, most of it utterly false. That didn't concern him—that he'd left his sister to pick up the pieces constricted his guts into a tight knot.

It was all out, all the dissembling over, and Lena began to sniffle again. As her shoulders slumped, Chester grabbed her arm and said, "It's alright, Lennie. It's alright. We're together again and we can face anything. Now, can we start with who these people are and what they're doing in our house?"

"Me and your brother already met, Miss Lena. I seen him on the front steps, squarin' off with Nigel, so I brung him on in here to Maddie," Bunk said, hoping to relieve Lena in her obvious discomfort.

She smiled at the piano man, his heart the biggest part of him, and said, "Thank you, Bunk. Chester must have been rather surprised by Nigel." She motioned with an unsteady hand toward the table. "And you've encountered Babette—Madame Arnaud—as well."

"*Enchantée, monsieur*," Babette said with a disingenuous deep bow of her head.

"*C'est un plaisir de vous rencontrer, madame*," Chester replied, looking confused. He looked back to Lena with pleading eyes, begging her to solve this puzzle for him.

Maddie nodded grave encouragement, her body all twitches and tics, more nervous than she'd been since her long-ago wedding day. Lena squeezed Maddie's hand in thanks and pulled her head and shoulders up, secreting the handkerchief in a skirt pocket. She took a few steps toward her brother.

"The banks were foreclosing after Papa's death and I had nothing. Maddie and I decided to let the empty rooms upstairs—we always did have too much room in this house, even when Maman was alive.

Madame Arnaud was one of our first boarders. That helped for a time, but the bank payments were too much. That's when Babette—Madame Arnaud—proposed a kind of partnership."

With the mention of her name, Babette gave Chester a showy wink and waved to Lena, urging her to continue. She was very eager to reach the *dénouement* of this delicious and sordid tale. Lena nodded to assure herself and drew another deep breath.

"Our business arrangement has been rather successful. So much so that I just paid off the mortgages this morning. I wanted everything cleared up before you returned, Chester, and here you are." Bunk was examining every scuff in the toes of his shoes and the adjoining floor. Babette smiled in deepest self-satisfaction, the cat among the pigeons.

"What exactly does this business partnership entail, seeing as it requires a piano player? And a doorman?"

Lena didn't have the strength to meet her brother's suspicious gaze. "We converted the house into... into a kind of... well a kind of local club where people gather and listen to music and dance if they've a mind to do so."

Running out of patience with the reunion, Babette hauled herself to her feet. "What our business *entails*, brother man, is six pieces of the finest ass money can buy asleep upstairs, a card room with a good rake for the house, a place for them with the money to puff some fine tea our reefer man brings, and since we got that sweet Prohibition, we tripled the price of our booze, too." Her declamation ended, Babette sidled out of the kitchen, flashing a knowing smile to Chester. She could almost feel the angry heat radiating from him as she floated past in a haze of tobacco and jasmine.

Lena watched as her brother's face went from confusion to stony rage and she recoiled from his bitter look. Grasping for something to soothe him, she stammered out, "I had no other option... really I didn't have a choice. The banks were bearing down on me and... and Mr. Davis said it was hopeless. I had to do something."

"So the something you did was connive with that woman to turn Maman's home into a *brothel*? What the hell were you thinking, Lennie? Our mother's house?" His voice rose with each word and Lena shrank back toward the sink where Maddie stood fixed by her own fear.

"I was off in the goddamn mud and shit and blood while you were entertaining men who shirked their duty to stay and profiteer? Is that it? And what exactly did *you* do to make so much money, Lena? How many men did *you*... entertain?"

She was collapsing with unsteadiness and said, "It wasn't like that, Chester. I didn't... that wasn't my part."

He stormed around the kitchen, pacing in undirected vectors from cabinets to sink, sink to pantry, pantry to back door. He finally settled long enough to turn again on his sister and stick the knife deeper. "Thank God our father's dead so he doesn't have to see the degradation of his only daughter."

She didn't recognize him—he seemed a stranger to her. This was not the brother she'd adored since she was old enough to have memories of him. This was some hard man, some brute who could wound her without hesitation. Her world was upended in the blink of an angry eye and Lena ran from his ravaging presence. Flying down the hall and up the stairs, she made for the meager refuge of her little room under the eaves.

"Oh, Mr. Chester!" Maddie said in a stricken voice. "Sweet Jesus save us now!" The old cook hurried after the girl she'd loved for twenty years and more, leaving Chester to his seething.

His breath came in rapid, ragged pants from the rush of blood pounding in his ears. He was startled by the sound of shuffling feet crossing the room as Bunk stirred from his frozen embarrassment. The big man came with short, swaying steps toward the madman in the green uniform. His jovial expression had turned weary and careworn. Bunk stopped a foot from Chester and studied the young officer, shaking his head in deliberate motions. "You may be some fancy soldier with a shiny medal or two, Chester Dawkins, but you also the biggest damn fool I seen since I got off my mama's tittie."

"This is none of your concern. This is *my* house and that is *my* sister," Chester said with a glance at the ceiling and the rooms above. The archness of his tone did nothing to allay Bunk's concern.

The big man put a beefy hand with a pointing finger up by Chester's face and said, "She ain't my sister, but I've taken a shine to that fine young woman and have looked after her and Maddie best I could while you was off in France. And I can tell you this, Loo-ten-ant, she done what she done for you and for no other reason."

"She turned my mother's home into a whorehouse for my sake?"

"You 'bout as blind as a man can be if you can't see that," Bunk said. "She'd have cut off her own good arm to keep a home for you to come back to. She couldn't see no other way."

Chester turned to look out the window, not wanting to hear more from this stranger who knew too much of his family's business. Bunk stretched out his arm and grabbed Chester under the chin, turning his head back to face him and squeezing a good deal harder than necessary. "And don't you ever again say anything makin' your sister out to be some kind of whore like that no-account Babette. That ain't how things was or is—and you can take that as Gospel, soldier boy."

He let go of Chester's chin with a jerk and forced a wide smile back across his face. "Now if you'll excuse me, Lieutenant Dawkins, I need to git back to my piano."

Bunk disappeared into the sitting room and Chester dropped into a chair. He ran a hand over the oilcloth and noticed it was new. He couldn't remember what the old one looked like, only that this was something else that had changed. As an improvised tune of long arpeggios drifted back, Chester found that, try as he might, he couldn't recall his mother's face.

CHAPTER FIFTEEN

Ned

Bobby Tobin still filled the house on 5th Street, although he would never set foot there again. His photographs were on the mantle in the sitting room, hanging up the stairway and along the hall, even in the dining room. No telling how many were in Pa's room, paper ghosts haunting every space, trying to fill the void left by his death. But Bobby had been too big for that, bigger than life itself. Surely bigger than Ned.

The newness hadn't worn off. Ned felt strange and out of place in his old room, the one he'd shared with Bobby all those years. It still looked out over the same narrow backyard where Bobby had made him spar and where he'd received endless bloodied noses and blackened eyes. It hurt every time, but it taught him not to cry. Never, not for any reason.

Bobby was gone and nothing could change that. He felt somehow foolish, this bitter sorrow at the loss of his brother. How many had he buried in France? How many had they lost that day on the Somme? Each one was somebody's brother. Each entitled to their portion of his grief, too. But Pa couldn't blame him for those deaths.

As the war hysteria swept the country, the inevitable grumbling at the corner taverns and barber shops started over fit men like Bobby not doing their part, not pulling their share of the load. Bobby felt it more than most, since to the swell of hectoring from the old veterans of Antietam and Cuba were added asides about his little brother doing a double share. Bobby succumbed like most of the others and joined up in April of '18.

The most puzzling and tragic aspect of the Spanish influenza was that it took the youngest and strongest, not the oldest and weakest. No one could explain why. Ned watched it strike a quarter of the 369th in little more than a month, with one in ten of those never coming home. He couldn't bear to imagine Bobby dying the way he saw those men in France, gasping and starving for air as they drowned in their own overflowing lungs. So the great Bobby Tobin, felled by no man in the ring, was carried away on the 12th of October, 1918 in an overcrowded New Jersey Army hospital by a little bug he couldn't see, let alone fight. He wouldn't have reached the front before the war ended—his regiment was demobilized having never fired a shot in anger.

The death of his eldest son wrought terrible changes in Emmett Tobin. Although Renie struggled to keep Charlie and little Bess clear when their father was in one of his drunken rages or sullen depressions, the house their mother filled with such warmth had become a cold and tense place. The neighbors were well aware of the changes. No one condemned his turning to the bottle. Sure, isn't drink just the good man's weakness, after all? And no one deserved to numb himself with the whisky more than Emmett Tobin, having buried both his wife and grown firstborn. So the neighbor ladies added Emmett to their rosary intentions and did their best to help Renie protect the younger ones from the worst of their father's grief. The neighbor men listened with patience to Emmett's ramblings at Murphy's, once a busy corner bar before Prohibition, now a thriving cigar store. Murphy sold precious few cheroots in front but a great quantity of whisky and beer in the back.

For Ned, it had been a whirlwind departure from France. He'd stayed with the 369th through the end of the fighting and, as a last tweak of General Pershing's nose, helped ensure the men of the 369th were the first of the Allies to reach the Rhine two weeks after the shooting stopped. In a final *beau geste*, the French insisted their American comrades lead the march to the river border with

Germany. Ned and Fabien Aubert stood together watching Colonel Hayward kneel on the muddy banks, fill his cupped hands, and drink the river's water with a satisfied grin. Of course, when word of this stunt got to American headquarters, the regiment was ordered to Brest for immediate embarkation. They'd been first to the Rhine and as a result would be the first home. They got their parade up 5th Avenue, all the way into Harlem, and were now returned to the New York National Guard under the less bellicose command of the new governor, Al Smith.

The American headquarter's rush to get their troublesome colored regiment out of Europe kept Ned busy for twenty hours a day since he refused to allow these men—his men—to suffer the indignities on their way out of France that they'd endured on their way in. This had left little time to search for Adèle. He'd managed an overnight to Paris, where he scrounged a room at his old haunt, the Hôtel de Crillon, planning to visit the *École normale supérieure* in Sèvres the next morning to see if they kept any information on their graduates. But the plan gave way to a stuporous drunken night in the darkest corner of a bistro behind the Opéra after the desk clerk retrieved a long-undelivered telegram from his sister Renie telling of Bobby's death. He'd resolved on his return to the States to seek assistance from the French consul in New York, to write Adèle's father in Albert and to drop a line to old Marcel at *Le Coq Main* in Amiens. That judgmental *concierge* would toss any letters from America addressed to Adèle's old apartment in the rubbish, of that he was certain. The result was that he left France having made no plans with Adèle.

Since demobilization from a slapdash Army camp halfway out Long Island and his return to Boston, Ned had written Adèle a half-dozen times. He'd sent a telegram to her father's address. Overseas mail service was back to normal, so either Adèle had never returned to Albert or Amiens, or she was choosing to ignore his letters. He stopped writing altogether as the second possibility etched itself with acid corrosiveness into his thoughts, overcoming what little rational resistance his exhausted and battle-scarred mind could muster. Besides, his family and his father's neglected businesses were in such a fragile state, he had little time for self-pity or chasing what felt like a long-lost lover.

That was how Ned found himself standing behind the counter in his father's candy store on East Broadway inventorying jawbreakers and taffy bites. He'd convinced himself he was just there to help out until Pa got his legs under him again. The mind-numbing sameness of days in the stores was at first soothing, not requiring much thought about anything in particular. This forestalled the need to plan any future for himself or anyone else.

His dismissiveness was the way he'd found to deal with the constriction in his stomach each time he thought of Adèle. The knot had gotten a little smaller over the few months he'd been home. Early on, he sometimes joined his father at Murphy's, but the pathetic state of Pa as the drinks went down was too unsettling. Ned hated feeling sorry for him and the whisky wasn't helping much. The routine at the stores was a better relief.

Just as he dumped a big jar half-filled with black licorice snaps into the brass bin of the shiny green Toledo scale, the little bell over the entry jangled. He'd made a game of predicting the emotional state of entering customers from the sound of the bell as it rang above the door. This time it was angry and insistent, so he heaved out a long sigh and turned.

He was met by the irate face of his sister Renie propping up their drunken father dangling by an arm thrown over his daughter's shoulders, slipping and bobbing on feet that might as well have been in skates. Ned flipped up the end section of the counter to let her drag Pa toward the back room where he'd slept off a daytime drunk more than once since Ned's return. As Renie slid sideways through the opening, Ned took their father's other arm and pulled it over his own shoulders, easing his put-upon sister's burden. She was tight-lipped with anger and embarrassment, but her eyes betrayed her deep concern.

They plopped Pa down on a scratchy dun-colored sofa that once sat under the front parlor windows before Ma had replaced it more than ten years ago with something more fashionable. Ned picked up the dangling legs, feet tapping to some unheard reel, and dropped them without ceremony on the sofa. Renie gave a few head shakes and a tongue cluck, more out of obligation than anger. She'd watched him spiral down for months longer than Ned, after all.

Back in the front, Renie resettled her clothes and smoothed her hair. She drew herself up with all the self-confidence she'd inherited from their mother and said, "He's getting worse not better, Neddie. What's to be done about him?"

Turning back to the scale and the pile of sticky black licorice, Ned studied the weight and jotted it down with a blue pencil on the inventory sheet. Without looking back to his sister, he replaced the licorice on an eye-level shelf and pulled down the adjoining jar of crystallized ginger. It clunked onto the scale in large clumps.

"Good man's weakness, don't they say?"

Renie was having none of it. "That's a lot of malarkey and well you know it, Edmund Tobin. This is beyond a little sadness chasing a drink or two. He's wrecked entirely." She grabbed his elbow and tugged hard to make him face her.

"He lost his favorite and blames me for it. It was my war in Pa's reckoning." He turned back to the scale, shaking off her grip on his arm as he bent to the inventory.

She tugged at his sleeve again. "You've had that chip on your shoulder about Bobby since I was old enough to remember and I suspect even earlier than that," Renie said. "And don't you think we all knew you were Ma's favorite yourself? You've got to be shed of all that or we'll lose him certain."

"Ma's long gone, Renie. Pa never had much use for me, less now that Bobby's gone, too. If he wants to drink himself to an early grave, that's his business." Ned jerked back his arm and took up his insincere interest in the candy inventory again.

"That war made you hard, Ned. Don't let it destroy you and all those around you." She stood staring at the side of his head as he went through the motions of preoccupation. Her accusing gaze wore him down, even without looking up. Closing the ledger, he set the blue pencil across the scratched leather cover and leaned on his palms. He stood suspended, still feeling his sister's eyes boring into him.

Renie tugged at his sleeve by way of encouragement. From the back, Pa mumbled a few incoherent words. Ned ran a hand from his eyebrows to his chin, trying to smooth away his uneasiness. There was no use pretending anymore.

"The war made me a lot of things, Renie. I suppose hard may be one of them."

She stroked the smooth poplin of his sleeve but kept silent. She knew he had more, maybe much more to say now that he'd begun.

"It was terrible in too many ways. So much pain and… and so much noise. Noise all the time."

"It must have been awful."

"It was. And so many gone. Good men." He swallowed hard a few times before he continued. "But it was so… so damn… *exciting*. I was scared half to death most of the time, but it was… almost *thrilling* every time I came out of a barrage or an attack in one piece… I don't think any of us ever felt so *alive* as we did in France… in the trenches."

She glanced all around the candy store. "This must seem dead as a tomb."

"That it does."

"You just can't seem to settle back into life here, can you?"

Leaning with his back against the counter, Ned fished a pack of cigarettes from his trouser pocket and lit one. He took a few long drags, then looked straight at Renie for the first time since she'd brought Pa in from Murphy's. "It'll never be the same for me here. And I'm so antsy, I might explode."

She blinked back emerging tears then leaned in next to her brother and slid under his arm. He squeezed her tight against his side. Neither felt any need to break the silence. Ned finished his cigarette and stubbed it out in an old tobacco tin he used as an ashtray. Renie wandered toward the wide front window and stared out at the mix of autos and horses making their way along Broadway. It was half past two, so the crush of children out from school was still a half hour away. Pa had gotten an early start. She slid her hand into the embroidered pocket of her skirt and produced a letter. She studied it for a few seconds, then straightened her shoulders and turned back to Ned.

"This letter came yesterday for Pa. With a postmark from Ireland. Since he doesn't see to any of his mail anymore, I opened it thinking it was likely news of the death of some relative or other." She came back to the counter with even steps and slid the letter across.

"It's from Kevin, the schoolteacher from Glenador. Eldest son of Pa's cousin Mick. He's concerned about the agent, some Mr. Nugent, whose been managing the farm since Granddad passed just after you left for the war. We wrote you, remember?" Ned nodded, recalling the crumpled letter that caught up with him at the Newfoundlander's depot in Scotland. He'd never met his grandfather, none of them had, but with Pa's retold stories of growing up on the farm a few miles outside Tipperary Town, Granddad comprised a misty second-hand memory familiar and comforting enough to Ned that he'd been grieved with the news.

"Pa says they knew each other as lads, this Eamon Nugent, but Cousin Kevin seems to have reasons for mistrusting him." Ned was listening, but glanced vacantly along the long shelves and big glass jars while she spoke. Renie needed her brother's full attention before she went on, so she moved in front of him, craning her neck to meet his face until he finally laughed a little and gave her hand on his sleeve a tight squeeze.

"Alright. You've something to say to me, Renie, so out with it."

She placed her other hand along his cheek, not stroking or patting it, just letting the warmth of his face warm her palm. Their mother had often done the same, not being one to fuss much over a crying or frightened child, but reassuring in her way. "Ned, you're lost here. You're not much good to Pa in his present state and you're no good to yourself. Why don't you go look after Granddad's farm, see what Cousin Kevin's so concerned about? Poor Pa would be every kind of thrilled at the thought of one of us being in Ireland."

He placed his bigger hand over hers, then slid it to his mouth and kissed her fingers with more affection than he had shown anyone since his return. He said in a quiet voice, near a whisper, "Renie, that's a lovely thought, but what in God's name do I know of farming?"

"It's a poor country and you'll find plenty of men ready to work our land for small wages. Perhaps some of the others just home from the war like you." She let go of his cheek and shook off the ripple of sentimentality that had passed between them. Hands on hips, she added, "Pa will stake you as well or he'll have to answer to me for it. He's tight as a drum and has more money than Croesus tucked away."

"What about the stores? He's in no fit state to see to business."

She waved a hand at him. "Bah, you've done your bit so it needn't worry you any longer." Ned watched a remarkable transformation as Renie's high cheeks reddened and she looked away, one hand about her throat. She alternated nervous glances at Ned's face, then over his shoulder at not much of anything. "You'll remember Joey McInerney, from the McInerneys in the big house over on 9th Street?"

Ned smiled and gave a little teasing nod, "Yes, I believe I do. Bit of a beanpole when we were kids, wasn't he?"

"Well, he's grown to a fine man. He joined up with the Yankee Division and they filled him out," she said, a touch of defensiveness in her voice. "We've been walkin' out from time to time on Sundays, taken in a few dances down at the parish hall as well. He's asked me to marry him."

As will happen at such moments even with adult siblings, Ned regressed to adolescence with eyes wide in mocking surprise, a taunting smile creeping over his lips. "Why Irene Tobin, you've a fancy man then?"

She glared the insincerity right off her brother's face. "There's been none of that. And if you'd kindly lift your filthy thoughts from the gutter?" Affection for his dear sister who deserved every kind of happiness replaced the teasing look. She went on. "I've a mind to accept his proposal. We'll live at our place with Pa and the young ones and Joey can help look after the stores in your stead. Unlike you, *Major Tobin*, he's more than thrilled to be safe and sound back here in Boston." She looked down while she smoothed her skirt and added with much less sureness, "And he's a handsome enough fella." Then, to convince herself as much as Ned, added, "Really he is. And not over fond of the drink."

Their heads turned as their father gave out a snort and mumbled again. They snapped back toward the front of the store as a happy out-of-school bell jingled above the door.

CHAPTER SIXTEEN

Adèle

Léonie was right about the freezing. Even this late into spring, the dampness seeped in through the walls. So while the peace conference at Versailles consumed important men's thoughts, Adèle was covered in nothing but gooseflesh, occupied with not shivering during Diego's interminable exposures.

"*Alors*," he mumbled, sliding an exposed plate out of the back of his boxy camera. The taciturn Spaniard had moved from grunts to occasional syllables over the year she'd known him. It wasn't much of an improvement, but he could produce the most beautiful pictures. She slid the *papier-mâché* mask up over her forehead and rubbed the red indentation it left on the bridge of her nose. Diego paused his rummaging and shuffling long enough to toss Léonie's old shawl to her. The worn silk chafed across her nipples, hard as dried beans.

"*L'autre*," Diego muttered, nodding to the collection of Signie's masks sitting on the low side table just out of the camera's view. They'd been through all but one, so Adèle scooted down the chaise and picked the last from the table. It was a Plague Doctor, the long nose drooping nearly a foot from the bone-white mask with its fishy glass eyes. Signie had found an 18th century book with wonderful engraved plates of *commedia dell'arte* scenes and was entranced by the stylized masks and costumes for each stock character. The book, which he could never afford to purchase, had been procured, he said, "in trade rather than cash from that dear, sweet little bookseller."

Signie had been experimenting with Diego on a collage project with nude photographs of mangled and scarred war veterans but was very unhappy with how it had progressed. Even after redoing the portraits of the wounded men wearing nine masks and odd bits of costume he'd made from the plates in his book, he wasn't satisfied. He was the first of the wounded men to pose, donning nothing but the half-face black mask and tall white sugar-loaf hat of Pulcinella, the horrible jagged scars and missing chunks of flesh from his hip and groin drawing the inexorable gaze of every viewer.

He hit upon the final format for his photographic study one drizzly afternoon while sitting in Léonie's apartment watching Adèle nurse little Édouard. He'd decided on the spot that what he needed was a Madonna for his collage, a Madonna also naked except for a mask. This had morphed, through several enthusiastic discussions with a rotating cast of artists and persons of less identifiable livelihood, into nine photographs of his Madonna wearing a different mask in each. It had taken the better part of a month to convince Adèle that only she would suffice as his naked Madonna, having been the original inspiration.

The apartment was more often than not occupied by one nude woman or another so Adèle had grown rather blasé in the presence of bare breasts and naked *derrières*. Since the masks were large enough to disguise her face, in the end she agreed. She reckoned there were precious few men left alive who might recognize her when viewed from the neck down. No one since Ned Tobin, although he might still be in France, either above or below the ground. Six months since the fighting ended and there were still hundreds of thousands of Americans in France and across the border in Germany.

When Édouard arrived early in August, Adèle had returned after just three weeks to her job at the munitions factory, claiming she had been stricken with the Spanish influenza still rampaging through France. The women she worked with were well aware of the true reason but the sanctimonious bosses accepted her proffered excuse. Old and stooped Madame Leblanc across the landing had been thrilled with the few francs Adèle could pay her to look after the baby and the dear woman brought the infant to a tiny café near the munitions factory during Adèle's lunch break so she could nurse him. Signie, who was entranced by the squirmy little man from the first, was up and down the stairs every hour from the gallery to check on him, so Édouard was in good hands. However, when the horrendous shelling that had consumed all the factory's output ceased on the 11th of November, the layoffs of the *munitionettes* began the next day. Some of the women who'd been there the longest were kept on for a few months, just to keep production ticking over and the Germans nervous. By March, the factory was shuttered and dark.

With competition biting into Léonie's earnings and the loss of Adèle's factory wages, things were rather tight for the inhabitants of the damp apartment in rue Vavin during the winter of 1918 and into 1919. By February, Adèle had found piece work translating articles from Parisian newspapers for American reporters sent to cover the peace conference. Although she could do this work from home, she couldn't bring herself to fire Madame Leblanc, who doted on the little boy and needed every *centime* of the little money she was paid.

Once the scrum of reporters and the burgeoning mass of government functionaries began arriving for the peace conference, another surprising line of work opened for Adèle. One of the American reporters asked if she could arrange a visit for him to the Somme and Verdun as well as the American battle sites in the Argonne and along the Meuse. In the end, he asked her to accompany him as translator, the Americans generally being rather deficient in French. Soon after, British families—grieving parents, heartbroken wives and sweethearts—trickled over to France in search of graves or, if there was nothing to bury, the places where their boys had fallen. After her reporter friends referred a few of these sad people to her, word of mouth made Adèle Chéreaux, much to her surprise, a sought-after battlefield guide.

After her first few tours—some day trips to the Marne, others overnight to Ypres or Cambrai—Adèle purchased a musette bag from one of the innumerable sidewalk vendors of war surplus. She carried maps and a notebook for jotting locations of unmarked cemeteries and village cafés reputable enough for repeat visits. She also used her bag to carry odds and ends she picked up along the collapsing trench lines. Since she'd picked up the brass fuse ring from the British 16-pounder shell in the field behind her father's house outside Albert, she'd become fascinated with the detritus left by the carnage. Not large things—she had no interest in the tall shell casings that were turning up as umbrella stands or floor ashtrays in cafés. She was drawn to small things—buttons and buckles, munition pouches and tobacco tins. Things that had been touched and used by soldiers, the details of their lives at the front. When she dumped out her musette bag after each trip, she was startled by how many items she'd accumulated. Léonie found Adèle's collection amusing, albeit a little morbid, but Adèle had lost one—and possibly two— lovers to the war, so it seemed understandable.

Since the avant-garde artists, in particular the Dadaists who'd just emerged in Paris, eschewed conventional shapes and forms, there were more frames in the gallery than art with which to fill them. At Signie's suggestion, Adèle took to wiring or gluing her battlefield *objets trouvés* in patterns and clusters on remnants of gesso-covered canvas or art board cut to fit abandoned frames. Since some were heavily carved and gilded from the last century, the effect was often shocking and provocative. Léonie of course loved them and the walls of their commune-apartment sprouted a new installation every month or so. The steady parade of true artists, charlatan *poseurs*, and one or another of Signie's indifferent lovers began to note Adèle's creations with grudging admiration.

As Adèle lay shivering on the chaise, the final mask pushed up over her hair with the nose poking up like a unicorn's horn, the door flew open as it did whenever Signie made an entrance. He dashed over and removed the mask with annoyed fussiness. "You are to treat my creations with more respect, Madame Chéreaux. These are not to be worn like a paste jewelry tiara atop your lovely tresses." He fluffed out her hair, cascading it over her pale shoulders, then nodded with approval at the aesthetics of his quick handiwork.

Diego grunted and stooped behind his camera, motioning with a jab of his hand for Signie to return the mask to his model. While Adèle shimmied out of the threadbare shawl and tossed it to the floor, Signie untied the black silk ribbons and placed the mask with utmost particularity over Adèle's nose and cheeks. When he retied the ribbons behind her head, they vanished into the glossy ebony of her unbraided and tousled hair, yielding what Signie found a stunning effect. With the softened focus Diego used to contrast with the unforgiving high resolution of the wounded men in the photographs, the mask would float on her face without visible attachment. It was exactly what he was after. He was now confident his grand collage, *Notre-Dame de la Boucherie*, would cause tremendous provocation at this autumn's avant-garde salon at the Grand Palais.

With the last of the exposures complete, Adèle went to the lone bedroom she shared with Léonie and little Édouard to put up her hair and find something warm to wear. Since it was already nearly dusk, she slipped into a flannel nightgown and then wrapped herself in the green peignoir she'd brought from Amiens. She smiled recalling how her beloved old silk robe had become, at Diego's insistence, an unwilling prop in one of her earliest poses. By the time she wandered back to the sitting room, a small group had gathered. Léonie was back from the market and shelving a few tins of fruit and a bottle of milk in the tiny kitchen. Madame Leblanc had returned with the baby who was happily enthroned on Signie's lap and gurgling at the silly faces the little man was making. Adèle retrieved a royal blue box of Gitanes from the square dining table and passed them around. As was her habit, Madame Leblanc placed one in her lips and slid a second under the collar of her blouse. Léonie waved away the offer of a cigarette and lifted Édouard from Signie's lap, shoving him out of the upholstered chair with her hip. The infant sniffled around in her chest hunting for a nipple, eliciting adoring smiles.

They all settled except Diego, who continued his eternal fiddling with his equipment. He picked up a stack of exposed film frames, snaking his way between the chairs and couch in the crowded room. As he passed Léonie, he caught his foot on the curled edge of the faded Persian rug and the stack of frames fell to the floor with a horrible clatter.

Everyone in the room startled at the sound. Madame Leblanc clutched her chest in fear for her health but a long drag on her cigarette soothed her. Adèle yelped then giggled at herself. Signie, however, stood leaning against the kitchen door jamb, directly across the room from Léonie and Édouard. Without a word, he went to the kitchen and returned with two copper pans. He walked behind Léonie, who looked at the pans but shrugged and returned to dandling the baby. Without warning, Signie banged the two pots together and the room jumped a second time. Except little Édouard.

"Signie, you unbearable shit, what the fuck are you doing?" Léonie said, turning to shoot him an annoyed glare. He hobbled around to the center of the room, crossing to Adèle.

"Adèle, would you go over and call to Édouard. Right in front of Léonie." She shrugged and did as he asked.

"Édouard, *mon petit*. Maman loves you very much." The little boy studied his mother's face as she cooed to him, smiling and bubbling and kicking out his legs. She turned to Signie and spread her hands with a shrug.

"Now could you go behind Léonie and say the same things?"

Adèle had humored much stranger requests from him these last months, so she did as he asked. The little boy made no attempt to find his mother or turn his head. A sharp chill ran down her spine as Adèle repeated the words much louder. Still, the baby made no attempt to find her.

She stared across at Signie, terror-struck by her realization.

Signie breathed out, tears streaming down his cheeks as he stepped toward her. Adèle staggered into his arms.

"Oh no... no, Signie. Not Édouard..." Adèle teetered on the sharp edge between fearful panic and maternal concern. "He's *deaf*? My perfect little boy is deaf?"

"Oh, *ma chérie*," Signie said, smoothing her hair with gentle strokes, "he's still perfect."

CHAPTER SEVENTEEN

Ned

Horses were back on the farm for the first time since 1915. Pa's agent, Eamon Nugent, had sold off the mares and foals to the army just a few weeks after old Charlie Tobin had passed in his sleep. The big roan stud, renowned in all the adjoining counties and beyond, went to a breeder in Roscommon who'd done business with Ned's granddad for years and wasn't a man to let such a fine opportunity pass.

On his rounds before breakfast, Ned released a gaggle of snorting mares from the long stable, waving them through the paddock and onto a pasture thick with ryegrass and white clover. Cousin Kevin had gifted him a young and impetuous herding dog of no recognizable breed a few months after his arrival last May. Kevin said a proper Irish farmer needed a decent dog for respectability. Trotting beside Ned, the animal darted after the horses once they cleared the double stable doors, yipping and snapping at their heels. Ned hadn't a notion how to train a farm dog, but Kevin assured him the beast was from a distinguished line and would sort himself soon enough. Ned hadn't settled on a name so he used a variety of titles and profanities depending on the state of the dog's behavior and his own nerves. The dog responded, begrudgingly but well enough, to whatever Ned yelled. He let the dog sleep on the flagstones before the fading embers in the big kitchen fireplace. Cousin Kevin accused him of spoiling the animal, but Ned appreciated the sounds of him in the house at night.

Being a man with a deep and abiding suspicion of lawyers and all their wily craft, Granddad never drew up a will so the farm and all his worldly goods passed by intestacy to Ned's father and his two sisters. The aunt who settled years ago in Glasgow Ned met for the first time during the war when he was at his first regiment's depot in the Scottish Borders. The other aunt emigrated to New South Wales at eighteen and was known to him only by spidery handwriting on a few envelopes delivered to their house. After Granddad's death, Pa wrote Eamon Nugent and asked him to tenant out the fields and rent the house using what was needed for upkeep of the place and Nugent's own fee as agent. At Pa's specific direction, the remainder was split between his two sisters and posted by bank draft twice each year. With his business and the half-dozen houses he owned and rented out in Boston, Pa didn't need the money and thought it a kindness to the sisters who were by now almost strangers. Renie had written to the aunts and informed them of the new arrangements for the farm, promising Ned would send a little money as soon as he'd brought in a crop.

With the $2,500 Renie shamed Pa into handing over, Ned did what work the neglected house and barn required and, with assistance from an old horse trader friend of his grandfather's, restocked the stables. They'd yet to find a new stallion up to the standard demanded by the reputation of the Tobin farm. For this year, they covered their new mares with a big chestnut stud— known to sire fine tall hunters—from an absentee Englishman's estate north of Thurles.

Grandma died when Pa was eleven and granddad never had the itch to remarry, diverting any romantic urges into his farm and horses. He'd moved in the widow of one of his shirttail relations as cook and housekeeper, then set about transforming his farm and stables into as prosperous an enterprise as one was like to find in east Tipperary during those twilight years of Queen Victoria's reign. The blue slate roof on the house was a reminder of the family's success, since most of the neighbors still slept under thatch.

It hadn't struck Ned as a sudden revelation. Rather, over the nine months he'd been at the farm outside the tidy village of Glenador, his indifference and irritation with everything and everyone plaguing him since his return from France began to dissipate in fits and starts. Some days, he was awful company for man or beast. Other days, he worked himself to exhaustion with Brian McNamara, the neighboring farmer who helped tend the fields and horses in exchange for a promised share of the crops.

Often accompanied by his two rangy teenage sons, Brian McNamara drew from a deep well of patience with this American who'd came to Ireland without a single farming skill other than the trench digging he'd learned in France. Since Ned was nothing if not dogged, Brian taught him while his sons teased the citified American over his cluelessness of matters they'd known almost since birth. The physical strain and uncomplicated honesty of the hard labor was a tonic to Ned and his edginess had smoothed from months of rising with the sun and collapsing into bed six days every week.

He hadn't been inside a church but a handful of times since Ma passed, but now welcomed the respite of a well-earned Sunday. He adjourned with the men to the pub afterward, standing his rounds and, with reluctance at first, sharing a few stories from his time in the war. He'd soon discovered he was related, with varying degrees of attenuation, to half the congregation. Since he was a tall and strong American (well fed since his earliest days, it was generally held), the unrelated mothers and aunts were anxious to keep a hook in him for his matrimonial potential. That he was now the proprietor of what was one of the finest farms in the county until old Charlie Tobin had taken ill (God rest his soul) only burnished Ned's allure for these canny ladies with a keen eye for man-flesh.

From time to time, he was stabbed by thoughts of Adèle. Soon after his arrival in Ireland, he'd sent a few more letters passing on news of the farm. He hadn't expected a reply, but the ritual of writing and posting moved him over some threshold and he hadn't written since. She still crept into his thoughts more than he wanted and he struggled with lingering regrets. He also grappled with fear, late at night when the dog or the wind woke him, that he might have lost his only chance at happiness.

Having finished their breakfast of cold bacon and yesterday's bread, consumed by both him and the dog with little thought and less savor, Ned pottered about the stables mucking out the odd stall while he waited for Cousin Kevin and Eamon Nugent. They'd sent word they wanted to speak with him about pooling resources to purchase the neat ten-acre field and cottage adjacent to the farm that old Bridie Comerford (the relict of P.J. Comerford, the tobacconist, God rest his soul) was wanting finally to sell.

Long before they turned up the graveled lane, Ned could hear the sputtering of Eamon's boxy black Model T laboring up the hill. He hung the manure fork on a rusty hook outside the tack room, brushed his hands against the back of his brown woolen trousers, and sauntered out to the forecourt framed by the stable, the house and the fieldstone hay barn with its new thatched roof. He leaned on his haunches against the high red wheel of the shiny jaunty car he'd repainted last week and lit a cigarette. Although Eamon had sold off the wagons and other equipment, Ned found the two-wheeled wagon, thick with dusty pollen, in the back of the hay barn. He'd hauled it into the daylight and set to work. Ned asked Brian to show him how to harness and drive a draft horse after the planting was in and they'd cut enough turf to keep their fires going through summer.

The engine's thrumming sharpened as the Ford turned up the lane. Eamon hit the klaxon horn as they approached, the wheezy ooh-ha starting the dog barking. Ned ground the cigarette under the toe of his boot and watched the automobile approach. He noticed three heads behind the flat windscreen, one with the pinned-up brown braids of Kevin's wife Maire wedged between the two larger men on the single bench seat. The little Ford stopped a few feet from the jaunty car, the dog yapping as Eamon pulled the hand brake with a metallic scrape. Ned stepped to open the passenger door and Cousin Kevin extended a hand as he ducked out. Maire held a basket covered with an unbleached square of rough linen in her lap as she slid across the tufted leather.

"I've a fine soda loaf just out of the oven and a jar of my blackcurrant jam," Maire said, motioning with her head and quizzical eyebrows at the house. "Sure, mustn't you be living on wishes and prayers, with no woman about to feed you." Ned motioned her toward the door and she clucked her tongue all the way into the house, headed for the kitchen to store the bread and see if Ned was caring for himself at all.

"I thought you said old Mrs. Comerford would only leave Glenador in a box headed for the churchyard, Eamon?" Ned asked, preempting the endless pleasantries that accompanied even the most casual encounter in Ireland. He was given much social latitude, being a Yank with modern ideas, and he took full advantage.

"Ahh now Ned, you can't hold a man to account for his opinions, what with the whole world spinning off its center all around us," Eamon said. From the first, Ned found the agent a little unctuous for his taste, but Pa vouched for him, albeit from forty-year-old memories. "Everything's been topsy-turvy since that no-good Breen from Donohill and his hooligans killed those policemen north of Tipperary Town. Those west Tipps have long been a shifty lot of stone-throwers, to a man."

Ned looked to Kevin, knowing reports of rebel activity in the area would've reached him in Glenador. Taciturn as ever, he pursed his lips and gave a slow nod.

"That trouble hasn't made it to east Tipperary, Eamon. What's it to do with Bridie Comerford selling up?"

Eamon fished a plaid handkerchief from inside his coat and mopped his forehead. "Oh, it's not the rebels, Ned boy. It's her sister Margaret's girl down in Cork City who's been after terrifying the old dear with letter upon letter, even a telegram if you can believe such a thing. So she's decided to move in with her niece." He folded the handkerchief, drew it across his upper lip and slid it back inside his coat. "So there you have it—life, death and miracles."

"Is she wanting a fair price?" Ned asked Kevin, who again answered with a silent nod.

Being the local school teacher, Kevin was the best informed man in town. From the mouths of babes he learned more each day than he'd ever a mind to pursue on his own initiative. It was a good thing he kept his own counsel closer than any man Ned had ever known. At first, Ned took his cousin's quietness for anger or resentment, but soon abandoned his mistaken assumption. The deciding factor in this turnabout of opinion was Maire Tobin. She radiated enough ebullience for the both of them, bubbling over with cheerfulness and an unaffected geniality that endeared her to Ned from the first. He figured there must be more to Kevin or he'd never have attracted the eye of Maire. Short and buxom with broad shoulders and a jutting chin, she was broadening around the hips a little after two children in three years. She wasn't a great beauty, but most called her handsome and she showed every sign of being a woman who would age into her looks remarkably well. Maire Tobin was also the only person on God's green earth upon whom Cousin Kevin smiled with any regularity.

"So what's your proposal then?" Ned asked.

Now that they were down to brass tacks, Eamon jumped back in. "Well now Ned, we figured we'd split the purchase money three ways. Brian McNamara's eldest boy, Liam—you know him, yeah?— he's ready to take on a field of his own. He's a steady worker and what with his Da to look over his shoulder, he'll make out well enough. We'll split the harvest with him, same as you do with Brian, and divide our half three ways. I've a likely tenant for the cottage. We'll split the rent three ways after expenses for keeping the place presentable and all," seeing Kevin and Ned nodding along, Eamon slipped in, "and a small fee for myself as agent as well."

With an arch grin, Ned said, "You're still trying to claw back that agent's fee from me, aren't you, Eamon? Wouldn't my Pa be disappointed in his old childhood chum?"

Kevin added in a murmur, "I'd have no trouble finding us a tenant, Ned. Maybe we raise the money just between the two of us?" He stared across at Eamon with a deadpan that gave nothing away.

Eamon tittered and patted the air with his thick hands. "Now there's no use in that kind of talk. We're all the best of friends here. Let's just say I'll lend my professional services free of charge in the interest of the... the joint enterprise?"

Ned was settling for the first time in six years. The mares swelled with growing foals, the lengthening days brightened his mood, and he began feeling less an interloper on the farm and in the village, having gained considerable skill and knowledge in the nearly ten months since his arrival. His dog seemed to understand, too, showing a little more eagerness to obey his profane commands.

He was still a city boy at heart, however, and after nearly a year of the bucolic life in Tipperary, Ned decided to treat himself to a few nights away in Dublin. He found himself craving the sound of traffic and the smell of dirty streets. Brian and his boys were happy to look after things while he was gone, so Ned went a day ahead into Clonmel and checked into a small hotel near the Westgate. He bought himself a fine new suit of clothes and a dark grey fedora. He ate a big dinner at the hotel, slept on clean cotton sheets, and rose early to have a full fry-up for breakfast before catching the first train to Dublin.

He wandered the city, including a stop at a bookstore behind the Four Courts where Kevin asked him to return a wrapped parcel he said was some books in Gaelic. Americans were enough of a curiosity to elicit endless questions and long conversations, as well as free drinks in pubs. That he was an Irish American with family in Tipperary and Clare made him everyone's distant cousin. The hurly-burly of traffic in the streets and the crowds on the sidewalks were familiar and cheering, but by the third day he was ready for home again.

A dairy farmer returning from deliveries in Clonmel dropped him at the head of his lane. Ned leapt from the wagon, shouted his thanks, and trotted up the gravel. He smiled at his excitement and wondered what his brother Bobby would have said of his little brother, the Irish sodbuster. When he reached the forecourt, he dropped his small brown suitcase, the one he'd carried with him since he was commissioned an officer by the British back in 1916, and gave a good look around. The place was neat as a pin, Brian McNamara not being one of those lay-abouts who lets a place get untidy. Then he noticed the door on the hay barn was a little ajar. He stepped inside, letting his eyes adjust to the dusty gloom, wanting to see if any animals had gotten into the grain he stored there for the horses. Glancing around, he noticed the loose hay they kept forked up against the wall had been trampled and pressed down. He walked over to look for any telltale signs of a large animal and found a brown cloth cap tossed against the stone wall. Bending to pick up the cap, Ned smiled.

Looks like young Liam's been entertaining one or another of the local girls.

He laughed to himself and pondered how he'd tease Liam when next he saw him, shutting tight the barn door as he walked back into the daylight, sun breaking between the growing patches of cloud.

Probably rain later…

The next afternoon came on warm for late March, so Ned was in his shirtsleeves lunging one of the mares while Brian McNamara unhitched another from the jaunty car. "That's fine now, Ned," Brian said over his horse's neck. "Give her a bit more line. Keep your whip still—she's doin' fine, don't worry her with the whip." Ned slipped six inches of line through his right hand and hid the short leather crop behind his back.

The mares hadn't been worked while Ned was away and Brian didn't want to put a cold horse into harness, excited as they'd be after four days' leisure. Ned had learned how to lunge the mares passably well and he felt a little surge of confidence as he watched the sleek brown mare trot, even and steady, at the end of his lunging line.

I see why granddad fancied these animals. She's a beauty—her foal should be a grand one come summer.

Ten minutes later, the two men were swapping out horses when Brian stopped and looked out toward the road, a twisty boreen paved in loose gravel with a strip of stubborn grass running down the center. Ned turned toward the intruding mechanical sound of an automobile engine—more like two. As the vehicles crested the rise northwest of the farm, they saw silhouettes of a Ford and a much longer and taller Crossley Tender with heads and shoulders bouncing along in back.

"We best get the horses inside," Brian said, sliding off the halter he'd just seated over the grey's dappled nose. "No tellin' what they're about." He nodded toward the road. By the time the mares were back to their stalls, the two vehicles rounded in the forecourt, blocking the entrance to the barn and the house. The driver of the black Ford, one of the local Royal Irish Constabulary who worked from the tiny two-man barracks in Glenador, dropped his feet to the ground. From the passenger side, a military officer with immaculate boots and an odd uniform emerged.

Ned took a few steps forward to meet the local constable, putting on what he hoped was a disarming smile, and said, "Well, what brings you out to my farm this fine afternoon, Sergeant Boyle?" The policeman was jumpy, Ned could see from the first. Brian stepped next to him and removed his cloth cap to wipe his face and head.

"Oh, 'tis just a bit of nothing, I'm near to certain, Ned," Sergeant Boyle jittered out in his discomfort.

The officer stepped close to Ned and stared with eyes cold as a fish for far too long before speaking. "So you're the American farmer?"

"Not much of a farmer, truth be told, but as to being American, I plead guilty as charged." Ned's humor fell with awkward flatness.

"I am Temporary Inspector Teesdale. Mister Tobin, is it?" Ned nodded, eyeing the Englishman. He wore tan khaki breeches above his spotless riding boots and a navy blue tunic that looked like those Ned had seen on London policemen during his wartime convalescence. He glanced over the man's shoulder and noticed eight or nine others dressed the same but carrying Lee-Enfield rifles, so familiar to Ned from his time in France with the Newfoundlanders. These men spread across the forecourt in pairs, two staying with the vehicles and two heading to each of the farm buildings. An older man with sleeve chevrons stepped up behind the inspector.

Look of an officer about him. The other must've been a sergeant-major, with that big mustache, Ned thought.

"More precisely, it's Major Tobin," Ned said with a little self-deprecating brush of his waistcoat, knocking off a few strands of hay, "Late of the United States Army and, for a few years before that, of His Majesty's Royal Newfoundland Regiment. Wounded at the Somme, as a courtesy to the Crown."

Sergeant Boyle, desperate to add something of value to the conversation, interjected, "Why Ned, wasn't Inspector Teesdale himself an officer with the Yorks and Lancs on the Somme as well?"

The Englishman did not acknowledge the constable's words. Instead, Inspector Teesdale gave Ned another languid stare, sniffing a little before proceeding. "I see. It is not uncommon, I am told, for Irish Americans to hold strong Fenian sympathies?"

"I couldn't speak to that, Inspector, only to myself. And I have no interest in anyone else's fight, having already had one of my own in France. I'm just looking after my grandfather's farm. I never set a foot in Ireland until last spring and I've been grateful none of this current nonsense has come near me, so far out in the countryside that the good Lord himself might lose his shoes." Ned gave the officer another unrequited smile.

"Sergeant Boyle tells me you just returned from three or four days in Dublin. Did you find anything amiss on the farm?"

Ned saw no need to dissemble and said, "Nothing more than the door to the hay barn a little ajar." One of the Englishman's sandy eyebrows rose a little. "But it looked to me like one of Brian's boys was entertaining a local lass, what with the pushed down hay. And he left his cap, so his father here might have surprised them, eh?" He looked to Brian to join in, but was stunned to silence by the agonized look on his neighbor's face as he gave an almost imperceptible shake of his head and stared with furtive eyes.

"Ah, I see." The Englishman turned and stepped back to the former sergeant-major and murmured a few words. The sergeant-major double-timed to the vehicles and gave directions to the guards, then motioned to the other six men. When one of the men returned from the back of the Crossley with yard-long lengths of wood, two in each hand, Ned's stomach clinched tight. He saw the ends were wrapped with dripping cotton strips and caught a faint whiff of kerosene. One of the men produced a lighter and struck it a few times, igniting each of the torches in turn before handing them over to the others. Two went to the house, two each to the stable and hay barn.

Ned lunged toward the pair heading for the stable but Sergeant Boyle grabbed his arm with one big hand and held firm. Brian gave Ned an oblique head shake and pointed toward the men who'd been guarding the vehicles. They now stood ten yards closer with rifles leveled.

"For God's sake, my mares are in there!" Ned pleaded. Boyle held him fast, whispering meaningless words of apology.

Temporary Inspector Teesdale stood before Ned, feet apart and one hand on his pistol. "We have it on good information your farm was used in your absence as a safe location for three men suspected in the murder of a magistrate in Offaly last week. It would seem they used your hay barn for hiding, Major Tobin, not your friend's son for a tryst."

The hay barn, full of combustible grass, was already flaming through the thatched roof. Ned saw a man upstairs in the house setting ablaze the curtains in a front bedroom. From the stables, the man who'd entered with a torch was now trotting back toward the Crossley empty-handed. His partner slammed the door and ran the wooden bolt home.

Ned listened, horror and rage pulsing through him, to the terrified whinnying from inside.

CHAPTER EIGHTEEN

Chester

Chester Dawkins and Benny Sharpe were two of the best dressed men on Lenox Avenue, but Tuesday stretched before them like a day in the trenches without the shelling. They occupied a bench in front of Mallow's Barber Shop, just north of 126th Street, watching without much interest as teenage runners cycled in and out, always heading through the battered green door at the back.

Chester idly read words painted on vehicles as they inched down Lenox. *National Delivery Company—5 Columbus Circle. Kold King Ice Company. Say it with Flowers—Premier Floral Gardens.* He lit another cigarette and flipped the match to the curb. *Coca-Cola in Bottles.*

The biggest numbers game in New York City was run from here. It was where the money was counted by two middle-aged sisters with thick eyeglasses, aunts of the Numbers King who had come up to Harlem ten years earlier from the Virgin Islands. With all the easy money and generous wages during the war, his game had exploded, offering the biggest payouts in town. The King held his business close, trusting his aunties with the cash and his security to a loyal group of cousins and friends from Saint Thomas. Mallow was happy to keep his mouth shut and his back room clear in exchange for inflated rent and free protection.

Benny sat listless as an old hound but his eyes followed every passing woman under the age of fifty. A few older than that, truth be told.

In normal times, neither Chester nor Benny would be caught lazing about in the middle of the afternoon. They were on a forced hiatus, however, until the decorating and equipping of the Club Sheba was completed in a few weeks. Their boss, one of Harlem's most respected and ambitious colored gangsters, saw how the dust settled after Prohibition went into effect last year. Since the lax efforts at enforcement could be avoided altogether with reasonable payments to various police captains and sergeants, the boss had decided to upgrade their prosperous but discreet buffet flat operation in a townhouse down the street from St. Nicholas Park.

Tremont Bottling Co's High-Grade Soda Water—All Flavors. Chester reversed his crossed legs and readjusted his grey fedora. *Langendorf's Royal Breads.*

Chester quickly regretted his reunion confrontation with Lena and had gone off on a week-long binge with a few obliging men from the old regiment. During one of those hazy evenings, he'd run into Benny who offered to let Chester sleep on the sofa in his musty walk-down apartment. During his bender, Chester's remorse had been exacerbated by both what he learned of the lawless state of Harlem and the amount of liquor he consumed. After sobering and cleaning up, he returned to his parents' house and threw himself on his sister's mercy, overflowing with apologies. After much hugging and many tears, they adjourned to the kitchen where Maddie commenced feeding him as if he were at risk of starvation. They spent the afternoon, the three of them, talking through everything that had happened since Pop's death and what Lena had done to save the house. Chester was both astounded by his little sister's tenacity and saddened by all she'd endured.

After exhausting the subject, Lena urged Chester to tell them of his time away at the war. While he spun out what he'd seen and done in a flat monotone, Lena sat across from him, dabbing at the tears that refused to stop welling in her horrified eyes. Maddie comforted herself by fussing about the stove and sink with only an occasional head shake and cluck of her tongue. What was clear by the end of that long wrenching afternoon was how much both of Clarence and Delphine Dawkins's children had been scarred by the past few years. But they'd survived and resolved to make a new place for themselves.

Saratoga Chips—Wafer-Sliced Dried Beef. Chester stood and tugged at his collar, stuck his hands deep in his trouser pockets, and looked back to the street scene. *Sheffield Farms Select Ice Cream. Mohawk Carpet Mills—Amsterdam, N.Y.*

Pop's old lawyer and Chester's former boss, Henry Davis, had died just a few days before the Armistice. Chester made some half-hearted inquiries with other lawyers, even called on Major Fish, a Dutch blue-blood officer from the regiment who'd returned to a lucrative law practice in Midtown and was now, it was said, headed for election to Congress in November. With the downturn after the war and Chester's late return home, he'd found no work. But he spoke French, wore a tuxedo well and was light-skinned enough to join Benny in lending a little class to the boss's operation.

Benny shifted and sat a little straighter, giving his striped tie a surreptitious tug to smooth it, as three teenagers came giggling by with sly side glances, trying on ill-suited vampy smiles. They were dressed in their best daywear, hemlines to the knee and cloche hats tugged down over their ears.

Chester had stayed on with Benny, thinking it best to keep himself away from the relationship Lena had hammered out with Babette Arnaud. He couldn't deny they'd made a great success and set the standard for high-class buffet flats, catering to the appetites of wealthy Negroes and even wealthier Uptown whites for jazz, alcohol, gambling, marijuana and sex with pretty colored women. There were scores of little private clubs like this sprinkled throughout Harlem—some guessed more than two hundred—so it wasn't as if Lena's operation was an island of illegality. It was this model Chester's new boss had emulated and, with much more capital at his disposal from his other illicit operations, had now surpassed. In its spacious new location on 133rd Street, the Club Sheba would be the first of a new generation of Harlem speakeasies, a full-service supper club with a jazz orchestra. A twelve-girl floor show was in rehearsal in the basement of a nearby old Dutch Reform church in anticipation of the grand opening in a few weeks' time.

There was still one problem, and their boss had given Chester and Benny the assignment to find a solution. With their move to an expanded operation, they were expected to fulfill roles beyond that of well-spoken and handsome decorations who did the occasional bouncing of unruly clients. The day-to-day operations of the club were to be their responsibility, while their boss saw to entertaining the well-heeled customers. Since word had spread of the Club Sheba's imminent opening, white gangsters with interests in dozens of less opulent buffet flats banded together to show the uppity Negro owner they didn't appreciate any enhanced competition. They had leaned on their suppliers to cut off sales of premium liquor, leaving only bootleggers with rotgut whisky and rough gin willing to sell to Chester and Benny. Without top shelf booze, the club would fail, regardless of the legginess of the floor show. The few suppliers who quietly agreed to sell them decent French or British or Jamaican product were quoting prices the business couldn't possibly absorb.

So they sat on their bench, counting numbers runners cruising in and out of Mallow's Barber Shop, no solution to their problem in sight.

"We've put together enough small lots of champagne and spirits to get us open," Benny said.

"If things go the way we expect, that won't last more than a few weeks," Chester said, a cigarette dangling from his fingers. "After that, we'll have to pay extortionate prices to any supplier willing to deal with us on the Q.T. We won't stay in business long, not with the payroll the boss is racking up for musicians and chorus girls."

"Might need to buy where we can, until we find some other way," Benny said.

Chester flicked his cigarette across the sidewalk and into the gutter on Lenox, then slapped Benny on the shoulder with the back of his hand.

"Maybe we ought to run our own booze."

Both men burst into laughter as they rose and ambled back to check on the two Barbadian artists who were supposed to have completed the mural behind the bar a week ago.

After three weeks of sawing and painting, the club reeked of sawdust and linseed oil, but the boss wouldn't let anyone open the doors to air the place. No one was to see the Club Sheba until the big unveiling on Saturday night. As workmen finished up the kitchen and storerooms, the ladies of the floor show moved their rehearsals to the club, scuffing the new flooring on the low stage with each tap and scrape. Chester and Benny sat at one of the round cocktail tables, watching this first dress rehearsal, although the skimpy sequined tops and minute silver lamé skirts the dancers wore could hardly be described as "dress."

"Alright, alright ladies! Let's take ten minutes," Chester shouted above the solo pianist, the full orchestra not joining rehearsals until tomorrow. "Then let's run the whole show again before we break for lunch."

Benny was gazing off across the big shadowy room, two bare bulbs in unshaded floor lamps near the stage providing the only illumination. Chester slapped his arm to bring him out of his wool gathering. "We still haven't solved the booze problem. At least not for the long run."

Sliding back to face Chester, Benny said, "We've scraped together enough stock here and in the walk-down at your house to get us through two, maybe three months. Unless we're a bigger success than even the boss imagines."

"That's not much breathing space. If we do make a big go of it, those Italian and Irish gangs are going to squeeze the suppliers selling us even a few cases at a time."

"Alright ladies, on stage," called out the choreographer, an old New Orleans tap dancer named Antoine. "You heard the man. Let's run it from the top before we break for lunch."

They sat smoking, minds wandering over the hundred details still to be ironed out before the grand opening on Saturday. Chester was startled when the skinny kid from the regiment they'd hired as a barback limped up beside him and bent down to whisper, "White man out front. Says he wanna speak with Lieutenant Dawkins."

Another reporter or some thug from one of the Downtown gangs trying to flatter himself inside for a peek, Chester thought. "Tell him we open Saturday and he'll have to wait 'til then like everybody else, Fred."

"I don't know for sure… didn't say his name or nothin'. Been awhile and he's white, y'know… but I swear that man out there look like Major Tobin."

Two very surprised faces turned in unison to Fred, then Benny and Chester jumped from their seats and dashed for the entrance. They each grabbed one of the long brass handles on the pair of heavy doors and yanked, revealing Major Edmund Tobin, squinting from the sunny sidewalk into the murkiness of the club. As the two men stepped into the light, all the annoyance in Ned's face drained away and he reached out a hand to Chester.

"Saints preserve us, if it isn't the heroic Lieutenant Dawkins," Ned said, pumping with one hand and slapping Chester's shoulder with the other. "And the valiant Lieutenant Benjamin Sharpe, as I live and breathe," he extended his hand and grasped Benny's with an enthusiastic shake. Benny gave a little twitchy smile, reminded all at once, even two years on, of his second-fiddle status in the eyes of the Major. He still smarted from the acclaim heaped on Chester in France. Benny had taken a piece of the same trench with most of his men alive to brag about it. More than could be said for Chester, even with his *Croix de guerre*.

With much chuckling over familiar insults regarding age and dress, the three wandered back into the darkened club. Benny pulled a third chair to the little cocktail table. Without a word, the skinny bar-back brought a bottle of whisky and some glasses, then limped away from the three officers, smiling at the familiarity. The three raised glasses and Ned said, "To the fallen."

"To the fallen," Chester and Benny echoed. New cigarettes were lit all around and they sat glancing across the table and shaking their heads with boyish grins.

"What brings you to New York, Major?" Benny said, never comfortable with the intimacy of silence. "Last we heard, third-hand rumors had you in Ireland. And farming?" All three burst into renewed laughter.

"Indeed I was, Benny. A true Irish gentleman farmer and breeder of some lovely horses, too." Chester saw a darkness pass over Ned's face, although Benny missed it. "But the civil strife you've likely heard about finally reached my sleepy corner of east Tipperary."

"You'd think those Irishmen would've had their fill in France," Chester said, his own smile fading with Ned's.

"And Gallipoli," Benny added, still the stickler for military precision.

Ned downed the remnants of whisky in his glass and waved it toward Chester, who refilled it. "Ahh, you don't know the Irish, me buckos. We've been scrapping for one fight or another since time immemorial. I just didn't think this particular one would be my fight, having done His Majesty some service in France before joining you pitiful slackers."

"Won't you go back, after the fighting is over? Isn't that your grandfather's place?" Chester long ago learned to detect when there was something below the Major's nonchalance. This was just such a time, recalling Ned's flash of sadness at the mention of the horses. Chester looked across at Ned and said with a quiet sigh, "It's gone, isn't it? The farm?"

Ned patted the back of Chester's hand flat on the tabletop, next to his whisky glass. "Burned to the ground, Chester. Those lovely horses with it."

"Jesus, sir. What happened?" Benny asked.

"Seems a few of the rebel lads shot up a magistrate in his bed while his wife watched. While I was away to Dublin for a few days, they took it upon themselves to spend a night or two in my barn, which the Royal Irish Constabulary discovered by means unknown to me." Ned drained the second whisky.

"You couldn't have known. And they still burned your farm?" Chester said.

"It's an ugly kind of war. Brothers and cousins shooting each other down, no telling who the enemy might be. It was easier for us, the Germans being the ones in grey to the east." Chester refilled all three glasses while Ned took a long drag from his cigarette and exhaled through his nostrils. "So I took every shilling I had on deposit in the Bank of Ireland and boarded the first steamer leaving Queenstown. It deposited me six days ago at the Hudson River docks."

"Major, when did all this happen?"

"Exactly nineteen days ago, Chester. And I figured no place better to seek my fortune than here, where I have so many comrades from our wasted youth in France. I visited Beatrice Freeman yesterday and she mentioned where I might find you."

Benny leaned in and slapped Ned's forearm. "Well, we'll do whatever we can to help. What is it you have in mind, Ned?" Chester and Ned twitched at Benny's presumption.

"Haven't a clue, Benjamin. I've considered a million things and settled on none, other than not going back to work in 'dear old Pa's' candy store." Both the younger men burst into laughter again at the thought of Major Ned Tobin selling sweets to greedy children, then straightened themselves after seeing Ned's flat expression.

"I thought I might make my way to Newfoundland and catch up with the lads from my first regiment," Ned said. "Now as for you two, it appears you've found success a little closer to home. I assume that with these lovely ladies will come ample illegal alcohol?" Benny smiled with self-satisfaction while Chester studied his palms, suddenly embarrassed at Ned learning what kind of businessman he'd become. Ned wasn't surprised to find Benny cocksure as ever. He was touched that his good opinion still mattered so much to Chester.

"Bah, there's no harm at all in giving a man a decent drink if he's a taste for it," he said, searching to reassure Chester. "This whole Prohibition was the butt of many a joke in Ireland. From what I've seen these past few days, seems the Volstead Act is going unenforced. Would I be correct?"

"Besides those holy rollers in the temperance societies and a few old women in the churches, you'd be hard-pressed to find anyone who supports Prohibition," Benny said. "The police and judges are making hay while the sun shines from the bribes we all pony up each month."

The morning rehearsal was winding down, the dancers already retreating to the dressing room. Ned watched as they disappeared through the swinging door behind the stage. "I thought I had a stable full of beauties in Ireland," Ned said, returning to the conversation. "All rather… fair, aren't they?"

This was Benny's particular area of expertise. "We worked for over a month finding them. We'll dance eight at a time, which gives us some reserve for sickness or injury, maybe a little time off."

"Might have to contend with a few chest colds, those costumes being a tad small, wouldn't you say?" Ned said.

"Those costumes on those legs will pack them in from Harlem *and* Downtown. That's why we only took on light-skinned girls—more appealing to the white customers," Benny said. "And to the colored men with the kind of money it'll take to frequent the Club Sheba."

"So how did you two get the capital for a place like this?"

Chester studied his hands again. "We... we manage the club. The owner prefers to stay out of the day-to-day, so he leaves that to us."

"Well, two respectable businessmen. My, how my lads have grown," Ned said.

Benny beamed, oblivious to Ned's sarcasm, and said, "I've been with the boss since just after the victory parade. He was standing drinks for the boys at a blind tiger he ran over on Lenox and we fell to talking. He was one of the first to see the potential in the Prohibition law and the fact that no man was going to be denied his liquor. I brought Chester along after he got home later last summer."

Chester leaned in, shoulder to shoulder with Benny. "Problem is we've become victims of our own success. The big white gangs—the Irish and Italians, even the Jews and Germans—they've all combined to choke off our supply of good liquor. They see us as unwanted competition for the white clientele who come for the jazz and the women. They've either set up or taken over nearly every speakeasy in Harlem, as well as half the buffet flats, even some of the tea pads for puffing reefer. They'll only allow a few smaller bootleggers to sell us third-rate rotgut."

"That wouldn't do for a first-class place like the..." Ned looked around and noticed in the muted light the elaborate wall paintings and wide chandeliers.

"Club Sheba," Benny interposed.

"Like the Club Sheba," Ned repeated. "Why don't you bring in your own stuff?"

"A few Negro owners tried, down from Canada through Watertown and Massena, but the white gangs hijacked their loads. Killed all the drivers and crew last time. They've got the border and most of Long Island and the Jersey coast sewn up tight," Chester said. Ned retrieved a pack of cigarettes and offered them around.

Then he produced his battered trench lighter, the very one he'd used to charm two naive second lieutenants. When he handed it across the table, Chester rubbed it between his fingers.

"Seems a long time since Spartanburg," he said. "We've a few of our own war stories now." He passed the lighter to Benny.

Ned studied Chester through the haze of blue smoke. *He's changed. Things haven't turned out how he'd thought they would back home.* The silence between them was comforting to Ned, the old familiarity and trust of the trenches descending since even Benny was talked out now. They'd done things together no one should have been asked to do. That would bind them, like it or not, to the end of their days. Pinching a flake of tobacco from his tongue, Ned said, "I bet those gangs don't know Newfoundland—that's not Canada. Most would think it's the edge of the world."

Benny's irritation lifted as he turned to Ned with astonishment. "I bet they don't." Then just as fast as he'd brightened, his face fell. "But that doesn't get the booze into the States. The gangs have every reputable port along the East Coast under their thumbs—Bayonne, Atlantic City, Newport, Boston. Not much chance of us getting your Newfoundland booze into the country."

Ned stared back at the desultory Benny with undiminished confidence. "How many of the *disreputable* ports do you think they know? Unlike a South Boston lad who traveled the whole of the Maine coast as a cornerman for his boxer brother's fights?"

Chester shifted in his seat with nervous excitement, wetting his lips and working his hands as the thousand details of such an operation sped through his brain. "You'd be willing to take this on, Major?"

"That I would, Chester, my lad. But we'd need some starting capital. I only have a few hundred dollars left after paying everyone I owed in Ireland and getting myself some New York City kit." Ned spread his arms and shot the white cuffs from under his blue serge sleeves.

Benny cut in and said, "If the boss thinks we can break the gangs' embargo... let's just say we can hold the bag while he shovels in the money." Chester nodded in agreement.

Ned looked hard at them, the eager lieutenants once again. He took in a long, deep breath and said, "You'll have to make this worth my while, gents. I'd need a sustained cash flow out of this little venture."

Pouring a final round to seal the nascent deal, Ned added with icy seriousness, "I've a few scores to settle in Ireland."

The kitchen was in its lunchtime routine, with Maddie alternately feeding and shaking her finger at Bunk Hill while Lena counted receipts and updated the books from the previous night's trade. She'd moved this daily chore from her father's old study—now the card room—to the kitchen months before. The book-lined study had such an unremitting smell of tobacco smoke and stale liquor that spending much time in there made her sullen for hours afterward. She hated that she now saw Papa's precious retreat only in terms of gross revenue from the house rake. Maddie and Bunk knew well enough how much money was coming in and going out, so there wasn't any need to keep secrets from them anymore. Babette trudged in for coffee at regular intervals, leaving cigarette smoke and too much French perfume in her wake. Maddie dispersed these remnants of Babette with a waving dish towel and disapproving grunts. Convinced that Lena wouldn't cheat a partner if her life depended on it, Babette left her younger *protégée* to the tedious chore of bookkeeping without interruption.

On her third trip of the morning, Babette lingered in the kitchen, her ample bottom leaning against the sink. She sucked at her cigarette holder and watched Lena scribbling in the familiar green ledger with the cash box flipped open beside her. She was still puzzled by Lena's tenacious honesty, even a few years into their illicit enterprise. She doubted the girl had stolen a single dollar, the thought of which pushed up a rueful smile on her well-tended scarlet lips.

With a long and showy sigh, Babette said, "Lena, *ma chérie*, we have a meeting today at two o'clock. You're free then, *n'est-ce pas?*" Lena laid her pencil under the last line she'd checked and turned toward Babette, curious why her partner was resorting to French this early in the day.

"I believe I'm free, but what sort of meeting?" Lena watched Babette hesitate and give a few distracted blinks.

She looks a little jumpy. What's this about?

Babette went for her cigarettes in the deep front pocket of her dressing gown, her best new turquoise silk one, Lena noted. She fussed for a very long time before answering Lena's simple question. "It seems that our silent partner wishes to make himself known to you." All three of the other kitchen occupants were watching, struck by Babette's unusual fidgetiness. A line of perspiration had beaded along her upper lip, threatening her careful morning makeup. Lena had never seen the supreme confidence of her partner waver like this.

She's terrified of him.

"Well, if that don't beat all," Bunk said with a hoarse chuckle, "The boss-man hisself gonna make an appearance." Maddie silenced him with a sharp glare then returned her suspicious gaze to Babette.

"He won't be doin' no appearin' to the likes of you, Bunk Hill," said Babette, back to her Carolina voice. "He don't have any interest in some fat layabout piano man." She gave a purse-lipped nod and glanced to Maddie. "And no kitchen help. So you two just keep yourselves out the way come two o'clock. And don't be snoopin' behind no doors neither."

It surprised Lena that the identity of their silent partner wasn't such a surprise. He'd been a regular and free-spending customer since their earliest days. What unsteadied her was that he was also the customer who'd made repeated inquiries about her availability for hire. It also explained why Babette never let the matter lie, even after repeated angry rejections from Lena. And now he sat in an unruffled pose across the green baize card table in Papa's study, eyeing her as he'd done these many months.

"I'm somewhat surprised to see you, Mr. Wright," Lena said, struggling to shake the chill from his silent staring. "You've spent your money very freely in a place where you might have enjoyed yourself at no cost at all."

Cyrus Wright smoothed the front of his vest with a little tug at the pointed hem. He was dressed with as much care and discernment in daytime as he showed in his nocturnal appearances.

"Just priming the pump for the customers," he said with a wide handsome smile spread below cold eyes that froze her again. "I didn't want them to know I was an owner. Until Madame Babette and me were sure, I didn't much want you figurin' it out either." He spoke with a very deliberate cadence, as if thinking over each word before it reached his lips. Sometimes he slipped and sounded a little off, making Lena doubt his education had been of the formal kind.

"That was very generous of you, Mr. Wright, given that Babette and I have kept two-thirds of the money you spent here."

"Just another little investment in the business, Miss Dawkins. Which reminds me of the point of my visit today." The smile remained, but his eyes hardened and narrowed a little. He turned to his right and gave a small nod to Babette.

That's why she's on the other side. This is two-against-one.

The sweat was back, glistening beneath the powder on Babette's upper lip.

"*Ma chérie…*"

So it's fancy Babette at the table then, thought Lena.

"You must see that Mr. Wright's position concerning…" she swept her glance and cigarette holder around the room, "…our business has been silent but *d'une grande importance*. You must agree, *oui*?" Lena stared daggers across the table, adding to Babette's already substantial edginess. "We wouldn't have had the money even to open without his investment. And as you've said, he's spent freely here and brought in most of the big paying customers, too."

Lena turned to Wright—she couldn't recall if she ever knew his first name—and examined him with great care. It was obvious this was rehearsed and he'd decided Babette would deliver the bad news that was surely on the way. He smiled with placid confidence, a crocodile awaiting its next meal. The chill left her, replaced with hot welling anger.

Exhaling a long stream of smoke, Babette continued, "And I've carried most all the *paying* work in the front of the house. And upstairs." She settled down, a little sense of injustice steadying her under Lena's withering glare. "You've not been much more than the housekeeper. Not that I haven't tried to bring you along in the other... aspects of the business." She turned and nodded to Wright with arched eyebrows.

The silent partner sat, silent and confident in his catbird seat.

"Mr. Wright and I are prepared to make you an offer to...alter our business relationship somewhat. In a way that's fair to each of us."

They're forcing me out, is that it?

"Say what you need to say, the both of you," Lena said, rigid and determined.

"We mean to be fair to you, *ma chère* Lena. We're offering you two choices. You may remain a full one-third partner if you agree to join the... staff in the front of the house entertaining the customers, many of whom have admired you very, very much." She turned and nodded again to Wright.

Lena shot from her chair, slapping both palms on the table, the sound muffled by the cloth. "You want me to whore myself to any man who comes through the door with a few dollars in his pocket? In my own mother's house? Maybe in my own mother's bed? You must be insane, the both of you."

"Oh no, no, no. You misunderstand. You're only to... to enchant the other customers. Any other duties..." she pointed to the rooms upstairs with a quick glance, "...would be limited to Mr. Wright's needs exclusively."

"So this is all about not taking no for an answer, Mr. Wright?"

The reptilian smile unwavering, he gave a slow nod, eyes already searching beneath her clothing.

Turning to Babette, she said, "You mentioned two, Beulah"—enough of this French play-acting—"so what would be my other option?" Not taking her eyes off Babette, she could still see Wright leaning back in his chair as his smile broadened, about to watch his hand played out.

"You can pack your bags and take your uppity high-yeller ass to the street, sister-girl," Babette said, with remarkable confidence, "but of course with a fair monthly rent for the continued use of your *très jolie petite maison*." With a victorious flourish, Babette spread her arms wide, taking in every inch of Lena's home with proprietary self-assurance.

Wright extracted an exquisite silver watch from his vest pocket and clicked it open, considered the time, then closed it with a demonstrative loud snap. "And a fair rent would be… let's say, bein' friends here, $35 a month?"

Lena pushed hard against the table, shoving it into the pair seated across from her. She was not fragile and delicate like Maman, to the surprise of her two erstwhile partners. Babette slammed down her hands to push herself up with frightening slowness and rounded on Lena.

"$35 sounds right fair to me," Babette said, not showing any sign of sympathy. "And you listen here, missy high-and-mighty. Who do you think been payin' off every cop 'round these parts to keep us clear of trouble? You think he can't get his lawyer-man to pull a lease with your signature right outta his dusty old ass? And don't think for a minute them judges he been payin' wouldn't throw you right out the courthouse door you try to make any trouble." Lena was shaking with anger and fear, steadying herself with a few fingers on the edge of the table.

"You take my advice, you bed down with this here fine lookin' man and stay in the business." Babette poked a finger below Lena's waist and added, "Can't for the life of me figure what you savin' that for anyway. Might just as well have a little fine livin' while some man with money still want you."

The tension was broken by a pair of jovial voices entering the house. Lena recognized one with relief. She couldn't make out the words, but she heard the two men laughing and chatting as their footsteps echoed down the hall, headed for the kitchen. Lena rushed to the door and flung it open, the doorway framing the startled faces of Chester and Benny. Behind Lena, they saw the woman well known to them as Madame Babette standing by the card table. And seated on the far side, their boss.

17th of November, 1920
St. John's

Dear Benny,

I'm sure everyone's looking forward to Thanksgiving in New York. They don't celebrate that up here and I feel a little let down with no November holiday coming. It's already awful dark and gloomy with still a month before winter.

I've been on four runs since September and feel a little less unsure of myself now. Who'd have thought a kid from Harlem would end up on the deck of a cod schooner? St. John's is as lily-white a place as you can imagine and that made Lena and me edgy at first. These are good folk up here though, and they've made us welcome. It's refreshing being surrounded day in and day out by white men who haven't grown up with Americans' opinions about the "Negro Question."

You asked about the syndicate partners up here, whether they're trustworthy. From what I've seen—and with long days at sea, I've seen and heard plenty—what you see is what you get. The ship owner and master, Jack Oakley, had as hard a war as anyone and tries to make up for his bad wounds by working twice as hard. He knows every inch of his ship and I swear he can hear her speak sometimes. The Ricky Todd was his grandfather's, named after Jack's dad and uncle, and he's run her decks since he was old enough to walk.

Geordie King had a tough time in the war, too, but doesn't seem as affected as Jack. He's friendly and open, always quick with a joke and to lend a hand. He pays too much attention to Lena for my liking, but I guess any man who's not her brother can't be blamed for that. All my reluctance about that sort of thing comes rushing back when I see him mooning over her. This isn't America though. As for business, I don't believe Jack or Geordie would know how to cheat us. Together with their loyalty to Ned Tobin, we don't have any cause for concern. These Newfoundlanders aren't New Yorkers.

We added the brother of Deirdre Oakley, Jack's wife, to the crew not long after we got the ship seaworthy. He'd come unannounced from Dublin. I'm not altogether sure what to make of him. He's an excitable type and ended up here after some trouble back in Ireland. We've become friends through our shared city boyhoods, although Dublin sounds smaller and friendlier than New York. Lord knows I've heard enough about the place. I'm stuck with an Irishman and a pair of Newfoundlanders, all born with too many stories in their heads.

Things are running smooth as you'd want on this end. We've got reliable suppliers in St. Pierre, Halifax, and here in Newfoundland. No one here seems any more concerned about their Prohibition laws than people in the States. The police and officials require a lot less bribing, too. Can't figure how anyone thought people would give up their drink just because some busybodies thought they should.

I don't see why the booze and the money won't keep flowing! I'll see you at one of the Maine ports whenever you decide to come along with the trucks again. I know the club is keeping you busy and the drivers don't need you or Ned breathing down their necks all the time. Most are from the regiment anyway.

> Best regards from way up North,
> Your old comrade in arms
> and new partner in bootlegging,

> Chester

CHAPTER NINETEEN

Lena

The New Year's dinner was winding down and Deirdre Oakley, after several hours careening between kitchen and dining room, looked to Lena as if she might drop mid-step. They'd started the washing up while the men went out on the back stoop to smoke and tell lies about their last run down the New England coast. Ned Tobin said he'd come up to Newfoundland from Boston to celebrate the dawn of 1922, but Lena suspected it was to check on his rumrunning associates in St. John's, including her brother. Their operation was proving very lucrative and she knew well enough how suspicion can grow with revenue.

One of the men had stayed inside to haul dirty plates to the kitchen, or so he claimed. Lena didn't mind, since his true purpose was flirting with her. Geordie King was a big, bluff man who'd suffered much during the war and looked a decade older than his twenty-six years. Chester told her Geordie had almost died from fever in Gallipoli, then was shot and gassed in France. Still, even with this past suffering, his lined face could light the room when he teased and smiled and laughed with her. He'd made this strange place a little more bearable.

"Deirdre, you're dead on your feet, my poor maid," said Geordie. "You get yourself into a chair in the sitting room and let Lena and me finish up here. Go on now." Deirdre made to shush him, as was her way, but she was too exhausted to argue. She gave them a weary smile, tossed her apron over the back of a kitchen chair and trudged down the hall toward the front of the house, one hand working the small of her back.

This was one of only a handful of times she'd been alone with Geordie since coming north to St. John's, Chester having suspicions about Geordie's intentions. With neither the time nor inclination for stepping out with men back in Harlem, she rather enjoyed Geordie's attention. She thought him a fine-looking man, too.

It wasn't just Geordie's company she enjoyed. She'd found the Newfoundlanders welcoming and guileless compared to folks back home. It had begun to feel like everyone in Harlem was on the make. First it was the new arrivals from the South looking to mop up as much of the easy wartime money sloshing around New York as they could. After the Armistice, everyone scrambled for the even faster money to be made from Prohibition and the insatiable demand among the white population for anything to do with jazz, including the Negroes who played it. This accounted for the runaway success of the business she and Babette had operated.

When Lena refused Cyrus Wright's ultimatum, Babette was true to her word and had Nigel turf Lena out the next day. The paltry $35-a-month rent they'd forced her to accept stopped once she and Chester left for St. John's. That didn't matter, since her brother was making many times that with each trip down the Maine coast. Still, it rankled that outsiders, wallowing in the corrupt stew of post-war New York, had been able to force her out of her own home with such impunity.

She and Chester were self-conscious fish out of water when they'd first arrived in St. John's back in June. After a few weeks of stares, they realized they were about the only colored people in St. John's— probably on the whole island of Newfoundland—and that people were more curious than hostile. For Chester, at first spending ten or twelve hours every day at the dry dock with the others, and now weeks at sea slipping in and out of Maine outports, it took some time getting accustomed to this new place. He was connected to his partners second-hand through Ned Tobin, the only person who knew everyone involved before they'd launched the enterprise. And Ned had come back from Ireland changed in some way Chester still didn't fully understand.

Deirdre Oakley took Lena under her wing from the start. Her Jack had also suffered during the war, carrying a bad limp, a withered right hand, and a scarred face from his wounding on the Somme. Deirdre herself was new to St. John's, having arrived barely a month before Lena and just married to boot. However, as an Irishwoman in a land filled with half-Irish natives, she experienced much less of the strangeness Lena felt.

But Geordie King remained unchanged since the first time she'd laid eyes on him. Despite all he'd suffered, he seemed always to be hearing a little joke or some pleasant music no one else could perceive, a half-smile on his face. Even the rare times when conversation turned to France, he was less affected than the others, including Chester. Geordie seemed more nostalgic for the friends he'd lost, not wounded somewhere deep and untouchable like the rest.

"So Chester mentioned you ran a boarding house while he was away having a grand time in France?"

So that was to be the story, she thought.

Lena busied herself spreading and straightening the tea towels drying on a wooden dowel near the stove. Avoiding Geordie's lingering gaze, she expanded on her brother's fib. "Yes. Our father died just a few months after Chester left with his regiment. That's when I discovered Papa had mortgaged our house to the hilt to get by after Maman passed." She smoothed a towel again, recalling the fine linens her mother favored. "They said he died of cardiac failure, but his heart was broken long before it stopped beating." She chanced a look, surprised to see Geordie's eyes filling a little.

He's sentimental for such a big man.

She felt a little braver now that she'd slipped into the comfortable little lie. "The only way I could keep our home for Chester's return was to take in boarders. I did a little bookkeeping, too… a few other odds and ends to get by." Geordie watched her, entranced with the tale.

I could tell him the moon was cheese and he'd believe me, wouldn't he?

"When Chester had the offer to come up to St. John's, I thought a change and a little less… responsibility would do me good."

Geordie crossed his arms on his chest, sleeves rolled to his elbows from the washing up, and leaned back against the drainboard of the long sink, devouring her with his eyes. "Isn't it my good luck your brother fell in with bad company like us and brought his lovely sister to our little island?"

Why doesn't his stare make me uncomfortable?

Out of options for diversion, Lena sat herself on one of the kitchen chairs and gave a smiling nod to Geordie, inviting him to take one, too. She sat at the head of the rectangular table and he chose the seat to her right, scooting his chair closer. His eyes never strayed from her face, but Lena could only return staccato glances and little smiles. They sat in silence, the unintelligible murmur of the men's banter on the back porch interrupted now and again by bursts of laughter. Although they'd sat down to dinner at noon, the meal and stories stretched almost three hours. With the washing up done, twilight was descending. It had been a little warmer than usual with only a light breeze, so comfortable enough in coats to sit outside.

"The temperature'll drop now the sun is headed down. That'll drive them inside I'd expect," Geordie said, the last words coming with a show of sighing disappointment.

"Chester and I should be going. You and the others, too, so Deirdre can have a rest."

Not just yet though…

"You're right there, my lovely maid. That one"—he motioned down the hall with his chin—"wouldn't know how to sit still with guests in her house." He shook his head with such affable affection for Deirdre and her Irish ways that Lena smiled, then without thinking much about it, placed her hand over his on the tabletop. She felt a little pulse of excitement run through her when he turned up his palm and wrapped his large fingers around her slender ones with surprising gentleness.

"You met her during the war, didn't you?" Lena said, watching his index finger rub, light as a feather, along the base of her thumb. His hand was ruddy and rough from work on the schooner, contrasting the supple golden tan of her own. His touch relaxed her with its feeling of safety, but she also felt a rising warmth below her stomach that spread in a steady flow.

I could get used to this man. No one up here would give us dirty looks.

"I did, but only in passing for a day or two. She was a sister—a nurse to you Yanks, yeah?—at a field hospital on the Somme. Jackie and I were both hit that first day, Jackie much the worse, and I brought him there. I can see her still, plain as day, standing in the ambulance parking with a paraffin lamp in her hand, ordering everyone around just as she does to this very hour." He squeezed her fingers with this little jab at Deirdre's bossiness. She smiled her agreement.

"But I'd bandaged Jack's head as best I could—you can see the scars still—so she never saw his face. He was hurt so bad that as soon as they were sure the bleeding in his leg was stopped, they got him on a hospital train and sent him back to Blighty—to England."

"So they met again when Deirdre went to London to work? By chance?"

"You've seen the two of them together. No chance meeting there. The Fates chose them for each other long before London, I'd wager." His expression made it clear he thought the same was true of them.

Doesn't lack for confidence, this one. But always been the perfect gentleman, few times Chester's left us alone.

The kitchen door opened letting in a flood of crisp, dry air and four men bumped through rubbing their hands for warmth. Geordie made no attempt to move his hand, but Lena slid hers away with regret, not before Chester saw what had been going on.

"We'd best be leaving, Lena. Let Jack and Deirdre have a little peace and quiet," her brother said, a little snappish. Lena flashed a last private smile to Geordie, patted his hand, and went to retrieve her coat from the front hall.

Ned Tobin turned to Deirdre's brother Sean and placed a hand on his shoulder. "What do you say we leg it up to The Blue Puttee and have a drink or two in the backroom? Leave your sister and her devoted husband to their privacy for a few hours?"

"A dram would not go amiss," Sean said, then to Jack, "You'll let herself know I'm off then?"

"Ahh, don't we all answer to your big sister, Sean, in ways great and small?" Jack offered his left hand—the right was curled and useless—to Chester, then to Ned. "So we'll see you both down at the quay tomorrow morning? We've some small repairs to do on the *Ricky Todd* before we sail again."

"Aye, Jack," Sean said, then gave a big wink over at Ned, "just not too over-early?"

"Out the back and off to your whisky, you pair of scoundrels. I'll make your excuses to my dear wife." Jack limped over to the back door and swung it wide for them, while Chester went to fetch his sister home.

Behind its storefront, The Blue Puttee maintained a well-stocked speakeasy. Since it kept up pretenses by selling the best ice creams and phosphates in St. John's, the shop was popular front and back, with both drinking men and their families. Its peculiar name, chosen by the veteran owner, was from the insult-turned-nickname their regiment received from the British Tommies upon landing in England with their unique-colored leggings. Their navy blue puttees were soon abandoned for British regulation khaki, but the name persisted nonetheless.

Pulling his overcoat collar up against the rising chill, Ned said, "It's done then. You've your treaty and your independence." He leaned forward as they climbed up Prescott Street toward Military Road. The speakeasy was a short walk from Jack and Dee's home, but a vertical one.

"We've our independence, Ned. As much yours as mine or any other Irishman's. You suffered loss, too. And didn't you say your old man is a Fenian from way back?" Sean was bouncing up the pavement, energized by the news they'd received just a few days earlier of the Anglo-Irish Treaty.

"I got what I wanted sending weapons to shoot up those bastards who burned my farm," Ned said. "I suppose it won't hurt in Pa's estimation that I did my bit for Ireland. Not that it matters."

"He still struggling with the *craythur* then?" Sean asked. Ned gave a terse nod, staring straight on. "The drink is a terrible thing for many, but sure doesn't he have reason enough, losing both your Ma and your dear brother? And isn't it the good man's weakness, after all?"

They were the same platitudes Ned had heard and spoken a hundred times both sides of the ocean, but they rankled today and he bristled at Sean's well-intentioned words.

"More a weak man's weakness. In the war, it was liquid courage for officers without the stones to lead their men over the top. In Ireland, it was more a way to duck responsibility than a result of misery from what I saw." Ned quick-timed a few steps to stay ahead of Sean. "I've had enough of weak men."

As they trudged uphill, a rising westerly stung their faces. The unseasonable fair weather was behind them, blowing off on the winter wind. Sean paced up next to Ned and jammed his hands deep into the pockets of the pea coat Deirdre had bought him, hunching his shoulders and turtling his chin down to his chest.

"So we're just respectable rumrunners of a garden variety now, eh?"

Sean's toothy grin proved enough to shake Ned from his funk. He slapped the younger man's back and said, "That we are, Sean Brannigan. That we are. And I look forward to pocketing 100% of my proceeds and allowing the Irish Free State to finance her own defense."

"A *Free State*," said Sean, wanting to hear the words again. "'Twill be a grand thing, won't it? I wish my Da had lived to see this day, like yours."

The slate-grey sea slid beneath them, white-capping as it rolled back from the sharp prow of the *Ricky Todd*. They were just off Penobscott Bay and would make their way into Rockland as soon as the sun went below the horizon. Chester didn't mind being the forward watch this time of day, the sun settling behind the low ragged line of the Maine coast in descending curtains of orange, then red, finally purple just before dark. Geordie wasn't looking well, fading as the day went on. He'd brought a nasty chest cold aboard with him, although it was hard to know how much of the hacking was from the virus and how much from his gas-compromised lungs.

When they finished dropping the last cargo tonight, Geordie could sleep the rest of the trip. They could handle the run back to St. John's well enough without him. Chester was amazed how much the one-handed Jack could do once they'd had new brass winches, usually seen only on racing yachts, installed in a Halifax shipyard several months back. Jack ground so hard at a winch that he could trim a sail faster than two of them working the sheets by hand.

Sean Brannigan had jumped ship back in early April. Ned Tobin put the word out in the bigger New England ports and Sean was spotted in Boston boarding a ship bound for Queenstown and Southhampton. If newspaper reports of the turmoil in the Irish Free State were right, Sean would be home choosing sides in a civil war. With the new winches and the amassed experience of the *Ricky Todd's* crew, they'd decided not to replace Sean and distributed his share of the profits among the remaining partners. They weren't fishing or unloading their own cargo, so three men could keep up the appearance of an innocent coastal schooner since most of their progress came from the twin engines Geordie had mounted belowdecks. The sails were mostly for show. Still, Jack insisted they keep her well-trimmed, not wanting other ships' masters to think the *Ricky Todd* a slack vessel.

Probably time we ended this. Enough money put aside to do whatever we want, Chester thought. *We've been lucky so far.*

Deirdre insisted after a near miss with the Coast Guard that this be one of their last voyages, continuing only until they cleared out the warehouse stock and gave Ned Tobin and the New York partners a chance to make other arrangements. Benny had written that several Negro-owned swanky clubs were springing up in Harlem, so the white gangs' boycott on selling them premium liquor was starting to crack. In the end, money was all green, regardless whose wallet it came from.

Suppose we can go back to New York and sort out the house. Never has sat well with Lena. Maybe I'll look for a partner and open a law office. Or start my own club.

Through the roar of the wind coming over the deck, Chester heard a few cracks. As he puzzled over the strangely familiar sounds he couldn't quite place, the nose of the schooner swung hard. All breath left him in one sharp huff as he fell across the coiled hawser in the bow. He struggled to his feet and heard yelling but couldn't make out the words. Placing a foot on the rail and a hand on the jib boom, he pulled himself up to see what was going on aft.

Splinters flew from the mainmast as punctured sailcloth shredded in the wind. He heard the cracking again. And he remembered.

Machine gun fire...

He saw Geordie scrambling forward, waving his arms to get down as the impacting rounds strode up the deck toward the bow. Before Chester could react, they reached him.

Oh Christ, no...

His chest turned inward as three bullets slammed into him. He couldn't inhale as he slumped to the deck, his throat straining to pull air into his ravaged lungs. He was beyond registering the awful pain.

Oh no...no...not like this...

His body spasmed and a shower of bright crimson erupted from his mouth. The hot blood spattered across the teakwood and rolled down his chin, soaking his shirt front.

Lennie, I'm so sorry... Jesus, not like this...

He gave a second heaving jerk as his eyes rolled back, Geordie's rushing footsteps echoing, distant and muffled, in his fading hearing. His mother appeared in his darkening mind's eye, lovely as when he was a child.

Je ne veux pas mourir...comme ça... parmi des étrangers...

Hands were on him, indistinct but insistent. His head lolled with Geordie's shaking but he was past feeling as a million brilliant lights flashed within his head.

Maman, j'ai peur... je suis seul... où es tu, Maman?

Geordie bent close, his ear just touching Chester's lips blued from shock, desperate to hear his friend's words. From the gurgling whisper, he could make out only *"maman, maman"*—and he understood. Chester Dawkins, a fearless soldier who had faced death in the field and prevailed, who had won France's highest honor, was now a frightened boy. And like so many dying men over whom he'd stood witness in the squalor of the trenches, this little boy, too, helplessly craved the comforting embrace of his mother.

Oh, Maman... Maman... tiens moi, Maman...

Then the lights faded, dying cinders floating into a depthless, welcoming black.

She hadn't slept since they'd brought Chester's body home. All she'd managed was collapsing for a few minutes, her mind exhausted from the crushing sorrow. It was an awful pain, a physical pain, more so than when Maman or Papa had passed. Chester was all that was left to her. She'd debased herself, flouted the law, made common cause with people she should have spurned out of hand, just to keep a home for him. She always knew he'd take care of things, take care of her, when he returned from France. That simple certainty kept her going through two torturous years.

The pillows needed punching up. Geordie was sliding off toward the wall, away from Lena's seat next to the narrow iron bed. She'd no recollection of how he got there, into the little bedroom at the back of her and Chester's house. Just her house now, although Chester had been laid out in a fine wooden coffin before the sitting room windows since they brought him home and the undertaker had seen to him.

The low muttering of women's voices and clinking dishes seeping up through the floor ended after a quiet snick of the front door latch. Deirdre Oakley and her mother-in-law had seen to the mourners who came back for the food and drink after the graveyard service. As she'd made clear to Deirdre and her broken-looking husband, she'd no interest in anything beyond seeing her brother put in the ground. After riding back in silence from the cemetery, Lena went directly upstairs and back to Geordie's bedside.

Not right for him to look so old already, she thought.

His sandy hair was limp and dank on his forehead, the spidery lines around his eyes and mouth he'd brought back from France etched in deep furrows. She pulled his wide shoulders up with one arm across his chest, poking and centering the downy pillows before easing him back. He gave a clutch of pained coughs as she settled him. The skin on his face and backs of his hands was lifeless grey, damp with remnants of the fever that felled him moments after carrying Chester's body into the house. The doctor, the quiet one from the war, said it was pneumonia and Geordie was lucky to be alive, bad as his lungs were already.

Couldn't help Chester. I'll do what I can to save this decent man.

Geordie's people—his father accompanied by one or the other of Geordie's sisters—came morning and evening, same as the doctor. Deirdre and the women from her husband's family came to make meals that mostly went uneaten. They knew better than to intrude.

The coughing cleared Geordie's head a little, kept him from nodding off. He blinked, then squeezed his eyes tight before opening them wide. She leaned in close and a crooked smile formed on his parched lips. A glass of water sat on the nightstand which she'd used to wet her fingertips and moisten his lips while he slept. She lifted it to his mouth, holding a handkerchief under his chin. He smiled again, eyes focusing on her face.

"You've done… too much."

She didn't say a word, tipping the glass a little again, wiping under his chin.

"My sisters can come…"

Lena straightened her back and replied to his meek protests with a wan, faraway smile. She slid her hand under his. He squeezed with what little strength he had, sending a thrill of relief, stronger than any sensual desire, right through her.

This one won't die. Not here. Not with me.

In the persistent silence, Lena looked without flinching into his rheumy invalid's eyes. She had none of the coquette left in her, not anymore and not with this man. With the fingertips of her free hand, she stroked his cheek, featherlight and all the more intense for it. He let his eyes close and open with each pass of her hand along his face, giving out slow exhalations—more quiet sighs—in time with her motion. A solid knot rising in his throat at her tenderness, he moved his weak free hand up to capture her fingers in the midst of a pass along his cheek. He rolled his head to the side and buried his mouth in her hand, inhaling the clean soapy smell and moist warmth. He kissed her palm, then her fingertips, but the physical effort and weight of emotion exhausted him. She leaned over the bed and brushed his fever-chapped lips with hers. No one watching would have sensed much passion, but it sent healing waves pulsing through them both.

"I don't want anything but... to take care of you." A solitary tear slid away without any movement or sound.

In the slanting afternoon sunlight her skin, stark against the black mourning she wore, shone gilded and flawless.

He looks at me like he's never seen a woman before...

"I might survive... so I can... marry you, Lena Dawkins."

She didn't look away. Not for a moment.

Form 1204

WESTERN UNION TELEGRAM

NEWCOMB CARLTON, PRESIDENT

GEORGE W.E. ATKINS, VICE-PRESIDENT   BELVIDERE BROOKS, VICE-PRESIDENT

St. John's Newfoundland, 3:42 PM May 28, 1922

RECEIVED AT   New York City

Mr. Benjamin Sharpe
        % Club Sheba
        133rd and W 7th

Chester killed at sea STOP Buried here STOP No plans return New York STOP

Lena Dawkins

CHAPTER TWENTY

Ned

It was like falling through pond ice in the dead of winter, the telegram from Deirdre. His brother Charlie was working alongside him when the boy in a Western Union uniform hanging big off of him entered the store with a brisk and efficient ring of the bell above the door. Charlie watched his brother read the creased yellow paper, then stare through the glass-paned door at the telegram boy remounting his bicycle.

"Renie says telegrams bring nothing but bad news," Charlie said, eyes pleading for contradiction.

"It's Chester. He's been killed." The Western Union boy was out of sight, but Ned went on staring.

"The man who served with you in France? Who works with you on… that other business?" Ned nodded, watching the cars, most of them black, rolling by the storefront.

Deserved better, Chester. You deserved better than that.

"I thought you were shutting all that down?"

"This was to be the end of it. Coast Guard caught them off Maine and shot up the schooner."

Although a little unsure how a man of seventeen should react, Charlie placed a hand on Ned's shoulder and said, "That's sure hard luck, Ned. I'm sorry you lost your friend."

He's a good boy. Always wants to do the right thing.

"That's good of you to say, Charlie."

Giving his brother a little pat, Charlie broke away and went back behind the polished counter. "You should go, Ned. No need for you around here. The kids will be in after school and you'll not want to be here for that brouhaha." He reached around the pass-through to the back room and lifted Ned's hat and jacket from a peg, walking it around to his brother.

"Yeah," he said, slipping an arm into the coat Charlie held for him. "Maybe go toast Chester's memory at Murphy's. Pa's been there for hours, more than likely." Charlie saw him out the door with a pained smile at the mention of their father and the local tavern.

Emmet Tobin hadn't been in Murphy's that day. Ned swayed his way home well after dark, having foregone his father's favorite bar to spend several hours at a similar establishment near the South Station. After the long walk home, he entered, not roaring but hardly sober, to find his sister Renie slumped in a chair in the front parlor. The remnants of her girlhood freckles stood out clear against her cheeks, whitened by exhaustion.

"Well, I see you've been drinking to the memory of your old pal." She was too tired to get her dander up, too tired of endless confrontations with drunken men in her family. That would change soon enough. "Charlie told me about your telegram."

"What's got under your skin, Renie? You look like death."

Pulling herself up straight and proper, as Ma had prompted a thousand times in simpler days, Renie rubbed the heels of her hands into her eyes before answering. "He's upstairs on his last legs. The doctor just left not ten minutes before you staggered in." There was no accusation in her voice. She was stating the facts as she knew them, waiting for Ned to take them in.

"What are you talkin' about? Last legs?"

"He's dyin' upstairs, Ned. Doctor said his heart's been failin' more than three years, since he took up drinkin' so fierce after Bobby died. Just like himself to hide it from the rest of us. Stubborn old goat. By the time I sent Bess to the store, you were already off on your tear. We couldn't find you at Murphy's either."

Ned swayed a little as he stood outside the narrow pool of light falling beside Renie's chair. He studied the lamp producing the spill of illumination, tracing the silver and brass filigree over the round amber shade.

Renie must have bought that. Don't remember it from Ma's time.

There was a dark maroon band around the bottom of the shade, glowing a saturated red from the bulb behind it.

Blood red. Not bright blood, from arteries, kills you fast. Slow blood, the kind oozing from veins.

"It came on so quick. When he was still abed at noon, I went up and he was deathly grey and wheezin' so terrible. That's when we fetched the doctor and the whole story came tumblin' out of him. Since he was... drunk... so much of the time, I suppose we wouldn't have noticed anyway."

She can hardly say the word. Our drunken Pa. Our sot of an old man. Jesus, how well they learn, mother to daughter. On and on.

Rising with sad purpose, Renie crossed the few steps to her brother and squeezed the arm hanging down at his side. She thought she was wrung out, but the tears came again, wanting to share with the brother she'd adored as a small girl and loved so dearly still. "You have to go to him. Charlie and Bess are up there now, but you send them down. There's no need for them to know whatever it is you two have left to say to each other." There was no bitterness. Protecting the younger ones was all she was after, as she'd done since Ma passed ten years ago. She'd have to let go of that soon when she started to show. No need to announce it to the world yet. She'd whispered it to Pa a few hours ago but didn't know if he understood or even heard.

Ned patted her hand against his arm, then turned reluctant and resigned to the hallway.

"His asthma's come back fierce from when he was a boy," Renie said to her brother's back. "It makes a distressin' sound in his chest. Doctor said there's no tellin' what'll kill him first, that or his heart." She wandered toward the front window, wrapping her arms about her to drive away the chill. "Not that it matters in the end," she muttered to the glass as her brother's slow footsteps on the worn oak treads echoed back like a muffled drum.

The door to the bedroom was ajar and Ned heard his little sister, Bess, sniffing between quiet sobs. Charlie was speaking in an indistinct voice, more toneless than Ned had ever heard. When he'd pushed the door open, its squealing top hinge intruded on the somber hush and startled the two at the bedside. Bess rushed over and tossed rag-doll arms around him, burying her face in his smoky shirtfront.

She's glad for the excuse to get away. Too much to ask of her.

Charlie spotted the telltales of drunkenness, having had ample opportunity with Pa, and grimaced at Ned with disappointment. "He still manages a few words. Not many, so go easy."

"Maybe give me a few minutes alone with him, Bessie? Why don't you go have a look in on Renie," he said, peeling her away and smoothing her ebony hair. "You, too, Charlie."

She has Pa's look about her, the black Irish. Such thick shiny hair. Like Adèle's.

They left without complaint and Ned moved to the end of the double bed, his knees touching the brass foot rail. He could feel the metallic cold coming through his trouser legs, the hardness pressing against his flesh. He leaned in, smarting his shins. Although the lids were closed, Ned could see Pa's eyes working behind them in rapid, furious jerks. Pa's fingers picked at the chenille bedspread and up the front of his pajamas without purpose, other than trying to keep the breath in him.

The sound of Pa's constricting lungs was awful, rails and rasps grating deep in Ned's ears with each labored breath. He was sober enough now, the buzzing of the whisky in his head settled to a high hum. He'd seen younger men die like this, during the influenza in France. It seemed impersonal then, not like the intimacy of the deaths at the front lines. Organs exposed and blood running out onto the hands of buddies unable to help. This was a lonely struggle. A solitary ending.

The chair Charlie had occupied was still at the side of the bed next to the nightstand. The only illumination came from the tiny porcelain lamp Ma had put on the dresser, in front of the big beveled mirror, its cloth-insulated brown cord trailing along the cherrywood before dropping down to the outlet above the millwork molding. Half the light was reflected from the mirror, the rest filtered through the rose-colored lampshade. Ned was soothed a little by the softness it gave to the room as he sat on the edge of the chair, near his father's head.

"Pa, it's Ned. It's your boy, Edmund." There was no immediate response and Ned's eyes wandered up the wall, to the foot-long crucifix with the writhing Jesus and the folded-over fronds from Palm Sunday mass stuffed behind. To one side was the hand-tinted prayer card of Leo XIII that Ma had put in a gilt frame, to the opposite side an aquatint of the Perpetual Heart.

Didn't do Ma much good, did you? Not doing too well by Pa either.

The wheezing hitched and quieted a little as Pa moved his head back and forth a few times, settling to the side nearest Ned.

"Pa, it's Ned. Why didn't you tell us you were in such a bad way?"

His eyes fluttered a little, squinted, eased open. Ned was stunned how deep they'd sunk since yesterday. Worse, the bright green had faded almost to dull grey.

Jesus, color of German uniforms now.

The dying man focused on the shadowy form next to him, then gave a little nod of recognition.

"Why didn't you tell us, Pa?" This seemed a safe way to show concern. Even that was more than he felt.

"No matter... wanted no fuss."

Ned studied the corded tendons in his father's neck and protruding veins along his temple. He was making a mighty effort to get enough wind to speak.

"Not... not much left... to say... between us, Ned."

"No, I expect not, Pa." He glanced across the room at the lamp and noticed the silk fringe along the bottom of the shade was swaying, even though the door and windows were all shut tight.

Must be the heat from the bulb. Like the waves from the big shells.

"I never... wanted you... at the war."

Christ, not this again. Even at the last.

"But you came... back to us... and did your bit... for Ireland."

Fucking Ireland. Always fucking Ireland.

"I did that for me, Pa. I'd a personal score to settle, not some... misty grievance... like the rest of you... of those fools." Despite himself, tears began to well in Ned's eyes, bitter ones, not sorrowful.

"No matter... she's free... free." The old man's eyes rolled back as he ran out of breath, his chest constricted. He choked hard, then with a huge strain, claimed a deep inhalation. He refocused his eyes enough to confirm Ned was still beside him, then opened his parched mouth to speak again.

"I've not... much longer. Send Bobby... I'd have him... here... when I go."

Ned wiped at his cheek with the back of a hand, a few scalding tears having escaped. He stood with a loud scrape as his chair slid backward.

"Sure Pa, I'll send Bobby right up."

Renie heard her brother's footsteps come down the stairs with more determination than on his way up. Bess knelt on the floor at the side of the chair, her head in Renie's lap, still sniffling. The older sister stroked the girl's hair and hummed a mindless tune.

They were both startled when the front door slammed, listening to the fading footfalls as their brother strode down the sidewalk into the drizzly moonless night.

On Board White Star Line
"Celtic"

Dear Renie,

Not much time to get this to the Purser before we sail, so just a few lines.

I'm going back to Granddad's farm. There's nothing here in Boston for me and I can't see any way past that. I loved the farm and I'll love it all the more after I've rebuilt it.

There's nothing I'll regret leaving behind but you, Charlie and Bess. I'm sorry for leaving everything to you, but you've always been the strongest of us all.

> *With my dearest thoughts and hopes*
> *we'll meet again, I'll always be*
> *Your loving brother Ned*

An efficient young lady with tightly wound hair set a small coffee tray on a battered desk dominating the dingy office on the shady side of Dublin Castle. Ned leaned forward and lifted a cup, the joints in his chair complaining.

Quite the important man now is our Sean, Ned thought, looking over his old rumrunning colleague. *Not a very fine suit, but a suit all the same.*

"So, you're back in the land of your forefathers then, Ned?" Sean Brannigan asked. He looked more a teenage boy in borrowed clothes than a police officer. Such was the way of things in the new Irish Free State, what with so many more experienced men barred from public jobs after choosing the wrong side in the Civil War. There were still a fair number locked up in Kilmainham, including de Valera himself. Some say he'd not have dodged execution in '16 but for his American citizenship. They were being released in a steady stream now, the Irish exhausted by the hate and violence, determined to put it all behind them.

"I'm back to reclaim my farm, that's all."

The office would be gloomy in the best of weather, but between the heavy February rain pelting the window and the pall of cigarette smoke hovering at eye level, it was a dreary and depressing place.

"About that, Ned. After your telegram, I made inquiries about your farm down Tipperary way. We found a number of records left by the Brits after the Treaty—mostly to stir up trouble amongst ourselves. You'll be honored to learn there were files on you and a few of your relatives in that neighborhood. I asked the lads at the barracks down in Cashel to nose about, too."

The secretary knocked once and opened without waiting, invisible from the neck down as her formless charcoal skirt and jacket merged with the gloom. "The file you requested, *Ceannfort*, on the Tobin farm," she said, setting the brown folder dead center on Sean's desk before leaving the office with equal briskness.

"*Ceannfort?*" Ned asked, taking another sip of coffee.

"That's 'Superintendent' to you heathen Yanks. We're all over fine

Gaels now, what with our Irish ranks and such." Sean flipped through the first few pages of the file to see if there were any new additions. He closed the cover and slid the folder across the desk.

"Go ahead and take a gander. I suspect it'll be somewhat of an education."

Straining in the dull illumination, Ned began reading the dozen or more pages attached to the back of the folder with brass fasteners. Some were handwritten notes, most smudgy carbons of typed reports. There was a pencil-sketch map of his farm. The papers weren't in chronological order, so they told a jumbled story. The first recounted the burning of his farm by the Black and Tans. The signature at the bottom read, "Teesdale." The bastard even provided a helpful estimate of how many horses they'd burned alive.

Behind this was a summary of reports from informants, by which every Irish rebellion from time immemorial had been plagued. There was some mundane information about himself—military experience, Pa's family—and one very interesting entry. It seems his taciturn and bookish cousin Kevin had been a rebel operative in east Tipperary ever since his return home as schoolmaster in 1916. And he was the one responsible for hiding the gunmen in the barn while Ned was away in Dublin.

That goddamn Kevin. He could've used his attic and got his own house burned.

Sean watched with curious detachment the variety of expressions passing over Ned's face while he read. The next few pages involved actions of the fugitive gunmen that had hid in his hay barn, providing details about the magistrate they'd killed, as well as a short history of IRA activity in Offaly where the assassination occurred. When Ned turned the page, his head jerked up to glare at Sean, who looked back with perfect aplomb.

"Jesus, Sean."

"No idea 'twas your farm and wouldn't have cared much at the time. I'd more pressing concerns."

Ned scanned the page again. There were photographs pasted across the top—two head-and-shoulder police photos, one a grainy and distant snapshot. The rightmost was a clear picture of a younger Sean Brannigan. He turned to the last page in the file, a terse informant's report. Glowering with rage, he closed the folder and slid it back across the desk. Sean noted his shaking hand. He exhaled a slow stream of smoke from his nostrils and continued.

"You'll find this out soon as you get to Tipperary, so I might as well tell you now. Your cousin Kevin is gone."

"And to where did he emigrate in such haste?" Ned said, his mouth twisted in angry sarcasm.

Sean rubbed a hand along his chin and looked away, but it was too late to stop, "Below the turf. He was deep in with the IRA. The British lifted him in the summer of '21, back when we were at the rumrunning. He was court-martialed here in the Castle. The Crown forces were anxious to make a big show of the execution, so they sent him back home to Tipperary. They shot him in Roscrea, against the back wall of the police barracks. Surprised you didn't hear of it."

"He didn't deserve that. Whatever he'd done to my farm. No more than you did, Sean."

The two sat in silence while the ragged ringing of a telephone in the outer office was followed by muffled mumbling from the nun-like secretary. The heavy receiver clunked down, followed by a single sharp knock.

"*Ceannfort* Brannigan, the... the Chief Superintendent...rather the..." she said, grappling for the term. Sean interjected, "*Príomh-Cheannfort.*" She gathered herself and went on, "Yes, the *Príomh-Cheannfort* wishes to see you in his office as soon as possible." Sean handed her the file. She spun on her sensible heels and left.

Spreading his hands in a show of helplessness, Sean rose and came around to Ned, extending a hand, his smile tinged with pity. Ned grasped the hand, mind careening from the revelations contained in the innocuous brown folder. A face, a wide smiling face, flashed through his thoughts.

"And what of Maire? Kevin's wife? And his children?"

Sean eased him toward the door. "Still down in Glenador, far as I know. Though the Lord only knows how they're surviving."

The last six months of rumrunning supplied plenty of money since Ned hadn't needed to bribe port officials or buy rifles anymore, not that he hadn't pocketed a fair share for himself all along the way. He might have something due him from Pa's will, too, but he wasn't interested in finding out. Back in Glenador, a letter from Renie was probably waiting for him at the tiny fieldstone post office with the green letter box and smell of musty newsprint and pipe smoke. He hadn't bothered to stop in yet.

Brian McNamara was none the worse for wear, although Ned had heard neither hide nor hair of him for over three years. It was a unique trait of the Irish, Ned found, the uncanny ability to pick up a conversation wherever it last ended, be it thirty minutes or thirty years ago. This had somehow been lost when they crossed the ocean and picked up the restlessness and impatience of the Americans around them.

"You've a mind to bring the horses back then?" Brian said. He stood beside Ned, both staring at the burned-out shell of the hay barn, the worst damaged of the buildings from its thatched roof and piles of tinder-dry hay.

"More than a mind," Ned said. "I've a great need to do it."

Brian flashed a satisfied grin, then looked back to the ruins of the barn. With one sharp nod, he said, "Right, by the looks of that fine suit you arrived in yesterday, you must have a little brass in your pocket?"

Ned saw Brian was already formulating how to get the farm running and tipped his head with a knowing smile and a raised eyebrow.

A second nod and Brian continued. "We'll be spending a good deal of it. That barn should get a slate roof when we rebuild her. Slate'll cost you dear, but it's cheaper over the years when you don't have to bring in a thatcher each and every summer. And it'll last longer than you and me. Safer from fire, too."

"Done. Whatever we need."

Brian whistled his admiration. "Well, well! Off to Amerikay to seek your fortune, was't? Like many a good Irishman, your own dear father among them?"

Ned enjoyed this backhanded admiration from a man he so respected. "This particular Irishman knew damn well that all the other Irishmen in America—Germans, Italians, and Poles, too— weren't about to forego their drink just because of some law."

Brian shook with amusement. He looked over at Ned in the solid farmer's clothes he'd purchased in Clonmel a few days earlier. His corduroy trousers were stiff with sizing, his cloth cap unstained by sweat, and his collarless shirt and grey waistcoat bandbox new. That would change soon enough and Ned looked forward to dirtying them with honest farm labor.

"So you made your fortune bootlegging? Isn't that what they call it? You were some kind of gangster then?"

"Hardly. We were rumrunning from Newfoundland and Nova Scotia, doing our best to avoid the gangsters," Ned said.

"Well, my boys are forever reading about them in the papers and puttin' on the Chicago voices. Or such as they think passes for Chicago voices. They'll tackle you like footballers with all their questions when they find out what you were up to."

Ned thought it best to leave out his funding shipments of guns to Ireland. With so many on opposite sides of the Treaty and the Free State, better to play the innocent American, at least until memories faded. Word would get out, everyone having family and friends on the other side of the Atlantic. Irish of whatever stripe or color enjoyed nothing better than knowing everyone else's business.

"Let's start with the stables, so we can get the horses in as soon as possible. Then the barn. The house will wait until those are done." Ned lifted his cap and made a long scan of his fields and wood lot, then turned and traced the crooked lane that ran from the burned-out hulk of his house through the double row of ash trees up to the narrow main road. Four years ago, one of the old men at the pub told him these trees were taller than the house even when he was a boy. So they must have been planted by Ned's great- or even great-great-grandfather, probably in the years after the Great Hunger. There were some trees missing in the gap-toothed line, lost to disease or wind or a need of wood for hurling sticks. A few more were missing big branches or had jagged scars from cankers. He turned back to the wrecked buildings and said, "It's only me here, after all."

Brian had seen him like this before, as he'd seen others who'd been off to France or gone through the viciousness of the rebellion against the Brits. Still, there was something new in Ned, another layer of regret. The farm would bring him back soon enough.

Tugging down his cap to shore up his mood, Ned shoved his hands into his trouser pockets and motioned with his head for Brian to follow to the house. "You told Eamon Nugent to meet us here as I asked in my telegram from Dublin?"

"I did."

Brian was sure Ned's reasons for wanting to see Nugent weren't limited to the Comerford place, which they still held as tenants in common with Kevin Tobin's widow. It produced good rents paid out twice a year, and Ned's Dublin bank account contained all of his accumulated share. Ned was unaware of Brian's repeated demands and threats to ensure the slippery Eamon sent those semiannual payments.

"And the boys? How are they getting on?" Ned stopped behind the fading red gate that hung uneven on one hinge and tugged as it scraped along the edge of the stone garden wall. Stepping up the gravel walk, he stopped to inspect the damage. The place was still smoldering when he'd turned his back and fled for America in 1920. Half the roof caved when the ceiling beams burned, but the other side escaped with a few scorched strips along the front edge. The windows were gone, some exploded by the heat of the fire, others in jagged shards from passing boys heaving rocks.

Me and Bobby would've done the same, not so many years ago.

"Oh, the boys are grand, right enough, and thanks for the asking," Brian said. "Liam married that youngest O'Fallon girl. You know, from the O'Fallons with the farm below Ballykeefe?"

He nodded, not an idea who the O'Fallons might be. "Nugent wrote that Liam and his wife are our tenants now?"

"Aye, and makin' a fine go of it. You won't recognize the very place," Brian said, proud his son had turned out such a capable farmer. "And wouldn't you know it, they're to make me a grandfather come harvest time."

"That's fine, real fine. A grandfather?"

Could that be possible? He isn't but a few years older than me, surely?

"And what of young Tommy?"

"Grown taller than any of us and tearin' through all the girls of the county, much like his brother before him. He'll settle down soon enough."

The familiar *pudda-pudda* of a Ford engine intruded. They walked back to the forecourt, sprouted in weeds, and watched the little black car chug up the lane with Eamon Nugent jammed behind the wheel. When the man himself emerged, Ned was struck by how hard the drink had aged his father in comparison with the fleshy Eamon.

Extracting himself from the narrow door, Eamon stumbled toward Ned, extending his hand from five yards away and blathering out condolences. "Oh, poor Emmett Tobin! That he'd be so young and yet below the ground in a faraway land! The news of it near killed myself as well, Ned, so dear he was to me. Friend of my youth and now gone!"

The stiffness in Ned's handshake and the twitching of his awkward smile were lost on Eamon Nugent, who thought himself more clever than most men. It was not missed by Brian McNamara, who was now sure there was more to this meeting. He stepped a little closer.

Ned stared with cold eyes at Eamon Nugent and said, "We need to discuss the farm."

"Oh, the Comerford place is a jewel, a very jewel, Ned. And young Liam and his Fionnuala, haven't they done wonders with the place? And always on time, even early with the rent." Eamon was unctuous as ever, not a hair out of place as he spun out his endless exclamations of good or bad, happy or sad.

The ferocious look on Ned's face chilled Brian to the bone.

"Not the Comerford place," Ned said, much to Eamon's confusion. "I mean this farm. My farm." Ned glanced at the burned-out house, then turned his head toward the charred stone walls of the barn. Finally, Ned turned with aching slowness to the stables. Brian could still hear the horses' agony, just as he knew Ned could.

Turning back to Eamon, his face dripping menace, Ned said, "You know why Constable Boyle and those auxiliary thugs showed up here, don't you, Eamon?"

The wind dropping from his sails, Eamon said, "Why I haven't the first notion, not being anywhere near here when... when the sad events of that day..." He trailed off, withered into silence by Ned's accusing stare.

Brian stepped next to Ned, his back to Eamon. "Ned, there's no good to be had ploughin' all this up. What's done is done." Ned ignored him, eyes never straying from Eamon Nugent's panicked face.

"Yes, you do. You were informing for Dublin Castle. I saw the file. It was shown to me by an old rebel friend who's a Garda superintendent now. Seems he spent a night or two in my barn right before it was burned."

Eamon shuffled his feet, scratching in the gravel with the tips of his polished brown shoes. "Now you can't be listening to all sorts of wild rumors. There's many a begrudger who'd say anything to harm a man with even a bit of success."

"I'd wager you were informing for some time before they came here, too. And you were paid well for it, weren't you?"

There was nothing left for Eamon to say. His face was red with embarrassment and fear, not yet knowing how this scene would play out. His eyes darted back and forth to the open door of his Ford, dearly wishing action could follow desire. The air between the two men was thick and cold with threat. Brian knew better than to intervene, taking a step or two back. Every muscle in Ned Tobin's body was taut with loathing for the man before him.

"You're to leave here. Take whatever you've begged, borrowed or stolen these many years. From my father, too, I know. I'm sure from many others. Get out of Tipperary. Out of Ireland."

This rallied Eamon a little, and his long-curated mask of civility dropped with sudden anger. "I'll not be driven from this land, not by the idle threats and precious feelin's of a trumped-up American! Yer just like yer father, always thinkin' yerelf above me and mine! Lookin' down yer long noses at me!"

Ned stepped uncomfortably close and said, "I've a few boys who might appreciate knowing of your activities during the War of Independence. I hear they go in for their own rough kind of justice. Isn't that right, Brian?"

The farmer shifted uneasily and said, "Ned, don't do this. There's no need."

Still fixed on Eamon Nugent, now covered in flop sweat, Ned said, "There's a great need, Brian."

Eamon worried his hat between his hands and said, "Alright, I'll leave, right enough. No need to tell the old IRA lads anything at all. I've a sister over in Liverpool."

As Eamon made for his car, Ned grabbed his arm and jerked him to a halt. "There'll be one last thing before you leave, Eamon. You'll sign over your third of the old Comerford place to Maire Tobin."

Brian had arranged for Ned to stay with Maire and her children and she was glad for the little money it brought. She moved herself and the children into the attic of her modest house just up from the little green in the center of Glenador so she could take in lodgers for the two bedrooms. That produced a tiny income, nothing steady mind you, but with her share of rent from the Comerford place it was enough to keep body and soul together for the three of them. Both the rooms were empty when Brian asked her to take in Ned.

Ned told her he'd be back before dark, no later than five or half five. She heard him at the front door and left the kitchen to greet him in the hall. She could tell even as he was taking off his cap and coat that something was uneasy about him.

"Well, right on time you are, Ned Tobin," she said, reaching to take his coat. When he turned, there was a hardness she'd never seen in him before. "You look as though you've seen the devil himself, Ned. Whatever's the matter?"

He passed her without looking and said, "You might come sit with me for a few minutes, Maire." He went through to the dining room and pulled out a chair for himself. "There are a few matters we need to discuss. You've never been anything but kind. I'd have things straight between us."

The last two years had worn on her. The first threads of grey appeared in her nut-brown hair and there were worry lines where before there'd been only traces of laughter. She was thinner, too, skimping on her own meals for the sake of the children.

"I visited an old friend, a trusted friend, in Dublin before I came back to Glenador. He's with the Garda now, a superintendent of police."

"What's that to do with me then?"

"He told me of Kevin's activities with the Republican Brotherhood and the IRA. And that he was responsible for hiding some rebel gunmen in my barn. While I was gone to Dublin." Her reaction convinced Ned she knew nothing of this. It wouldn't have been brought up at his court-martial and Kevin was wise enough to keep his wife well clear of any guilty knowledge.

"Oh, Jesus, Mary and Joseph! He brought the Tans down on you?"

Ned nodded, saddened to bring fresh grief to his cousin's widow. "I'm past blaming. And Kevin's well past being blamed, God rest his soul." He wanted to be angry with Kevin, but he'd been a good and loyal friend. He'd just been more loyal to his cause than to a distant cousin.

Maire produced a crumpled handkerchief and sobbed into it. He leaned across the table and took her hand, easing it away from her face. "I've other news I hope will cheer you."

She sniffed and blew, turning hopeful, exhausted eyes up to his face.

"I'll take the other room. It's still empty?" He withdrew a wallet from his back pocket and produced three five-pound notes, dropping them on the table. Maire stared down at the white bills, the red rosette around the "5" in the center like a splotch of blood on a clean bandage.

"And who is to be taking the second room?"

"You and the children," he said, sliding the bank notes closer. "I'll not have you shivering in that attic room another night." She squeezed his hand and smiled down at the table, humbled by his generosity but grateful for her children's sake.

"And there's another matter that concerns you directly." She couldn't imagine what could be better news than fifteen unexpected pounds, even in notes from the Bank of Ireland, so she looked back at him a little confused.

"Eamon Nugent has decided to join his sister in Liverpool to live out the rest of his days."

Her confused look now shifted to outright shock. "Why would he do such a thing, with all his business dealings, his comings and goings around these parts?" She blew her nose again.

"No telling, but since he won't be here to look after his interest in the old Comerford place, I suggested he sign his share over to you."

"Get on with yourself, Ned Tobin! Eamon Nugent never did a good turn for man nor beast unless 'twas for profit." She turned away, not interested in hearing any more of this nonsense.

"Maybe he's making amends for past sins," Ned said in the same bloodless way with which he'd addressed the man himself not two hours before. "Regardless, that's his intention and you should have the papers from the solicitor by noontime tomorrow. Since I'll be occupied with getting my place fitted out again and with the new horses arriving and the planting coming on, I thought you might just as well have my share, too." Ned produced his cigarettes while he spoke, lighting one and waiting for her reaction.

Maire's puzzlement burned away as it dawned on her that this was a pure act of kindness, engineered by this peculiar American cousin of her dear departed husband. Up came the handkerchief again as tears filled her eyes. She jumped from her chair and threw her arms around Ned's neck, sobbing and laughing with relief.

After many more hugs and most of a shared half-bottle of port, Maire smelled the burning edges of the meat pie she'd left in her oven and ran to the kitchen to rescue it. The smell brought the children downstairs from the attic room. The boy was a gangly seven-year-old with the dark looks of his father—and of Ned's father, the black Irish running strong in the Tobin line. The other was a plump, cherubic five-year-old girl with her mother's dark brown hair. Ned rubbed the boy's head and tickled the girl's ribs as they ran round and round the table.

After supper, Maire sent the children off to play in the front room while she and Ned settled down to their coffee. Both were exhausted by the wild emotions of the day and were glad to be near done with it. It was just such a moment of full bellies and tired bodies that allowed for impertinent questions. And Maire Tobin was nothing if not impertinent a good deal of the time.

"Ned, you're a handsome enough man and still young. You seem to have done right well for yourself. How is't some woman hasn't got you to the altar and settled you down?"

She nearly had to pinch herself, but it looked like Major Edmund Tobin, gentleman farmer, was blushing at her table. He hesitated a little, giving no reply as his thoughts slid away to somewhere she couldn't know.

"Was there never anyone? In America? Someone who you might have settled down with?"

He traced the rim of his coffee cup for a moment and said, "There was someone... quite special. Not in America. In France... during the war."

"What happened to her? Did you lose her?"

"During the last German push. She left for somewhere, I couldn't find out where. I was off at the front with my regiment and they needed everything I had. I did write... at our special place...in Amiens... and to her father's house in Albert." She covered his hand with hers and nodded encouragement.

"Never heard a word. She had my address in Boston, but I never heard from her there either." He pushed back from the table. "Meaning she doesn't want to be found. At least by me."

There was such hurt in the telling, she knew it wasn't done for him. "Ned, when the horses are settled and the spring crop is in, you need to leave things to Brian and his boys for a few weeks. Get yourself to France and try a last time to find your...."

"Adèle. Her name was Adèle."

She shot him a chastising look, "Her name *is* Adèle... and you need to find your Adèle and settle things. I can't bring my Kevin back, dear as I wish it, but you don't know if that's true with your Adèle."

"Go to France, Ned."

CHAPTER TWENTY-ONE

Adèle

At least nothing had fallen off Signie's masterpiece. They'd stored it in one of the assembly sheds at the old munitions factory. The owners had returned to making milk cans and cheese presses and, there being less demand for such homely products, several of the factory buildings stood unused and neglected. Signie badgered Adèle until she'd agreed to ask if they could store some of the larger works by the avant-garde artists there, those that couldn't be accommodated in the overflowing Galerie Myrmidon. The Dadaists in particular were fond of creating outsized works made of any imaginable collection of things. Such a pity they'd declared themselves dead before splitting into surrealists and social realists, communists and anarchists. But there was to be one last gasp for the Dadaists before disappearing beneath the surface of new artistic conventions.

"My God, it needs a good dusting," Adèle said, "but at least it hasn't mildewed." The big canvas-covered board—really several planks joined by a carpenter's apprentice with whom Signie had been sleeping— provided the mounting for the *assemblage* of items from Adèle's scrounging and Signie's photographic *collage* or *montage* or whatever they were to call it. This was the form on which he'd finally settled for his grand project. The canvas background alone had been the source of endless argument, with every artist and hanger-on who passed through the apartment having an opinion as to gradation and hue. In the end, they'd settled on a cascade of colored bands, each blending into the next, starting with a rich blood red at the top and ending in jet black almost two meters away at the bottom. After the 1922 show in which it was unveiled, they jammed it against the wall in the undersized storage room of the gallery. A few months later, *Notre-Dame de la Boucherie* had made its way to its current resting place.

"I find the dust adds a certain patina of authenticity, unifying this great work of our hands," Signie said, slapping at Adèle as she flicked a handkerchief over some of the objects, taking care the linen didn't catch on any protrusions.

"Perhaps of *your* hands. More a work of my bare breasts." Much as she struggled against it, Adèle still flushed when she saw these photographs of her wearing masks and little else. The wounded men revealed so much more, including the small man beside her, so she had little reason for embarrassment. This was a powerful creation, a searing indictment of the folly of the War and those who kept it grinding through those four long years.

They'd hand-tinted the photographs of Adèle, the eponymous Madonna of the work, starting with the huge enlargement at its center. Signie called this the "altarpiece Madonna" and since the effect was quite striking in contrast to the crisp focus and stark lighting of the black-and-white images of mangled men, they'd colored all the smaller prints of Adèle as well, interspersing them among the pictures of the men and the objects.

"They look like holy cards, don't they?" Adèle said, inspecting one of her smaller selves. "Like the ones the sisters gave as prizes to the girl with the best behavior or finest cursive."

"Or most obsequious bovine behavior," Signie added. "I thought your parents were atheists?"

Dabbing at a few objects again, Adèle said, "They were, but they so appreciated when their darling girls won anything at school. It made the nuns think they were converting us, too." Signie slapped at her hand a second time.

"Why did you agree to show this again?" Adèle asked.

"Because Picabia asked me. For his final Dada extravaganza or whatever we're calling ourselves now that we're dead."

"Let's hope he doesn't try to hang himself or drink rat poison again."

"Oh, he's over the depressions and suicides. He's taking shocking amounts of cocaine instead."

She sized up the *assemblage* once more, not for artistic merit but for size and weight. "And we're expected to get this across the river to the Théâtre ourselves? What is it he wants this for? Isn't he doing a ballet or something?"

"Oh, there's to be a cinema film at the intermission, too. That lovely dark-eyed René Clair is providing it," Signie said. "I hope he has more talent with a camera than he does in bed. Both he and that woman of his—like a couple of fish laid out on ice in the market. He does always smell wonderful though, I suppose because his father sells soap in Les Halles."

"Signie, please. Stay to the point. Why does Francis Picabia want an *assemblage* for his... performance?"

Signie gave a little sniff at being hauled back from his sexual reminiscing. "It's to go in the lobby. He's collecting a half-dozen works including one of those *portraits mécaniques* he did while he was in New York and Alfred Stieglitz wasn't able to unload on some American collector with more money than taste. Picabia hates those candy-colored brothel paintings that prig Maurice Denis did in the lobby of the Théâtre, so he wants something to shock the audience as they walk in. I agreed on condition that my work would go beside the entrance to the bar."

Adèle began fussing with her handkerchief again. "If it's to be in that kind of light, we must clean it. I won't have this looking like it came out of your granny's attic."

"Let's see if we can move it into the light over by the doors. We can give it a good look, see what needs to be repaired." Signie tried to heft one side. "The damned thing weighs a ton. Maybe we should wait until Léonie gets here." He shoved an abandoned munitions crate to face his masterpiece and sat down, patting the wood slats beside him for Adèle. He produced a slim case from within the long opera coat he wore over a pale yellow shirt and huge umber cravat. He offered her one of his usual cigarettes of Indonesian clove tobacco rolled in magenta papers with gold foil tips.

They sat without speaking, comfortable together as a dotty old married couple. Having not seen the fruits of their joint labor for almost two years, they looked with fresh eyes, reacquainting themselves with the work and accompanying memories.

It really is extraordinary, Adèle thought.

Her eyes settled on the photograph of Signie in a conical white hat and drooping black mask that left his mouth and chin exposed. She knew the lack of facial features, those things to which the human eye is most drawn, lent striking immediacy to the terrible damage and twisted scars beneath his torso. The missing piece of his right pelvis, ripped away by German shrapnel, or perhaps it was French, left a large concave scar. Diego had positioned him to catch the depth of the horrible wound in perfect profile. His testicles were gone, replaced with hard puckered flesh, and his penis was reduced to a flattened stump from which Army surgeons fashioned a rough urethral opening. Above and below those injuries, his skin was as white and unblemished as *crème fraîche.*

Reaching for the hand lazing on his crossed legs, always left over right, she gave him a quick squeeze and smile. She saw how her own skin had the slightest tinge next to his. She never thought of herself as olive-complected—it didn't have that appearance lying next to Léonie's freckly skin that she hid under prodigious amounts of powder when posing for postcards.

The household they'd created around themselves and little Édouard would seem strange and decadent to a respectable conservative family like Léonie's in Orléans. Adèle thought from time to time how it might be better for Édouard, maybe for her as well, if she were to marry again. She'd had an offer from the widowed headmaster of the rather exclusive *lycée* where she tutored the sons of old money and new in English two days a week. The idea of being cared for, of being able to relax and let go of planning next week, next month, next year, appealed to her in moments of exhaustion or worry. But she'd put her suitor off more than once and he'd moved on to marry the widow of an artillery captain who managed to survive until the last month of the war, leaving three children and no resources beyond a paltry pension from a begrudging Republic.

There were still physical needs. She'd just turned thirty-two and sexual desire continued well past that age. She'd taken a couple of lovers over the last few years, more out of craving than affection. Neither had lasted long and she was glad of that each time. Their household was so filled with nudity and sensuality from Léonie's modeling—and occasionally Adèle's, too—it seemed natural, almost inevitable, the first time the two women fell into bed together. Léonie struggled a little at first, not looking to fall into the maw of unrequited love again. It surprised Adèle, that first time, how much she enjoyed sex with another woman. There was a sureness and confidence, combined with gentleness. She also enjoyed her thunderous orgasms from Léonie's meticulous ministrations.

Signie joined them after blithely stumbling upon one of their sweatier sessions. Having lost his primary sexual organ, he made up for it through unflagging generosity in delivering pleasure to his partners, male or female. And he never tired of designing new combinations and positions for the three of them. Most times this was exciting. Other times, they collapsed in convulsions after attempting some circus stunt he'd dreamt up. All three enjoyed the sex as a needed release and a pleasurable way of nurturing the affection between them.

Their pleasant arrangement didn't interfere with Signie's wanderings or Léonie's fervid pursuit of other alluring women. But for Adèle, it was enough. Besides, she had little time for outside lovers with her son always her priority.

Quick scrapes of shoes sounded across the cavernous space. Adèle turned to see Édouard scampering toward her, right hand open and palm up, chopping toward his chest, signing *Maman, Maman* over and over in his excitement. He would turn six in August, so an adventurous visit to this mysterious building was very thrilling. Adèle ground the foiled end of the cigarette under the toe of her beige shoe. For some reason not clear to her, she didn't like Édouard seeing her smoke. The boy loved the smell of Signie's special cigarettes, however, and she could see him sniffing at the spice hanging in the air as he approached.

Léonie trudged behind the boy, a market basket over her arm. She wore outsized white flannel trousers and a short French sailor's jacket over the requisite striped undershirt. Adèle was pleased Léonie had forsaken the monocle she'd taken to wearing that made her look like a half-startled owl with a crest of red-hennaed feathers.

"We came to fetch you for a picnic in the Luxembourg. And to find someone else to chase this little shit of a dervish." She caught up with Édouard just as he slammed into his mother, throwing his arms around her legs. Léonie bent and kissed the boy on the top of his head and hugged him with her free arm.

"Do not call that precious boy a little shit, you enormous turd," Signie said after Léonie had kissed him on the mouth and taken what was left of the clove cigarette from his hand.

"There's a real advantage in raising a deaf child, Signie. Think of those poor parents who must be scrupulous with their language." She then kissed Adèle on the lips, ruffled Édouard's hair, and plopped down on the munition crate in the spot Adèle had vacated. She looked with displeasure at the small amount of remaining cigarette and snapped her fingers at Signie, who dutifully produced his case. She took a long drag while studying the *assemblage* with pouted lips.

"I still don't think the background's right."

Édouard tugged his mother's skirt, then slid his hand from his throat to his chest, looking up with knitted eyebrows. *I'm hungry.* Adèle pinched three fingers near her temple. *I understand.*

"We have a starving boy on our hands. Let's go to the park," Adèle said. "We can come back later and see to this monstrosity."

The Parisians had fallen head over heels for jazz and the musicians who provided it. Ned knew as soon as he arrived in this Paris liberated from fear that he'd find Jugs McGowan easily enough. It only took asking an American piano player, who in turn asked the American on clarinet, to discover where Jugs was working that very afternoon.

He was jammed with his trio on a little corner stage in the back of a smoky café on the Place de la Madeleine, right in the shadow of Napoleon's neoclassical heap that had been claimed by the Church at the end of the Age of Reason. Across from the tiny stage, workmen stood at the bar, saving a few *centimes* on the price of their *café cognac* and *vin ordinaire*. The tables were filling with the better sort of patron, most coming from work in a government office or cutting afternoon lectures across the river. When Ned entered, he picked out Jugs immediately, sitting on a chair at the front edge of the stage, blowing smooth and easy like he was born to it. Jugs scanned the crowd during a piano solo and spotted Ned. He flashed an enormous smile, his eyes crinkling as he shook his head up and down, then sideways a little. He held up a finger to Ned, took his solo, and ended the tune. Turning to the other musicians, Jugs suggested they take their break a little early.

Stepping down from the tiny stage, Jugs wiggled past a few crowded tables and made his way to Ned. "Well, I'll be goddamned if it ain't Major Tobin hisself, right here in Paree. I'll be goddamned." Jugs swiveled in reply to a tap on his shoulder. An eager young man in wire-rimmed glasses began stuttering ecstatic compliments on his playing. When the avid fan stepped back to his friends, Ned motioned to the corner table and signaled to the waiter. He ordered two drinks then sat down across from his old corporal. "Two Yanks meeting up, I figured we ought to baptize the occasion with a whisky or two."

Ned smiled across at the fine and steady man, always true to his friends and his music. The whiskies arrived and he raised his glass. "To the Regiment."

Raising his glass, Jugs added, "And to them we lost," his smile fading. They locked eyes in the middle of the noisy café and remembered in silence. No one noticed, although many would have understood.

"So what brings you all the way back to France, Major Ned? Heard from somebody somewheres you turned farmer at your grandpappy's place in Ireland?"

"That's a long and troubled story, but more or less correct, Jugs."

"Well that's a good thing, 'cause I sure had a big laugh when I heard it. Hate to think it was for nothin'." Jugs hailed the waiter and mouthed for another round across the noisy clutch of tables then refused the offer of a cigarette. Ned lit one and looked across the little table, recalling that last battle, the one with the little Renault tanks, when Jugs and Chester Dawkins were two of the few from that left flank who made it out alive.

"I'm sure you heard Chester Dawkins is dead."

Jugs slumped, having sat in this very café with the young lieutenant during those glorious months after the Armistice when they'd been toast of the town. "Heard he was rumrunnin' and the revenuers shot him up."

"I was in business with him and some of the lads from my first regiment. They got caught just off Maine and the Coasties strafed the deck. It was to be one of the last voyages—we'd decided to wind things up."

"Damn shame," said Jugs, hanging his head over the table. "Goddamn shame."

"Chester was in business in New York with Benny Sharpe and some money man they worked for. You remember Lieutenant Sharpe? He commanded the other flank, when you and Chester took that machine gun." Jugs nodded but Ned noted a little suspicion cross his face.

"Figures that Lieutenant Sharpe would be involved. He was jealous as any man could be of Chester Dawkins. He onboard that boat when Lieutenant Chester got killed?"

"No, he and I didn't work the rumrunning, just the distribution in the States once we landed the stuff. Chester and his sister moved to Newfoundland and he helped crew the schooner we used to run the booze."

"He wouldn't find hisself around no danger, Lieutenant Sharpe. Not if he could help it none. Always more worried how his uniform looked than whether his soldiers's fed and warm."

Ned gulped half the second whisky and held the glass between his hands on the tabletop. "I miss Chester, too, Jugs. One of the best men I've ever known." Jugs looked down into his own glass and watched the amber swirls bloom as he dribbled water from the tiny pitcher the waiter brought with the second whisky, knowing how Jugs took it.

"But something else brought you back, Major? Besides bringing me news I already had?"

They'd known each other frightened, exhausted, furious, like any two men who came out of the wretched war alive, so Ned had no misgivings. "I've got some unfinished business. You remember there was a woman here?"

"Lot of talk about that 'mong the men. Sergeant Freeman told me once you had a sweetheart up 'round Amiens, but you lost her when the Boche made that big push."

"More or less. I was there a few months after the Armistice. Took a taxi all the way out to her father's house in Albert, too. Deserted, full of starlings and bats. All I got in Amiens was from a waiter at a place we used to know, said she went to Paris when the Germans advanced. Figured you were as good a place to start as any, seeing how the French can't get enough of you jazzmen."

"I got a few connections inside the government might help. They come in a few times every week, no tellin' which nights though." Jugs sipped his whisky, then said, "Tell you what. Might be a few of them goin' to this new show at that big theater over on the Avenue Montaigne. Supposed to be some avant-garde shindig. All the hep people going to be there, maybe one of them government men." Jug gave Ned a sly smile and added, "My girl Yvette's dancing in the show, so you can see how much one Frenchy girl loves this here jazzman."

Jugs had to play a last set before the next band took over, so by the time they strolled out of the café, Ned had another three whiskies in him and was looking forward to the walk to clear his head. They headed toward the river to shortcut behind the Grand Palais, but they'd still make the theater with little time to spare before the curtain. Although the way Jugs spoke of the wild production, a curtain might not be needed tonight. They turned up their collars and pulled down their hats against the thick mist that often passed for spring rain in Paris.

From up the Avenue Montaigne, the square building sat haloed, its sharp lines and bas reliefs indistinct through the mist. The facade of the Théâtre de Champs-Élysées was brilliantly lit above the moving reflections on the wet pavement. The patrons shuffling toward the doors spanned the sartorial spectrum from opera-clothed mavens to the plainest workers. Or perhaps communist intellectuals dressed like workers.

Jugs's girl had left tickets at the *places réservés*, so Ned wandered the grand foyer while Jugs went to the will-call window. Anticipatory conversations hummed from a dozen or more clusters of people gathered in the lobby, punctuated by bursts of boisterous laughter emanating from the crowd spilling out of the bar across. Through the press of patrons, he caught glimpses of curious paintings set on bare steel easels along the walls either side of the twin staircases curving up and around both sides of the lobby. The stair railings were formed in repeating arcs that reminded Ned of the ironwork over some of the entrances to the Metro stations. These were simpler though, cleaner, less extravagant.

Lovely this place. Beautiful.

Glancing down the elegant sweep of the left stairway, his eye caught on the strange artwork propped between the bottom of the stairs and the entry to the bar. As people passed through his line of vision, he glimpsed photographs and odd objects mounted on a large canvas that looked to be dripping blood in melting waves. Walking toward the easel, he couldn't piece together what he was seeing. All the photographs seemed to be of masked people.

Are they all naked?

Drawing closer, he saw that black and white photographs scattered across the canvas were of maimed men with every variety of horrible wound—missing arms and legs, mustard-scarred skin, a face chewed away by shrapnel or infection. One was of a little man with no genitals and a mangled hip.

Didn't need reminders of this.

That was, he noticed, only half the pictures. The others were of naked women, wearing the same masks as the men, all carefully tinted in lustrous colors. There was a single large photograph at the very center, with the smaller ones arrayed around it like an elaborate triptych.

One way to sell girlie pictures. Call it art.

The objects between and around the photographs were arranged in patterns. Ned now saw they were remnants of the war and studied each with care. One was a spent ammunition belt from a Vickers machine gun, mounted in a long undulating wave, like a draftsman's curve. Another was a cluster of spent brass rifle casings, a hodgepodge of shells from friend and foe alike, laid out in a sunburst around one of the tinted pictures. There was a pair of banged and scratched German field glasses peering up toward the man with no genitals.

Why would anyone dig up this junk and try to make art from it?

As he continued examining each object and photograph in turn, Ned was discomfited by a hollowness in his chest and a sudden uneasiness that settled over him.

Jesus, what a fucking waste that whole cock-up was...

He looked over the pictures of the women again, shaking off his sudden funk. With a realization they were all the same woman, his interest piqued. The model's face was obscured by each mask, her hair covered in some by a hat or crown that matched the particular mask she was wearing.

Damn fine-looking woman. Probably some whore they paid to lounge around naked.

In the photo at eye level, to the right of the big central picture, she wore the smallest mask, one that just covered her eyes and the bridge of her nose with a wide black oval but no hat or scarf. The only other accessory was a silk robe draped in the crook of her left elbow and hanging to the floor. It had been tinted a light green over the detail of its Chinese pattern. He stared at it, an odd familiarity rising through his whisky haze.

Then he noticed the thick, lustrous black braid arranged just so over her left shoulder. The strong line of her jaw. The slight unevenness of her breasts.

"We best be gettin' inside, Major."

Ned reddened and stammered like a boy caught stealing apples. "Who... where can I... who can tell me... I need to know who made this... this picture."

Uneasy with all the people—all the men—leering at Adèle, Ned careened around the lobby in a frantic search for a manager's office, Jugs following with growing concern.

"Maybe best ask the man who made up this show. Yvette said he's some half-Cuban, name of Pickabee or some such. Why you need to know so bad?"

They were back by the barroom again. Ned turned to confront the *assemblage*, transfixed by the big central photograph of Adèle. He glanced to the hand-lettered placard at the base of the work. "'Our Lady of the Butcher Shop' it's called."

Jugs was struck by the forlorn look of neediness that had come over Ned. He seemed to have aged a decade. He watched while his old major stared unblinking, lips parted and head tilted to one side, at the naked woman. Jugs was stunned when Ned brushed his cheek with the back of a hand. This was her, the woman Ned had returned to find. He stared down at his shoes, embarrassed at having leered at the pictures like every other man in the theater.

"We best try to get backstage and find that Pickabee." He took Ned's arm and guided him outside and down an alley that ran to the rear of the theater. As they approached the backstage entrance, the door flew open and an usher strode out, letting the last-minute chaos spill into the grimy narrow space. Jugs stepped through the door before it swung closed, pulling Ned with him. Immediately, a young man in shirtsleeves holding a notebook with a strip of sequined material spilling from the end moved to block their way.

"*L'entrée est interdite!* You cannot come in here! *Sortez!* You must go!" The stage manager began shooing with his hands, pushing them back toward the door.

With his most endearing lost-boy grin, the one that had charmed Yvette that first time, Jugs said, "We have something urgent for Monsieur Pickabee. We must see him."

The stage manager gave a sardonic sniff and said, "That would be Monsieur *Picabia,* I assume? Absolutely impossible. We are just three minutes before curtain."

Ned saw that the curtain concealed a large cinema screen with dancers in evening wear gathering behind it. In the dim work lights, random flashes came off an entire wall of shiny silver disks. While he watched, a lighting operator ran a dimmer up, illuminating the bare bulbs mounted in the center of every reflector. Ned looked back to the stage manager through dozens of orange blooms, residuals from the unexpected flash of brightness.

"Perhaps you can tell us, so we need not bother Monsieur *Picabia,*" Jugs said, demonstrating his fluency with careful pronunciation. "Who made that big picture near the bar? The one with the naked people and trash on it?"

"Fiantrien, Signie Fiantrien. I arranged the delivery with him myself." The manager was outraged by something done or not done by a subordinate and made a rush for him. Ned caught his arm a little harder than necessary and said, "Where can we find M. Fiantrien?"

Gasping at the affront, the stage manager spit out in great indignation, "At the Galerie Myrmidon, near the Gare Montparnasse. Ask for him there." He wrenched his arm away and strode over to the offending underling, tearing into him with all the more fervor because of his offended dignity.

This was something he needed to do alone, although Jugs had offered to go along. A *gendarme* at the entrance to the train station in Boulevard Montparnasse directed him to rue Vavin and the red-trimmed front of the gallery. He tugged at the door and it hitched on its warped frame. An odd man sat on a high stool at the back of the small gallery, flipping through a magazine. He looked up and, seeing a smartly dressed man who had been better fed than any Frenchman of the same age, hopped to the floor and ambled toward the front of the shop with a rolling gait. Ned stopped dead as the little apparition smiled at him, dressed in tight trousers with a billowing shirt and elaborate cravat that must have been fashionable early last century.

"*Bienvenu à la Galerie Myrmidon, monsieur.* How may I be of service to you?"

There was something familiar, although Ned couldn't imagine why. "I saw a work at the Théâtre de Champs-Élysées by an artist, a M. Fiantrien. I was told he might be asked after at this gallery." Ned was startled by the little man's immediate paroxysms of fussing and preening.

"Ahh, *monsieur*! But you have met the artist!" Signie said, appearing to Ned as if he might explode, so pleased he was with himself. "For I am Signie Fiantrien, creator of the *assemblage* you so admired at the Théâtre."

It hit him then. This was the poor man with the damaged hip. And no genitals. A hero of the Republic.

"I believe your Madonna is... well, I believe she may be an acquaintance of mine."

Although the accent was fine—a bit northern for his taste, but fine nonetheless—Signie detected an American undertone.

"I have only recently come to Paris and happened upon your work completely by chance. Of course, I might be wrong, since all your models were masked." Ned gave a quick but intentional glance downward to Signie's waist, but the little gallery manager had been beyond embarrassment for some years.

"You understand I must respect the privacy of my models, *monsieur*. So may I ask the name of your old acquaintance first?"

"She was a close acquaintance, and not so old, while I was stationed near Amiens during the war. She was a schoolteacher," Ned said, watching Signie's preening turn to anxious twitching. "Her name is Adèle Chéreaux."

It was so obvious, Signie knew. Little Édouard's round face and apple cheeks, so unlike his mother's. The vague Celtic look of his green eyes and freckly skin.

"May I ask your name, *monsieur*?"

"Tobin. Edmund Tobin. Ned among friends."

Signie turned to the back of the shop, saying over his shoulder, "Please come with me. I fear I am suddenly feeling faint." Pulling himself up on his stool again, Signie invited Ned to take a lower chair against the wall behind the little counter.

Flipping open his cigarette case, Signie offered one to Ned. Seeing the color, Ned declined and took one of his own. Signie seemed to be waiting for Ned to produce a flame, so he held out his lighter and flicked the wheel. Cigarettes lit, the two staggered into an uneasy conversation.

Signie drew a deep breath and straightened himself. "Adèle is a dear, dear friend of mine. She has mentioned to me she once knew an American, an officer she called Ned, whom she loved most dearly." The last words stabbed Ned. Signie noticed the shaky hand as the American lifted the cigarette to his lips, looking vacantly at a white canvas with three intersecting colored lines. "She said they lost contact when she fled Amiens in the spring of 1918 and never found each other again. She always assumed he had either been killed or gone back to his life in America." There was no indignation in Signie's voice and this drove the words that much deeper. The shaking was quite pronounced and Signie knew Ned was clinging tenuously to his composure.

"She is as lovely still as when you knew her. And as kind."

There was no resistance left, not after these years of self-delusion and loneliness. He let the hand with the cigarette hang down as his head sank. Signie watched as the broad American shoulders shook with soundless sobs. The silence was broken only by Ned's sniffing back his running nose, dragging his sleeve across his face.

"I will take you to her, Ned Toe-been. But you must accept that her life has changed these years without you. I do not know what you can expect from her."

"I came because I must know. All the unanswered letters. I can't leave Paris without knowing."

Signie appraised the man sitting below him while he finished his magenta cigarette. He regained his feet and touched Ned's shoulder to signal he should follow. When Signie opened the door next to the gallery and started up the stairs, Ned was at his heels, not understanding until the first landing that Adèle must live above the gallery.

The little man's interminable progress was unbearable to Ned, knowing Adèle was so near. As they made the final landing below the dirty round window, Signie turned. "I must insist you wait here, just for a moment, but you must wait." Ned nodded, rubbing his hand across his sweating face and neck. The door to the right opened only enough for the little man to slide through.

Adèle sat at the wobbly dining table with a small stack of travel books, a red *Guide Michelin* on top. She was scribbling in a small notebook, her map case slung across the back of the chair opposite. She didn't look up at Signie's entry, knowing too well the sound of his walk.

"Have you closed the gallery already? Édouard is across with Madame Leblanc, if you want to fetch him." She pointed with her pencil, still not looking up. He crossed over to the table and stilled her writing, his hand over hers. Her head jerked up in irritation. Then she saw the look of him.

"Whatever is wrong, Signie? Have you had bad news?"

"I've had news," he said, stroking her face. "I don't yet know whether it's good or bad." Terrified by his pained look, her chair clattered over backward in her rush to stand.

"What are you talking about?" She had both hands on his narrow shoulders, shaking him a little more than gently. "Signie, you're frightening me!"

Before he could answer, the door drew open again. Her hands closed over her mouth as she teetered.

"Adèle?" he said, less a question than a declaration to himself. Tears streamed down his cheeks, something she'd never seen before. The years had changed him in other ways, too. His face was a little gaunt, thinner than before, his eyes deeper and sadder. Most of his old sureness, some would have said arrogance, was missing.

What has life dealt you these seven years? There would be time to hear all of that. Now there would be time.

She half staggered, half ran across the room and he folded his arms around her. She smelled the familiar scent of him, tobacco and bay rum, her face buried into fabric much finer than his old khaki. She felt his lips kissing her hair, again and again, as her sobs joined his in an outpouring of relief and long-ago love. Pulling away from his chest, she put her hands on both his cheeks and scrutinized his face, finding all the familiar things there. She stood on her toes and kissed one eyebrow, then the other, then his nose and finally his lips, hard and full.

"Where have you been, Ned?"

"I wrote to Marcel in Amiens, to your father's address in Albert…"

She let go a few short sobs and said, "Poor Marcel didn't survive the war by more than five or six months. He couldn't go on with his grandsons dead and so many others' returning."

"What about your father? I wrote. I went to the house before I returned to America, trying to find you, even a word about you."

Signie had retreated to the modeling corner, seated on the edge of the old chaise draped with carpets. He was too far away to reach the door before Madame Leblanc stepped through holding Édouard's hand.

CHAPTER TWENTY-TWO

Lena

The only white man in the house sat across the big kitchen table from Babette with a relaxed smile creasing his face. After noting his irregular coughing, she began directing smoke across the table at him. He gave no indication of noticing and his untroubled look unnerved her. But Babette had long experience intimidating men of every size, shape, color, and thickness of wallet.

Another big man, this one wider around by half than Geordie, ambled into the kitchen, a folded newspaper under his arm. Unlike Babette, the piano player had taken an immediate liking to Lena's new husband. Sure he was a white man, but at least he wasn't an *American* white man and that gave him greater stock in Bunk Hill's book. Maddie was finishing up the lunch dishes, while Lena stood at the window, looking out over the familiar backyard. She and Chester had grand adventures there when they were too young to walk to the park alone. She didn't have as fond memories of the park. That was where Chester and his friends learned to tease and tug hair. With a little pang of guilt, she recalled how her brother failed to stick up for her as often as he might have done.

This isn't much like home anymore, she thought. *Maddie's still here though. She's the last thread to Maman.*

Lena didn't want anything to do with the looming negotiations. Geordie had insisted they visit New York City, partly to settle the situation with her house. With Chester gone, she was sole owner, in law at least. With two rumrunning shares, Chester's and Geordie's, they didn't need the money, but her husband had a keen sensitivity to unfairness. This was a matter of principle and he wouldn't be denied setting things right. She'd agreed on condition she be kept out of it. Truth be told, Geordie also wanted to see New York City, see what all the fuss was about. And he wanted to know where his wife grew into the fine woman he adored. Although she'd never mentioned it to Chester after they moved to St. John's, she'd felt the empty ache of homesickness, too.

Just a few months after Chester was killed, they'd married in a long dusty office upstairs in the St. John's courthouse. The single window behind the old commissioner looked out over the harbor, its glass rattling from the wind blowing off the water. Jack and Deirdre Oakley stood as witnesses with Geordie's father and sisters smiling through happy tears. Lena had stopped searching them for signs of hesitation, chiding herself for slipping back into the wariness she'd carried with her everywhere in the States.

Her husband's health was restored after his terrible bout of pneumonia, at least as much as his gassed lungs would allow. They'd come down to New York a few weeks after a lighthouse trip with the Oakleys and Geordie's last surviving boyhood friend, Will Parsons, along with Will's tiny English wife. The men had journeyed up to Jack's uncle's lighthouse each summer since they'd turned twelve. The other two from their band of pals died in the war and Geordie spoke of them with deep affection. Their ghosts filled every nook of the lighthouse during their visit, but they were fond spirits. With Deirdre pregnant after years of trying, the trip was a last opportunity for the men to visit their beloved lighthouse together since the Parsons were relocating to London. During walks along the sea cliffs, the grey-blue ocean dotted with random June icebergs, Geordie had insisted on the trip to New York City after Lena came clean regarding the real use to which she'd put her house and how she'd been turned out by her partners.

"*Alors, Monsieur* King. Now what is it you so urgently wanted to discuss with me?" Babette was in full flow, confident she could turn this rube from up north to her advantage.

"Can we agree that you're sitting in my wife's kitchen?"

"*Bien sûr, Monsieur le Roi*... oh, *excusez-moi, Monsieur* King." She gave a contrived little twitch of her mouth, Babette Arnaud having moved miles past anything as obvious as eye-batting or winking.

"And that these rooms are my wife's rooms? These windows my wife's windows?" His curious smile remained, invariable and inscrutable, after each rhetorical question. Babette concurred with a languorous blink and tiny nod.

"Then I should think it only fair, since you've used my wife's home without her consent and without paying rent these last four years, you might be anxious to make an offer to purchase her property."

"After dear Lena and her brother, *pauvre homme—quelle triste*, abandoned me and our investor, we assumed she had abandoned her property as well. For which I took on the considerable financial burden of maintaining *au maximum*."

Brushing aside the French sugarcoating, Geordie replied, "We're reasonable people here, Mrs. Arnaud. And I believe we understand each other quite well, don't we? I expect you to make an offer, full market value plus back rent, for my wife's family home. And I expect that offer today."

Lena never turned from the window. Maddie heard everything but kept herself at the sink, although the tense set of her shoulders spoke enough. Bunk sat in the pantry corner pretending to read his newspaper, marking every spoken word. Lena was too important to Maddie and him to abandon her to the sole care of her unknown husband. Not with that snake Babette slithering around.

Babette saw Geordie's unnerving half-smile melt into a straight line. The transformation that came over the amiable face, every line of his past sufferings visible around the now-menacing sunken eyes, would be chilling were she a woman subject to chills.

Pulling the cigarette from its holder and poking it without ceremony into her mouth, Babette threw an arm over the back of her chair, letting her best continental posture fold into a slouch. "And when I tell you to go fuck yourself, Big Man, what you gonna do about that?"

"Have you dragged out, if that's what you want. By the police."

The room echoed with the harsh laughter emanating from Beulah Tubbs of the Carolina rice flats. "You sure not from 'round here, Mr. King. Ain't a policeman within fifty miles not bought and paid for. My money-man partner got them all sewed up, least those care about squeezin' colored folk here in Harlem." She continued with her throaty laughter, enjoying the empty silliness of his threat.

The hard look remained, stubborn as the smile had been. "But the last thing twisted coppers want is attention from above. Before you laugh at me again, you might want to know a mutual friend, a former comrade of mine and Chester's—you might have heard of him, Major Ned Tobin?—suggested I look up the old commander of Chester's regiment. Had a very friendly meeting with Colonel—well, now Mister—Hayward. Very successful lawyer, close advisor to the governor they say. Told him Lena's whole sad story. He even let me listen in on the telephone call he made, right then and there, can you imagine that?—to the… what's he called down here?… the District Attorney for the island of Manhattan."

He had Babette's full and unamused attention now.

"Being a fair-minded man, I asked Mr. Hayward to give me a chance to reason with what he called our 'adverse possessor'—that being you—before asking the District Attorney for assistance on our behalf. Or the federal authorities." Watching Babette's nervous squirming, Geordie slipped his enigmatic smile back in place. Nothing could have unnerved her more.

"Alright, Big Man. I'll arrange a meetin' with my partner. Your sweet little bride there knows him well enough, don't you, baby girl?" A little disappointed this didn't get a rise from Lena, she went on. "Let's make it five o'clock, in the card room. He's the one gonna have to make a decision this big."

Lena had forgotten how long Babette's heavy jasmine scent lingered after she left a room and the odor stuck at the back of her throat. After her ex-partner stalked out of the kitchen and banged up the stairs to her front bedroom, Maman's old room, Lena turned back to her husband like a sleepwalker awoken. Jumping up to lead her to a seat at the table, he sat close, her icy hand warming in his. Maddie fussed at the stove and produced a cup of tea for the stunned Lena. It was clear to Geordie his wife had taken in much more than she'd let on.

Bunk rejoined the table, squinting with concern while mopping the July sweat from his broad forehead. "Miss Lena, don't you mind that Babette none. Cyrus Wright ain't gonna bring trouble down, not with his other business. Shoot, everybody with a few dollars and a bootlegger is opening up a place like that Club Sheba of his. Most of 'em just for fancy white folks from Downtown, too. He been using this house for after-hours, for his special customers and high-rollin' hoodlum friends. You wouldn't believe the money movin' through your Papa's old library these days."

Maddie stopped her scurrying for a moment as she passed near Lena, sliding an arm around her and hugging her head against an aproned hip. The old cook gave Geordie a worried look, then turned back to her make-work.

"She'll throw you on the street—just to spite me—if Geordie can't force the sale," Lena said. "He'll see you're blackballed in every club and bar in Harlem, Bunk." The big piano player shot several looks at Maddie's back, but the cook carried on without turning.

"Oh, I been a lotta kind of black in my day, Miss Lena, so don't you worry 'bout me none." He gave a few longer stares at Maddie. "Don't you worry one minute about me. We...umm... I got other plans anyways." This brought a jerked-up head from Maddie, who turned and studied Bunk with pursed-out lips. She answered his imploring wide eyes with a single slow nod, then turned back to her counter. Bunk heaved a long sigh, mopped his forehead again, and said, "See, Miss Lena, me and Maddie here... Well, you remember her man passed last year? I know she told you—I was sittin' right here next to her when she wrote the letter. Told you how he keeled right over playin' poker with his friends and woke up in the glory land."

Lena was past curious at the jumpy behavior of the preternaturally jovial Bunk Hill. "Yes, she did. I wrote her with my condolences." Geordie watched the scene unfold with amusement, releasing his wife's hand and folding his arms across his chest after a little bout of coughing.

Bunk shifted his substantial bulk in his complaining chair and stammered, "Well, see that's the thing, ain't it? Me and Maddie, well, we always pokin' fun and teasin' each other... you remember that?... and you know I never thought myself much of the marryin' kind.

Well, when she finally stopped her slappin' and finger-waggin', turns out our Maddie here thought maybe I *was* the marryin' kind."

"Bunk!" Lena turned to Maddie, who was trying to hide her smile by bending low over the sink for no discernible reason. "Oh, that's wonderful news." Lena went to the old woman who had raised her as much as her own mother. Wrapping both arms around her, Lena hugged the broad, strong back, pressing her cheek against the flowered calico dress. Maddie nodded to herself and ran a hand under her nose. She reached back and patted Lena's hip, pretending to keep on uninterrupted with her work.

With that unruly cat finally out of the bag, Bunk relaxed back to his usual affability. Geordie gripped his shoulder and pumped his hand in hearty congratulations.

"What will you do when you leave here?" Lena asked.

Bunk assumed his accustomed storytelling posture, handkerchief in one hand, thumb of the other hooked through a suspender. "Oh, Maddie's man—he was a good man, you know—he left her a little somethin', along with the house. That's 'nough for us to keep body and soul together, least 'til we get the business opened up."

"You're starting a business? Bunk Hill, businessman?"

"Now Miss Lena, don't look surprised as all that. After you left, I put a nice pile aside… let's just say, Babette ain't the only one knows how to skim. Plenty for us to start our restaurant. With jazz music, too. There's not a man in this city won't love Maddie's cookin'—and I'm the one sampled it all." He rolled out a big low laugh, patting his belly and wiping his forehead. "So we put us together what they call a men-yoo with all my favorites. And I'll play the piano and bring in some other players when we get enough business."

Maddie came over to the table drying her hands on her apron, a sight that brought years of memories flooding back to Lena. She stood beside Bunk, a chapped and wrinkled hand on his big shoulder. Lena felt her tears swell as she memorized the happy look of the two, wanting it etched in her mind. Then Maddie lifted her hand and slapped at the side of Bunk's head, a half-hearted swat that he laughed away.

Papa's study was filled with the tensed feel and forced affability of a poker game, everything but the cards and chips. There were other kinds of chips held around the table and no one knew with certainty who had the most. A pall of smoke formed a corona around the protruding bulbs of the green-shaded chandelier Babette installed when they converted the library to a card room almost seven years ago. Cyrus Wright was in the center, asserting his seigneurial privilege, Babette at his left. With his chair pulled back far enough to show he knew his place, Benny Sharpe looked immaculate, the light pinstripe of his carefully cut trousers retaining perfect perpendicularity even with his legs crossed. Sitting in shadow, Benny studied Geordie King, trying to recall if he'd been this thin while delivering booze to the Maine outports.

Lena perched on the edge of her seat, shoulders erect and back not touching the chair, hands folded in her lap, a childlike imitation of her mother. She'd also moved her chair away from the table far enough to signal it was her husband with whom they'd be dealing.

"Well, Benny," Geordie said, "I haven't seen you since you brought those drunks to unload us at Jonesport. If I recall, they smashed six cases of good Irish whisky." Benny smiled, placed his cigarette between his lips, and followed his boss's orders to keep his mouth shut. "And Mister Wright? Seems we were business associates for some time without even knowing it."

The money man was relaxed as a speakeasy owner threatened with arrest could be, lounging back but unable to keep his eyes from wandering over to Lena. Geordie knew of his previous indecent proposal, but was unfazed in his knowledge this was the last either of them would see of Cyrus Wright.

"And despite our previous relationship, you've come to New York to squeeze me, Geordie?"

"No squeezing involved. You've a choice here. Pay my wife a fair price and back rent or get your girls and your booze and your customers out of her house," Geordie replied. Babette wanted nothing more than to slap the placid smile right off his face.

"Madame Arnaud tells me you've been talking to some Uptown lawyer, maybe the District Attorney, about our little enterprise here? Sounds like squeezin' to me." Cyrus was leering outright at Lena now. Geordie knew it wasn't about sexual desire. Cyrus was trying to provoke him into blowing up the meeting.

Benny leaned to stub his cigarette, the full light shining off his smooth hair, then settled back into shadow and recrossed his legs. His eyes never left Geordie's face.

"Seeing as how you're a stranger to our ways, let me tell you what'll happen if the D.A. or federal agents or anyone else I don't want messing in my business shows up. There are a lot of bad men would be pleased to do me the favor of puttin' a bullet in your head."

The calm smile never varied and Babette knew this was going somewhere bad. Geordie folded both hands on the green baize, his ribcage pressed against the edge of the table. His smile grew as he sized up Cyrus Wright anew, now that he'd threatened murder.

"I've died four times already, Cyrus. If fever in Gallipoli, bullets on the Somme, German gas or pneumonia didn't kill me... well, you mistake me for a man who's afraid of dying."

Everything stopped in the hot and close room while Geordie and Cyrus Wright waited to discover which of them was bluffing. Behind the confident facade, Cyrus's thoughts ran at breakneck speed, toting up the probabilities, the known costs and likely benefits. He also saw that Geordie King was doing nothing of the same, having already made his decision.

"Perhaps you'll excuse me and my associates for a moment?" Cyrus rose with great care, easy and relaxed. The other two followed. After the thick six-panel door closed, Geordie and Lena heard muffled voices in three octaves. Each was having a say, but the money man would make this decision. Lena looked straight ahead, fearing even to glance at her husband, tenuous as she was under the withering reptilian gaze of Cyrus Wright. Geordie watched the back of the door in silence.

After they returned to the card room and settled, Cyrus flashed a winning smile. "My associates believe it may be in our best interest to avoid any trouble. Much as I hate to swallow a threat from any man, I've been convinced to agree to your offer."

Geordie had discussed terms with one of Bill Hayward's junior attorneys, so knew the fair price. "As you're well aware, the value of real estate in East Harlem went through the roof during the war, but we don't want to be profiteers. That said, let's say $28,000 for the house and its furnishings, except for any small items my wife might find of sentimental value, of course."

"$28,000 then," said Cyrus, turning toward Benny to issue instructions.

"And four years' back rent," Geordie said.

"Come now, Geordie, $35 a month? I just agreed to give you almost thirty large for this shack."

"This premium location for your... enterprise was worth ten times that in rent. But I'm a reasonable man, so four years at *$200* a month. Let's call it an even $35,000."

"Agreed. Madame Arnaud will be picking up the back rent from her own purse."

Babette opened her mouth to object, then decided she wanted no part of the danger still lingering between these two men. "Of course, *mon cher*."

"We can forego the customary handshake, if it's all the same to you," Geordie said as he began to stand. He could hear his wife's respirations as she struggled to keep calm.

"There's one other thing I feel, what would you say, honor bound to tell you," Cyrus said, his pleasantness giving Geordie a flicker of concern. Lena's hands tightened in her lap as she pinched the cloth of her skirt to still them.

"Benny here, seems he found himself in a jam awhile back when we were rumrunning. Ran into a roadblock, hauling a load of your fine liquor from one of those shit-hole towns up the Maine coast. Revenue agents from that new Bureau of Investigation, weren't they, Benny?"

All the studied nonchalance drained from Benny Sharpe, since he had no idea why his boss was doing this. He worked the wooden arms of his chair with sweaty hands, head turning from face to face, looking for support or escape.

"Well, Benny got himself arrested and was looking at a long, long stretch in prison. But then those federal agents offered a deal, letting him walk away if he told them when and where they could intercept the ship hauling his hootch down from Canada." Geordie was glaring at the unnerved man across from him as the realization of what Benny Sharpe had done hit home.

"Of course, I was the one told the Bureau where they'd find Benny. I could've told them myself where to find your ship, but figured this way I'd get you boys killed or in prison, since you'd decided to shut down our very profitable enterprise. And I'd have something to hold over Benny, just to keep him honest. Too bad only Chester got himself shot up."

Stammering random words with his head turned to Cyrus and Babette, Benny didn't see it. For a big man who'd lost much of his strength to wounds and sickness, Geordie came across the card table with shocking agility, landing on Benny's chest. The two men tumbled backward off the chair to the floor, slapping hard against the wall. Lena jumped to her feet and screamed, short and throaty, with terrified eyes watching her husband slam Benny's head against the dark wainscot.

Cyrus Wright had already left the room, Babette fleeing at his heels. Lena heard his vicious laugh rolling back down the hall all the way to the door. Back in the kitchen, Bunk heard Lena's scream and hurried to the card room. Seeing Geordie was near to killing Benny Sharpe, he pulled him away with a bear hug around his shoulders and chest, there being more strength in Bunk Hill than most would guess.

Benny staggered to his feet, trailing dark red smears as he hauled himself up the wall. Lena came over to Benny and struck his face with an echoing smack. As he teetered backward, she slapped him again. Benny slid to the floor whimpering with fear and pain. Geordie wrenched free and grabbed the lapels of Benny's fine suit, dragging him to his feet and nailing his back against the wall. Lena laid a hand on her husband's flexed arm, her light touch still weighty enough to penetrate his runaway rage.

"No more. You're a better man than that," she said in a shaky whisper. Geordie pushed away when he felt the battered man's urine soaking through his own trouser leg.

In a quiet voice, Lena continued, "You have to see Colonel Hayward tomorrow, to thank him for his help. You make sure he knows who was responsible for Chester's death. He'll see to it the other men from the Regiment know soon enough."

She came close, the tip of her nose almost touching his bloody ear. "Benny Sharpe, I want you to live a long time with what you've done. There's been enough killing."

CHAPTER TWENTY-THREE

Ned

The last of the work was underway, the painters perched on the rough scaffolding almost done whitewashing the second story of the rebuilt farmhouse. Ned had begun sleeping there once the roof was on and the new windows in. The kitchen survived the fire intact, so Maire had it up and running in short order with help from the carpenters and painters. She'd been working for Ned, doing some housekeeping and a little cooking. He allowed her whatever time she needed to look after the children and tend to her lodgers, so the arrangement was good for them both.

She saw a change for the better after his three weeks in France. He told her much of what transpired—she was certain not everything—including the revelation he had a six-year-old son. Once he found Adèle, she'd brought their son to Ned's hotel each day. Past the initial shock, he was over the moon with being a father. They'd gone to the Tuilleries and the Luxembourg, big parks in Paris Ned had told Maire, and eaten ices and things called *crêpes* they bought from street vendors. Since the boy had been born deaf, his mother or one of her housemates always went along to sign so the boy could communicate with his father. Ned came back with a book in French he was using to study sign language every night. Some mornings, too—Maire had seen him sitting in the kitchen practicing with his hands, mug of tea and book on the table, when she arrived to start her day.

Maire thought Adèle had left Ned on cruel tenterhooks with her request for time to consider his offer of marriage. So for the master of the Tobin farmstead, everything was left unsettled, including when he would next see his son. But farms demand attention, especially with brood mares arriving from across Leinster and Munster almost daily. Brian McNamara kept a quiet overwatch, since Ned Tobin had come back from France more distracted than he'd ever seen him before. Of course, with his becoming a father— and of a half-grown boy—there was no faulting him for a little wooly-headedness.

These French women are powerful choosy, given how many of their own men lay dead after that bloody war, Maire thought. *No sense throwing a fine catch like Ned back.*

Paring the large pile of potatoes sitting in a blue willow-patterned bowl on the table wasn't providing her much diversion. Her eyes jumped every few seconds with undiminishing curiosity to the beige telegram envelope she'd placed at the far end of the table in a futile attempt to forget about it.

I spent too much on that new Stafford chinaware. Maire's mind wandered over a hundred unrelated things. B*ut Ned insisted we spare no expense.*

She scanned the freshly painted cupboards and the new soapstone sink, then right around to the repointed stonework of the big fireplace with its glossy new fittings.

Telegrams bring nothing but sorrow, that I know well enough.

She looked down at the hundredweight sack of coal delivered just yesterday, slumped like a fat old drunk beside the new stove Ned ordered sent down from Dublin on the train. It took Ned, Brian, and both the McNamara boys to manhandle the big brute into place.

It's coal himself must have, dear as gold it is. And with his own woodlot close at hand and a turf bog just down the road.

There was cold bacon and a good cheese from the dairy up in Cashel for the midday meal, along with the tatties and a pitcher of buttermilk sweating under a tea towel in the sink, set on the stone to keep cool.

Holy Mother of God, let it not be woe from his family in America. The Tobins both sides of the water have already had more than their due.

Ned and the McNamara men had been haymaking all morning and would return hungry as plough horses. This was the first mowing, put off late into June because of steady rains in May.

'Tis a fine house right enough, and with all the brass Ned's been throwing about to kit it out, he means to stay for good, I'd wager.

She'd helped with all the purchases for the house—had made most of them with little more than a nod from Ned. She only convinced him with difficulty to consider some good used furniture, at least for the guest bedrooms upstairs.

Everything new, everything shiny for himself and his American ways.

He was strange about a few things. Last month, the painters started on the doors and shutters, painting them the same crimson red they'd been as long as anyone could remember, when Ned stopped them and told them to choose a different color, a new color. He didn't care which one, he said, so the doors and trim now sported a lovely green that Maire chose for the befuddled painters.

Could just be news of some horse. Bah, no farmer would spend good money on a telegram when a penny stamp would do.

Laughter and the crunch of boots on gravel floated in through the kitchen windows, shutters thrown back to catch the breeze.

Saints be praised, we've a little sun and warmth finally.

Maire set down the small knife and walked over to the alluring envelope, sliding it into the wide pocket of her apron. When the men threw open the newly hinged and repainted gate at the front of the house, Maire was standing in the doorway, hands on hips.

"You're in earlier than I'd expected and the tatties aren't even on the fire yet," she yelled over. "Now go wash yourselves and have a smoke or two. I'll put the kettle on while you wait."

All four turned for the hand pump around the kitchen side of the house, but Maire called out, sliding the envelope from her pocket. "Ned, you'll want this right away, I expect." He saw the familiar shape and color, walking over to Maire with an extended hand and a puzzled look. He slid a dusty thumb under the flap and extracted the message. Reading over the telegraph clerk's spidery copperplate writing, his face brightened in a broad smile.

"Well, don't keep a girl waiting all anxious, Ned Tobin. What does the bloomin' thing say? I've been fretting with the nerves since it arrived midmorning."

Ned scanned it a second time before reading it out. "*Édouard says must see new father. Will arrive 15 Aug for extended visit. Will wire train details from Dublin. Study book please. Adèle.*" Maire wasn't much surprised when he wiped at his eyes. Fathers are a sentimental lot, even the freshly minted ones.

Folding the telegram into his trouser pocket, he said, "I best clean up. I could use a smoke, too." She smiled with relief as he disappeared around the side of the house, toward the sounds of splashing water and teasing McNamara boys.

The grey gables of the station in Thurles vanished into the overcast and soft mist. The moisture collected and pattered down from the cold iron grillwork of the footbridge that spanned the tracks, leading to the #2 platform, the one for trains up from Cork. Waiting for a Dublin train, Ned had a little cover from the weather beneath the eaves of the station. He'd tried sitting inside on one of the hard varnished benches but found he was too jumpy for that. The soft weather calmed him a little, that and the chain of cigarettes he lit, one from the other, while leaning against the chilly stone wall.

His careening thoughts came in such a rush that he seemed to be thinking of nothing at all—maybe everything at once. The only thought upon which he could rely was that his son was arriving on the 11:13 from Dublin. With the boy's mother, with his Adèle.

Extended visit, she said. She's coming to stay. They're coming to stay.

It was the only explanation. Of course she'd come to marry him so they could raise their boy together here in Tipperary. She was half-British anyway, so it wouldn't be so strange for her. Less than it had been to him at first.

Such a long time coming. So much behind us.

A crystal-sharp image flashed through his thoughts and his breath caught. He had the smell of her lavender scent in his nostrils, felt the heavy thickness in his fingers as he loosened her thick braid, shaking out the twists of jet-black hair over her bare shoulders. Pulsating heat spread from the pit of his stomach downward to his groin and upward to form a knot deep in his throat.

A distant high and breathy whistling shook him from his daydream. Back along the wide curve of southbound track, he saw thick billows of pearl grey smoke rising above the rooftops on the north side of town. He flicked his last cigarette to the pavement and stepped forward to within a foot of the platform edge. Four or five others emerged from the station and joined him in craning their necks and squinting for the Dublin train. The black round face of the engine appeared around the bend, its smoke tapering off as the train slowed in its approach. As the passenger carriages slid beside the platform, brakes squealing against the wet iron wheels, he could see passengers through the windows, a few rising to collect hat boxes and valises from the overhead racks. Some of the compartment doors opened before the train had stopped, anxious travelers ready to be done with their confinement.

Ned looked along the carriages, not sure where they would emerge. Just down from where he stood, a compartment door swung open, splitting the "Western" in the gold-lettered name of the railway running along the dark green side. Two adult hands held the smaller pair of a little boy, who jumped the foot or so down and began exploring his new surroundings the moment his shoes touched the platform. The round head with the tousled mousy brown hair turned toward Ned. With an excited smile of recognition, the boy looked back to the compartment, snapping his thumb and finger together near his beaming face. Ned recognized the sign from the book Adèle had given him—*Papa, Papa, Papa*.

As Ned hurried toward Édouard, the same hands and black sleeves that had helped the boy down shoved a fading carpetbag out through the door and Ned shouted over the hissing steam brakes, "Adèle! Adèle! Here! Over here!"

The mist had turned to rain while he was waiting. It ran around and off the brim of his fedora, dripping onto the shoulders of his coat. He'd worn a good suit to meet the train, gotten to Thurles early so he'd have time for a haircut and shave, a shoe shine, too. It felt good to have a day with clean hands and a fresh shirt, to meet Adèle feeling a little like the officer she'd fallen for back in Amiens.

The hissing stopped and the voices of excited families drifted a thousand miles away. His vision narrowed as if peering through a soda straw. He placed a hand on the carriage to keep steady, fearing his knees would buckle. The dark sleeves were attached to a man's tuxedo jacket, covering shoulders that held a head with short-cropped hennaed hair and an eye with a monocle. As Léonie hopped to the platform in hot pursuit of the scampering Édouard, Ned saw a foot with a pale lavender spat reach for the platform with tentative little stabs.

As the boy wrapped himself around his leg, Ned gaped in crushing disbelief, willing another leg or arm to emerge from the passenger compartment. Léonie called his name, imbedded in a stream of French he didn't choose to understand. He stood frozen, little Édouard tugging at his trousers and signing *Papa, Papa* until a conductor, working his way from the rear of the train while fretting over a heavy watch in his palm, slammed the compartment doors as he hurried past.

16 rue Vavin
29th of July, 1924

My dearest Ned,

I'm so very sorry you discovered I was not accompanying Édouard without fair warning. That was heartless of me, I know, but I could think of no way to avoid it. For the sake of our son, I hope you'll forgive me.

My darling, I cannot marry you. No, that's unfair. There has been too much unsaid for too long between us. I choose not to marry you.

We were, in many ways, victims of circumstance—the bloody war, missed opportunities (coming so close at my father's house in Albert!), unreliable mail, upended lives. But most of our bad luck was of our own making. We both, you and I, made choices. You chose to return to America, then come back to France in circumstances that required everything you could give. I chose to run from Amiens when it wasn't really necessary and not to return when I might have done so. You've chosen Ireland and I've chosen Paris and we've both chosen new lives.

My first and last concern is Édouard's welfare. I am overjoyed he's found his father. He loves you so already. But he will start the école maternelle at the National Institute for the Young Deaf in September. This is where I know he will thrive and have as fine an education as you and I, even university I've been assured. I won't take that from him.

Nor will I take you from your farm. I saw what it means to you, how it has healed you, even with the horrible things done by the British. You have people there who care greatly for you.

I shall send Édouard to you every summer. You deserve to know your son and he needs his father. The other nine months of the year, well, you know he will be surrounded by people who love and adore him. And they love and care for me, too.

We lost our dear Madame Leblanc not long after your visit. We laid her to rest in the Montparnasse cemetery so she will always be nearby. Édouard likes to visit her on Sundays when the weather allows. We've taken her flat, too, so we've made quite a little commune for ourselves on the top floor above the gallery. Please know that I'm happy with the life I've made. Were I religious, I would pray you've done the same in Tipperary.

Perhaps we burned too bright? Perhaps we lived in a dream within the insanity of the war? I don' pretend to know, but we're forever linked by our sweet boy. That will have to do.

With all my fondest affection, now and forever,
Adèle

"Well, 'twas a fine visit with that dear little man of yours. Such a love he is, Ned. Such a love. My two had a fine time with him."

Maire set a mug before the dejected man sitting in shirt sleeves, a cigarette unsmoked between his fingers, his steady stare not straying from the burning turf in the wide kitchen hearth. Maire wouldn't burn coal in the fireplace, not with turf so much cheaper and near at hand. She thought it made a cheerier fire anyway, not like the hard heat of coal, bright like a forge. But she had to admit, the coal was much better for the stove, especially for her baking.

"And he'll be coming for his summers, too," she said, blowing across the top of her own tea as she settled in next to him, scooting her chair to face the fire, too. "That'll be fine, won't it? He won't grow up altogether French, will he? Three months each year we'll have to make a proper Irishman of him."

After a single long pull, Ned flicked the cigarette into the fire, walked over to a cupboard, and took down a whisky bottle. He poured a healthy portion into his tea and slouched back to the fireside. She tutted a little, as all Irishwomen were meant to do in the face of a man taking strong spirits, but said nothing. He hadn't fallen deep into the drink, as she feared he might when his son arrived without Adèle.

"I thought the worst when you brought Léonie and Signie through that door. But didn't they turn out to be a fine pair altogether? So good to your boy they are. They dote on him something shameless, don't they?"

Ned nodded a little and slurped at the fortified tea. "They do, they do at that. And I'm grateful. Would've been difficult talking with the little fella without them."

Maire slid forward on her chair and turned. Ned could see she was gathering herself to say something weighty.

"I've a few matters to discuss with you now." He looked her square in the eyes for the first time since they'd sat down by the fire. She deserved his attention, so much had she done for him since his return. He waited in silence while she took a deep breath before launching into a subject it seemed she'd been pondering for some time.

"She's gone from you, Ned, and she's not coming back." His eyes darted back to the fire and he gulped the whiskied tea. "No, you don't look away from me, Ned Tobin. You'll hear me out—you owe me that."

Sheepish in his avoidance, he turned back and said, "I do owe you that. And more besides. I'm listening."

Jesus, she's so much like Renie when she scolds.

"She made it clear as could be in that… sad letter she wrote you. She'll not be back." When he'd handed it to her, the second night after his son arrived, she cried agonized tears for him. He hadn't shed a one, at least not that he'd let her see. "Whatever her reasons might be, you need to accept them and be grateful she wants you part of Edward's... Édouard's upbringing. I'll tell you, it'd be a hard thing indeed for any mother to send her boy away each and every summer, away across the sea, as Adèle's agreed to do. I admire her for that."

And she speaks to me so much like Ma used to. Like a naughty boy.

He had nothing to say in reply, since he knew she was right. It hurt no less with the certainty.

"So, you can take to the drink until you lose this fine farm and find an early grave. Or you can count the blessings you have—and they're many, Edmund Tobin, many more than most will ever know—and get on with your life."

"'Tis better to have loved and lost? Is that what you're telling me?"

She could see he was angry still, although he was holding back, not looking to blame her. "Bah, that Tennyson was nothing but a bloodless Englishman, Kevin always said. There's no such thing as losing one you love being anything but lifelong painful." He saw she was angry, too, still angry for her lost husband. Not that she wasn't entitled. She'd had a hard time of it since he was shot by the British.

"You said a few matters to discuss," Ned said. "Maybe we can leave off Adèle for now?"

She looked him over with close scrutiny. "Just so. You've another choice to make, and I'll hear that choice this night."

He set his mug on the hearthstone and shifted to face her, waiting in silence.

"I've looked after you since you returned last year. And I helped put this house back together, and a finer house there's not to be found in east Tipperary." She glanced around the scrubbed kitchen with its fine stove and new fittings with proprietary pride. "And my children have taken to you, and to your little Édouard, as if you were their very own family. It's become a little... confusing for them. And for myself as well."

Is she blushing? Didn't think that possible.

"So, you'll need to choose. You can find yourself a new housekeeper, starting tomorrow." She was fiddling with the lower buttons of her blouse, her face a bright and radiant red.

Ned smiled and leaned closer. "And what would my other choice be?"

In a quiet and uncertain voice, she said to the fire, "You know very well what your other choice might be, Ned Tobin, and you don't need me to say it, do you?"

She might have thought half the night passed as they sat, the only sound in the big kitchen the hissing of the glowing turf on the grate. It was, in fact, only a minute or two later when she felt Ned's hand wrap around hers. He gave it a tight squeeze and said, "I shouldn't have let you buy that old furniture. We'll want to have something new upstairs for the children."

HISTORICAL NOTE

The First World War has long been almost a historical sideshow to most Americans, since the U.S. was late getting in and only had significant numbers of troops in combat for seven months. As a result, much of the extraordinary and heroic history of American participation in the Great War is sparsely known. Such is the case with the 369th U.S. Infantry—Harlem's Hell Fighters—as well as thousands of Americans who served as volunteers in Allied armed forces before the United States entered the War. This is the genesis of how, in this second volume of my *Sweet Wine of Youth* trilogy, Chester Dawkins of the 15th New York Regiment—federalized as the 369th U.S.Infantry—and Ned Tobin of Boston, late of the Newfoundland Regiment, found themselves in doughboy uniforms and as main characters in this novel.

Although the 369th was a famed historic regiment, I purposefully never placed Chester Dawkins or any other characters in a specified platoon or company. This was for two reasons. I'm generally not fond of "fictional biography" (with some notable exceptions) and this also gave me a lot of freedom with my plot and narrative. There is only one historical figure with a speaking role, Colonel William Hayward, a white Uptown lawyer, advisor to the Governor of New York, and founding commander of the 15th New York who led them throughout the War. A few others are mentioned but don't actually appear in the story—Captain Hamilton Fish, who would later became an isolationist Congressman from New York, and Lieutenant James Europe, the leader of the amazing regimental band that brought jazz to France and would be killed by one of his own drummers just months after the War ended. For the other characters from the regiment, I pulled first names and surnames from census records (which are searchable by race) from 1890 and 1900, so they are all historically plausible. (Babette Arnaud is an exception, being named after one of my favorite restaurants in New Orleans.)

There are, of course, other historical figures mentioned, and some with substantial detail. Most everything said about General John J. Pershing, commander of the American Expeditionary Forces (AEF), is supported historically, including his great resistance to allowing Negro soldiers to serve in combat units within the AEF. Ned Tobin's gambit to get the 369th assigned to the French Army has factual roots, since Pershing did send all four of the African-American regiments comprising the 93rd Division (Colored) to the French. It is historically accurate that Secretary of War Newton Baker strongly supported African-American participation in the War and that the otherwise segregationist President Woodrow Wilson concurred with this plan.

A word on word choice. Although it was very uncomfortable using the words "colored" and "Negro" throughout this novel, these were the historically accurate terms used within the African-American community at the time. (The terms "African-American" and "black" were not in usage until well into the second half of the 20th century.) I strictly rationed use of any racial slurs to those instances where they were essential to character development. For example, the only white character who uses the "n-word" is Ned Tobin's Irish immigrant father who lives in the Irish enclave of Southie in Boston, where some of the most virulent opposition to forced school desegregation would occur 50 years later. I put a period-appropriate and slightly milder version—the phonetically spelled "negrah"—in the mouth of a racist southern sheriff. Shocked Germans referred to 369th soldiers as *Schwarze* which was correct usage in that language at the time and a mild pejorative, meaning simply "black." Otherwise, I found no narrative need for racial epithets. I leave it to the reader to decide whether these were appropriate choices.

It may seem odd to some readers that there was discussion of lightness and darkness of skin within the African-American characters' dialogue. This too is accurate to the period and was much discussed by commentators and leaders within the black community, in particular Marcus Garvey. Lighter skin was widely considered more attractive and afforded decided social and economic advantages. That all the chorus girls at the Club Sheba—my fictitious nightclub catering to a white and wealthy black clientele—were chosen for their light skin is historically accurate. This was unsettling to write, but I found it an important aspect of the social context of the period that needed inclusion, particularly since Lena Dawkins favored her light-skinned Louisiana creole mother.

The two battle scenes are my invention, although I lifted aspects from historical sources, including medal citations for 369th soldiers. Although fictitious, I hope they are representative of the indisputable gallantry of the brave men of the 369th. The other experiences of the 369th were based loosely on historical fact, adapted to my narrative purpose. The stand-off with the sheriff in Spartanburg, SC, is my invention. The soldiers suffered a long string of humiliations and confrontations from the white population throughout their weeks at Camp Wadsworth, but I needed a set-piece event to make the point while keeping the narrative moving. This is also why I felt the need to give Colonel Hayward a speaking role. (He was originally in two other scenes which, alas, did not survive revisions.) The assignment of French advisors and the use of French rifles and equipment are accurate. Sadly, the "Secret information concerning Colored American Troops" issued by French General Headquarters to their field commanders and military governors is true and reproduced exactly with only light editing for length. It's almost certain this was requested—if not drafted—by officers within the AEF staff and pushed on the French, who would have done anything to keep the late-arriving and eagerly-welcomed Americans happy. It remains a horrific and inexcusable stain on U.S. military history. And it needed to be in this book.

The homecoming parade riot in Norfolk is an historical event and I included it as a representative scene of the racially charged atmosphere in the United States after the War. Unlike their white comrades, African-American doughboys were disarmed in France and returned to a country where little had changed regarding matters of racial prejudice and segregation. The middle months of 1919 would become known as the "Red Summer" from a series of two dozen or more incidents of racial violence—almost all instigated by whites against blacks—that broke out across the country. These horrendous events were clustered in Georgia, Mississippi, and Arkansas, but also included major incidents in Chicago, Omaha, and other northern cities. It's hard to imagine the overwhelming sense of injustice and disappointment felt by these brave men returning from fighting their country's war overseas only to be attacked by racists at home.

Republican France made no exceptions to conscription for clergymen, so Captain Fabien Aubert, S.J., is historically plausible. Sergeant Lucien Barthold is loosely based on a real *poilu* (literally, "hairy one") named Louis Barthas and is a small *homage* to his remarkable war notebooks only recently translated into English. (It's included in "Suggested Further Reading" at the back of this book.) I'll admit I loved creating the characters of Sergeant Barthold and Sergeant Freeman, as well as their curious relationship. It was very difficult for me to kill them, but the story demanded it and at least they died together.

The experiences of Ned Tobin in Ireland are in an accurate historical context. The killing of a magistrate in Offaly occurred about the time depicted, although the identity of the killers was my invention. The Auxiliaries—known to history as the Black and Tans due to the colors of their scrounged surplus uniforms—were all too real. They commenced operations in Ireland right around the time depicted in my story, although I nudged forward their arrival in Tipperary by a month or two. That Kevin Tobin was an undercover IRA operative and Eamon Nugent an informant has ample precedent in the history of the bloody Irish War of Independence and the tragic Civil War that followed on the heels of the British withdrawal in 1922. (This astounding history of Ireland from 1916 through 1924 will provide the milieu for the final book in the trilogy, *No Hero's Welcome*.)

The few scenes in Newfoundland and on the schooner *Ricky Todd* are a direct connection to my first book, *None of Us the Same*. Three of the four main characters in this book—Ned Tobin and the Dawkins siblings—are minor characters in *None of Us the Same*. Geordie King, Deirdre and Jack Oakley, and Sean Brannigan are also characters of greater or lesser importance from that book. (Sean and the rest of the Brannigan family will be at the center of *No Hero's Welcome*.) Several scenes dovetail directly with scenes in *None of Us the Same*, including Ned and Geordie's truck ride to visit Will Parsons and his Glamorgans, the New Year's dinner in St. John's, and Chester's death on the *Ricky Todd* (told from Geordie's point of view previously). The schooner *Ricky Todd* is based on detailed models of two cod schooners, *The Blue Nose* and the *Lloyd Jack*, photographs in various collections, and the description of the *We're Here* in Kipling's marvelous tale, *Captains Courageous*.

The French suffered more casualties than any of the other combatants in the First World War, losing almost 4.5% of their total population and just under a third of young men aged 18-30. That many French women did not or could not marry after the War was therefore a demographic reality. Advances in medicine allowed men like Signie to survive horrible wounds that would have proven fatal in past conflicts. The photo montage of maimed veterans was therefore plausible. The Dadaist movement was all too real, shining brightly for just a few years from the middle of the War and into the '20s before publicly declaring themselves dead in 1924. Although short-lived, their utter rejection of artistic conventions and dismissal of reason and rationality and progress had an outsized impact on the wider avant-garde movement, especially the surrealists and, some would argue, the post-modernists. They also perfected *collage*, with which every grade schooler is familiar to this day.

The self-assignment of new and ironic names was a characteristic of the Dadaists. For example, one of the leaders of the Dadaists, Marcel Duchamp, sometimes went under the assumed name (and cross-dressed gender) of Rrose Sélavy, pronounced in French "Eros c'est la vie." Therefore, Léonie Déchaîne (more or less, "unchained lioness") and Signie Fiantrien (more for less, "proof of trusting nothing") are plausible enough for my purposes.

Francis Picabia's stage extravaganza at the Théâtre des Champs-Élysées was real, as was René Clair's film contribution. You can see the beautiful art deco main lobby and sweeping staircases of the Théâtre on your next trip to Paris. Clair would go on to become one of the most innovative directors of the 20th century. New Yorker Arthur Stieglitz was an influential and innovative photographer and promoter of modern art in many forms, including the Dadaists. (During the War, he also discovered the drawings of a young woman from Wisconsin named Georgia O'Keefe.) The Galerie Myrmidon is, more's the pity, my own invention, although the area around Boulevard Montparnasse was a hotbed of avant-garde artists and Lost Generation writers immediately after the War.

With so many men off to war, many women in France and Britain took up munitions work, as did their American sisters after the U.S. entered the conflict. The skin and hair of *munitionettes* who worked in shell factories often took on a bright yellow tone from unprotected exposure to the various caustic explosive compounds and were known as "canaries." So the yellow tinge to Adèle and the newborn Édouard is historically accurate. And of course, with all those millions of young soldiers in France, the business of producing nude "French post cards" was very lucrative during and after the War. The period of the 1920's was also one of newfound freedom and openness for the gay and lesbian population of Paris and other major cities, so Léonie and Signie have a strong historical context. The *École normale supérieure de jeunes filles* was one of the first French universities for women and was originally located in the old royal porcelain works in Sèvres, just outside Paris. The *agrégation* examination was the preeminent academic qualification of the day and those who passed were called *agrégés* and considered the best of the best, monopolizing the most desirable jobs. It was indeed a big deal that Adèle and her husband were *agrégés*. And yes, the French Army went off to war in 1914 wearing bright red caps and pantaloons, just like poor Gilles Chéreaux.

I included a variety of written communications in this book for two reasons. First, these letters, telegrams, and military orders were a very efficient device for moving the narrative along. Second, reading these forms of handwritten (and slowly delivered, or not delivered at all) messages plays a role imparting a sense of the time in which these events occurred. People were accustomed to waiting for news, even of crucial events.

Although I took meticulous care to avoid anachronisms, historical groaners, and wild implausibilities, any such errors remaining are entirely my own. I can only promise to do better in *No Hero's Welcome* and other future books.

ACKNOWLEDGEMENTS

No book encompassing so many widespread historical events could have been possible without assistance from many generous people. Since I relied so heavily on African-American and, to a lesser extent, LGBT characters, I sought out more than the usual number of outside readers to provide some objective criticism of my choices. I'm a cis-gender white male writer, so I hope I've treated my disparate characters with sensitivity and respect without tipping into either lionization or caricature. I leave that to the reader's judgment whether I've succeeded.

The Imperial War Museum in London is the preeminent place to visit for First World War exhibits and archival sources. Their utterly unique World War I exhibits are an invaluable resource for historical fiction writers. Although the major military units in this book weren't British, the IWM provides a comprehensive look at the Great War and my notes and photographs from a visit there in 2016 proved immensely useful.

I imposed upon many talented and indulgent people to read various drafts of this book, starting with my wife, who gave me extensive notes for two drafts and also provided the final copy edit. Two historians of the period who are also experts on the 369th U.S. Infantry, Stephen L. Harris and Richard Walling, very generously read complete early drafts—in shockingly short amounts of time—and provided invaluable advice on historical context and detail, as well as recommendations on plot, narrative, and characterization. Two of my children were early readers. So many thanks to my daughter, Lindsay Driemeyer, and my son, Evan Walker, for their continuing enthusiasm for their father's literary projects. These very intelligent, well-read women graciously agreed to beta-read the book: Teri Collins and Mish Kara, who provided invaluable continuity checks with the first volume of the trilogy, as well as great insights for this book; Pam Kanner, who provided a sensitive understanding of the characters and settings that gave me both valuable feedback and welcomed assurance; and Kathy Phillips, another continuity reader from *None of Us the Same* and a fluent French speaker, who is the straightest-shooting beta reader for whom any writer could ask. In addition, Madame Mitsou Borgen, a native French speaker and mother of my dear friend Professor Christopher Borgen, read the entire manuscript and provided extensive notes, including assessing the many French words and phrases for accuracy, idiom, and aptness. Her suggestions were an enormous help to the authenticity of the story.

In the end, however, this is another story that wouldn't have seen the light of day without the patient support of my wife, publicist, talent manager, editor, marketing director and chief financial officer, Kathy.

ABOUT THE AUTHOR

JEFFREY K. WALKER is a Midwesterner, born in what was once the Glass Container Capital of the World. A retired military officer, he served in Bosnia and Afghanistan, planned the Kosovo air campaign and ran a State Department program in Baghdad. He's been shelled, rocketed and sniped by various groups, all with bad aim. He's lived in ten states and three foreign countries, managing to get degrees from Tulane, Syracuse, Georgetown and Harvard along the way. An attorney and professor, he taught legal history at Georgetown, law of war at William & Mary and criminal and international law while an assistant dean at St. John's. He's been a contributor on NPR and a speaker at federal judicial conferences. He dotes on his wife, with whom he lives in Virginia, and his children, who are spread around the United States. Jeffrey has never been beaten at Whack-a-Mole.

Connect with him on Twitter at @jkwalkerAuthor, on his Facebook fan page at www.facebook.com/jeffreykwalker or on his website at jeffreykwalker.com.

SUGGESTED FURTHER READING

Harlem's Hell Fighters and French Poilus: Any fictional work incorporating characters or events from the history of the 15th New York/369th U.S. Infantry, "Harlem's Hell Fighters," has to begin with Stephen L. Harris's definitive work on the subject, *Harlem's Hell Fighters: The African-American 369th Infantry in World War I* (Washington: Brassey's, 2003). In addition to his generosity to me as a fellow author, he is an incredible non-fiction writer and his book is a ripping good read as well as finely crafted history. I found Arthur E. Barbeau and Florette Henri's *The Unknown Soldiers: Black American Troops in World War 1* (Philadelphia: Temple Univ. Press, 1974) very useful to set the 369th in the broader context of African-American participation in the Great War. When fleshing out my characters from the 369th, I found myself lingering over the beautiful and haunting period photographs and other illustrations in Robert J. Dalessandro, Gerald Torrence and Michael G. Knapp's *Willing Patriots: Men of Color in the First World War* (Atglen, PA: Schiffer Military History, 2009). My feel for the life of the French *poilus* was best informed by reading Louis Barthas's wonderful diaries written during his service through all 51 months of the War, *Poilu: The World War I Notebooks of Corporal Louis Barthas, Barrelmaker 1914-1918* (New Haven: Yale, 2014, tr. Edward Strauss). This is the first book I'd recommend to anyone seeking insight into the life of the average

French infantryman. For the details of French Army organization, rank, uniforms and equipment, I relied heavily on Elizabeth Greenhalgh's *The French Army and the First World War* (Cambridge: Cambridge Univ. Press, 2014), and two thin volumes by Ian Summer, *The French Army 1914-1918* (Botley; Osprey, 2009, ill. Gerry Embleton) and *The French Poilu* (Botley: Osprey, 2009, ill. Giuseppe Rava).

Dadaists and 1920s Paris: My use of the Dadaists was something of a dare. In the spring of 2006, my wife and I dragged our three children to a huge exhibit of Dadaist collages, *assemblages*, multimedia works, and other creations—including random phoneme "Dada poetry"—at the National Gallery of Art in Washington, D.C. They unanimously hated it and it became a running family gag that we might drag them to something equally horrendous. My wife and I, on the other hand, loved it. (And my now-adult children have come to appreciate the Dadaist a bit more.) So my initial decision to use the Dadaists was admittedly a little tongue-in-cheek. It didn't turn out that way, given the wonderful manner in which the Dadaists unified Adèle's life in Paris with Signie and Léonie. And the Dadaists did indeed have much to say about the destructive lunacy of the War, as represented by Signie's magisterial *Notre-Dame de la Boucherie*—"Our Lady of the Butcher Shop." The single most important resource on Dadaism for me, in addition to lots of online imagery, was Michel Sanouillet's comprehensive history, *Dada in Paris* (Cambridge, MA: MIT Press, 2009, tr. Sharmila Ganguly). But Signie's *assemblage* is, regretfully, entirely fictitious.

Harlem in the 1920s: There may not be a deeper well of marvelous settings, characters, dress, speech and events—outside of major wars at least—than Harlem in the 1920s, the age of exotic speakeasies, jazz clubs, reefer dens, and dapper gangsters. This was also the beginning of the Harlem Renaissance, the age of W.E.B. Du Bois and Langston Hughes and Fats Waller. There is a substantial amount of online material relevant to this period and I availed myself of much of it. I also relied on three books: David Levering Lewis's *When Harlem Was in Vogue* (NY: Penguin, 1979), a wonderful edited volume collected by Lionel C. Bascom, *A Renaissance in Harlem: Lost Voices of an American Community* (NY: Avon, 1999), and Ron Chepesiuk's *Gangsters of Harlem: The Gritty Underworld of New York's Most Famous Neighborhood* (Ft. Lee: Barricade, 2007).

COMING SOON!

Book Three of the *Sweet Wine of Youth* Trilogy

NO HERO'S WELCOME

The horrors of the First World War devastated many a Dublin family and the well-known Brannigans decidedly were not spared. Struggling to get past their heartache, the family finds itself divided by both the rebellion against British rule and the wide Atlantic. Readers first met this provocative family through the eyes of eldest daughter, Deirdre, in *None of Us the Same*. Now comes their tragic yet hopeful story in the final volume of the *Sweet Wine of Youth* trilogy. How does devoted matriarch Eda Brannigan cope with the loss of her beloved husband, Daniel, on the bloody beaches of Gallipoli? Widowed with children to look after, can she make a new life for herself? And how does eldest son, Francis, horribly wounded beside his father, face a life of physical challenges, bleak memories and a troubling taste for the drink? Sean Brannigan, still a youngster when his father left in 1914, finds the camaraderie he craves in the Irish Republican cause, but how will he get on with Francis who unflinchingly supports the War? What of the two youngest Brannigans? Studious and ethereal Molly—Sean's "Vatican twin"—grown to a young woman, finds her first love in an Anglo-Irish government clerk, but is he really the man she believes him to be? And what about the youngest, quiet and easily overlooked Brendan, who is a keen observer and remembers more than he'd ever let on? Follow the exciting story of the Brannigans, centered around Eda's bustling pub, The Gallant Fusilier. Can this loving family endure the violence and intrigue of the Easter Rising, the bloody struggle for independence and a bitter civil war?

Coming Summer 2018.

Stay in touch!
Sign-up here to receive early notice of book releases:
jeffreykwalker.com

CPSIA information can be obtained
at www.ICGtesting.com
Printed in the USA
LVHW091137191219
641031LV00035B/825/P